THE HUNTSMEN

TONY J FORDER

A DS Royston Chase novel

First published in 2021 by Spare Nib Books

tonyjforder.com
tony@tonyjforder.com

Also by Tony J Forder

The DI Bliss Series

Bad to the Bone

The Scent of Guilt

If Fear Wins

The Reach of Shadows

The Death of Justice

Endless Silent Scream

Slow Slicing

Bliss Uncovered (prequel novella)

Standalone

Fifteen Coffins

Degrees of Darkness

The Mike Lynch Series

Scream Blue Murder

Cold Winter Sun

To the good men and women who take
enormous risks on our behalf working
for police services around the world.
#FundThePolice

EIGHT-YEAR-OLD MANDY RADCLIFFE COWERED beneath her cotton sheet as the first low rumble of thunder caused a loose pane of glass in her bedroom window to shudder. She was terrified of storms, and the one heading her way sounded as if it might give her bad dreams for the rest of the night. Rigid with anticipation, she waited for the expected flash of lightning. When it failed to materialise, she pushed back her cover and sat up in bed, wondering if she had somehow misheard.

The second clap came only seconds later. Once again it was muted, but preceded on this occasion by a piercing blaze of light; as if a lightbulb in the sky had been abruptly switched on and off, leaving its flickering presence resonating in her eyes. Mandy gasped and wrapped a hand over her mouth to stifle a cry. Her subsequent unease resulted as much from the vision as the sound. She didn't quite know what she had seen or heard, but if it was a storm, it was unlike any other she had experienced before.

Curiosity winning the day, Mandy decided to be brave. She clambered out of bed and padded barefoot across to the bedroom window, intending to close it. As her hands reached out, the sound came again. Not a rumble after all, she realised. More like a sharp but deep pop. The explosion of light again came first, only this time she was in a position to see it was not in the sky at all, but low to the ground, somewhere beyond the neighbouring farmland.

Her tiny heart leapt and began to beat more rapidly, this time in excitement. For, while Mandy hated the thunder and lightning brought by a heavy storm, she loved a firework display. And what she had heard and seen coming from the farm across the field and through the knot of trees, surely had to be bangers being fired off. Bangers always came ahead of the rockets and Catherine wheels and Roman candles and fountains, which meant her neighbours were about to have the kind of fun she always missed out on.

Cautiously, she glanced back over her shoulder at her bedroom door. She was not allowed to go out alone at night, but knowing it was wrong had not always prevented her from doing so. Provided she remained on her own front lawn, her parents would not scold her too severely if she got caught.

Thinking only of the fun others were about to have as they gathered for the display, Mandy hurriedly tip-toed downstairs, where she let herself out of the house, snicking the front door closed behind her. The warm air meant she was unconcerned about being outside wearing only her nightdress, and she often played barefoot on the grass, so being without her slippers did not bother her at all. As for letting herself back inside, she knew which rock to shift in order to find the spare key. She stood on the stone doorstep for a few seconds, gathering her composure, before summoning up her courage and sprinting across the lawn.

Another banger exploded somewhere ahead of her. This time she saw no flare of light. *If you get closer*, she told herself, *then you'll be able to see everything. You'll enjoy it so much more.*

Crossing the road on her own was forbidden, because of the cars that hurried by along the stretch of road outside her home. Mandy held her breath. She saw no traffic, heard no roaring engines. Excitement battering away at her heart, she shuffled forward. At the low kerb she stopped to look both ways as she had been taught by her parents.

Go on. Why are you waiting? Just this one time. Mummy and Daddy will never even know you were gone.

Mandy steeled herself. She looked left and right one last time. Only when she was certain the road was clear did she dash across to the safety of the opposite narrow grass verge. Panting, she glanced back over her shoulder. The thrill of it all was almost too much to bear.

The thin wire fencing around this part of the field had gaps wide enough for her to climb through without snagging her nightdress or scratching exposed flesh. Once beyond the flimsy perimeter she started running again, over a stretch of open land that stood between her home and the farm where two or three times a year people seemed to have such great fun. Several more bangers had gone off in the meantime, and Mandy was eager to watch the entire display from the beginning. She put some extra hustle into her stride, panting but beaming with delight as her loose hair flew wildly behind her.

The woods were the only part Mandy did not like. She and her friends swapped stories about them, and she'd heard a lot of fairy tales devoted to the eerie nature and creepiness of dense woodland and the creatures who inhabited them. Regardless, she ignored the scary legends and endless possibilities. If you wanted to get to the farm you had to pass through the thickets, so she continued on her way, more slowly once in among the trees, but equally determined.

She was not about to miss out on the festivities. More bursts of light and sound told her the display was about to move into full flow, and she simply had to be there when it did. Following a route she felt sure would take her where she needed to be, the dim glow of sunset guiding her way, the eight-year-old came to a grinding halt when the trees and undergrowth around her suddenly erupted with the rustle of swift and sudden movement.

Mandy gasped. Put a hand to her mouth. Held her breath.

Had the nightmare creatures of the woods found her?

She heard branches being thrust aside, the pounding of footsteps both soft and heavy. Something was moving between the trees and it was headed her way. She wanted to run, told her legs to move as fast as they were able, but they disobeyed her command. Monsters lived in the woods, so too ogres and witches and all manner of horrible beings. She remained rooted to the spot in petrified silence, waiting for whatever it was to materialise and pounce upon her.

A shape emerged through the gathering gloom, growing larger as it moved ever closer. White, flapping, moaning… *a ghost.* At the point at which she became terrified beyond screaming for help, Mandy saw that she was wrong. It was not a ghost at all, but a girl. Older than herself, wearing a long flowing nightgown that rippled as she ran. The girl's eyes were wide and her mouth hung open. She sped through the trees with both arms outstretched and flailing, bearing the brunt of the stabbing branches as she burst through them without breaking stride.

'Run!' the girl screamed as she spotted Mandy.

Mandy remained motionless.

'Run!' the girl screamed again. This time the voice seemed to erupt from the very centre of her being.

Then came the flashing light of another banger.

The deep crack of its explosion.

The girl in the flowing nightgown fell forwards and sprawled face first onto the ground, where she lay still and silent. On her back, something dark began to spread out across the stark whiteness of the gown.

More movement now.

This time when she looked up, barely able to draw breath, Mandy saw a man striding purposefully towards her.

A man who carried a rifle.

He stopped walking when he spotted Mandy. A smile flickered across his face as he raised the weapon and gazed along the barrel aimed directly at her.

ONE

IT LOOKED AS IF the carnival was in town as Detective Sergeant Royston Chase approached the Beckhampton roundabout on the A4. Blue and white lights danced over twin strands of solid red in the distance. He'd been warned to expect a long line of traffic, the tail end of which he encountered half a mile from the scene of a multi-vehicle collision. Drivers had been instructed not to turn around in search of a detour, the open lane being kept clear for emergency vehicles.

Chase took the oncoming side of the road with blues and twos announcing his presence. The juices in his stomach roiled, providing a familiar acid reflux burn; it had been a long time since he'd attended the scene of a road collision. He was puzzled as to why he had been summoned, the duty officer running the circus alongside the roads traffic crews having asked him to attend.

A number of vehicles caught in the jam had decanted their cargo, drivers and passengers staring ahead, some engaging in idle chatter, animatedly gesturing with their hands. The closer to the scene, the more ambitious they became. Several had their phones out, taking photos or using the video app. Chase did not understand the desire to store visual reminders of death, destruction, and injury for future edification. As he rounded a left-hand bend, he drew level with a small white van. He noticed the driver's door hanging wide open and a man standing on its roof filming the carnage in the distance.

Chase braked to a halt. Powered down the passenger side window. 'Hey!' he called out, leaning across the centre console. 'Get down off there. Show some respect, will you?'

The man flapped a hand but refused to tear himself away from the action.

'Do I have to come up there to make you stop filming?'

This time he got the driver's attention. A young man in his early twenties, still all greasy skin and alarming pimples. 'It's a free country. There's nothing to say I can't film what I see.'

'There's me,' Chase replied. 'I realise you're probably desperate to get that up on social media for all the other ghouls to see, comment on, and make sick jokes about. But let me tell you what will follow. Full and graphic images of the colonoscopy I'm about to give you by shoving that same smartphone up your obnoxious arse.'

White van man remained on the roof of his vehicle. He glared at Chase, yet lowered the phone. In a less aggressive tone, he muttered something about having rights. Despite the man's relative youth, Chase thought he ought to know better. There was no time to teach him the error of his ways, however.

'I have your number plate on my forward camera,' he said. 'If I see anything on Facebook or YouTube or wherever, I'm coming for you. Understand?'

The driver whirled away in disgust. The phone went into his pocket.

Chase drove on as far as the first cordoned-off area. He flashed his warrant card at the uniformed officers manning the tape. One of them directed him towards a bank of vehicles parked on the grassy verge. Police, ambulance crews and the fire service were already hard at it, though it was obvious to even a casual observer that the bulk of their work was finished and they were tidying up behind them. Other than his SUV, only one other vehicle was not sporting emergency service livery. Chase recognised it as a mortuary van.

Stepping out of his Volvo, he was immediately assaulted by a cacophony of sound. Voices in a state of controlled agitation despite being raised; metal groaning, occasionally shrieking from the torture of being twisted against its natural form; a low rumble of diesel engines and generators; hydraulic screeching as tools either compressed, cut, or levered; glass exploding, pumps running, feet scrambling…

As for the vehicles involved in the incident itself, it was hard to see where some started and others ended. Chase eventually picked out six distinctive forms, once pristine, now mangled together as if forming some grotesque art instillation. He inhaled the odour of warm oil and chemicals from fire suppressing foam. There was no sign that any of the vehicles had caught alight; melted electrics came with their own bitter tang, which was not present in the balmy night air he breathed.

One misery spared, he thought. A shudder rippled between his shoulder blades; being trapped alive in a burning car was one of his worst fears.

The duty Inspector who hailed him from a distance was a man Chase knew well. He and Trevor Shipman had worked together at the Swindon city police HQ based in Gablecross. Both had been promoted to sergeant on the same day. Shipman retained the uniform and rose up a rank to Inspector five years later, while Chase shifted sideways into CID. There had to be a good reason for Shipman to request a detective attend the scene, even if one was not immediately apparent.

By the time his friend broke away from the team he'd been talking with, Chase had gloved up and got himself suited and booted in full forensic protective gear. The two men did not shake hands because of it, but nodded at each other instead.

'How're things in the sticks?' Shipman asked behind his mask.

Four months ago, Chase had been posted to the tiny village of Little Soley, becoming its only detective in the process. Located in the foothills of the North Wessex Downs, the police station was situated in the hamlet's oldest remaining building. In its time it had served as both a library and village hall, and now housed something far less salubrious in the eyes of most locals – as Chase had come to discover. These days, he had the run of the place, with the sole exception of whichever PCSO happened to be serving the community on any given shift.

'Sticky,' he said in response to the question. 'And more than a little soul-destroying at times.'

'I can imagine.'

'Believe me, Trev, you can't.'

Shipman shifted his stance. 'Grin and bear it for a while longer, Royston. They'll have you back at HQ the moment they realise what they're missing.'

'I wonder. If they haven't missed me in four months, perhaps they never will.'

'They'll miss your mind. You know that. You run rings around most of them in CID. In time they'll forget about your… foibles, and will be only too happy to welcome you back.'

Chase grunted, unconvinced. 'Anyhow, what do you have going on here that you thought might be of interest to me? Looks like any old RTC to me.'

'In many ways it is,' Shipman said, turning to look at the scene of devastation, tangled wreckage blocking the road and roundabout. 'But the reason I requested CID is anything but usual, I can assure you.'

'That's me intrigued. Give me the broad strokes.'

'One vehicle, a Land Rover Discovery, came hurtling down the hill from the far side and failed to stop at the roundabout. Went straight onto it, flipped on the central mound at high speed, and crashed down into vehicles which were either on the roundabout or waiting at the junction to access it. Six vehicles altogether, including the one that caused all the chaos. First police responders recognised the Land Rover immediately. Not the first time they've encountered the driver. Apparently, he's stopped on a fairly regular basis by patrols late at night. His motor often has to be towed out of hedgerow or a ditch. And all because he's had a few too many. Only, this time he really screwed up. Found dead behind the wheel.'

Chase pursed his lips. 'With that kind of history, if he still has his licence, I'm assuming he's either important or a celebrity.'

Shipman snorted. 'Are they not usually one and the same?'

'Not in my world they're not.'

'In this case, Royston, it's the former. In fact, he was once the Chief Constable for the area.'

'You mean Ken Webster?'

'The very same.'

If he could, Chase would have whistled. It wasn't a skill he had mastered as a child. 'No wonder he was treated so leniently by patrol. Still, I'm not quite sure why his death in an RTC warrants a CID callout.'

'It doesn't. He doesn't. But the other occupant of his vehicle does.'

Chase ran through the logical connections. 'Not his wife, I take it?'

Shipman shook his head. 'Far from it. A female minor in a state of complete undress. Also deceased, I'm afraid.'

'That *is* interesting. Now I understand why you chose not to identify Webster across comms. Must be my lucky day.'

'How so?'

'Had you done so, there's no way they would have sent me out here. It'd be the Chief Super, somehow managing to prise his backside out of that foul leather chair behind his desk. This is not something he'd want bandied about, fuelling rumours. He'll want to clamp down on it from the start, before rushing off back to the safety of his office. So tell me, how minor are we talking about when it comes to this girl?'

'Very. Hard to know for sure, but she's just a kid, Royston. And that's not all the bad news, either. Not only was she naked, but she was in the process of giving Sir Kenneth oral sex when the incident occurred.'

Chase blew out a puff of air. Even the thought beggared belief. 'How on earth can you possibly know that?'

Shipman hung his head. 'The poor thing must have slipped her seatbelt off when she went down on him. She was ejected through the side window when the Land Rover slammed into the roundabout. When we found her, she still had half of Sir Kenneth's dick in her mouth.'

TWO

CHASE MANAGED TO GRAB a few hours' sleep after getting home from the callout, but he was up and out of the house again ahead of the traffic. The road through Marlborough could be a pain, but was quiet and easy to navigate at that time of day. He pushed on through, making his way back towards the crash site. Things always looked different in daylight, and without all the emergency vehicles and personnel he'd be able to get a better feel for the incident.

He was approaching Manton Down when he took a call from Shipman, who was about to end his shift. 'You must be exhausted,' Chase said. 'How many fatalities in the end?'

'Five. Another expected to go the same way, plus two critical who are fifty-fifty.'

'Those five include our minor?'

'Yes. We're not ready to release full details to the media as yet. Nor precise figures, for that matter. The longer it takes for people to work out for themselves that we have an extra body, the happier everyone here will be.'

Chase could imagine. For the men and women on the ground it was another day, another job. Not so for the senior leadership. 'While I understand that from their point of view, she's the only victim I'm concentrating on. I don't suppose you have a name on her yet?'

'Nowhere near.'

'Okay. I understand you want to get off, Trev, but do you mind asking the exhibits officer to give me a call? I'd like to go over the victim's clothing with them.'

'There's no clothing to go over.'

'I realise she was naked when they found her, but–'

'I know what you're about to say, Royston. You'd expected her clothes to be in the Land Rover somewhere, or strewn over the crash site, maybe. As did we. They weren't. We never turned up a single item. And we're as puzzled about that as you are.'

Chase didn't know how to react. The girl being fully naked when giving Sir Kenneth oral sex had been a surprise, but hardly a shock given the precise circumstances. Yet if the young kid's discarded clothes were not in the vehicle and had not been found at the scene of the RTC, then that implied she was already naked at the time she entered the Land Rover. Which made no sense to him at all.

'I'm going to have to give that one a bit more consideration,' he said softly. 'It's changed my line of thinking altogether.'

'Which was?'

'I'd imagined she was a runaway or homeless, and that he'd picked her up off the street on his way home from somewhere. Only, now I'm confused.'

'Join the club,' Shipman said. 'And whatever you have in mind, Royston, you'd better make it quick. Senior leaders are due to meet in less than an hour. Our Knight of the Realm's family received the death knock in the early hours, and have been rattling chains ever since.'

'Where are they? Up at the farm or on their Cornwall estate?'

'Cornwall. His wife is busy seeking media blackouts and assurances from the emergency services that Sir Kenneth's name will not be released in any official statements until her legal team say otherwise. As soon as she's done with all that overwhelming grief, I dare say she'll find time to drive up here.'

Chase smiled. He enjoyed his friend's cynicism.

'I was going to take a fresh look at the scene,' he said, 'but I think I'll turn around and head out to the estate instead. If I can get an hour alone with the staff there, I might discover something of value.'

'The key thing is to get a head start on the case. Establish yourself as the lead investigator. Be hard to elbow you out once you do.'

'I'm not so sure about that, but it's a good thought.'

Shipman wished him luck before hanging up.

Chase knew he'd need some. He was too low on the totem pole to be handed such a high profile investigation. He was also out of favour, which didn't help. Not that his win record wasn't impressive. But he had a habit of rubbing people up the wrong way, his bluntness a sharp tool. He was a self-confessed square peg, and the police service was all about smooth, round holes. Not that he was some sort of dissident or maverick – far from it. Being outspoken, however, made some people uncomfortable. His only chance of staying anywhere near this case was if he discovered something important at an early stage. Removing him afterwards might come across as a bad move, particularly when the full story inevitably broke. He already knew what his argument was going to be. All he needed was to find the right key for the door he wanted to open up.

He found a convenient spot to turn the SUV around and headed back the way he had come. The day was becoming typically autumnal: a weak sun tried valiantly to poke its way through a low sky filled with wispy cloud cover. Leaves were in the process of turning yellow and red, beguiling deep shades revealed as the trees started to store nutrients in their roots in preparation for winter. This was Chase's favourite season, and the drive opened up the landscape to provide spectacular views of the sweeping countryside in a pleasing state of flux.

It took him twenty minutes to reach Little Soley. On the other side of the village, close to the county border, Webster's Farm and Produce spanned twelve-hundred acres. In the mid-1800s, a plot around the grand stately home and gardens had been developed into farmland. It was later purchased by Sir Kenneth's grandfather, whose money came from livestock farmed in both Scotland and New Zealand. Over time, a reduction in farming led to a reduced array of produce, but the name remained. These days they kept a few sheep and pigs, but if farming was in Sir Kenneth's genes, it had skipped a generation.

Chase recalled meeting the man on one occasion, shortly after taking up his post at Gablecross in Swindon. Their brief exchange wasn't memorable, but since being based in the village he had become increasingly aware of the regard locals had for the farm and its owner. He needed to act quickly if he was going to grasp the nettle of his case, but he also had to do so with decorum and tact.

Neither of which were his speciality.

The farm lay off a rough track of compressed dirt, mud and gravel. Chase was unsurprised to discover a patrol car parked across the entrance, whose wrought-iron gates stood wide open. He didn't recognise either of the two officers sitting in the vehicle, and assumed they had been sent over from Devizes. Chase came to a halt and held his warrant card up to the Volvo's windscreen.

Instead of moving aside, the car barring his way rocked as the passenger climbed out. He adjusted his cap before sauntering over. Chase already had his window down. He looked up and gave a smile.

'Morning, sir,' the officer said. 'Do you mind telling me your business here today?'

Chase had not anticipated being asked any questions at this stage. Even so, he was ready with an answer. 'I've been sent to get an early start interviewing the staff. I'm based in the nearby village, so I drew the short straw.'

He shrugged as if he didn't really want to be there.

'We had no word you were coming, sir. We were told to keep things sealed up here until Lady Jane arrives sometime this afternoon.'

'Sealed up against the media, gawkers, and personal callers, not me. Look, you can give them a call at Gablecross if you like, but don't expect anyone to be happy at being dragged out of important meetings to deal with a routine matter.'

The officer looked at him for a few seconds, as if weighing up his words. Chase hoped the man did not call his bluff. After a moment, the uniform shrugged and gave the kind of smile that suggested this was all beyond his pay scale. 'Good luck,' he said as he turned away. 'They're all taking it pretty hard from what we could tell.'

Seconds later, the patrol car started up and shifted forward, leaving room for Chase to slip by behind it. His vague knowledge of the estate told him it consisted of a small lake, several fields separated by dry stone walls, and acres of dense woodland. The curving, tree-lined drive beyond the entrance was in good condition, winding around to emerge from what felt like a dark tunnel onto open land. As the SUV passed through a baroque-style archway, the main house revealed itself, together with an array of outbuildings.

Chase was impressed with his first sight of Webster Manor. Constructed of local limestone from the Chilmark quarries during Elizabethan times, it compared favourably to other grand homes in the area such as Corsham Court and Bowood House. Although this was not a tourist attraction, Chase was certain its design and opulence would draw visitors from all around the world. Both the central porch and its flanking wings had angular gables, with a clock tower rising above a clutch of octagonal minarets. At three storeys with windowed attic space, the solid-looking pile reeked of privilege and vintage elegance.

As he pulled up in the vast courtyard outside what he presumed to be the front entrance, a door opened and a tall, reed-thin man came out onto the stone-paved steps. Chase realised his arrival had been noticed. Either that, or arrangements had been made between whoever this was and the officers back at the entrance. Irrespective of how he had been alerted, the man waited at the top of the steps for Chase rather than descending to greet his visitor.

He wore casual clothing with a perfect fit, a distressed brown leather waistcoat, and boots that looked as if they might cost more than most police officers took home in a month. Upright, his dark brown hair wavy and unstyled, he had an unmistakable air of aristocracy about him.

'Good morning,' Chase said, once again offering up his credentials for inspection. 'I apologise for bothering you at a time like this, but the sooner we get our preliminary questioning out of the way, the sooner you can all go about your usual business. And you are?'

The man shook Chase's offered hand. 'Miles Radford. I'm the estate manager. We're preparing for the arrival of her Ladyship. I know you have a job to do, Sergeant, but can this really not wait?'

'I wish it could. Believe me, I have no great desire to be here at a time like this. However, it's crucial that I obtain as much information while minds are still fresh. I'm sure you're about to get an awful lot busier, so there may be no better time than right now.'

Radford didn't like it, but he gave a stiff nod and led Chase inside. To many, the immediate interior would almost certainly be a let down by comparison to the home's imposing façade. No Baccarat chandelier hanging in the entrance hall. No family portraits by the greatest artists of their time hung in gold frames upon the vast walls. No tapestries or antique vases in protective glass cases. Chase liked the more austere elegance. He approved when taste exceeded wealth.

He followed the estate manager into a narrow side room, which looked as if it had once been a store cupboard. 'My own offices are at the back of the building,' Radford explained. 'I thought this would do, given the time constraints.'

Chase nodded, happy with the arrangement. When asked if he wanted a drink, he declined. Reluctantly. He was thirsty and could have used a coffee, but he was also waiting for a phone call that might yank him off the case before he'd really begun investigating it. When they were both seated, he focussed on the details he regarded as a priority.

'We are attempting to discover further information about precisely what took place last night, Mr Radford. Tell me, did Sir Kenneth have any guests staying here?'

If the man was surprised by the line of questioning, he did not show it. 'Not currently. As you might imagine, a wide variety of friends and acquaintances have enjoyed Sir Kenneth's hospitality on many occasions here at the manor. However, during this stay he was here to relax and to complete some business.'

'I see. So you would not have expected anybody to be in the vehicle with him at the time of the incident?'

Until that moment, Radford's face had been as implacable as the limestone blocks used to form the house. He tried hard to maintain his composure, but Chase spotted a pulse in the man's sunken cheek and concern passing across his eyes.

'Are you telling me there was somebody with Sir Kenneth, Sergeant? Because if that's true, it's the first any of us have heard about it.'

'No. Not exactly. Without meaning to be indelicate, it was a tough scene to work. We're not entirely sure on numbers as yet.'

There was relief in Radford's nod. 'I see. I can only imagine. In that case, all I can do is tell you that when Sir Kenneth left the house earlier yesterday evening, he was alone.'

Chase caught the implication. 'You saw him leave?'

'I did. I spoke with him for a brief moment as he pulled out of the garage. I was on my way home.'

'And this was what time? Approximately.'

Radford looked up and to the left. 'Around six-thirty.'

'I see. Is it possible that he met up with somebody while he was out and was bringing them back here with him? Was that the kind of thing he did?'

'Anything is possible, I suppose. And yes, on occasion I'm sure Sir Kenneth returned home with a friend or two for a nightcap. Equally, he might have been giving one of the neighbours a lift back to the village.'

Chase nodded, pretending to consider the possibility. He wasn't getting a great read on Radford. The estate manager was calm and collected, but the one momentary slip suggested an unease with the thought of his boss having had company. Or perhaps knowing that the police were aware of it.

'I take it the house is staffed day and night?' he said.

Radford surprised him by shaking his head. 'I understand what you mean, Sergeant Chase. But no, there are no live-in staff here when Sir Kenneth alone is in residence. Residential staff take care of Lady Jane. Where she goes, they go. Sir Kenneth is... was, more independent.'

'So he pretty much came and went as he pleased, and nobody would ever know if he invited a guest back to stay overnight.'

'What are you implying?' Radford's gaze narrowed. As did his mouth. 'If you're suggesting Sir Kenneth entertained other women during his wife's absences, the answer is no.'

'I wasn't implying anything of the sort,' Chase said, maintaining a neutral tone. 'But, as you pointed out yourself, sir, you'd hardly be in any position to know for sure one way or the other.'

Radford cleared his throat and pushed his shoulders back. 'I know my employer, Sergeant. I know what kind of man he... was. He and Lady Jane were devoted to each other. If you have evidence to suggest otherwise, then please say so. If not, I'd rather you move on.'

Chase raised both hands defensively. 'I intended no offence. And I wasn't fishing. I have to ask such questions, irrespective of the victim's standing in the community.'

'I'm sure you do. But if it's scandal you're looking for, you won't find any here.'

Try telling that to the underage child your boss had going down on him last night, Chase thought but did not say. Instead, he did as suggested and went in another direction. 'All scandal aside, it seems to be pretty common knowledge that Sir Kenneth enjoyed a drink or two and didn't let the thought of driving home while under the influence prevent him from doing so. That's not gossip, sir, it's a matter of record. My first thought when I was given this information was to wonder why a man of Sir Kenneth's means didn't have use of a driver, or at the very least hire a taxi whenever he went out.'

Radford shifted uneasily in his seat. 'I'm sure I don't know the answer to that. Nor was it my place to ask.'

'But you were aware of it, yes?'

'I'd rather not say.'

'Fair enough. I can drop it for the time being. Tell me, then, Mr Radford, which were Sir Kenneth's favourite haunts when he did go out for the evening? I don't see him propping up the bar of some country pub.'

Radford took a breath. Chase thought the man was again contemplating not answering. But a moment later he said, 'Sir Kenneth was a member of a club of sorts. It's exclusive, as you might imagine. They have locations all around the country, but the closest one to the manor is just outside Calne. On the road out of town on the way to Chippenham.'

Chase nodded, giving that some thought. 'Are we talking Rotary-style, or something more along the lines of the Freemasons?'

The man arched his eyebrows. 'Interesting. Most people assume they are one and the same. You have experience of either yourself, Sergeant?'

This time, Chase smiled, ignoring the blatant deflection. He shook his head and enjoyed watching the man's face sag once more. 'No, sir. I'm not one for such things. I do enjoy a good read, however. I like to educate myself. You never know who you might come up against during an investigation. So, which of the two most appropriately describes the club Sir Kenneth joined? Rotary or masonic?'

At this, Radford drew himself up to his full height. 'Sir Kenneth was not a joiner of such clubs. He was, in fact, a co-founder. It's a club enjoyed by a number of influential people from a good many areas of society.'

'Not a whole lot of road sweepers, I don't imagine.'

Something frosty glazed over Radford's eyes. 'Oh, you'd be surprised.'

About to ask for further details, Chase's flow was interrupted by his mobile phone. He excused himself, turned away to read the name on the screen. He knew his time was up if he answered it. Instead, he swiped towards the red circle and prepared to make the most of the delay he had bought himself.

THREE

THE POLICE STATION IN Little Soley was built from a combination of grey Georgian brick and the same limestone used on the Webster Manor house. The two-storey building stood on a sharp bend in the road running through the centre of the village. Its rear garden extended down to the river Kennett, a gravel path leading to a small landing dock. Inside the front entrance hall, a single staircase swept around to the left as it wound up to the first floor, whose rooms had long-since been abandoned. On the ground floor, DS Chase had use of a substantial main office, with a smaller room to the back. On the other side of the hallway lay another large room, as unused as those upstairs. The ground floor also included a kitchen which in turn led to the building's only toilet and washing facilities.

Oil-fired radiators kept the place above freezing in the winter, but even in the summer the rooms failed to hold their heat. Whatever remained clung to the high ceilings. The station was a grand old building in Chase's view, and he did not miss the company of fellow detectives. He tended to work out of the smaller office to the rear, leaving the open area to the PCSOs. He got on well with all of them, but the turnover made it difficult to form a bond with people who were mostly passing through on the way to somewhere bigger and better.

By the time he got back, the front desk was staffed by Alison May. At twenty-one, she was the youngest PCSO Chase had worked with. A slight, somewhat timid creature, she was nonetheless bright, helpful, and above all dedicated. Nothing was ever too much trouble when it came to serving the local community. She was on a one-in-six rotation, which meant she shifted between five other stations dotted around the Wiltshire countryside during a six-week period. The young woman was Chase's favourite of the Police Community Support Officers, because while the others were as undoubtedly eager to please, she was the quietest of them and usually left him alone.

'Afternoon, Sergeant,' she said as he came through the door. It was almost twelve-thirty. After leaving the farm, Chase had continued on with his original journey to inspect the crash site once again. Having eventually had his fill of a grim scene that was still partially closed off to traffic, he'd grabbed a bite to eat and a mocha at the Caffe Nero in Marlborough. By the time he had finished his lunch, Chase knew he could no longer avoid the inevitable and had driven back to the village, fully expecting the worst upon his arrival.

'Hi, Alison. How are you today?' He offered his most winning smile.

'Right as rain, thanks. Rushed off my feet as usual.' She laughed at her own joke, then her face grew serious. 'Detective Superintendent Waddington is waiting for you in your office, sir. He didn't look exactly... happy when he came in.'

Chase leaned both elbows on the counter, resting his chin on both fists. 'Really? How did he look? Exactly?'

May stooped forward, lowering her voice conspiratorially as she said, 'Like somebody had thrown up in his soup bowl.'

Chase took a deep breath. 'The more you get to work with me, Alison, the more familiar you'll become with that look on the faces of more senior officers. There's something about my obvious charm and charisma that goes right above their heads.'

'It does? Imagine that?'

The Superintendent stood with his back to the door looking out of the window at the garden when Chase walked into the office. Waddington paused long enough before turning to show who was boss; even though his rank achieved the exact same purpose perfectly adequately.

'Ah, there you are, Sergeant,' Waddington said. 'Glad you eventually found time to pop by.' An average man of average height and build, his physical appearance belied an inner strength and a firm conviction. Mostly he was convinced of his superiority, it seemed to Chase, who immediately affected surprise.

'I've been busy chasing up a new inquiry, sir.'

Waddington brushed a fleck of lint from his suit jacket before folding his arms. 'I'm well aware of that, DS Chase. What I would like to know is why you have been avoiding my calls?'

Chase added a deep frown to the affectation. 'What calls? I've not received any calls… ah, I wondered why I hadn't heard from anybody other than Inspector Shipman today.'

He took out his phone, glanced at its screen and nodded. 'No signal. I thought that might be the case. It can be extremely sketchy around here at times, sir.'

'Are you seriously going to stand there and tell me the reason you've not taken my calls or replied to my messages all morning is because of signal failure?'

'It's more of a weakness than a complete failure, sir. I think the system is being overhauled. You can never tell what you're going to get these days.'

Waddington abruptly shook his head and took out his own phone, eyeing Chase with scepticism. He stared at it for a moment, tapped in a number. When nothing happened, he set his jaw and got down to the business he'd driven over from Swindon to discuss.

'Please tell me you've not yet visited the Webster farm,' he said.

'Wasn't I supposed to, sir? It seemed the most logical place for me to start?'

'So you have? Did you interview anybody, man?'

'Yes, sir. The estate manager. Man called Radford.'

The Superintendent closed his eyes and exhaled with a huff. When he looked up, he fixed Chase with a sullen glare, before seeming to reach a decision. He took out his phone again, saw that it still had no signal. He picked up Chase's landline instead, leaving his mobile open on the contacts page while he dialled a number.

'Adrian, it's me,' he said. 'Yes, they have signal issues here in Little Soley, which is why I'm using the station phone. I need you to do two things for me: first, contact the patrol officers outside the Webster farm. I need to know if Lady Jane Webster has arrived, and if not I'd like an ETA if they have it; second, arrange for an Airwave device to be assigned to DS Chase and then get it over here, please. Yes, get back to me as soon as you have an update for me.'

Chase knew the Superintendent had been speaking to his Personal Assistant. His thoughts followed the course of the conversation. He could guess Waddington's intentions – to inject himself into the case as Senior Investigating Officer, brushing Chase aside. Easily done provided he spoke to the estate manager before the newly widowed woman arrived. Not impossible afterwards, but it then became a potential minefield littered with banana skins and eggshells.

The best strategy was for Chase to remain silent and wait for Waddington to commit. And yet he couldn't quite help himself.

'Good thinking sending over an Airwave device for me, sir. Can't imagine what we're going to do without them.'

The existing service communication structure was due to be replaced by an Emergency Network System, having been delayed on two previous occasions. Now there was talk of further interruptions, pushing the project back by years. Chase was aware that Superintendent Waverly was on record as supporting ENS, though some suspected his familial links to the partner provider, EE, had something to do with that.

Waddington gave him a withering look. 'ENS is back on track, Sergeant. And this issue with your mobile phone service is precisely why we need to upgrade to a system capable of delivering in rural areas like this.'

'If you say so, sir. Only, ENS will rely on both Motorola and EE, the two same companies currently not delivering either of us a signal we can use.'

The landline rang, releasing the increasing tension within the office. Waddington snatched it up. Chase immediately saw it was bad news – for the Super. He suspected Lady Jane had arrived at the manor, or that her arrival was imminent. The farm was only a few minutes away, so Chase guessed the former. That gave him hope. Miles Radford would have updated Sir Kenneth's wife the moment she got there, informing her of the initial interview with Chase. Replacing him with a more senior officer was by no means unusual, but in this instance, her Ladyship was bound to be interested in what Chase already knew. More importantly, she would want to know what he intended to say and report. She would also have far greater influence over a mere DS than she would a DetSupt. No chickens were being counted, but he thought he was in with a chance.

'Good news, sir?' he asked amiably.

Waddington was unable to keep the scowl from his face. 'All right, Sergeant. Time for an in-depth chat, I think. Please begin by telling me exactly what you and the estate manager, Mr Radford, discussed. And do not omit a single word you two exchanged.'

FOUR

WHILE SUPERINTENDENT WADDINGTON TOOK stock of the discussion they had just finished, Chase attempted to think several steps ahead. Mentioning the media at a time when nerve endings were frayed was bound to add a further layer of stress to the situation. The word coming down from the current Chief Constable was to keep as much detail as possible under wraps until the investigation team had completed their various reports. Working against that was a naked, deceased child, and the item found in her mouth.

This was not simply a matter of police officers drawing a defensive blue line and keeping quiet. Other emergency services had attended. An ambulance crew had spent time with the girl. As had the crime scene investigation manager, whose technicians photographed and videoed the entire crash site. Finally, two mortuary attendants had whisked the girl away in one of several vans sent to the incident. In many ways, the police were the least of it. Irrespective of their intention to keep this snippet out of the media briefing and from appearing on official records at this early stage, they could not prevent tongues from wagging and lips becoming loose at the sight of a hefty bribe from journalists looking for an edge.

'Tell me what your next three moves are, Sergeant,' Waddington eventually said. 'If you are to remain on the case, I want to know how you intend to approach this tense and fragile stage of the investigation.'

Chase was ready for him. 'People other than Sir Kenneth have lost their lives, sir. He may be our focus here inside this office, but we have to operate in the wider sense.'

'Of course. That goes without saying.'

'And yet I thought it better said than not, sir. Just so's there are no misunderstandings between us. Witnesses at the scene described what happened, and an array of emergency service workers were involved in removing Sir Kenneth from the wreckage. I'm told his bloodwork is unlikely to make for good reading in respect of alcohol levels. I don't see how we can avoid following that particular path – even if we wanted to. There is also no doubt that he caused the RTC. I'm sure his vehicle will be examined forensically in order to check out tyres, brakes, and suspension, but I'll put a rush on it.'

Waddington let out a frustrated sigh. 'And beyond branding Sir Kenneth a drunk-driving killer?'

Chase frowned. 'It's not a question of anyone branding him that, sir. It's what the known facts and witness statements are telling us. Unless SCIT find evidence of brake tampering, it really doesn't look good.' The Serious Collision Investigation Team took on the unenviable task of scrutinising road traffic collisions in which death or serious injury occurred. Their expertise in such incidents was invaluable in helping the police investigators and the families of those involved.

Waddington issued another sigh, this time accompanied by an irritated gesture for Chase to continue.

'As I think you are probably already aware, sir, it gets much worse. At some point in between Sir Kenneth leaving home yesterday evening and reaching that roundabout where he apparently lost control of his vehicle, he gained a passenger. I'll want to know where he went and at what stage of the evening that young girl joined him.'

'Presumably your intention is also to speak with Lady Jane Webster?'

Chase shook his head. 'No, sir. Not quite yet. I fail to see what she could add at this early stage. She's bound to be defensive, so the more evidence we have the better. I'm more interested in the young girl. Once I've established who she is, and where she was when she and Sir Kenneth met, I then need to look at why she was naked and engaged in a sexual act with him.'

'Is that entirely relevant at this juncture?' Waddington asked, clearly unsettled at the thought of raking up dirt on a man of Sir Kenneth Webster's standing. 'The evidence we have at the moment is a decent enough indicator of what took place, but the official report will be our true guideline. We don't have all the facts as yet, Sergeant.'

'With respect, sir, we do have those eye witnesses who will today make statements attesting to what they saw. And what they saw was Sir Kenneth's Land Rover driving downhill too fast, hitting the roundabout and catapulting into the air, before slamming into a number of other vehicles when it landed. According to our people on scene who were among the first to speak with those who avoided the worst of the carnage, some of those same witnesses saw the young girl being flung out through the window of the Land Rover as it took off. And as circumstantial as it may be until we get the forensic and pathology reports in, the fact that Sir Kenneth is missing half of his one and only penis and the naked kid happened to have half of one in her mouth, doesn't sound like a coincidence to me.'

The room was silent for a moment. Chase realised he'd said too much and phrased it poorly. But as much as he wanted to keep this case, he was not about to be steamrollered into following a sanitised route.

Waddington regarded him with ill-concealed distaste. 'Sir Kenneth and I once had a close working relationship. We were members of the same golf club, and often enjoyed a round together. So, please, spare me your vitriol. But also, despite my relationship with the deceased, I won't ask you to overlook any issues you consider pertinent, Royston. What would be equally wrong, however, was if you set your priorities in such a way that your investigation became elevated by emotion and therefore sidetracked.'

Chase took a moment to compose himself before responding. 'I hear what you're saying, sir. I understand how difficult this may be for you personally, and for the job in a much wider sense. This is sensitive information and it requires handling appropriately.'

'Good. I'm glad to hear you say that.'

'Even so, are you telling me his having a naked young girl in that vehicle and receiving oral sex from her at the time of the crash, is a sidetrack? Because I would dispute that, sir. As tragic as it is, the resulting carnage and loss of life is only one element of this case. Carnage – need I remind you – quite possibly caused by what was being done to Sir Kenneth at that precise moment. The other significant factor is the poor kid who was with him.'

Waddington raised a hand in defence. To give him his due, he looked chastened. 'You'll get no argument from me there, Royston. Of course her presence in the vehicle requires our full attention. I'm merely debating the order in which you appear to want to investigate the collision and the resulting deaths.'

Chase gave himself time to think. It wasn't that he failed to understand the Superintendent's position. He simply didn't care. Waddington was a decent enough copper, but he was also the kind of man who buckled beneath the weight of pressure from above. Irrespective of his personal inclinations, the man was only ever going to do what he was told.

'Sir,' he said. 'You'll surely agree that identifying the girl is something we must do as soon as possible. She will most likely have family, and they will want to know how and why she died. I'm not suggesting we provide them with the precise details at this stage. Not immediately. Perhaps not at all if it can be avoided. But the fact that she was in that Land Rover is not something we can keep from them. I doubt they'll have second thoughts as to the order in which we investigate what happened. Do you?'

The resignation on Waddington's face and the loss of tension from his shoulders told Chase he'd made his point. He decided to use that as a pivot to take it further.

'I'm not naïve, sir. I do realise how much of a mess this is. And given the stature of Sir Kenneth, and the circumstances in which we found him, I also understand why certain people will want to circle the wagons. But the reality is, news about the kid, how she was found, who she was with, and what she was doing at the time of the crash, will come out. I'd be surprised if it doesn't come up in the very next media briefing. It's too juicy a piece of gossip. If you're imagining how awful the prospect of that is, think how much worse it will appear if we're not even looking into it.'

After a moment of further reflection, Waddington said, 'I hear you. And of course I appreciate the ramifications. There's no lid big enough to put on this. I've been handed the shitty end of the stick, and all I can do is make the best of it. That's why I'm still wondering if I should take over this case and run it from Gablecross.'

They'd reached the point where Chase had to step up or step back. These next few moments might well determine his entire career. Part of him thought he should let Waddington run with it, to act as the lightning rod for the storm headed their way. But another part – the larger, he hoped – knew that in the Superintendent's hands, the unnamed girl would be regarded as nothing more than a by-product of the fatal crash. Chase decided he couldn't allow that to happen.

'Superintendent, I can see why this warrants being taken under the wing of a senior officer working out of headquarters. I'm not immune to Sir Kenneth's profile. But there is another way of looking at it. I think having a local officer, based in a local station, investigating a local dignitary, sends out a message to those beyond our immediate world. It's the common touch we always say we try to provide but seldom do. Serving our local communities equally is a policy people are well aware of, so a local DS heading things gives the right appearance. Then there's a more personal consideration…'

Waddington's head jerked up. 'Which is?'

'The shitty end of that stick you were handed is passed over to me and remains firmly in my hands. I'm the one left holding it if it all goes wrong. And it will go wrong – let's not even debate that. With everything you already know, do you really see any way of avoiding upsetting certain influential people? That's without taking into consideration the details we've yet to discover. Sir, whatever the outcome, this is not an investigation from which any winners will emerge. But to put it bluntly, when it does go wrong, would you rather see your face or mine plastered all over the news?'

It took a while, but eventually the Superintendent responded. A tight frown revealed his bemusement. 'Why would you put yourself in that position? What you're volunteering for here might well kill your career where it stands.' He shook his head. 'I like you, Royston. I always have. But I don't understand you. I never have.'

'I imagine there are many differences between us, sir. When you and those above look at what happened, you immediately think of Sir Kenneth. And when you think of him, you think of the role he once held here in this county. Right from the off, you start to wonder how to avoid scandal and the kind of overbearing pressure that can be exerted when somebody of his prominence gets caught up in something unsavoury and sordid. Me? My first thought is for that poor young kid. And not only about the life she lost too early, but also the circumstances that led her there. Oh, and I don't suppose this hasn't crossed your mind, but for me another train of thought follows on….'

Waddington's low groan was one of increasing despair. 'I'm almost too afraid to ask.'

Chase nodded. 'I can imagine. Because when I think of Sir Kenneth and that naked young girl lying dead on that roundabout, I can't help but wonder how many others there might have been in the past.'

FIVE

WADDINGTON LEFT THE STATION intending to speak with Sir Kenneth Webster's wife, leaving Chase to continue with his inquiries as agreed towards the end of their discussion. Their only remaining moment of conflict before the meeting ended had come when discussing the media. The Superintendent was adamant that Chase join him at Gablecross for a briefing later that evening. Chase had wanted nothing to do with it.

'What's the point?' he'd argued. 'We both know you won't want me up there answering questions.'

'I don't intend for there to be any questions. I will make an initial statement, after which I'll introduce you as the man in charge of the case. Your statement will focus on the remit you have been given, which is to find out the cause of the crash. You're capable of handling that without causing any controversy, surely?'

Chase had sensed it was a potential deal breaker, and so had reluctantly agreed. He had a couple of hours before they were due to meet again on the other side of Swindon. If he allowed a half hour for the drive, that gave him ninety minutes to himself. He dialled a number for the county Roads Policing Unit, asking for the collision investigation office when he got through. He told them who he was and the incident he was seeking information about, hoping that would secure him an actual person rather than an answering machine. The voice he heard next told him he'd been successful.

'Hey, Royston. How are you doing, sweetheart?'

Maggie O'Donnell had been running crash investigation crews for as long as Chase had been a detective. She was short and wide and bustling, and when on a roll you'd jump out of her way. Her approach and attention to detail were legendary. A senior member of her team would have attended the scene itself, but it was O'Donnell's eye and thoughtful process that often put the pieces together even when working against the clock.

'I'm calling you about this mess,' he said. He smiled to himself. 'What does that tell you?'

'I don't envy you. I've heard of making a silk purse from a sow's ear, but I can't imagine anything palatable arising from this sorry tale.'

'I take it you've heard the full story, Maggie?'

She sucked in some air. 'Let me see... drunk Knight loses control of his steed, wipes out a number of people, including himself. Oh, not forgetting a dead child with a mouthful of his cock. Have I missed anything?'

Chase winced. She had a way with words. And a knack for making him feel uncomfortable with how she used them. 'No, I think that pretty much sums it up. When you say he lost control, how confident are you that there was no mechanical malfunction?'

'Completely. From the evidence gathered at the scene, I'd estimate he hit that roundabout at approximately seventy miles an hour. The paved rim around the traffic island was stripped away by the initial collision, and both front tyres burst on impact if the shredded strips of rubber are to be believed. There were no tyre marks on the road to suggest the use of brakes. And before you ask, the brake pipe itself was intact and in good working order. Oh, and the discs and pads were also functioning. Our naughty Knight simply failed to apply them.'

'I wish I could say I was surprised. Any revelations at all, Maggie?'

'Not so far. Of course, our primary focus today has been on his Land Rover. My understanding is that the event I just described was also witnessed by several drivers uninvolved with the collision. I can't speak as to his intoxication, but his motor was not to blame.'

Chase thanked her, promising to meet up for a coffee or lunch next time he was in the city. He mentioned his media briefing, and O'Donnell said she'd see how she was fixed for time when he was done.

His next call was to obtain an update on witnesses. He learned that all statements from those who observed the incident were in. Four survivors had yet to be spoken to, their condition prohibiting a formal visit from the police. Chase didn't think they would be needed, though they would add weight to what was already an impressive litany of evidence. He next turned his thoughts to where Sir Kenneth and the unidentified female victim may have met.

The notepad device provided by his employers sat unused in a desk drawer. Chase pulled it out and powered it up. There was a computer at the front desk, but he could hear Alison May busying herself out there and he wanted some solitude when running the web searches he had in mind.

He first of all searched for information relating to Sir Kenneth, which resulted in several million hits. A link to the man's Wikipedia page was close to the top, but Chase knew how easily the information on the site could be corrupted. There were far too many newspaper articles to contemplate wading through. He narrowed the search by adding clubs and pastimes as keywords. On an educated impulse, he also included Freemasonry. He'd scrolled halfway down the page when an entry caught his eye.

The link took him to a feature in a society magazine. In an opinion piece, the journalist speculated as to Sir Kenneth's secretive interests, specifically in regard to his having achieved the rank of Chief Constable. According to the article, evidence existed of Webster having been a member of a provincial grand lodge based in Salisbury. It went on to theorise that he had left the masons behind when he instigated a coalition of like-minded people to form a similar but wholly new organisation. Speculation went as far to suggest this new group was limited in both numbers and interests. This was much more in line with the secretive society the Freemasons had once been. At least, that was Chase's take on what he read.

A further search, now including fresh information and keywords taken from the article, led him to a site whose efficacies he doubted. The site appeared to exist to cater to the tastes of those who enjoyed conspiracy theories. It was there, surrounded by links referring to the twin towers, 5G and hoax pandemics, that he spotted something alluding to a new secret organisation to rival that of The Knights Templar. Chase took a deep breath and threw himself down the rabbit hole.

The page bore no author's byline. It comprised only three paragraphs. But Chase felt the jolt of adrenaline like a static-electricity shock as it rocketed through his veins. Whoever had written the item made it crystal clear that their theory was unconfirmed. Despite this, they alleged the club was called Tier One, and that the co-founders were Sir Kenneth Webster and media mogul Colin Shakespeare, also recently knighted.

A search for Tier One resulted in links to rifle scopes and miscellaneous optical solutions, plus car sales and career contracts. Tier One Organisation fed him the meaning of tier one companies. Adding the word "secret" brought him back to familiar sites associated with historical groups, including the site that had provided him with the name. He was going around in circles, but to Chase it felt as if he had a solid base from which to start.

Remembering his chat with Trevor Shipman the previous night, he placed calls to local nicks at Devizes and Monkton Park in Chippenham. He was fairly certain that road traffic patrols covering the area from Little Soley to Chippenham stemmed from both stations. He also put a call in to Gablecross, leaving a message asking for Inspector Shipman to contact him when he arrived back on duty.

Based on what his friend and colleague had told him, Sir Kenneth's drunken jaunts were commonplace. That being the case, there was the distinct possibility that the patrol crews knew some of his regular haunts. One of them might well be the Tier One club. All he needed was an address. Without mentioning his deeper interest, he asked to be called back by any officers with relevant information concerning the man's drink-driving offences.

Which reminded him about the club's co-founder. Colin Shakespeare was a name he was familiar with, though he didn't know a great deal about the man. Once again, Google was his friend. Sir Colin had started out producing a single local newspaper and had ended up running a media empire, including cable TV and mobile phone companies. Unlike many similar business owners, Shakespeare had remained in the UK and resided in Corsham, close to Bath.

Chase found no surprises, nor anything unsavoury attached to the man's history. His biography spoke of a man whose honesty and integrity had led to him creating a national symbol heralded internationally as an employee-friendly enterprise. If he had skeletons, they were hidden well. Yet the same could be said of Sir Kenneth – on the surface, an ex-cop who made it to the top within his chosen profession. A man who had married well; an equal to his own solid stock. If a man with his background and upbringing could wind up in a vehicle with a naked underage girl, was it so far-fetched to think of Sir Colin doing something similar?

Exhaling a long breath, Chase sat back in his office chair. He had to wait for other people to respond in respect of his first two courses of action. However, the third, and to his mind the most important, was to identify the dead girl. He stretched his imagination wider, recalling all conversations relevant to the case so far. As he mused, he caught hold of a stray thought as it was about to slip by him.

Trevor Shipman had mentioned Lady Jane Webster seeking injunctions to maintain a media blackout. Whoever had delivered the death message would have supplied only the most basic of details relating to the RTC. So why had Sir Kenneth's widow not wanted the media to report on what, at that stage, would have merely been a dreadful road accident? Was she aware of his inclination to drive when intoxicated? Or did she perhaps know a great deal more than that?

SIX

CHASE LEFT LITTLE SOLEY early for the media briefing and hit little traffic along the way. He made it to the Gablecross police station in Swindon ten minutes ahead of schedule. The corporate-style building wasn't to his taste. The layout was wasteful and inefficient in his opinion, but it fitted in with its surroundings and gave the right impression. After checking in at the desk, he immediately sought out Trevor Shipman, hoping to catch up on any fresh findings from the night before. His friend happened to look up as Chase approached the shared office, and gestured with his hand that he'd be a couple of minutes.

The corridor thrummed with activity as he waited. A few familiar faces smiled and nodded a greeting, and several people stopped to talk. When you were sent to the Wiltshire equivalent of Siberia, the rumour mill was never slow in churning out gossip and speculation as to why. Chase maintained an upright stance and a knowing smile, hoping it projected confidence. When Shipman eventually joined him, the uniformed Inspector spoke to him in a hushed voice.

'I hear you've been busy trying to contact our patrol crews.'

Chase conceded the point, wondering why his friend sounded concerned. 'Naturally. You said yourself they knew Sir Kenneth's routine pretty well. I thought they might be able to help me.'

'I understand, Royston. *I* do. Others might not. So, do yourself a favour and take a step back from it. I assumed you'd look beyond their actions when I told you about the arrangement they had with him. Most of the crews ignored his drunk driving because of who he was. Plus, they assume the current incumbent would unofficially prefer they turn a blind eye. And they are not wrong about that.'

'And the others involved?'

'May be on the take.'

Chase was disappointed. 'So now you're warning me off, Trev?'

Shipman lowered his voice until it became little more than a whisper. 'I'm saying nothing. And while I'm saying nothing, I'm deliberately not saying that if I were you, rather than talking to the men and women out there who still want to keep their jobs, you might consider having a word with those who no longer give a stuff. Such as the officers who have jacked it in, or retired. And, by the way, neither am I saying I might have a name for you.'

'And you're doing a bang-up job of avoiding saying anything.'

Shipman clapped him on the upper arm. 'Good. I hope I've made myself unclear.'

'Opaque as mud.' Chase looked down at his feet, surprised at how scuffed he'd allowed his shoes to become. He thought about everything his friend had and had not said. When he looked up again, he gave a nod of resignation. 'Maybe I shouldn't have made those calls. On the other hand, wouldn't it be expected of me, as the man responsible for investigating him?'

'That's just it, Royston. You're not investigating Ken Webster. You're investigating the circumstances of his RTC. You're also attempting to ID the young person who accompanied him.'

Chase agreed, offering a shrug. 'Fair enough. Slip of the tongue. All the same, it would look a bit odd if I didn't pursue that particular avenue. Wouldn't it?'

Shipman nodded. 'Pursue might be too strong a word. Look into, maybe. Of course you'd have to ask around, especially if his blood work comes back as expected. And you've made those inquiries.

You did your bit, Royston. You had no response. You left it there. That's all anybody needs to know.'

Chase didn't like what he was hearing. 'Who got to you since we last spoke, Trev? Are they putting pressure on you from the point of view of the RTC itself?'

He got no reply this time. Shipman only stared back, unblinking.

After a moment, Chase winked and laid a hand on his friend's shoulder. 'I'm saying nothing, Trev. Just like you. After you don't tell me who not to speak to, that is.'

Ten minutes later he was being prepped for the briefing. Superintendent Waddington was not a happy man. In fairness, that's how he always came across to Chase. The DSI's edginess was apparent in every mannerism, and when he spoke his voice caught at the back of his throat which had to be squeezing tighter the closer they got to meeting the media.

'I need a direction. I need to feed these bastards something they can't throw up at me in return.'

'You need a distraction,' Chase replied. He blinked, having not expected to say that.

'What do you mean by that, Sergeant?'

Chase eyed his boss, then slipped his gaze sideways across to the senior media officer who had joined them. 'We're not there,' he said. 'Nowhere near. All that we have learned so far only makes things worse for Sir Kenneth. From what I understand, the hospital is holding up its end of the deal. They're blanking the media in respect of confirmed fatalities. We know that won't last, but we can at least defer to them and make it clear we are not willing to speculate when it comes to life and death.'

'Good. Yes.' Waddington nodded. 'So why the distraction?'

'Because we will have to provide them with that number at some point, sir. Tomorrow at the latest, I suspect. By that stage we'll no longer be able to ignore the young girl. The only way the media won't smell blood is if we distract them somehow.'

'And how do you propose we do that?' the media officer asked.

'I have absolutely no idea,' Chase said. 'That's your speciality, isn't it?'

*

The fifteen minute session was tolerable. Waddington began by informing the gathered TV crews and assorted journalists of his short visit to Webster Manor, and his subsequent conversation with the grieving widow. He had offered his assurances on behalf of Wiltshire Police. An in-depth investigation would be carried out, but currently there appeared to be nothing more to report beyond that of the tragedy itself and the deaths arising from it. When Chase's name came up, his role was described as working under Waddington's supervision in a position supporting both Inspector Shipman and the investigating team. Not important enough to be prominent, but a usefully significant figure when the shit started flowing downhill.

The latter was not mentioned out loud, but the implication was clear to everyone in the room.

Chase was hoping to leave as soon as the briefing was over, but Waddington had other ideas. A meeting had been arranged with the wider team tasked with investigating the fatal RTC, and there was no question of Chase not being involved. The meeting room on the first floor was large, and it needed to be. In addition to Superintendent Waddington, Chief Superintendent Crawley had also been invited to attend, as had Trevor Shipman, Maggie O'Donnell in her role as head of SCIT, the Collision Investigation Unit boss, Marcus Hinds, and completing the full set, Anne Joiner, the Senior Investigating Officer sent from Roads Policing. Each of them also seemed to have a lackey with them to take notes, except for Waddington. Chase took this to mean his role at the meeting was to act as the Superintendent's personal assistant.

The Chief Super got the ball rolling by insisting all subsequent proceedings and discussions were to be sealed. Everyone in the room was invited to speak freely; a statement that drew a warning glance in Chase's direction from Waddington. He pretended not to notice, though it had lacked subtlety. Crawley finished his opening speech by outlining the process, during which each area of the incident was to be examined in chronological order.

That put Shipman up first in the crosshairs.

He kicked off by providing a brief outline of the call he had taken, describing how the first responding officers had spotted Sir Kenneth's vehicle among the wreckage. Upon closer inspection, it was immediately clear to them that the man had not survived. They then went on to reveal that witnesses had described the driver of the Land Rover as being entirely responsible for the devastation at the roundabout. It was only after he'd arrived at the scene that Shipman was advised about the man's passenger, her condition, and the circumstances surrounding her presence there.

'Let's all be adult about it,' Crawley said at that point. 'A naked, underage girl was found with part of Sir Kenneth's penis in her mouth. It doesn't take a postmortem to confirm what that means.'

Hinds from CIU quickly told his story. His entire involvement amounted to contacting SCIT and instructing Maggie O'Donnell to send a team out to the scene because multiple fatalities had occurred. The Serious Collision Investigation Team used specialised equipment, testing brake fluid, window tint depth, tyre depth and pressure, vehicle brakes and suspension, and anything else that may have been a contributory factor in the collision.

They also mapped the scene using GPS and direct line of sight surveying equipment to plot the location of every vehicle involved. In addition, their role was to identify marks and scuffs on the road and disturbances to the roadside vegetation, to help build a more complete picture of what happened. They also sought to understand the behaviour of the drivers involved in such collisions. This included testing eyesight, breathalysing drivers, testing for drug use and seizing mobile phones.

O'Donnell declared herself satisfied with the work of her dedicated officers and technicians. 'I've examined my chief forensic investigator's report, studied video footage, examined photographs, and familiarised myself with all relevant details. There is no doubt in my mind that the evidence concurs with witness statements.'

The SIO from Roads Policing stood – as others had done – to lay things out more clearly. 'Current fatalities number six,' Anne Joiner said. 'But we are expecting that number to increase, possibly to reach a final total of eight. That is a substantial figure, more commonly associated with motorway pile-ups. My remit is to ensure all data is complete and correct, and to work with legal teams in any subsequent inquiries.'

All faces turned to the Chief Superintendent. The meeting had confirmed rigid compliance between policy and procedure. Strict adherence was to be expected at any time, but with this particular RTC, the investigation into its cause was taking place beneath the stern gaze of the public. Families had lost lives, and they needed to know who to blame.

Up to this point, Chase had kept quiet and gone about the business of taking notes. With a silence in the room to fill, he found himself speaking without realising what he was about to say. 'The elephant in the room remains the underage girl,' he said, his eyes still on his notepad.

When the hush continued, broken only by the clearing of throats, he eventually looked up to see he had become the focal point of attention. He sought out Trevor Shipman, who was almost imperceptibly shaking his head. But Chase realised others in the room expected him to continue, and so he did.

'With all due respect to Sir Kenneth, this is not something we'll be able to sweep under the carpet. Eventually, somebody is going to start totting up the number of drivers and passengers and realise they are not all accounted for. That not all the fatalities are accounted for, to be more precise. Their attention may also be drawn to the fact that the mortuary is holding one victim too many. It will come out. Trust me on that. This is far too juicy a prospect, and someone will get rich on the back of it.'

'And your point is?' Waddington demanded to know.

Chase could only admire how the man both threw him to the wolves and demonstrated who was in charge with that one simple question.

'That we are well and truly stuffed no matter what. If we sit on the information, we are made to look either incompetent or corrupt when the details eventually spill out. We cause uproar and wild speculation if we release anything without being fully aware of what precisely happened in that vehicle driven by Sir Kenneth. Yet I am of the opinion that we get ahead of it as soon as we are able.'

'Am I right in thinking you are currently looking into this particular aspect?' Crawley asked.

'You are, sir.'

'And you are at what stage in your investigation?'

'Given the time constraints, I'd say preliminary.'

'What can you tell us, DS Chase?'

'That yesterday evening, Sir Kenneth left Webster Manor on his own, driving his Land Rover. The rest you already know.'

This sent a hubbub of chatter around the room.

'That's it?!' Crawley said, incredulous.

'In terms of hard facts, yes, sir. The estate manager, man by the name of Radford, confirmed that he saw Sir Kenneth drive off. There are no guests staying at the manor, and Sir Kenneth was unaccompanied at the time. Between then and the RTC, which you are all aware of, we have a gap of around five hours. Those are the known facts, though if you want insinuations and speculation I can also provide them.'

Crawley spread his hands. 'Go ahead, Sergeant.'

Chase nodded and paused for breath. He did not like to be the centre of attention at the best of times, and these were anything but the best of times. He went on to relate the information available to him, outlining the routine acceptance of Sir Kenneth's driving while under the influence. He mentioned Radford's educated guess that his boss had intended to visit his club, which was located near Calne.

'As far as I've been able to ascertain, the club goes by the name of Tier One. Its co-founders were Sir Kenneth himself and Sir Colin Shakespeare. As yet I've not been able to locate the club's premises, nor have I been able to confirm Sir Kenneth's presence there last night. And, of course, that still leaves us with an unidentified victim who appears not to have been reported missing. All of which poses a vast number of questions in need of answering.'

SEVEN

HOME FOR ROYSTON CHASE was a detached house in the small village of Shrivenham, over the county border in Oxfordshire. The UK Defence Academy was a close neighbour, where the best and the brightest were prepared for high office and a world of secrecy. His property had been ideally situated for Chase when he worked out of Gablecross, but since the change he spent an hour a day commuting.

The plus side of being shipped out to Little Soley was the improved weekly hours. Since being posted there, he'd seen little in the way of major crime, and certainly nothing requiring an overtime requisition. That might be about to change, and Chase felt the first tingle of excitement in quite some time.

Prior to leaving Gablecross, he'd caught up with Maggie O'Donnell. 'Anything worthwhile from Ken Webster's mobile phone?' he asked.

'Not so far. Certainly no leads on where he'd been that night, nor who his passenger was. We'll keep on trawling through the data, though.'

'How about GPS history? Can we trace his whereabouts that way? I'm particularly interested in where he was after six-thirty yesterday evening.'

O'Donnell gave him a curious narrow stare. 'Oh, yes? Why six-thirty?'

'That's the time he left his farm.'

'Interesting.' Her eyebrows arched.

'In what way?'

'Because twenty-one minutes past six is when he switched his phone off. It never came back on.'

The conversation replayed through his mind as he locked the car and walked along a short path leading to his home. His friend had presented him with yet another barrier, yet to Chase the act of switching off the phone suggested Sir Kenneth had already known the kind of evening he was in for. The thought process intrigued him, conjuring up all manner of possibilities.

He pushed open the front door and breathed in the delicious aroma of steak pie nearing completion. He wondered what he had done right to earn himself one of his favourite meals on a weekday evening. He took off his jacket and hung it on a hook by the front door, which he had closed as softly as possible. He approached the kitchen by stealth, but after only a couple of paces a pocket-sized human missile launched itself at him and two arms wrapped around his thighs.

'Daddy, Daddy!' his seven-year-old daughter cried gleefully. Her pink cheeks shone and bulged around a wide smile of pure delight. A straggly mop of black hair flopped across her shoulders.

Chase scooped her up off the carpet and held her high. 'Uh, you're getting too heavy for this,' he said, exaggerating the buckle of his knees. 'How are you doing, chicken lips?'

She gave him the kind of look it had taken her mother many more years to perfect. 'Daddeeee.' She rested her forehead against his, her gorgeous big eyes brimming with mischief. 'I've told you before, chickens don't have lips.'

'What? Of course they do. How do you think they give each other kisses?' He proceeded to plant smackers all over his daughter's face. She squealed in delight, her chuckle making him laugh.

'Chickens don't kiss each other, silly.'

Chase looked at her for a second with his mouth wide open. 'Are you insane? You think they peck each other with their beaks? That would be crazy.'

'No, you're crazy.'

'No, you're crazy.'

'No, you're crazy.'

'No, you're crazy to infinity and beyond.'

His daughter hunched her shoulders and giggled, squirming out of his arms as he put her back down. 'To infinity and beyond!' she roared, holding her arm upright, her tiny hand forcing a fist.

Maisie had come as a surprise package. Chase was thirty and focussed on his career when their daughter was born. His wife, Erin, had her own business producing individualised books for children. Neither of them were prepared for parenthood, not even nine months later when Maisie arrived. Now that she was in their lives, he often wondered why they had waited.

He was no dummy, and Erin outshone him in the raw intelligence department, so they were not naive enough to believe that the sweetest little girl who ever drew breath wasn't at some point in the future going to become a raging hormonal nightmare on two legs. But they both lived for the moment, adapting to circumstances as they arose.

Where Erin had gradually brought along a successor from the inside to run her company from the day she stepped aside to focus on giving birth, he had cut back on his hours knowing that in doing so he was also shelving any career advancement he might have been planning. Which became moot when a scuffle with a fleeing suspect had led to him falling backwards on a flight of steps, smashing his head open and causing a minor brain bleed and some swelling.

As a couple, he and Erin had taken it in their stride. Getting up again was what counted, not that you fell in the first place. It had helped them both being cut from the same cloth, and nothing Maisie had done since being born suggested she had not inherited this trait from them. As Chase watched his daughter skip back into the kitchen, he felt an ache descend upon his heart like an anchor. Not one that threatened to drag him under, more hold him firmly in place to provide a sense of stability.

Erin had already popped the tops off two bottles of beer. It was their daily treat – something to take the edge off the day and to look forward to each morning. They kissed and hugged, then each gave a satisfied sigh after taking that first gulp of chilled Peroni.

'How'd it go today?' Erin asked. Chase always told his wife about his cases, omitting the gory details but making sure she understood the severity of the crimes he dealt with. It helped their relationship, because she had come to terms with the rhythms of his moods and distractions depending on the kind of investigations he worked at the time.

'We made some progress.'

'You didn't get a great deal of sleep, I bet. What time did you eventually make it home?'

Chase shook his head. 'I have no idea. I was worried I might disturb you, so I got a bit of kip on the sofa, but pretty much tossed and turned.'

'From what you said this morning, it sounds like a disaster waiting to happen. Let's hope it's someone else's disaster sooner rather than later.'

'That may not be the case. I think I'm stuck with it.'

Erin eyed him suspiciously. 'Stuck with, or fought to keep? I know that look, Royston.'

He took a swig from his bottle and grinned. 'Let's just say I found it intriguing enough to want to stick with it a while longer.'

His wife said no more about the matter. They ate dinner, put Maisie to bed, watched a bit of TV. They each had another beer, but did not move on to wine. When Erin said she was headed to bed, he told her he'd be up soon.

She smiled at him and said, 'I won't stay awake. If you join me before midnight I'll be staggered.'

She knew him well. The first couple of days with a new major case prompted a predictable response. He worried and fretted over the investigation until it started to take shape. It was his way, and she accepted it. Chase loved her all the more for that.

What had been described by the estate agent as a potential fourth bedroom was in effect hardly large enough to be a storage cupboard. But Chase had created a small office out of it, and after saying goodnight to Erin, he took himself into his own space and sat down at the tiny desk. He pulled over a lined pad and began scribbling notes to himself. When he was done bullet-pointing the salient investigative moves taken so far, he leaned back in his chair and sent his mind in search of further answers.

Seemingly, nobody had recently reported missing a young girl whose description matched that of their victim. Chase found himself once again thinking of her as a runaway; somebody Sir Kenneth could easily have spotted either walking the streets of Calne or perhaps sleeping rough in a shop doorway. The substantial matter of her missing clothes aside, it was the most likely scenario he could think of, which meant trawling through various databases.

Inevitably his thoughts drifted to Maisie, safe and secure in her bed. It was impossible to imagine her leaving home and living on the street in a few years' time. Neither he nor Erin would ever give her reason to run away, but he was all too aware of the physical and chemical changes she would undergo, and the other influences that had yet to enter her life. His own sister had left home shortly after her fifteenth birthday. She was gone for little more than a week, but he vividly remembered the strain and stress his parents had endured every day she was missing. It prematurely aged them, and altered their perceptions of who and what they were.

As for Ken Webster, Chase held only contempt in his heart for the supposed pillar of the community. He'd asked the question earlier in the day, but again he wondered how many girls there had been before this one. Had he stripped them naked, too? Had he forced them to engage in sexual acts with him? He winced at the thought of the man's penis being bitten into by the girl's teeth clamping down at the point at which the Land Rover slammed into the roundabout, before being ripped off entirely as she was abruptly flung in the opposite direction by the next impact. For a brief moment he was even glad of it; happy to know that the man had endured that moment of agony immediately prior to losing his own life. He had caused the girl to lose hers, but what might have become of her had they both made it back to Webster Manor that night?

Chase recalled an investigation he'd worked while he was still in uniform. Although not as young as this girl, a woman new to being homeless had been lured away from her spot by the offer of some hot food and warm lodgings for the night. In mid-January the temperature plunged close to zero, and on clear nights the ground frost lay like a thin carpet of fresh snow. The price she had been willing to pay was to have sex with the man. The price she had eventually paid was to be repeatedly raped by a gang for several days before being thrown back on the streets.

Sitting alongside a female constable while the woman related her tale of brutality and drug-fuelled sexual abuse, Chase had felt only loathing for the animals who had treated her with such contempt. He volunteered to take part in the ensuing investigation. It was his first time working with CID, and he'd found the experience exhilarating. He never once forgot the terrible incident that had led him there, and had remained in touch with the victim as part of her liaison team. But he was also overtaken by a sense of place, a feeling that this was where he needed to be. Driven to find the poor excuses for human beings that had physically and sexually abused the homeless woman, Chase had dropped everything else in his life at the time. On the day the team arrested and charged six men, he knew this had to be his future.

Each of those men was a drug user, which became the lame excuse for their repulsive behaviour. Their lower class status, an inability to hold down a proper job, and the ensuing poverty this caused, was also used in mitigation. All six were found guilty and given prison sentences. Their deprived backgrounds had not saved them. Would Sir Kenneth's privileged upbringing and heady career save him?

Chase vowed there and then that it would not, if he had any say in the matter. Landed gentry and their ilk were experts in covering up their examples of low morals and poor judgement, and they could also afford the best legal representation money could buy. But in his view, there was simply no explanation feasible nor forceful enough to explain away the events leading up to the crash. Nor Sir Kenneth's role in them. Whoever this young girl was, the man had to be held to account. Nothing else would be acceptable to Royston Chase.

He wrote himself a few more notes before calling it a night. He felt he might need all the forbearance he could muster in the days to come, but this was a fight he very much wanted to be in the middle of. No matter what the cost.

EIGHT

When chase arrived at the station the following morning, PCSO May's face bore all the hallmarks of a cat having dined on both a canary and a full pot of cream for breakfast. 'Don't tell me,' he said. 'You won the lottery and you're handing in your notice.'

May's grin widened. 'Oh, no. It's so much better than that.'

'You do look extremely pleased with yourself, Alison.'

'I am, sir. Savouring the moment, you might say.'

'Okay. You have my full attention. What's up?'

'Your blood pressure in the very near future.'

Chase groaned. 'Please tell me Superintendent Waddington isn't here.'

Through a chuckle, May said, 'No, the Super is not here, sir. But you do have a visitor waiting for you in your office.'

Chase closed his eyes. Ah, yes. Before leaving Gablecross the previous evening, he'd had to sit and wait in the Superintendent's office for Waddington to discuss something with his boss. Upon his return, the Super appeared put out. Agitated, he shifted endlessly in his chair, causing Chase to wonder if the man had some form of ADHD. When he spoke, his voice was clipped.

'Evidently, DS Chase, you are to have some assistance for the duration of this investigation.'

He'd imagined being partnered with Alison May, but the Chief Super had other ideas. Crawley was about as keen as Waddington himself on the idea of Chase running the inquiry, and had insisted that he did not do so alone. No debate, no argument. Chase was being joined by a female detective who had recently transferred across to Wiltshire Police from another area.

'Wipe that smug grin off your face,' Chase told PCSO May, jabbing a stern finger across the front desk. 'It's unbecoming.'

'Yes, sir. I'm having a little trouble not laughing, that's all.'

Chase sighed and thrust both hands into his pockets. 'She can't be that bad. Please tell me she's not that bad.'

'I couldn't possibly say. We exchanged only the briefest of greetings.'

'Which is all you needed to set off that smirk of yours?'

'In this case, sir? Yes. You'll know why as soon as you lay eyes on her.'

He left May to it, certain he heard her smothering another laugh as he walked away. Pausing outside his own office, Chase took a deep breath. He suspected May was simply trying to wind him up. Put him off his game. He fully expected to push open the door to find a perfectly normal…

To begin with, the woman was sitting in his chair. Sprawled, more like. Both feet on his desk, crossed at the ankles. She wore heavy brown boots, and what looked to be black denim trousers. Over a rusty-orange roll-neck sweater, she had on a midnight blue leather jacket with black tassels on the seams of both arms. Chase's gaze continued to travel north…

The Detective Constable he had been sent looked older and more clapped out than his own grandmother. Moreover, a granny with a face that Heath Ledger's Joker might have had second thoughts about when he caught sight of his reflection in a mirror. As Chase entered the room and completed his fleeting assessment, the woman remained where she was. Cupping both hands behind her head, she said, 'About bloody time. I'm gasping for a brew and I could find no tea bags. Be a love and put the kettle on, will you?'

At first he made no reply. She rolled her eyes as he hovered over the threshold. 'You're not one of those men who think the women should always make the tea, are you? Times have changed, cupcake. Perhaps you haven't noticed. Though judging by this musty old room and your equally ancient haircut, I could be wrong.'

Chase stood rooted to the spot. 'And you are?' he said.

The new DC both groaned and sighed. She struggled up out of the chair, stuffed both hands into her jacket pockets, and nodded in his direction. 'Morning,' she said. 'I'm DC Laney. Claire. You're DS Chase, I assume. There, introductions over. So, how about that cuppa?'

'I'm sorry,' Chase said, mustering all of his composure, 'but you do understand that I'm the more senior officer of the two of us, yes?'

Laney winked at him, seemingly undaunted. 'Of course I do, love. But I won't hold that against you. Is that the meet and greet done with?'

'No. It isn't.'

He deliberately held out his hand, knowing she could not refuse to clasp it under the circumstances. He tried hard not to stare as he took a pace forward, but noticed her hand first snake out and then jerk away as she took a step back, almost falling into the chair she'd heaved herself out of. 'What the bloody hell is up with you?' she said, her voice climbing in both pitch and volume.

'Nothing. I just...'

'You just what? I saw that look pass across your face. What was that all about?'

'Nothing, really. I thought you'd be younger, that's all.'

Her mouth fell open. She glared at him for several seconds before responding. 'And I hoped you'd not be a complete tosser, so I guess we're both disappointed.'

Chase shook his head. 'I'm not disappointed, as I had no expectations. I was taken by surprise, that's all. To be honest, I'd forgotten all about you being assigned to me until Alison told me you were here.'

'Alison? Alison who?'

'Our PCSO at the desk.'

'Oh, you mean the fluttery little blonde.'

'Alison May, yes. Anyhow, I thought Superintendent Waddington mentioned you were winding down your time ahead of retirement. I must have got that wrong.'

'How so?'

'I hadn't realised you were already retired and had come back.'

Laney exhaled rapidly and rammed both fists into her hips. 'What the fu… How bloody old do you think I am?'

'Mid-sixties?'

'Excuse me?! You cheeky bastard! I'm closer to fifty than sixty. What kind of thing is that to say to a woman? To anybody, for that matter. I may look a bit old and crusty, but I don't expect to be told I do.'

Chase had no idea how to react. In his eyes her face was more condemned than lived in, and he suspected it had endured all kinds of toxic abuse over many decades. Currently it was growing dark, eyes screwing up tight.

'I'm sorry,' he said, averting his gaze before she incited some other careless remark. 'I do that sometimes when I get nervous or confused. I don't mean to offend. Also, it has nothing to do with you being female – if you were a man with a comb over or an obvious wig, I'd have reacted in a similar way. And please believe me when I tell you it's not so much your puffy skin or deep wrinkles, it's more the heavy makeup.'

His words did not have the desired effect.

Incredulity took over. 'Is that right? Aw, thank you. Thank you so much. I'm so glad it's not my podgy flesh or crevices so deep you could hide a submarine in them. That's such a massive relief. And what's wrong with my makeup, anyway?'

Chase's mind returned to Heath Ledger, but on this occasion he managed to stop himself from saying so. 'You look a bit like a clown,' he said instead.

This time her nostrils flared and her mouth screwed up into something resembling an anal sphincter. 'Say that again! Go on, say it again and I'll claw your face to shreds with my old hag nails.'

'You can't speak to a senior officer like that,' Chase told her.

'And you can't speak to a... human being the way you did.'

'Well, don't ask me leading questions.'

'Use your filter, man. Use your bloody filter.'

'If I could, I would. Believe me. It... it goes missing sometimes.'

Laney reset her features. Bemusement replaced fury. 'Seriously?'

'Seriously.'

She huffed a long sigh of frustration, turned away and threw her arms up in the air. 'Jesus! Why do I always wind up working alongside the bloody cranks?'

'Would you like that cup of tea now?' Chase asked for want of anything else to say.

*

'You do know you can't smoke in here?' Chase said.

DC Laney's response was to take an extra-long drag on her cigarette and then blow the smoke in his direction. She even wafted it his way with her hand. 'And yet, I seem to be doing precisely that.'

She had made a cup of tea for herself, which she slurped down while it was still close to boiling. She had not asked Chase if he wanted a drink, and given the circumstances, he didn't blame her. He felt guilty, and realised he had probably offended the woman. Not knowing what to say, he stood and stared in her direction and tried his best to look remorseful.

Laney stared back at him, becalmed. Over the rim of the mug she said, 'So, what's your problem, Sergeant?'

'What do you mean?'

'This lack of filter business. I'm assuming there's a medical cause. It's either that or you're making excuses for being a complete dickwad, and right now I wouldn't take bets on either one of them.'

She was sitting on the right side of his desk this time. He took his own chair, buying time to think of how much to tell this scary woman. Although she looked as if she could take care of herself, he felt he owed her an explanation.

'I had a fall. Smacked my head on a concrete step. It caused a bleed and then a blood clot between my skull and my brain, which put pressure on it. I was operated on to relieve that pressure, and on the whole recovered pretty well from my surgery and the initial damage to my brain. However, among a whole litany of side-effects, I have moments when I lose my inhibitions. Verbally, at least. If it was physical as well, I'd probably be out of a job. Or, at least, the job I want to be doing.'

Laney made no immediate reply. She appeared to study him. Then she stubbed out her cigarette on the side of her mug and dropped it into the dregs of her drink. 'You weren't giving me some old shite simply to cover your arse, then? You actually do have a physical problem and weren't just being horrible to me.'

'I do, and I wasn't. But I'm sorry, all the same. Most of the time I don't mean to offend people, and I don't like it when I do. It can be extremely embarrassing, not to mention distressing at times. For all concerned. Like I said before, it has nothing to do with you being female. The thing is, unless somebody pulls me up on it the way you did, I very often don't even realise I've done it.'

'So you are capable of saying precisely what pops into your head. And you have no control over it whatsoever?'

He thought about that for a moment. 'I have coping mechanisms. I try to slow down my response times when in conversation. This often allows that aspect of my brain to catch up and apply the filter. But when I'm confused, taken by surprise, or simply forget to relax, then that control occasionally escapes me.'

Laney nodded. 'That must be difficult to deal with.'

'It can be.'

'But, essentially, all you are doing is saying what you think.'

'That's correct.'

'So let me get this straight: you're sorry for phrasing things the way you did, but in fact you still think I look like an ancient, puffy, wrinkled, version of Ronald McDonald?'

Chase winced. 'Don't ask,' he said. 'Please don't ask.'

For the first time, DC Laney chuckled. 'It's okay. I'm a tough old bird. It takes more than a few insults to drag me down. As for the fags, I yearn to be a chain smoker because I enjoy things to excess. But don't worry, this is an occasional bad habit, and I won't do it again in here.'

'I'm happy to hear it. So, what's your story, Claire?'

'You mean how has this old bag ended up in the arse-end of nowhere with you? Mine is a much simpler explanation. I get on the wrong side of pretty much everybody. I have a mouth on me, and I'm not afraid to use it as a weapon. You've probably noticed. Unlike you, I have no brain injury to blame.'

'Then why are you this way?' Chase was genuinely interested. He liked to study people, especially those he worked closely with.

'Hard to say. I drink too much, smoke too much, fuck too much. I don't conform, and I don't give a crap. I also have a bad habit of pissing the wrong people off, which is why I've gone from DI back to DC in the past decade. I have a little over two years to go before I reach my fifty-fifth birthday. To our twunty bosses I'm a bad smell lingering long enough to grab my early pension and run.'

Chase had been told some of it and guessed the rest. What interested him beyond the bare facts of Laney's story was not why she had been posted to Little Soley, but the timing of the move. If he needed assistance on this case, was Laney the right person to provide it? She seemed not to care about anything other than drawing breath and eking out her time in order to take the pension pot she considered her due. What exactly was she able to offer him? Or the investigation?

But then, perhaps that was precisely why those strolling the corridors of power had sent DC Claire Laney. Because maybe they wanted to hinder rather than help.

'You're not going to go to sixty, then?' he asked.

'I could do. They certainly couldn't make me quit. But I think another two years is all this… tired old body can take.'

Chase gave a sheepish smile. 'I can only apologise once again.'

Laney waved away his words. 'Don't worry about it, love. Those were my own words this time. It's the way I feel about myself, and it's only going to get worse. I probably overdid it today in order to make the wrong impression. Shock value, you know?'

It was an honest assessment. Chase regretted his earlier statements, though they were not far off the mark. Beneath the thick layers of makeup and the unusual attire, she was clearly a genuine, forthright woman with strong opinions. An experienced cop, too. That counted for a lot.

'What's the job we're working on?' Laney asked him, snapping him away from his thought process. 'Forget all that nonsense earlier between us. As time goes by you'll find I'm a much better cop than I am a person. Tell me what you want me to do.'

Nodding to himself, Chase said, 'Claire, how much would you like to stick it to the people who dumped you here with me hoping it would be the last they ever heard from you?'

Laney leaned forward. Her smile cracked her makeup mask wide open. 'Go on,' she said. 'I'm listening.'

NINE

THE MARKET TOWN IN which Stacey Brownlow lived had been known as Royal Wootton Basset for over a decade, having been granted royal patronage in recognition of its role in military funeral repatriations which passed through on the way from RAF Lyneham en route to Oxford. Chase thought about those funeral corteges as he drove into the town, specifically recalling the increasing number of people lining the pavements between the spring of 2007 and summer 2011. The elevated sense of patriotism during that period was never better exemplified, and he had been a part of that crowd on several occasions..

Brownlow had not been fired from the police service, and neither had she retired. She had simply not returned to her job after giving birth to her second child. It was clear from the moment she opened the door to him and Laney that a third at least was on the way; and probably quite close to making an appearance.

Chase had not called ahead. Doing so gave people the option of talking or delaying, and invariably they chose the latter. His intention had been to take the ex-cop by surprise, and the look on her face told him he'd been successful. He wondered if she might refuse to talk once she knew why he and DC Laney were there, but after a momentary delay she allowed them inside.

Both detectives accepted the hot drinks Brownlow offered. Without waiting for a sly word from Chase, his new colleague offered to make it; a gesture he appreciated as it enabled him to break the ice. 'Thanks for agreeing to talk to us, Stacey,' he said, taking a seat in the small but tastefully decorated living room. He scrutinised an array of framed photographs lined up on a set of free-standing bookshelves. 'You decided to give up the job in order to raise a family, I see. Looks to me as if you made the right choice.'

One hand cupped beneath her bulging stomach, Brownlow followed his gaze. The smile she gave brought her entire face to life. 'Yes, I think so. Funny, for a moment there I thought you were about to lecture me about how the job I gave up was vitally important.'

Chase arched his eyebrows. 'Not at all. I mean, it is, don't get me wrong about that. But so is what you have going on here.'

'You have a family of your own, Sergeant?'

'I do. My wife and I have the one child. A daughter.'

'That's nice. Having children made my husband and I happier still, but I know it's not for everyone.'

'I suspect we'll settle for our little Maisie. She's more than a handful.' He smiled affectionately, knowing Stacey Brownlow would recognise its source.

Laney came in with their drinks. Chase waited for her to take her place on the sofa before he began. 'Stacey, at the door I said we wanted a word with you about Sir Kenneth Webster. I'm grateful to you for agreeing to speak to us. I also get the impression our visit wasn't entirely unexpected.'

Brownlow sipped from her mug before responding. 'As you will know yourself, the police jungle drums are loud, and I still get to hear them. I received one or two calls, I have to admit. Made a couple of my own, too.'

Chase leaned closer. 'My understanding is you were unhappy at Sir Kenneth receiving preferential treatment. Is that the case?'

'Yes, it is.' No hesitation. 'The man was a bad accident waiting to happen, though I only ever encountered him on two occasions.

On the first of those, he'd driven off the road down into a slight ditch and ended up buried in some hedgerow. The second time we pulled him over because he was wandering all over the road when we happened to come up behind him. I wanted to breathalyse him both times. But I was the junior partner and told to forget all about it.' Brownlow paused. Blinked twice. 'Now look at what he did. How do you think I feel about that?'

'I can only imagine. You must be devastated.'

'It's not your fault, lovely,' Laney offered. 'No doubt the officer you were partnered with was under instruction himself. Either that or had his own snout in the trough.'

Chase shot her a warning look. 'We can't know the circumstances, DC Laney. Better if we allow Stacey to speak for herself, don't you think?'

She offered nothing in reply, but he could tell she did not agree with him.

'Actually,' Brownlow said, 'I think your partner here is right, DS Chase. Mine was a great bloke, and we got on famously. Those two incidents with Sir Kenneth were just about the only times we fell out. I'm sure in his case it wasn't about money. He told me it was naive to imagine a scenario in which matters would be taken further. That the only ones in the firing line if we went through our normal procedures would be us.'

'And there I would have to agree with him,' Chase said, after sipping from his mug. 'I play by the rules as often as I can because I believe in them. Up to a point. But breathalysing an ex-Chief Constable with such a massive social profile, and perhaps having to arrest the man and drag him into the local nick, would almost certainly have been career suicide. It simply gets too political at those levels. That's the perception, at least.'

Perched on the very edge of her seat cushion, the heavily pregnant woman clasped both hands beneath her belly. 'I felt terrible letting him walk away. It didn't sit right with me, but I didn't want to harm my partner's ambitions. I didn't know what interference there might be from above, or even if there would be any. I suppose I simply wasn't willing to risk it on his behalf.'

Chase flashed a knowing smile. 'I notice you haven't mentioned your partner's name. That's commendable of you, but of course we can easily find that out if we need to.'

Brownlow nodded. 'If you must. That's fine, provided it's not from me.'

'Hopefully it won't come to that, Stacey. At this stage, I'm not intending to make anything formal regarding this aspect of my investigation. Bearing that in mind, you told us you encountered Sir Kenneth driving in that condition on two separate occasions. Tell me, was he alone both times?'

'Yes.' She half turned her head and her eyes narrowed. 'Why do you ask?'

Chase ignored the question. 'And what about others who patrolled those same roads when you and your partner were off duty? Any reports of unusual activity relating to our Knight of the Realm?'

'Such as?'

'Anything. Something out of the ordinary. Beyond him being a drunk driver, I mean.'

'Not that I ever heard, no.'

'Okay. How about this: I'm guessing he was headed in the direction of home on the two occasions you came across him. If that's the case, did either you or your partner ask him where he had come from?'

Brownlow searched her memory. She dipped her head before speaking again. 'I did. I have a clear recollection of that. I'm sorry, though. He didn't answer me.'

'Did you think he was being evasive? Or was he too pissed to understand what you were asking?'

'I got the feeling it was a bit of both. However, it didn't seem as if it was worth pursuing. Look, DS Chase, I'm happy to answer these questions. It's a small sacrifice given what happened the other night.

But the ex-cop in me can't help but wonder where your questioning is leading.'

He'd expected as much, anticipating her eventual response. 'I understand. We are simply looking to establish his whereabouts prior to the RTC. Intel so far suggests Sir Kenneth might have been running his own form of gentleman's club. There's a suggestion that this could be located somewhere on the road between Calne and Chippenham. Do you know anything about that, Stacey?'

Judging by the firm shake of her head and the look in her eyes, Chase did not think Stacey Brownlow was lying to them when she said she had never heard the rumour and had no idea where the club might be located. If not exactly eager to please, she did seem perfectly willing to share whatever she knew. Hers was one of two names offered up by Trevor Shipman. Chase had approached Brownlow first because, when he traced the other ex-patrol officer, he discovered the man had retired to his home city of Durham. Chase had hoped to get enough out of this visit to prevent them having to traipse up north.

He glanced over at Laney. 'I think that's about it from me,' he said. 'Do you have anything to add, Constable?'

'I do have one question, if that's all right by you?'

'Of course.'

His colleague turned her attention to Brownlow. 'Stacey, you worked this general area for quite a while. You say you heard no rumours about Sir Kenneth. Nothing above and beyond him driving around with a drink inside him. Nor do you know about this club he's supposed to have a stake in. So how about men picking up young runaways? Are you aware of anything like that going on around here?'

'Is that why I was asked whether Ken Webster was alone both times I encountered him?' Brownlow asked after a moment of stunned silence. 'He was with somebody when he was killed? Is that it? A homeless kid?'

Chase jumped back in. 'You know we can't comment on that, Stacey. And I'd strongly advise you to keep such speculation to yourself. Thank you for your help.' He put down his cup and got to his feet. 'Your cooperation is appreciated, and I understand your reticence regarding your old partner. Perhaps we'd all be better off forgetting what was said here. And not said, for that matter.'

On the drive out of Wootton Basset, Chase said nothing for a few moments while he gathered his thoughts. Eventually, when he felt calm enough to talk reasonably, he turned to Laney and said, 'What the bloody hell was that back there, Claire?'

She turned to him in surprise at his curt manner. 'What do you mean?'

'Those questions as we were wrapping up. You might as well have shown her our case file. The death of that minor is not a detail our bosses are keen to expose. You do get that, right?'

'I do. But she could have known something she hadn't put together with Sir Kenneth. It felt to me like a legitimate question in need of asking.'

'But did you have to be so obvious about it?'

'Yes. I thought that was the point. We're looking for information. As somebody who patrolled that area regularly for a number of years, Stacey Brownlow was in a good position to be aware of that sort of thing. Local intelligence.'

'And it didn't bother you at all that in doing so the way you went about it you were putting Ken Webster in the same little box as homeless young girls?'

Laney shook her head. 'No. Not at all. Brownlow used to be one of us. She knows how the game is played. I wouldn't have done that with a civilian.'

'But she *is* a civilian, Claire. That's my point.'

'Yes, but she still knows what way is up. She won't want a full inquiry leading back to her door, so she won't be telling anybody else.'

'And you know that for sure, do you?'

'You mean do I have one hundred percent confidence? No. But I'm certain enough to have chanced my arm.'

Chase blew out a lungful of frustration. He knew Laney was probably right; that the ex-traffic cop's experience and knowledge would most likely ensure her silence. Even so, it felt as if his new partner had taken an unnecessary risk. He took a couple of breaths and allowed his irritation with her to subside.

Laney seemed not to notice. Or if she did, she simply did not care. She was keen to know more about his plans for taking the investigation further. He didn't allow the fact that she had once been a Detective Inspector to influence his response.

'I have a lot running through my head,' he admitted. 'I'm only now trying to put it all into some perspective. Our unidentified victim disturbs me a great deal. She had no clothes with her at the time of the crash, which is something I'm struggling to get past. For me that puts even greater emphasis on where Ken Webster was that night and when and how he first encountered the girl. I do still suspect he may have been at this club he runs, but quite how his presence there relates to his eventual passenger on the drive home, I have no idea. I also think I probably need to speak to Lady Jane.'

Chase told his partner about Sir Kenneth's widow seeking a media injunction without being told anything other than the bare facts relating to the crash. Laney agreed it sounded suspicious.

'You think she knew about his inclination towards young girls?' she asked.

'I think her initial response implies more than a desire to suppress his reputation for drunk driving.'

'I don't know. These people get so up themselves they can't see clearly anymore. Her first thought might have been to protect her own status. She wouldn't want it sullied by accusations or, worse still, evidence against him regarding his alcohol levels. I'm guessing she was well aware of how he considered himself above all that.'

'You may well be right,' Chase acknowledged. 'Going for a media blackout seems like a complete overreaction to me, but then I don't live in their world. Also, we don't know there were other young girls. Not for sure. Until we can explain why this particular one was with him the other night, we may never know.'

'There had to have been others,' Laney said flatly. 'Or are you telling me this was pure coincidence? How bad would his luck have to be if the first time he tried it on with a young kid he rolled his motor and got them both killed?'

'I know. And I think you're right. Only, we have no evidence to back it up.'

'Yet.'

'Yet. Nor any idea how to acquire it other than the girl, the club, or his wife. And in that order.'

'Is your mate Shipman running down a list of reported runaways and missing persons?'

Chase shook his head. 'He will have nothing more to do with this beyond the RTA itself. I was hoping somebody would have claimed her by this stage. If they haven't by the time we get back to the station, I'll chase that up myself. The coroner will demand it, anyway.'

'I can do it if you like.'

He gave a sidelong glance.

'What?' she said defensively. 'You think you're the only good copper here? You're Mr Plod and Inspector Clouseau rolled into one compared to me, my love. My crumpled old face might have been around the block more times than a ten-quid brass, but so has the rest of me. When I put my mind to it, I can be a bloody good asset.'

Chase relented. 'In that case, fill your boots. There must be some way to find out who that kid was. The sooner we do that, the sooner we discover why she came within Ken Webster's radar.'

'And you'll be looking into the whereabouts of this club, I'm guessing?'

'Yes. Trevor Shipman was reluctant to go into any great detail, but I'm sure those patrol officers must have had some idea.'

'Stacey Brownlow didn't, and she seemed genuine enough to me.'

Chase agreed. 'If you're wondering why I'm headed this way and not across country, I want to have a drive around that area.'

'Between Calne and Chippenham? That's a lot of acreage.'

'True, but for at least part of that journey we have Bowood House and gardens along one side, so that cuts it down a bit.'

'Yes, but all you have is a rough idea that this club is located somewhere between the two towns, not how far off the main road you have to drive to get there. Other than the villages dotted around, you have plenty of farms and private land tucked away out of sight. If it's a secret club, I doubt this place is going to be signposted.'

He knew Laney was right. His urge to scour the area was as much in search of inspiration as it was any expectation on his part. Somewhere in the back of his head a small voice had niggled, telling him if he drove enough roads and lanes he'd eventually stumble across the place. It was a stupid idea, and his new partner had been right to call him on it.

'I don't know what I was thinking,' he said. 'Let's get back to the nick and do some real work. We don't have time to waste.'

'How about her Ladyship? You want to launch a stealth attack on her?'

Chase had imagined himself visiting the newly minted widow alone. Certainly without DC Laney. If Lady Jane Webster was half the snoot he expected her to be, someone like his new partner might cause her to have some kind of fit. But perhaps that was the precise reaction he wanted from the encounter.

'Yeah, why not? Tell you what, give HQ a call and ask if there's been any update on our girl's ID. Then have them start the ball rolling on mispers. Have them look for girls between ten and fourteen to begin with. You can pick up on that when we do get back to the station. For the time being, let's go and have a chat with our late Knight's Mrs.'

TEN

CHASE REALISED HE WAS pre-judging Lady Webster in a way he wholly disapproved of. He knew nothing of her character, and only his friend Shipman's caustic remark questioning the depth of her grief on the night of the crash had led to him thinking of her as anything other than a new widow in mourning. He made no mention of his intolerance to Laney, settling for mentally chastising himself.

The reason behind his instinctive dislike of a woman he had never met was her money and privilege. Landed gentry rubbed his ideologies up the wrong way. He was no socialist, and had no inclination to embrace civil war and anarchy in an attempt to rid the country of the elite. But he abhorred the kind of licence their wealth gave such people to live their lives by other standards. Lesser rather than higher, as was often the case. But Chase also knew he would never regard any other bereaved relative in the same way, and he didn't like what that said about him.

During the journey, he learned more about DC Laney's ignominious fall from grace. She had not willingly volunteered the information, but he wanted to know what kind of person his new partner was and why she had ended up working alongside him. He wasn't entirely sure which of them had been saddled with the other, and decided it could have gone either way. He found the notion both unsettling and amusing.

'Are you asking if my vices and unpleasant demeanour are the result of my demise or the cause of it?' she asked, cagily.

He thought of how clouded his approach to Lady Webster had been. He shifted his outlook a little. 'I'm trying hard not to speculate either way,' he said. 'Though I am interested in how our two falling stars have managed to collide.'

To his surprise, Laney smiled. To his greater surprise, it was a nice smile that changed her entire face. 'That's a good way of putting it,' she said. 'But I'd say yours is probably more on the wane rather than falling, whereas mine is in serious decline to the point of crashing and burning somewhere far beyond the horizon.'

Chase nodded. Shrugged as his hands gripped the steering wheel. 'So tell me about it. Looks as if we're stuck with this partnership for the time being, so we might as well get to know one another.'

'There isn't a great deal to tell. The truth is, I am this way by default. I am what it says on the tin. My real problem is that, rather than learning from my mistakes over the years, I've continued to make them and do so in such a way that I've burned all my bridges behind me. Nobody who ever worked with me can honestly have any issues with the way I did the job. I'm a bloody good detective, and my record speaks for itself. But we both know a person needs more than that in this business. Especially if you're female. If you want to get on in this job, you can't swear like a fishwife, drink like a fish, and fuck like… well, I can't think of a way of continuing the fish metaphor there, but you get my drift. You can't be a woman like that in today's police force.'

'Service,' Chase reminded her.

They exchanged grins at that.

'I don't know,' he said, risking several sidelong glances. 'I can't tell if you're screwing with my head or not. Having fun at my expense. I doubt you are as debauched as you make out.'

Laney took a breath. Exhaled slowly. 'Let's just say I'm not anymore. I don't do any of those things to excess these days. But I once did, and the past often trumps the present when it comes to reputation. I still talk a good game, though. And I won't bend over for any fucker.'

Chase grinned. 'Metaphorically speaking.'

'If you like.'

Two different officers were on duty outside the entrance to Webster Manor. Chase wondered if he would have to go through the same routine, but this time the flash of his warrant card was enough to secure immediate access to the estate.

He raised an appreciative hand as he drove on through. 'The moment we're out of sight they're going to put in a call to Waddington,' he said.

'I don't know the man. But from what you say, he's probably got his finger on the pulse of this at all times.'

'I don't doubt it. So I have to wonder why he's not put out a standing order to prevent us from speaking to her Ladyship without him also being present. No offence to you, Claire, but it only makes me more suspicious about his aims. I really am wondering if he's sitting back waiting for the pair of us to screw this up.'

'If that's the case, I suggest we do our best to disappoint him.'

Lady Jane Webster's personal assistant introduced herself as Harper. She had a kind, open face but sad eyes, Chase thought. He wondered why a woman who had no obvious job required the services of a PA, but he assumed her Ladyship was an ambassador to a number of charities. He had never fully grasped what it was wealthy people did all day.

The woman herself made them wait ten minutes before putting in an appearance. She wore a knee-length black dress, accentuating a slender body that looked a little on the frail side. A matching set of diamond necklace and earrings glittered as she made her entrance, immediately drawing the eye. Platinum rather than silver, Chase imagined. Not a single strand of her dyed streaky blonde hair was out of place. It was raised up in some fancy type of bun, pinned into rigid defiance, and about as solid as any of the pillars at Stonehenge. In her mid-sixties, she carried a superior air far more lofty than the one her own heritage had provided. The only daughter of distillery owners, Lady Jane had done extremely well for herself. She declined to sit, instead striking a pose beside the marble fireplace.

'So you're Chase,' she said, keeping her hands clasped in front of her.

'I am,' he replied. 'Though you're welcome to call me *Detective Sergeant* Chase.'

Her mouth twitched and her eyes flicked up to meet his. He held her cool gaze. He was aware that he had responded to her rudeness in kind, but this was one he was happy to have had slip through the filter.

'Our condolences on your tragic loss,' he continued, gesturing towards his colleague. 'This is DC Laney. We don't intend keeping you long, but we do have a few questions for you.'

'Then you had better sit down. And please, do make it quick. I have other matters to attend to.'

It felt like more of an order than an invitation, but despite his reluctance to follow it, Chase took a seat. Laney sat next to him on a long sofa upholstered in a silky striped pattern. They were in what the PA had described as the drawing room. Other than soft furnishings, four glass lamps sitting on separate wooden tables, and an upright piano, the main feature of the room was its magnificent library. Chase was fond of reading, but he didn't think these creaking old floor-to-ceiling shelves contained anything he might have read. You could smell the leather covers and the aged undisturbed pages within.

'Once again, we're sorry for your loss, your Ladyship,' Chase said, elevating his frown to a more temperate state. 'We wouldn't be bothering you at a time like this if it wasn't of the utmost importance and urgency.'

She peered down her long, thin nose at him. 'This is more about the young woman than my late husband, I take it?'

Chase silently cursed his boss. He had suspected it might happen, but considered Waddington too much of a coward to break such news to a woman of Webster's standing. He would have to re-evaluate the man entirely. Huffing a sigh, he said, 'Superintendent Waddington told you about that, did he? How disappointing.'

'He did. As a long-standing friend of the family, he thought to prepare me, should the media somehow get their grubby little hands on such a juicy piece of gossip.'

'I take it he merely passed this news on in conversation, your Ladyship. I have no record of him questioning you about it.'

'I believe he considered a formal interview to be inappropriate at the time. Given my distress, you understand?'

Chase sniffed. 'Hardly. More inappropriate not to once you've delivered the news, in my opinion. However, we are where we are. In which case, I'll press on. Lady Jane, I'm puzzled about something and I'm hoping you'll be able to clarify the matter for me.'

'I will do my best, Sergeant. Though I'm not sure what it is you expect me to know.'

'It's simple enough. Virtually the first thing you did upon receiving the news of your husband's death in a road collision, was to seek a gagging order on the media. That seems like a rather odd reaction to me. Tell me, were you already aware that your husband had somebody in the vehicle with him? And if not, did you at least suspect he might?'

Webster's features became more stern, and a flush crept into her cheeks. 'If you're asking me if I knew my husband entertained the occasional local floozy from time to time, the answer is yes. We had that kind of marriage.'

'How very Bohemian of you.'

'Indeed. I doubt you could understand.'

Chase allowed a smile to thin his lips. 'I doubt I would wish to. As for these local floozies, were they always children?'

The temperature in the room seemed to plummet in an instant. Lady Jane's fingers, still clasped at her waist, began to squirm. 'I beg your pardon?'

'I'm sorry, but did Detective Superintendent Waddington not mention the age of the young girl when he spoke to you?'

The look she gave him contained pure venom. Her eyes narrowed to the point where it looked as if they might have closed altogether. 'He did allude to some confusion over the young woman's identity, and that you were having difficulties ascertaining her precise details. Her exact age was one of those particulars in doubt, I believe. My understanding was that no evidence had arisen either way.'

'Hard evidence? No. But we are sure this girl was underage and therefore classified as a minor.'

A tic pulsed beneath her left eye. 'I see. Yet without evidence of that you cannot possibly know for certain, as you yourself stated. Nevertheless, was there any need to be quite so brutal in your own questioning?'

'I thought you'd appreciate my being direct with you.' Chase offered no apology. Nor would he.

'I'm not sure you recognise the fine line between being direct and being cruel, Detective Sergeant. Perhaps that is one lesson your superiors will make sure you learn when all this... unpleasantness is over.'

Chase inclined his head as if giving her suggestion some weight. 'I certainly think they would if they could, your Ladyship. We seek to include all types these days. Not that I have superiors. We refer to them as senior officers, of course.'

'The distinction is important to you, I take it?'

'Absolutely. We're not the military. I understand what you mean, though. Especially about the *unpleasantness*, as you described it. Strange choice of word. If I were in your shoes, I think I'd regard my husband being killed while receiving oral sex from a girl barely into her teens, as rather more than unpleasant.'

When the glimmer in her hostile eyes winked out, Chase knew his words had cut her to the bone. She had not been made aware of this fact, and he wondered if Waddington had left it unsaid so that Chase himself might blunder in to devastate the woman further.

Doing so held no pride for him, but it was something he'd had to know for sure.

'What I think my colleague is trying to say, your Ladyship,' Laney interceded urgently, 'is that when we assess the precise details, we are obliged to take into account all relevant factors. We understand and appreciate this is a time of grief and mourning for you, but a number of other people also died as a result of the collision. Including the young girl. It's our duty to do our very best for them as well, not just your husband.'

The widow turned her gaze away from Chase. She looked Laney up and down, wrinkling her nose in distaste as she did so. 'My dear,' she said eventually. 'Have you no decorum? I mean you no disrespect, but is that any way to present yourself here today?'

Claire Laney stared hard at the woman wordlessly for several seconds. Then she gave an insincere smile and turned to Chase. 'I gave it my best shot. She's all yours, Royston.'

'Now hold on a moment!' This time Lady Webster's tone was curt, genuine anger leaking through the thin veneer of stoicism. 'You are both guests in my home. I won't have you treat this matter as if it were some kind of sideshow.'

Chase paused before reasserting himself. 'I'd apologise for our lack of courtesy if I thought it would put a dent in that stiff upper… everything of yours. However, it would be remiss of me not to point out that your own civility has been sorely lacking. You may believe you got a raw deal because you haven't got a Superintendent at the very least following you around like a new puppy, pandering to your every whim at the expense of everybody else who was killed or injured at the same time as your husband. But I would be neglecting my duty if I didn't remind you that it was Sir Kenneth who caused those devastating deaths and terrible injuries. And while it might temporarily offend your sensibilities, I would not be doing my job if I failed to push you on the child – and I do mean a child, your Ladyship – being naked in that vehicle with your husband at the time. I need to know if his preference that night was unusual. I need to know where he might have found such a girl, and where he intended to entertain her. And it seems to me you are the best person to provide that information.'

Her pale face had become almost crimson with rage. 'How dare you?! How dare you treat me this way? Do not for one moment think that my grief will prevent me from reporting your abhorrent behaviour to the new Chief Constable.'

Chase shrugged. 'That's your prerogative. But if your grief is able to make room for petty retribution, then it will surely allow you to answer my questions. We came here today with no intention of insulting you, but I'm afraid it is your attitude that has allowed this interview to become contentious. Lady Jane, please tell me if you were aware of your husband's habit of spending time with female minors. Tell me if you know where he procured them, and where he entertained them. Also, I'd very much like to know the location of his club. Tier One, I believe it's called.'

She took a few beats, but he had to admire how quickly she pulled herself together. Still bristling, but in control once more she said, 'I haven't even laid my husband to rest, Sergeant Chase, and yet you want me to bury him deeper still? Is that what you expect of me? Is that the kind of spousal loyalty you are used to?'

'What I expect of you is the truth. I look into your eyes, I analyse your overall reaction, and I can tell.'

'Tell what?' She steadied herself, seemingly more resolute than before.

'That you knew. Or that you at least suspected. Which is why you wanted a media blackout. Not because your husband might have been drunk when he killed those people and himself, but because of the distinct possibility that he was indulging himself in sex with a child. And you couldn't possibly have that being reported. If you hold anything back, Lady Jane, we will find out the truth. It will be better for you if you tell us what you know right here and now.'

She did not appear overawed or cowed by their conversation. In some ways she seemed energised by it. She stepped away from the fireplace and drew in a deep breath. 'I'll have you both shown out. I have the beginnings of a migraine. Should you need to interview me again, I think it best done with my solicitor present. Superintendent Waddington assured me this would be a civil process, but I can see that is not how you intend to investigate the incident. My husband's status and wealth is an easy target. One you appear to have set your sights on. You will rue that decision, Sergeant. I'll make sure of it.'

Chase got to his feet, Claire Laney rising alongside him. He tapped a finger against the side of his head. 'Somewhere inside here lies my defence. The result of an injury sustained on the job. I think I'll be fine, no matter how long or hard you complain. I'm not so sure about you, your Ladyship. You clearly have a lot to hide, and it will not only twist your insides, it will eventually be drawn out of you. One way or another.'

'Is that a threat, Sergeant Chase? Do you actually have the gall to threaten me here in my own home?'

'No, that wasn't a threat. But I do have the impudence, so this is: between you, me, and DC Laney here, I think you might want to tell us what you know before the media break the story. These things have a habit of leaking out to the press. One cannot always control what one says. I'm sure you understand.'

Her face formed a dismissive sneer as she stood at her most upright. 'Do you honestly believe you can browbeat a woman like me?'

'A woman with compassion and tenderness at her core? A woman of immense understanding and empathy? A woman whose heartfelt sympathy goes out to those who also lost their lives. A woman who feels only revulsion at what her late husband was up to on the night he died? A woman like that? No, because in fact, a woman like that needs no browbeating. A woman like you… that's a different matter altogether.'

ELEVEN

'THAT WENT WELL,' LANEY said to him once they were outside and walking back to his car. She lit a cigarette and drew the smoke in with a look of immense satisfaction. 'What an absolute delight she was. We really must invite her over for tea and scones one day, Royston.'

Chase didn't feel like smiling. He was angry with himself. 'I blew it. I knew I would. I went into it in completely the wrong frame of mind. I allowed her sense of superiority to affect my judgement because she was precisely how I imagined her to be. She met my low expectations, and I punished her for that. I antagonised the woman, losing control of the interview in the process, and that was unprofessional of me.'

'So you blew your filter wide open. What was her excuse?'

'She had just lost her husband.'

Laney scoffed. 'That's even less of a reason to pretend your shit doesn't stink. Genuine grief drops your guard, to the point where any airs and graces you might have fall away because they're unimportant. Death is the great equaliser, only not in her case. She's an awful hag. I gave her the benefit of the doubt. I offered her the ideal opportunity to reel it back in when she got pissed off at you, and instead she sneered down her nose at me as well. She deserved every barrel you fired off at her.'

Chase stroked his chin. 'I'm not entirely sure that's true. I mean, I do think she knew what her husband was. But she mentioned loyalty, and she's protecting her husband's memory despite having been humiliated by him. Many would call that noble.'

'And I call bullshit. I get the Tammy Wynette concept of standing by your man. I do. But not when he's a bloody kiddy fiddler. How a wife can remain supportive of a husband who got his jollies playing around with little girls is beyond me.'

'Maybe I should have gone the whole hog and shown her the photo of her husband's cock in that poor girl's mouth. You think she had that coming, too?'

Laney took a final drag before dropping her cigarette to the ground and snuffing it out with her boot heel. 'Why not? Showing her the devastating reality of what occurred might have done the trick.'

They vented about it a little more, but as they emerged from the estate, Chase received a call. It was from the Cellmark forensic services lab at Abingdon, in Oxford. Chase had been expecting to hear back from them with the result of the young girl's DNA analysis, which had been processed as a matter of urgency given she remained unidentified.

The first thing the lab supervisor said to him was, 'You are never going to believe this.'

For a good few seconds after he'd heard the results, Chase didn't. Then he realised it wasn't some kind of practical joke, and the seriousness of the information struck home. After a short conversation between the detectives, followed by Chase digging through records via his phone and Laney using her own to locate an address close by, they made the short drive around the perimeter of the Webster Manor estate to the southern edge of Little Soley.

The detached cottage was set back off the main road, but not far enough for Chase's liking. The long and straight stretch of tarmac had a flat surface, and he imagined boy racers enjoying themselves along it at regular intervals. The property had a red slate roof as opposed to thatch, but at first glance it looked charming and cosy. It was only after they exited the car and walked up the flagstone path that the dilapidation became more obvious. Paint flaked from the window frames, and a dark stain ran the full height of the two-storey home beneath a gutter that looked as if it had not been cleaned in a decade or more.

Harvey Radcliffe opened the door to them wearing a stained Eric Clapton T-shirt at least two sizes too large for his clearly shrunken frame. Blue denim jeans hung low and loose on his hips. His white hair was tangled and unruly, offering pockets of tufted islands adrift on a sea of scalp. Silver whiskers suggested he hadn't shaved in weeks. He squinted at the two detectives through deep, bloodshot eyes ringed with bruises and puffy swellings of neglect. It was early afternoon, and the man reeked of alcohol. Chase introduced himself and Laney, telling Radcliffe they had come to speak to him about his daughter, Mandy.

The man gave a resigned shrug and turned on his heels, faltering slightly. He led them on unsteady legs into the cottage's living room, which was as dishevelled as Radcliffe himself. Chase's eyes immediately flitted between the empty beer, wine, and Jack Daniels bottles littering most surfaces, including the floor. All but one curtain in the room was drawn closed, creating a dark and oppressive atmosphere with clouds of swirling dust kicked up by Radcliffe's shambling gait caught in a single band of sunlight.

Radcliffe staggered over towards a reclining chair that had long since seen better days, lowering himself into it with obvious discomfort. Laney swept aside bottles and dirty dishes on the sofa to create room to sit, though pointedly she remained on her feet. Chase strode purposefully across to the front window and yanked the other curtain back to let in more light.

'Nice,' he said, admiring the open countryside beyond the road. Trees lined the deep valley between two hillsides directly opposite, like a daunting barrier formed over time by nature.

'Is it?' Radcliffe observed the window as if a long-forgotten relic had been uncovered behind the bedraggled and dusty strip of curtain. 'Can't say I've noticed in recent times.'

'As views go, that's a belter.'

'For you, perhaps. My wife and I used to sit at that window staring out waiting for our Mandy to come skipping up the path. I don't recall how many years we did it for, but eventually we couldn't take it any longer. Views are for people who still care about such things. What do you want with me, anyhow?'

Chase turned, regarding the man carefully. 'Sir, I realise we're going to appear somewhat dense at first, but please bear with us. Before we get to the purpose of our visit, I need to establish a couple of things with you. Our records indicate that you and your wife had a daughter, Mandy. She vanished from your home in the summer of 2001. Is that correct?'

'That's not what you people seemed to think back then,' Radcliffe mumbled as if to himself. On a small table beside his chair stood a wine bottle containing an inch or so of dregs. He cast a covetous glance over the contents, first licking his lips and then backhanding them.

Chase was curious. 'I'm sorry. Are you telling me your daughter didn't disappear overnight?'

'Oh, no. She did. My wife tucked her up in bed as usual and I read her a story. I worked long hours in those days, so it was rare for me to be home at that time of evening. I ran my own building company, and we were doing good business at the time. But I got home early that day. I remember the book: a Horrid Henry, all about the Tooth Fairy. I read it to Mandy, kissed her goodnight, and that was the last either of us saw of our little girl.'

'I'm guessing the implication of what you said a moment or two ago is that the police wondered if you'd had something to do with it.'

The man scowled as he shook his head at the memory. 'No won dering about it. Nothing of Mandy's was missing, so of course our girl couldn't possibly have run away. There was no sign of a break-in, so nobody could have entered our home to take her, either. Typical inside job as far as your people were concerned. They suspected us. Me, most of all.'

'It is standard procedure, sir,' Laney pointed out. 'A process of elimination. I realise that doesn't make things any better, but experience tells us to always look hard at the family first.'

The man made a sound of disgust in the back of his throat. 'Say what you came to say. I'm guessing somebody found her bones buried out there in a field and you lot think I did it.'

'Not at all, sir.' Chase thought he knew the answer to his next question, but asked it anyway. 'Sir, is your wife at home? I think she ought to hear what we have to say.'

'You'll have to shout. Loud, too. She's been dead these past four years.' Radcliffe smiled reflectively. 'You'd never have seen our home in this state while she was alive. It was clean and bright, and it matched her personality in those days. For quite some time now it has very much matched my own, I'm sad to say.'

'I'm sorry to hear that.'

Radcliffe shook his head and sighed. 'We were finished as a couple long before she passed. My Miriam never got over the loss of Mandy. And once you people put it in her head that I might have killed our little girl, my wife never looked at me the same way again.'

'You both decided to stay on here, though.'

'Yes. At first I was all for selling up and moving far away. Miriam refused to leave. Said she needed to be here when Mandy came home. She was convinced that's what would happen one day. Of course, it was sheer bloody nonsense. I was the only one of us who could see it, though.'

Chase moved away from the window to stand alongside his colleague. 'You believed your daughter was dead, I presume.'

'Oh, yes. Ever the realist, that's me.'

'I take it you wanted to get away from the awful memory of the night Mandy went missing?'

'Wouldn't you?'

Chase paused, but Laney jumped right in. 'Yet you remained living here despite the relationship with your wife breaking down, and then long after she passed. Why was that, Mr Radcliffe?'

He fixed her with a surprisingly benign look. 'Miriam changed my mind. Told me she understood my way of thinking, but said she preferred to focus on all the good memories she had of Mandy in this house. All of her memories, in fact. Over time, I came to see things her way. Sometimes it's hard to let go of the past. Other times it's damn near impossible.'

Chase sympathised. It was hard enough having your young daughter taken from you, because what it did to those left behind was unbelievably cruel. 'Mr Radcliffe,' he said. 'I asked you to confirm your family circumstances for a reason. I don't know any easy way to put this, so I'm going to be truthful with you. Sir, we've been unable to identify the body of a young girl we believe to be between twelve to fourteen years old. She was one of several victims in a road collision on Tuesday night. We've since spent some time carrying out a variety of tests, including the drawing of DNA. The result of–'

'What the bloody hell has any of that got to do with me?' Radcliffe snapped. Glazed eyes stared with incomprehension. 'Or my daughter? Mandy would have been twenty-eight had she lived. Can't you people get anything right?'

'I understand your confusion, sir. Please bear with me a little longer. There's a reason why I asked if Mandy was your only child. Because if she was, then there's really only one logical conclusion to what I'm about to tell you.'

'Just spit it out, man. Do your worst. You think I can be hurt anymore? Any worse than I already have been?' His fingers had moved to wrap around the bottle on the side table. Whatever lay inside would undoubtedly taste foul, but he was not far off throwing it back.

'Mr Radcliffe, our forensic lab informs us they produced eighteen exact matches between your DNA sample taken at the time of your daughter's disappearance, and that of the deceased young girl.'

'What?! Are you deliberately being hurtful? Are you trying to say you think I'm the girl's father?' Radcliffe started laughing, which broke up into a wet and hacking coughing fit. He eventually shook his head and waved Chase away. 'You're out of your tiny mind, man. Go bother someone else, why don't you?'

He started reaching to heft the wine bottle, but Chase gave him pause when he said, 'No, that's not what I'm telling you, sir. It means we have 99% confidence that you are her grandfather. In addition, while DNA in this instance cannot specifically tell us who the child's grandmother is or was, there is also a familial DNA link between the girl and your wife. In short, sir, our victim was your grandchild. Yours and your wife's.'

The man's ruddy complexion became pale, then quickly tinged with grey. His mouth hung open, revealing two rows of teeth long uncared for. He clawed overly long fingernails down both unshaven cheeks, the harsh sound clearly audible to Chase. Radcliffe blinked rapidly, but he remained mute and seemingly uncomprehending.

'Do you understand what we're telling you, sir?' Laney asked him, lowering her voice. Chase heard tenderness and compassion in it.

'No. No, I don't have a bloody clue. It's nonsense. It has to be. Miriam and I never had another child. Mandy was our beautiful daughter. She was all we needed. You must have this wrong. Somebody made a terrible mistake.'

'There is no mistake,' Laney insisted. 'DNA obtained from your daughter's toothbrush the day after her disappearance also gave us a hit. Your daughter, Mandy, was our victim's mother. Conclusively. Our forensic people confirmed this a short while ago. It's why we came straight here, sir. Do you not see how in some respects this may be good news.'

'Good… you see good news in this?'

'For you, yes. Not that you've lost a grandchild you never knew existed. That is, naturally, a terrible outcome. But the fact is you *had* a grandchild to lose. Mr Radcliffe, if Mandy was your only child, then she still might be alive. Sir, you've always believed your daughter to be dead. She still may be for all we know. But we do have conclusive evidence to prove that she didn't die that night she left here, nor any night soon after. Mandy survived childhood. She lived long enough to bear you a granddaughter. And there's no reason to think that she is not still out there somewhere.'

Radcliffe looked at her as if she were insane. 'But… that can't be. It simply can't be. Where has she been all this time if that's the case?'

Laney shuffled her feet on the spot and said, 'Sir, as mentioned previously, we have no way of knowing whether Mandy is alive or dead at this moment. But she did survive well beyond the night she disappeared from here. Long enough to give birth to a child of her own at the very least. In hindsight, does that influence your memory of what happened?'

The man narrowed his gaze while simultaneously drawing back. 'That was two whole decades ago. You've seen how I live. Too many empty bottles to count, and that's no more than a few weeks' worth. Have you any idea what that kind of drinking does to a memory?'

'Actually, I do. I'm a pretty sozzled old sow myself, Mr Radcliffe. I might not be able to drink you under the table these days, but I reckon I'd give you a run for your money.'

'Well, then. You expect me to think back and have any clear notion of what happened?'

'You seemed to do well enough earlier,' Chase said to him. 'Your wife tucking Mandy up in bed, you reading to your daughter. You were even able to recall the book you read.'

Radcliffe turned his contemptuous gaze upon Chase. 'That's because those details are seared into my brain, man. They are the details that sent me crawling off inside the bottle to begin with. I'm never going to forget them. They're like scars I carry with me everywhere I go. Not that I stray far beyond my own doorstep these days. But don't ask me to conjure up new memories. I'll only ever draw a blank.'

Chase understood. 'I guess you've asked yourself these questions over the years. Or something similar, at least.'

'You can be sure of that. Never any answers, though. That's what kills you slowly inside – the not knowing. It rots you away like a cancer. Hence my sterling efforts to drink myself to death. I want to get off this macabre carousel, Sergeant.'

'I can understand that, Mr Radcliffe. But you might well have something to live for. Whatever happened to your daughter that night, whether she walked out of here of her own volition or was snatched away from you and your wife, we now know that her life did not end that same day. Nor the next. Nor any day close to it. She could well still be out there, sir. And if she is, we'll find her.'

'And if she's not?'

'Will you be any the worse off?'

'Of course I will,' Radcliffe said in a hushed voice. 'Because then I will have lost both a daughter and a grandchild.'

'Then have some hope at least,' Laney said. 'Before we came to your door today, you were convinced that something awful had happened to your daughter. You believed Mandy was dead. Now we've come to you with evidence telling you she was alive, perhaps as recently as thirteen or fourteen years ago. That's something to hold on to, I'd say.'

He nodded. 'Definitely something to raise a glass to.'

Laney grinned. 'That's the spirit.'

Chase thought the man might have shut down, overwhelmed by the revelations. But a moment later his head jerked up and his eyes fixed upon DC Laney. 'Hold on a moment. You said you connected me to this dead girl through DNA?'

'Yes, sir. From a sample taken from her body.'

'Yet clearly you haven't spoken to her mother. You told me you don't even know if she's still with us. You say this poor young girl died in a road accident on Tuesday night. Who was she with at the time? Why haven't they come forward with the information you need? Were they also killed? I don't… I don't understand.'

Raising both hands to settle the man down, Chase said, 'I'm afraid we're unable to release any further details at present, Mr Radcliffe. All I can say at this time is that the girl was found alone, no family or friends with her at the time. Neither has anybody yet come forward to report her missing. We think she might be a runaway, but that is pure speculation on our part. There's nothing more I can tell you at this stage, I'm afraid.'

Radcliffe took this fresh news like an additional body blow. He slumped lower and deeper into his recliner. He moistened his lips, and Chase knew the man could not wait for them to leave so that he could find a full bottle to drink from.

'There is one other thing. You didn't ask if we knew who the girl's father was. The question was bound to come to you at some point, so it's best we address it here and now. The answer is we don't know. Obviously we also have his DNA, but there is no matching record on our database.'

Harvey Radcliffe sat in stunned silence, his body rigid, eyes moist.

'If you do happen to think of anything further,' Chase said, 'please do get in touch.' He took out a card and held it out for the man to take. After a few seconds, he set it down on the arm of the chair. 'In the meantime, rest assured that the moment we get any further details about your grandchild, or your daughter, we will be in touch.'

But Radcliffe had already switched off. He stared straight ahead, perhaps immersed in the summer of 2001 all over again. Chase made no judgement. If he and his wife had lost Maisie, he couldn't begin to imagine how the rest of his life would have panned out.

TWELVE

THE TWO DETECTIVES SAT in the car outside the Radcliffe cottage long after leaving the bemused man to his alcohol consumption. Using his mobile, Chase read a few salient reports, interviews, and evidence files connected to Mandy Radcliffe's disappearance. He found little to query, but since the lead detective on the case still lived within a short driving distance, he thought it worth their while making the trip. He called ahead this time to make sure ex-Detective Inspector Donovan Riley was available to speak with them, and on the way to Bath pit-stopped at Claire's Café which was located in the car park between a B&Q store and Carpetright in Chippenham. It was one of the cleanest roadside snack bars Chase had ever used, and their food was always tasty.

'However did you find this place?' Laney asked him as she munched her way through a fat cheeseburger dripping with juices.

Chase was already deep into his second hot dog. 'I spotted it here many years ago. Came to B&Q for something, felt hungry, gave it a whirl. There was a fair sized queue, as I remember. I find if these places are located on an industrial estate and doing good business, that's usually all the recommendation I need. Those burgers are bloody delicious.'

Her mouth full, Laney nodded and continued to chew. When she was done, Chase asked the DC what her impressions were of both

Lady Jane Webster and Harvey Radcliffe. 'To be perfectly honest with you, I don't know which of them has the worse life,' she replied, mopping her lips with a scrap of kitchen towel, which she then screwed into a ball. She took out a cigarette, lit it, and took a deep lungful before continuing. 'On the one hand, you have a narcissistic parasite with her nose so far up her own backside she must breathe every foul gas her intestines emit. On the other, you have a man wallowing so deeply in grief that he prays for the swift demise of his liver. Neither of them has any real life as far as I can tell. One pretends she has it all but must cry herself to sleep at night with that cold space beside her knowing she has nothing of any real value. The other is all cried out and thinking only as far forward as his next drop of booze. A sorry state, the pair of them.'

Chase digested those observations along with his food as they continued on towards Bath. Laney's insight had taken him by surprise, causing him to question the person beneath her exterior shell. On the outskirts of Somerset's largest city, just off the A4 in Larkhall, they found the Rose & Crown pub in which Riley had suggested they meet. Even in a fairly crowded bar, he was easy to spot. He had that cop look about him; a man whose eyes seldom shifted yet at the same time seemed to take everything in.

Retired these past five years, Riley had not yet allowed himself to go to seed. His finely cropped hair was more silver than grey, but it was clean and recently trimmed. The Van Dyke whiskers were the same colour, though they looked like a relatively new lifestyle choice. Not an especially imposing man, he was nonetheless broad and solid-looking. Chase picked him out before the man raised a hand in greeting. Laney offered to get them all a drink, and neither of them refused out of some old-fashioned sense of chivalry. To Chase it was one of the perks of feminism. His new colleague came back with their orders on a tray, and they each took a sip before Riley explained his choice of location for their chat.

'Our daughter and grandkids are over,' he told them. 'The place is a madhouse. I love them all to bits, but even before you called I was thinking of nipping out for a bit of peace and quiet. I'm sure you both know what I mean, right?'

Chase ignored the question other than giving a perfunctory nod. 'I wouldn't normally choose to bother you given you're retired, but as I mentioned on the phone, we have developments on the Mandy Radcliffe case and I thought you might be able to help us out. I also thought you'd probably be interested.'

Riley nodded, his meaty hands still wrapped around his pint glass. 'In books, on TV cop shows, and occasionally even in films, you get these old washout cops who talk about that one case that won't leave them alone.' He snorted and shook his head. 'We all know that's cobblers, right? By the time you've put in your years in this job, you've probably got a dozen or more of them that hang around your neck like Mr T's bling. The Radcliffe op was one I'll always remember, but for very different reasons.'

'How so?' Laney asked.

'Most of the ops that get their claws into you are children whose life hangs in the balance, or who you somehow manage to pull back from the edge. This was nothing like that. We never really got to know the kiddy herself. Never got a sniff, let alone get close enough to touch or attempt to rescue. Never closed it off, either.'

'I can see that. Makes it a real odd one. Do you recall what your feelings were about it at the time?'

Riley took another pull from his glass and nodded, running a finger and thumb down over his facial hair. 'As clearly today as I did back then. It was like one of those locked room mysteries. Mandy was put to bed in the evening, but in the morning she wasn't there. You approach a case having learned that much and you think of three possible scenarios: she walked away, she was taken away, or she was murdered by one or both parents. I thought the parents were a non-starter. That was my immediate judgement. The pair of them were as distraught as any couple I'd seen in my career to date. For me, there was no way they were putting that on.'

'But?' Chase prompted. 'I'm guessing there is a but.'

'Sure. Because when we looked at those first two possibilities, neither of them worked. If an eight-year-old girl is going to run away from home, she's at least going to get dressed. Her mother said she checked every item in Mandy's wardrobe and chest of drawers, but they were all there. The nightdress she was wearing when she went to bed wasn't lying around anywhere, nor was it in her laundry basket. She took nothing with her at all. Not her little bag that she carried around sometimes. Not her backpack. Not her pocket money, which she kept in a ceramic bear. Not even footwear as far as her parents could tell. It made no sense.'

'But neither did the notion that she'd been abducted.'

'Frankly, no. The front door was shut when the parents checked, caught on the Yale-type lock. It had been a hot night so some of the upstairs windows were open, but unless a window cleaner chanced by in the middle of the night, there was no reasonable way for anyone to enter through them. No sign of a ladder having been used beneath any of the windows. Downstairs windows and back door all closed and locked, too. Plus, no hint of a struggle and neither parent heard anything untoward.'

'Which left you with Harvey and Miriam Radcliffe.'

Riley nodded. 'I'd forgotten her name. The mother. But yes, we had to start looking at them anyway as a matter of process, but we really went to town on their backgrounds and their alibis. If I'd had to plump for one of them, it would have been him, but I didn't like either of them for it. It was a puzzle, except for when we learned of a time window we'd not previously considered. See, the kiddy was put to bed about seven-thirty. Mrs Radcliffe went to bed at around ten, her husband an hour later. We assumed Mandy was in bed at that time, so our time window was between eleven that night and eight the following morning when they found the girl's bed empty and no sign of her inside the house.'

Chase was already there with him. 'I'm betting neither parent checked on the girl before they turned in. So in effect, she could have left the house or been taken from it between seven-thirty and ten while both parents were still up.'

'Precisely. And although that was much riskier, either for the girl going off on her own or for whoever took her, it would explain a few things. You've seen their place, I take it?' Chase and Laney nodded in unison. 'So you know that unless there's traffic bombing along that road, which is actually one of the quieter stretches in the area, you can hear a gnat fart a hundred yards away at night. Both parents were certain they would have heard something had their daughter been taken or even walked out of her own accord. But with them both in the lounge with the TV on, it's less likely they'd have heard.'

This was news to Chase, and good additional information. He'd not seen it in the case files, but had pretty much only scanned them. 'I take it that hour's difference in them going to bed that night is why you'd plump for the father over the mother if you had to?'

Here, Riley faltered for a moment. He gave himself time to respond carefully. 'I don't want to mislead you. You're right, that hour does make all the difference. But I must emphasise once again that I believed them both.'

Chase took a beat or two before imparting the fresh information they had about Mandy and her daughter. Riley switched his gaze between them for a few seconds, perhaps hoping one of them was going to crack a smile and let him in on the joke. As he did so, he drank from his glass until it was empty.

'How is that even possible?' he finally said.

'That's what we're trying to find out,' Laney replied. 'Knowing she survived for another seven or eight years at the very least, how does it change the way you regard that case?'

Riley's response was immediate. 'Radically. There's no way that little kiddy walks out of there on her own taking nothing with her, wearing only a nightdress, no shoes on her feet, and manages to survive. Not without somebody spotting her at some point soon afterwards. Someone had to have known. Had to have helped her. Either that or she was taken.'

'Or willingly left home with another person,' Chase suggested. 'Think about it. It fits right between the two scenarios. I only dug into the case file a little, but I assume you had suspects other than Mandy's parents. If relatives were in the picture, maybe even a close friend of the family, it would have been possible for one of them to lure her out.'

'On what pretext? And to keep her all that time afterwards?' The ex-cop shook his head with some certainty. 'The Radcliffes were close. That was the word no matter who we spoke to. Mandy's school teachers, friends, her friends' parents, even the parents' own friends. Often at a time like that you get somebody who has a bad word to say and wants to get it off their chest and point the finger of blame. But not in this case. Mandy was a great kid, who loved her parents and they loved her back. She had absolutely no reason to go off with anyone else.'

'It could still be done,' Chase insisted. 'The lure. If they were really close. Somebody Mandy trusted implicitly. Someone she would never even think to question. Was there anybody like that in her life?'

This time, Riley leaned back in his chair to think about it. His eyes narrowed in concentration. Behind him a group of men stood at the bar staring at a TV showing a sports channel. They chatted, laughed, and drank. Nobody was taking an interest in the conversation at the table. If only they knew, Chase thought. If only they knew what had happened, and what might be about to happen.

When Riley spoke, he did so with conviction. 'All four grandparents were alive, as I recall, though not in the picture. One couple lived in Portugal, I think, the other in north Wales. Mr Radcliffe had a sister, and his wife had two brothers. None of them lived nearby, so they were seldom seen. Special occasions, that sort of thing. Nothing dysfunctional as far as I could tell, just not geographically close.'

'A friend, then?'

'I was coming to that. Let me get the next round in and I'll tell you all about him.'

It was all Chase could do to bring himself back down. Excitement had built steadily throughout the day, because he felt they were making headway. If this family friend was going to be their silver bullet or smoking gun, then Chase wanted to squeeze every fact from Riley and did not want to wait. He glanced across at Laney, who wore a half smile.

'What?' he said.

'You. It's like watching a small child anticipating opening his presents at his own birthday party. Fuck the cake and the clown, let me at those pressies.' Laney mimed ripping paper from gifts.

Chase chuckled. 'Not bad, Claire. Not bad at all. I suppose you could say I've been known to get a little intense at times.'

'I can tell. But be prepared for disappointment. I have a feeling this isn't going to be your bogeyman.'

'Why do you say that?'

She hiked her shoulders and the leather of her jacket creaked. 'Just a feeling. It's all a bit too neat for my liking. And I'm sure Riley and his team will have run it to ground at the time.'

'We did,' the man himself said as he returned to the table with their drinks. Chase had opted for a carbonated water, but Laney had gone for her second Screwdriver. If this was her stepping back from the booze, he wondered what she'd been like at her worst. 'His name was Paul Daniels, but this one was no magician. He was Harvey Radcliffe's oldest and closest friend. Best man at their wedding, Godfather to their only daughter. To Mandy he was Uncle Paul.'

Laney leaned forward, glass tumbler to her lips. 'Did he live in the area?'

'Close enough. In Devizes. They saw each other regularly.'

'What did you find on him?'

'Nothing. No record. He was single, but had lived with several women and was known to be a bit of a womaniser. A roofer by trade. We asked around before we spoke with him, but got no sense he was anything other than genuine.'

'And what did you make of him when you interviewed him?'

'If you mean did we get the impression he had something to do with it, then no. He was almost as broken up about it as Mr and Mrs Radcliffe were. He didn't have a decent alibi, as he was at home alone. But none of us fancied him as a suspect. And there was absolutely no motive that we could find.'

'What about him and Mrs Radcliffe?' Chase asked. 'You said he was a known womaniser.'

'Again, we considered it. Came up short. If it was him, then he fooled all of us.'

'Worth having another go at?'

'It's your time to waste. Your call. I don't think you'll find anything there.'

'The difference might be this fresh news we have. About Mandy having a child. It could spark something in him if he did something to her back then.'

'Like I say, your time. I'm confident in our assessment of him back in the day.'

'Was Mr Radcliffe aware of your interest in his best friend?'

'We asked him. Him and his wife. In general, not in terms of Daniels being a viable suspect or potentially knocking off Mrs Radcliffe. In fact, the man himself was there with them on one occasion when we stopped by. If either of them suspected their friend, they failed to mention it to us.'

Chase thought about it. Sounded like a dead end. But he kept coming back to how Mandy had left that night. He agreed with Riley: there was no way the girl walked away on her own. Abduction also seemed unlikely, given the complete lack of evidence. But Uncle Paul playing a game? *Don't tell your mum and dad. It's a surprise. Just slip out the front door and walk along the road – I'll find you and take you to get this wonderful surprise that only you and I can get for them.*

If the girl spoke up ahead of time, it'd be simple enough to brush off. Mandy's wild imagination. Laughs all round. And yet… Chase wasn't feeling a genuine pull towards that theory. There didn't appear to be anything in Paul Daniels's history suggestive of his liking for children.

'One thing did occur to me,' he said to Riley, 'and I've heard no mention of it so far. Did you ever ask the Radcliffes if Mandy had a history of sleepwalking?'

The ex-cop squinted hard. 'Now that you mention it, the subject came up during one of our team briefings a day or two into the investigation. I had a DC call the parents. He spoke with Mrs Radcliffe, but both she and her husband were firm in saying it wasn't something their daughter ever did – or at least if it had ever happened, neither of them were aware of it. It was an action, so it should be somewhere in the case files.'

Chase held up a hand. 'I'm not suggesting otherwise. It was just a thought.' Which was when another dropped into plain view.

'The Radcliffe home,' he said. 'Do you know the area well?'

Riley nodded. 'Very.'

'What's over the other side of the main road? Farmland and woodland, yes?'

'That's about right. The first main field belonged to a man by the name of Owens. He sold up many years later as I recall, but yes, he farmed that land at the time. Which we searched, and I do mean thoroughly.'

'Right. Then you've got the hills and dales and what looked like woodland in between.'

'That'd be the Webster estate. Sir Kenneth. And we did extend the search into the woods, but there's just too much open land in and around that area to cover properly. Nasty what happened to him the other night, eh? Pound to a penny he was pissed. The way I hear it, that was a common occurrence. This time he took other people out with him. Somebody will have to pay for that, I reckon. I pity the poor sods who have to run with the case.'

Chase smiled. He gestured towards Claire Laney. 'Indeed. That would be us.'

THIRTEEN

ON THE WAY BACK from Bath, Chase decided to drive the perimeter of the Webster estate – as close as he could, at least – to get a better feel for it. At its north-western edge he missed a narrow lane and had to make a U-turn further along the road they'd been driving.

'What do you expect to find out here?' Laney asked him.

'I'm not entirely sure. I'm hoping I'll recognise it when I see it.'

'Why do you even think there's something to see?'

Chase glanced across at his partner. 'Because I don't trust coincidence. I'm not one of those coppers who don't believe they exist – I accept there are coincidences happening all around us. But I've learned to be suspicious of them.'

'Which in this case is what?'

The tight lane narrowed further, wild hedgerow encroaching over both sides of the track. Chase could barely see around each bend they came to. He waited until they were on a straighter stretch before answering. 'We have a female minor who died having been in the same vehicle as Ken Webster. Now we discover that same minor was the daughter of a young girl who disappeared from her home twenty years ago. And the home she disappeared from happens to be the width of a field away from Ken Webster's property. I don't like those odds, Claire. I'm not yet sure what any of it means, but my mind is buzzing and my thoughts are scattered. When I get like this, I have to do something about it.'

Laney jerked her head up as Chase stamped on the brakes. He cursed, put the Volvo into reverse and pulled back twenty yards. He switched the hazard lights on and climbed out, Laney following closely behind him. The gap in the hedgerow was wide enough to take a vehicle, but less than a dozen paces along the dirt track a wrought-iron gate blocked the way. Chase walked up to it, wrapping both hands around its two supportive struts as he peered beyond along the track. The entrance lay at the shoulder of a crest, and some fifty yards ahead the trail disappeared over the rise and fell away out of sight.

Chase leaned into the gate, then pulled at it. Solid, it refused to budge so much as an inch. He checked for a sliding bolt and a padlock, but found neither. Then he noticed the sensor affixed to the equally sturdy gatepost. He glanced back over his shoulder to where his partner waited patiently.

'Does an electric gate strike you as something a bit fancy for a farmland entrance and exit?' he asked.

Laney stepped forward to join him, appraising the landscape and her surroundings. She nodded. 'It does. Unless you happen to know the landowner is a rich, ex-Chief Constable whose security while he was in the job would have been immense.'

Chase grunted, annoyed with himself at having overlooked the obvious. 'I suppose.'

'Why, what are you thinking, Royston?'

'Right at this very moment I'm wondering where that track leads to. That and how often this gate is used.'

'I'm sure Lady Jane would be thrilled to answer those questions.'

He raised his eyebrows. 'Perhaps not. Actually, I was thinking more about Miles Radford. As the estate manager, who better to ask?'

'That's one way of looking at it. The other is to assume it'd be easier to insist he excrete a pine cone than extract information from him at this precise moment. He'll have been warned off.'

Chase agreed with his partner's assessment. He regarded the gate once more before looking back at Laney. 'You got your wellies or hiking boots handy?' he asked.

'I have both,' she said. 'Handily, they are sitting in the boot of my car right where they ought to be. So, if you're thinking of doing what I think you're thinking of doing, count me out.'

He walked back to the Volvo and opened up its tailgate. After rummaging around for a few seconds, he fished a pair of sturdy boots out of a blue holdall. Laney laid into him as he stepped out of his shoes, pulled on the boots and began tying a lace.

'You do get that beyond the gate is private land, I'm assuming?'

'I know.'

'And you do understand the act of bypassing said gate and entering said private land is called trespass unless you happen to have permission or a suitable warrant?'

'I do. I won't be long and I won't go far. I want to see what's over that hill.'

'Okay. But I'm also sure you realise that trespass is measured by the act itself and not yardage?'

He closed the hatch and stamped his feet to make the boots more comfortable. 'I'll be five minutes. Less. And before you prattle on about trespass not being measured in time, either, let's assume I know what I'm doing is wrong. But, Claire, who is going to tell on me? It's just you, me, and the birds here.'

'And what if somebody comes along?'

'Perfect. The car is blocking their way in. If they pull over, you lean on the horn. I'll skirt around and find a way out further along, so by the time I rock up I'll be on the right side of the property again.'

Laney let go of a long sigh. 'You're going to be hard work, aren't you?' she said.

'That's the general consensus,' he admitted.

'Five minutes.'

'Count them off on your fingers and you probably won't even need your thumb.'

He turned and walked across to the gate. At approximately six foot high, but with cross struts welded to the vertical bars, it was simple enough to climb over. On the other side, he turned and flashed a wide grin. Spreading his arms, he called out, 'Hey, look at me. I'm trespassing. I made it, ma… top of the world.'

The old Cagney line from the film *White Heat* had stuck in his head. He had no idea why he'd used it, especially as he was about to climb even higher. But it made him laugh as he turned and started to jog before his partner could lodge a final plea. The incline was severe, the dirt path rutted and hard going. He stepped sideways and switched to the tall grass, which for some reason was easier to run through. As he climbed, the harsh sound of machinery filled his ears and grew louder with every step. He thought he heard voices somewhere in the distance. In less than a minute he reached the brow. Out of breath, he panted and surveyed the deep valley that lay beneath his feet.

A vast meadow gave way to a series of copses as it began to level out, after which the tree count rapidly increased and became heavier woodland. But Chase's eyes were drawn to the source of the sounds he'd become aware of during his approach. A yellow earth digger clawed at and digested large quantities of soil, before swinging around to cough up each mouthful into the back of a tipper lorry. Not far away a bulldozer pushed further mounds of earth into narrow heaped lines. In a shallow trench, a number of people gathered together to study what Chase assumed were plans of some description; blueprints, perhaps. A large caravan stood close by; presumably used by the workers to take their breaks and shelter from heavy rain.

Puzzled and more than a little disappointed by what he saw, Chase was startled from his deliberations by the deep blare of a car horn. He immediately moved further down the hill so that he could not be seen from the gated entrance. He jogged along to his right, grateful to find another sweep of hillside behind which to conceal himself. He began to ascend, and when he reached the crest he crouched low at first. Content that he was out of view, he made a dash for cover across open ground before reaching the boundary wall of thick shrubbery. A couple of minutes later he found a tree close enough to climb up and skirt along one of its heavier branches overhanging the partition of foliage. Eventually he managed to hang down and drop the final few feet onto the narrow lane that led back to the entrance.

When he reached the Volvo, Claire Laney was leaning against it, whistling as she scrolled through something on her phone. As he approached, she cursed and frowned at the device, before tucking it back into her shoulder bag. 'Bloody signal,' she complained. 'One minute it's fine, the next...'

'Who was it?' Chase asked.

Lines deepened on Laney's brow. 'Who was who?'

'Who showed up? Why did you hit the horn?'

Her face brightened. 'Oh, that. It was nobody. I got bored.'

Chase felt the flesh around his jaw and mouth tighten. 'You what? You made me scuttle around that bloody field and use a sodding tree to climb my way off their property because you were bored?'

'That's about the size of it, yes. You took too long.'

'That was never five minutes.'

'It felt like five hours.'

'I was going to take some photos,' he complained.

'Of what?'

'Some mechanical equipment I saw down by the woods. Looks to me as if they're laying the groundwork for something.'

'Fascinating. A farm erecting some sheds. How suspicious. Sketch it out for me when we get back to the nick. I think I have some crayons.'

He took a deep breath and slowly let it go, inwardly fuming but saying nothing.

Laney peered closely at him. 'What's got you so wound up?' she asked. 'So what if they're building something on their own land? Whatever it's going to be doesn't yet exist, so how does that help us now? Shouldn't we be focussing on what's in front of us? Something more tangible.'

Chase shook his head. 'To be absolutely truthful, I don't really know what's bugging me,' he confessed. 'Other than the fact that nothing about this whole sorry mess feels right to me.'

'So... pure gut instinct is making you feel queasy, is that what you're telling me?'

'That's about it, yes.'

'And you risked a trespassing charge and a bollocking from the bosses on that basis?'

'I suppose I did.'

Laney grinned and straightened. She patted him on the shoulder. 'Fair enough. You know, I think I'm actually starting to like you, cupcake.'

FOURTEEN

WITH CHASE STILL CHURNING the possibilities over inside his head, they continued on to the station. The building was locked up. Taped to the front desk, PCSO May had left a handwritten message to let them know she was dealing with a minor incident. They'd not been in the office five minutes when Superintendent Waddington called. After thirty seconds of having the signal drop out and back in again, he killed the call and rang the landline. His fury was nonetheless restrained.

'What on earth were you thinking?' he demanded to know. 'You had no reason that I can think of to visit Webster Manor, and certainly no right to talk to her Ladyship. But having taken such an unnecessary step, why did you feel the need to antagonise the poor grieving woman?'

'It was she who antagonised me,' Chase countered, hackles instantly alert and keen to rise. 'I merely gave as good as I got.'

'Lady Jane just lost her husband, for goodness sake! Your manner was completely unprofessional.'

'Is that so? You were there, were you, sir?'

'I heard all about your encounter, DS Chase. That was more than enough for me, thank you.'

'And you're only interested in hearing one side of the story, is that right?'

'Do I need to hear yours? I already know how difficult you can be.'

'So, then you'll also agree it's not always my fault. I lack control at times. This might well have been one of them. Though, and I say this despite appreciating your friendship with the deceased, the woman is not easy to deal with.'

'Be that as it may, I don't understand why you went there at all. You knew I'd spoken with her Ladyship. I told you everything she had to say.'

'And I'm sure you haven't completely forgotten one of our more basic tenets, sir: that memories are often improved twenty-four hours after being given devastating news. I wanted to find out if she knew who was in the car with her husband, or at the very least if she'd suspected somebody might be. And trust me when I tell you she was full of herself right up until I mentioned his club. That's when she threw up all the barriers and feigned distress at my overbearing attitude.'

Chase could almost feel his DSI composing himself during the pause that followed. Eventually, Waddington said in a cool, brusque tone, 'Let me make this abundantly clear for you, Sergeant. You are not to visit Webster Manor again without my express permission. You are not to talk to the manor's staff. And you damn well better not speak to Lady Jane Webster again, either. Please tell me you heard and understood my instructions, DS Chase.'

'I think I got the gist, sir.'

'Don't mess with me, Royston.'

Chase swallowed back his agitated temper. 'I wouldn't dream of it, sir. Clearly your orders will make it more difficult to proceed whenever we need fresh information. I'm assuming you will have to obtain it for us as and when required. Going through a third party always slows things down.'

'What more could you possibly need to ask her Ladyship?'

'I don't know the answer to that, I'm afraid. That's the nature of an on-going investigation. I'm sure if you think hard enough you can remember.'

Chase held the receiver away from his ear. The phone was dead. 'How rude,' he said, not quite managing to disguise the smirk touching his lips.

'I take it he's not best pleased?' Laney said. Having heard his side of the conversation, she was unable to mask her own smile.

'Not so's you'd notice. Look, he and Sir Kenneth were friends as well as colleagues. Possibly more for professional reasons than genuine affection, knowing Russell Waddington. But either way, I can understand why he's fighting me.'

'So why not give him an easier ride?'

A frown tightened Chase's brow. 'Because he's a senior officer, and I am duty bound to be a pain in the neck as often as possible where such luminaries are concerned.'

Laughing, Laney shook her head and said, 'You don't mean that.'

'No,' he said. 'But that's the way things seem to turn out.'

By this time, May had returned to the station. She barged into the office carrying two glasses of lemonade. 'I thought you two could do with a nice cool drink,' she said.

'You're an angel,' Chase told her, holding out his hand. Laney echoed his gratitude as she took her own drink. 'That's if we're still allowed to say such a thing to a colleague. Perhaps angels have recently been cancelled and I didn't get the memo.'

May's cheeks swelled. 'I think they get a pass, sir. And I have no problem being compared to one.'

'Good to hear…' He paused mid-thought, then said, 'Alison, you're still considering joining up, aren't you?'

'Yes, sir. That's my intention.'

'You have your degree already?'

'I do. Just.'

'Good. Tell you what, why don't you sit in with us while DC Laney and I talk over our day's work?'

May appeared shocked by the offer. 'Are you sure, sir? I don't know what I'd be able to bring to the table.'

'More drinks?' Laney suggested, arching her eyebrows. 'Perhaps a doughnut next time?'

Chase threw her a caustic glance before returning to May. 'A fresh set of eyes and ears for a start. I reckon you'll be good at this lark.' He turned to Laney. 'What do you think, Claire? Does PCSO May look up to the task?'

Laney set down her glass. 'We met briefly this morning, when I admit to not being at my best. Since then, we've nodded goodbye as you whisked me out of here earlier. I'm not sure I'm the best judge.'

Chase smiled enthusiastically. 'That's a yes, then. I have an eye for talent. I can tell things about people.'

'Really?' Laney stared him down. 'And what can you tell about me?'

'For reasons I think I'm slowly starting to grasp, you were deliberately chosen as a washout and a burnout to handicap my investigation.'

Laney's eyes widened. 'Thank you, my love. That's possibly the nicest thing anyone has ever said about me. Any chance I could have that quote printed out and framed?'

Chase smiled. 'The thing is, Claire, I'm willing to bet they were wrong about you. I don't think you're either. You made DI, and we both know that didn't happen because you kiss arse. Nor, admittedly, was it likely to have been due to your blinding charm and winning personality. Ergo, you must be a grafter. Someone who is determined and bright and gets the job done despite outward appearances and the barriers put in your way.'

Laney inclined her head. 'Okay, that was a little better. I can get past the bit about outward appearances. Do go on.'

He scratched the back of his neck, where the hairs were longer and starting to curl. 'If the intention was to scupper this investigation, I'm convinced they got it wrong sending you to me. A major case fell into my lap by accident, and by the time the senior leadership was aware, I was already digging into it. They didn't know what to do about that, and somebody came up with a plan to put two outcasts together believing that would make one larger and infinitely worse outcast. To my way of thinking, it's going to work the other way. I reckon we might each be the spark the other needed. You, Claire, could well be the flickering flame to my blue touch paper.'

DC Laney had been nodding along. When he stopped talking, she stopped nodding. 'That is one magnificently uplifting pep talk,' she said. 'Is this the point at which we start calling you skipper? Or coach, perhaps?'

Chase winked as he drained the last of his lemonade. 'Royston will do just fine, thanks.'

'Not Roy? We're not that close yet?'

'Never Roy,' he said with a shake of his head. 'I answer only to Royston. Now, let's have a chat about our day so far. Beginning with… Stacey Brownlow.'

He and Laney discussed their meeting with the ex-patrol cop. Chase's take on it was that although Brownlow had held a few things back, she had been honest with them in everything she had said. Perhaps there were others who knew where to find the mysterious club, who knew more about what went on there, but Brownlow had come across as credible. Laney agreed with him.

'I liked her,' she admitted, pushing aside her empty glass. 'She showed admirable loyalty to her old partner, even though they no longer work together. She also clearly disagreed with his approach to Sir Kenneth, but still she stuck with him. The partner might well be able to tell us more; the question being whether he would be willing to. I'd say it was worth a phone call at best rather than a long drive or train journey to find out.'

'Make a note to give him a bell tomorrow morning.' Chase glanced across at May, who had pulled in a third chair and was sitting alongside his partner. 'Anything to add, Alison?'

She bit into her lower lip. Looked between them. 'Is it all right if I didn't pick up on anything?' she said tentatively. 'I mean, you both covered everything as far as I can tell with my limited knowledge.'

'That's absolutely fine,' Chase said. 'If it isn't there, then it isn't there. We move on.'

Next up was the visit to Webster Manor. 'I found the climax to that interview more than strange,' Laney admitted. 'You broke through her defences piece by piece – which you did very well, I have to say – and you forced her onto the back foot when you brought up the subject of her husband spending time with minors. All as I would have expected. But what seemed to clam her up completely was when you mentioned his club. This Tier One place.'

Chase gave a thoughtful nod. 'Yes, I thought that at the time. I wasn't sure if the whole issue of the young girls had only just caught up with her, but she did seem to panic when I introduced the club into the conversation. The question is: why?'

'I have a suggestion,' May jumped in. 'I'm sure you've both already put it together, but I'd like to offer my thoughts first. Be nice to see how closely they match yours – if at all.'

Chase gestured for her to continue. She nodded and cleared her throat before speaking. 'You were both there, so you'd have seen the changes in her features and how she held herself. But from hearing your account of what was discussed, it seems to me that Lady Jane was terribly put out when you brought up the business about the girl. My guess is that wounded her deeply. However, the fact that she shut you down only when you spoke about the club could be because it's the place that ties the two together.'

'You mean the club might well be the place where our Knight of the Realm and that poor child first met?'

Laney raised a hand. With a faint grin she said, 'If I can butt in here, that's almost word for word what I was going to suggest myself.'

Chase gave a satisfied nod. 'Yes, I think you're both correct. She stopped our interview at that point because she did not want to discuss the place with us, fearing we'd make the connection. To me that says it's the key. It caused her to panic. I'd go as far as to say it frightened her.'

'I'll make a note for tomorrow. We have to take a hard look at this club. What it is, what it does, and most important of all, where we can find it.'

'Our number one priority,' Chase said. He turned to face May. 'Well done. See, I knew you had a future in this business.'

The PCSO flashed a shy smile and shrugged. 'I think it was simple logic.'

'Something in shorter supply than you might imagine, Alison. Especially in today's modern police service. But don't let that put you off – we need more of the right stuff.'

'What about Mr Radcliffe?' Laney asked. 'Did he provide us with any answers or leave us with more questions?'

Chase puffed out his cheeks. 'The poor man was almost too stunned to take it all in. So would I be if I found out the daughter I'd suspected was dead these past twenty years had been alive long enough to give birth to a child of her own. We tell him he had a granddaughter as well, and now he has neither. As for him being in the frame for Mandy going missing in the first place, I can't see it. I'm convinced she let herself out of the house, though I confess I'm not seeing why. But let's come to that, because something Donovan Riley mentioned got me thinking about that night.'

'Isn't that another key, another missing piece of this overall puzzle?' Laney said. 'As you indicated earlier, our victim's mother going missing from home in mysterious circumstances can't be coincidental, can it?'

'Doubtful. Make another note, because we have to follow up on that even though it's not our case. There is a connection, I'm sure of it.'

'Which still leaves us with the question of why Mandy Radcliffe has not come forward to report her daughter missing.'

'Which is significant only if Mandy herself is still alive and well, of course. She fell off the edge of the world twenty years ago. Our victim is the only proof we have that an eight-year-old missing kid survived. But until when?'

'This is so interesting,' May said, edging further forward in her seat. 'Don't get me wrong, I understand how horrible and disgusting it all is. But listening to you two hash it out is enthralling for someone like me.'

Chase nodded. 'Sometimes, Alison, talking about it is all we have.'

'I can understand that. So, can I ask about the child? Mandy's daughter.'

'Go ahead.'

'Did she have any distinguishing marks on her body? I'm thinking of tattoos, piercings, even a birthmark.'

'No. None of those things. Even her ears weren't pierced, which is unusual these days for a kid her age. Sadly, neither did she have any metal screws or parts holding bones together, so no way of identifying her through hospital records, either.'

'Dental?'

'We'll know more about them later, but word is she had no fillings, nor any other obvious signs of dental work, and her teeth were in bad shape.'

'So she was most likely neglected.'

'I'd say so. Okay, so let's move on to Daniels. The only suspect other than Mr and Mrs Radcliffe: what do we think of him?'

'Mr Daniels interests me,' Laney said.

'Me, too. If we go back to how Mandy Radcliffe left her home that night, he's still a potential suspect. We know that Mandy's parents didn't kill her and bury her out in the fields somewhere. I don't buy her walking out into the night on her own and somehow surviving long enough to have her own baby. Someone breaking in and snatching her doesn't work for me, either. No obvious sign of forced entry. Parents didn't hear a thing. But you know what does interest me? Mandy being lured out. And who better than family friend Paul Daniels?'

'You don't think it could have been her school friends?' May asked.

'We can't discount them,' Laney replied. 'It's a bit late in the evening, plus you'd have to wonder how they got there. But yes, it's a path we have to explore. That said, Mr Daniels seems the more likely and immediate candidate.'

'You think he lured the girl out under some pretence, took her and kept her?' Alison May's forehead first creased then flattened. 'Oh my God! You think he might still have her?'

'Stranger things have happened,' Chase remarked. 'Every so often one such incident comes out of nowhere, taking us all by surprise yet again. A visit to Mr Daniels is also high on our list. However, for your benefit, Alison, this brings me back to something I again mentioned earlier. Ex-DI Donovan Riley spoke about the area in which the Radcliffe cottage is situated. Across the main road opposite the front of the house is a field belonging to a farmer. On the other side of that field is the Webster estate. Before taking a drive around the outer fringes, it hadn't occurred to me how their land sweeps around in a curve, so I didn't realise how close it came to the Radcliffe home.'

'What are you saying, sir?' May asked.

'Claire and I agreed it cannot be pure coincidence that the daughter of a girl who disappeared into thin air within walking distance of Sir Kenneth Webster's property twenty years ago, turns up in his car all these years later. Is it possible for there to be no connection between these two events?'

'Yes,' Laney said immediately. 'Absolutely. Sorry to jump back into this, but although I agreed with you earlier, I'm going to cite the John O'Neill exception here.'

Chase fixed her with a bemused expression. 'What on earth is that?'

'John O'Neill was a senior FBI agent who believed Al Qaeda in the form of Osama bin Laden was going to strike at the USA. He grew sick and tired of the CIA withholding pertinent information from him. He was not the type of man to accept this without a fight. Eventually he was all but sidelined and shoved out of his job, though he effectively quit his post. He still firmly believed Al Qaeda were going to hit the US with a massive terror attack. O'Neill was less than three weeks into his new job when the twin towers went down. His new job? Head of security at the world trade centre. He died in the north tower. So, ever since nine-eleven, whenever somebody questions dramatic coincidence, I throw that out there. If that can happen, then it must be possible for that twenty-year-old case and this current one to be entirely unconnected, despite featuring both a mother and daughter separately in the same breath as Sir Kenneth Webster.'

Alison May blinked and turned to DC Laney. 'Is that all true? That stuff about this O'Neill man. Or is it one of those urban myths?'

'It's all true. I watched a TV show about it, and then checked it out later on.'

Chase nodded. 'And I'll also admit to having heard of even more bizarre coincidences than that. This one wouldn't be in that kind of league, I grant you. However, it's still more unlikely than not.'

'I expect that's because of your experience, sir,' May said. 'To me, the link seems tenuous at best. On the one hand you have a young girl killed while travelling in a car with Sir Kenneth, on the other you have a young girl who disappeared from her home a few hundred yards away from his property. Given the size of his estate, I'd think most homes in the area could be seen as being close to it.'

'And I would agree,' Chase said, nodding amiably. 'But for one significant factor: the girl who vanished from her home turned out to be our victim's mother.'

'You almost seem to be implying a degree of collusion,' Laney declared. 'That not only is it not a coincidence, it's actually deliberate. We know that can't be. Not given the way our victim died.'

'No, I'm not suggesting that at all. I can't really explain. Being able to reference Webster in relation to both cases is the issue. Yes, I admit, the first of those incidents is nothing more than a footnote. But when you introduce the mother-daughter relationship, it suddenly seems so much more.'

Laney gave a long sigh. 'I do see what you're getting at Royston. I can't deny it's an amazing turn of events. And I also see the deeper meaning: young girl goes missing close to Webster's property, young girl dies while in his vehicle. I think there's something there. I'm just not seeing what it could be. There needs to be an even closer tie-in to Webster in the case of Mandy Radcliffe. Certainly if we're going to chase it down as a formal lead.'

'You're right.' Chase paused to consider what they had. 'I'm not about to let it go, though. If it needs more substance, I'll try to obtain it. One place to start would be to find out where Sir Kenneth was the night Mandy Radcliffe disappeared. Meanwhile, how about we let Alison here have a crack at her disappearance. It's not on our immediate agenda, even if it's definitely related. Alison can follow up on a couple of things by phone. First with Mr Radcliffe, then perhaps Donovan Riley. See if they remembered anything else after we'd left. Perhaps probe where we failed to.'

'I'm up for that,' May said brightly.

Laney laughed. 'Sorry, but you failed your first test. Never volunteer.'

'I didn't. Did I?'

This caused a gentle ripple of laughter all round. 'Never you mind,' Chase said. 'It's a nice job for you to get your teeth into rather than standing at the front desk all day waiting for somebody to walk in to report their poodle missing.'

'Or that a sheep was looking at them oddly. I had one of those last week. Bit of a psychopath, it appears. The sheep, I mean.'

'You can see why they posted the best of the best here,' Laney muttered. 'These mean streets need taking care of.'

Chase grinned. He was enjoying the light-hearted nature of the banter. Theirs was a serious job, but occasionally it required a more flippant approach in order to get through the moments filled with darkness. 'Claire and I will put our heads together on finding out where this Tier One club is. That and taking a run at Paul Daniels.'

'I like that idea,' Laney said. 'Not a lot… but I like it.'

FIFTEEN

LATER THAT NIGHT, AS he and his wife stood in the kitchen discussing their day, Chase found himself doing so with a surprising amount of enthusiasm. He'd reeled off a digested version of the encounter with Lady Jane Webster when he caught his wife's puzzled look.

'What?' he asked. 'What's with the squinty eyes?'

'We?'

'What?' This time he shrugged.

'You keep using that word, Royston. Who's the "we" you're referring to?'

Chase coughed up a laugh and took a long swig of his beer before continuing. 'Oh, that's right. I forgot to tell you; I've been given a partner.'

'You have? That's quite a turn up for the books.'

'I know. Unthinkable.' He went on to describe his initial encounter with and impression of Claire Laney.

When her roar of laughter had become more of a gentle chuckle, Erin said, 'You're exaggerating for comedic effect, I assume?'

He shook his head. 'I kid you not. You'd think she got dressed and applied her slap in the deepest cave at Wookey Hole without the benefit of a torch or naked flame.'

'Now my imagination is racing. I'm guessing you're going to tell me she makes up for it with a cracking personality.'

His shoulders bounced as he chuckled once more. 'Not so's you'd notice. Her appearance is… unfortunate. And initially she came across every bit as scary on the inside as she was the outside.'

'Initially…?'

He nodded. 'You know I like to give time for people's true character to emerge. When she and I first met and spoke in the office she was indignant, surly, and had that kind of overtly aggressive personality capable of driving a person insane.'

Erin ignored her bottle for a moment to rub his arm gently. 'Ah, bless. But not my Royston.'

'I have to confess, she was almost too much for me. Still, after spending time with her on those interviews, I think I eventually found her good points.'

'Which are?'

'For one thing, she's more than decent at her job. I don't quite know what she did to get herself demoted from DI to DS and then down to DC again, but given her awful personality she must have been a terrific detective to have forced her way up to the rank of Inspector in the first place. She showed flashes of that today. It was nice working with someone you didn't have to brief all the time. She knows how to handle interviews; when to speak, when to keep schtum. And she has a sharp mind. What's left of it.'

His wife pulled back and narrowed her gaze. 'What does that mean?'

He tipped his Peroni and finished the last of it. 'Bit too much of that,' he said. He glanced around the room, saw they were alone for the time being. 'In fact, she said her problem was she drank too much, smoked too much, and fucked too much.'

Erin laughed. Put a hand to her mouth. 'She actually said that about herself.'

Chase nodded. 'Later on, while we were driving to meet with someone, she told me she must be the only woman in the police force to sleep her way to the bottom.'

This time they both laughed. At which point Maisie came running into the room, a sheet of paper flapping in her hand. His daughter showed him what she had painted that day while Erin served up their dinner. They sat down together at the dining table and Chase began to feel the minor physical aches and tweaks of frustration ebb away. His second bottle of beer helped soothe the way towards relaxation. He knew he'd be drawn back into the case before night fell, but for a while he was content to enjoy some down time with the two loves of his life. When you had this to come home to, it made what you saw, heard, and did during the day appear to drift away until it flickered out altogether like a candle being starved of oxygen.

*

Chase's mobile phone vibrated on the bedside cabinet, and its screen illuminated the bedroom at two in the morning. Erin shifted and turned beside him, hugging the duvet closer as she buried her head deeper into the pillow. Chase blinked his vision clear and answered without checking who was calling.

'DS Chase.'

'You don't know me, Detective Sergeant Chase, but we need to talk.' The voice was measured, authoritative and cultured.

Chase drew saliva into his dry mouth, raised himself up and swivelled, legs hanging over the edge of the mattress. 'What about? Who is this?'

'We're outside. You have five minutes.'

'Five… look, what's this all about? What do you mean you're outside? Outside where, the station?'

'No, Sergeant. Your house.'

The line went dead. The caller had hung up.

Running both hands down his face, Chase's mind finally caught up. He snatched a quick peek at Erin before slipping out of bed and padding across to the window. He eased back a flap of curtain. A dark car was parked across the entrance to his driveway. Its lights flashed on and off again. He reared back, but realised the stupidity of doing so given he'd already been seen. Still groggy with sleep, he assessed the situation while his heartbeat quickened. No matter which way he looked at what had just happened, it didn't make sense. And neither did it bode well, especially with Erin and Maisie in the house.

He moved quickly and silently back across the room, then snatched up his phone and thumbed through the call log. He assumed the caller would be listed as unknown, but he thought he might be able to get it traced. He opened his eyes as wide as he could, blinked some more. Then he frowned. According to the mobile, he had not received an incoming call since late afternoon. Had he imagined the whole thing? Was he dreaming?

Back to the window. Curtain flap drawn aside only by a sliver this time. If he was still sleeping, then the car remained a part of his dream. Chase took a deep breath, gathering his wits. Heart hammering to bursting point, he pulled on a T-shirt and jogging bottoms, stepped into his trainers, and quietly left the bedroom, easing the door closed behind him. His mind working frantically, he put on a windcheater jacket. From the utility room next to the kitchen, he pulled a small mallet from its hook on the wall. Its dense rubber end was perfect for paving, but could also do some damage if wielded as a weapon.

The Indian summer air outside had cooled significantly, but was not cold. Breath coming in short bursts, Chase crept along the path down to the twin gates sealing off the two-car drive. A harsh squeal from the one he opened to let himself out sounded so loud he expected lights to flicker on in bedrooms all the way along the street. He froze, but nobody stirred.

Chase heard the unmistakable sound of a car window being powered down. A face appeared from the back of the vehicle, which he recognised as a Jaguar. 'Jump in,' he was told. The window slid back up.

You're a confident sod, Chase thought. He cautiously made his way around to the offside rear door, thoughts whirring with each step. *What exactly fuels your arrogance?*

Three men sat inside the car. The two in front said nothing when Chase slid in, but the one in the back thanked him for joining them.

'Did I have a choice?' he grumbled.

'We always have a choice, Detective Sergeant Chase. You've chosen well so far. Let's hope that continues.'

Chase reached a decision. He'd been making up his mind about how to deal with the situation – whatever the situation was. Sitting back and hearing the man out was one option. Behaving as if he himself was in charge was the other. He opted for the latter.

'Before we go any further,' he said, 'I want your name, I want to know who you work for, and I want to know what you want with me.'

The man looked to be in his late fifties, with silver-white hair shaved close to the scalp. He appeared lean and fit. Average height and build. Tailored suit, complete with waistcoat. The man's eyes glimmered in whatever natural light the early hours afforded.

'You can call me Maurice. As for who I work for, that's an enigma even I've yet to unravel. Put me down as a civil servant. But I am happy to answer your final question, DS Chase.'

'That'll do for the time being. We can come back to the rest.'

Maurice seemed amused by the suggestion. 'I've popped by to have a chat about the investigation you're working.'

Chase gave a curt laugh of disbelief. 'People don't just pop by at this time of morning. People try to intimidate by calling on others in the early hours. That isn't going to work with me. So, please say your piece. I have an early start.'

Unruffled, the man nodded. 'Fair enough. It's actually quite simple. There are some police officers who go through the motions. They watch the clock, they abide by protocol and follow procedures. They tend not to exercise their minds too often. Men and women like that, who do as they are told and don't rattle cages, often find themselves in a good position when it comes to career ambitions, pension package, that sort of thing. Stability and security for themselves and their family.'

He turned to stare pointedly at the bungalow for a moment, then dropped his gaze back upon Chase. 'Others – those who fly too close to the sun – get their wings melted and tumble into the sea. I suppose that's where we come back to choice. This current investigation of yours, for example. I'm sure if you put your mind to it you could wrap it all up by this evening. I mean, who's to say where that young girl really came from on Tuesday night? Witnesses have been known to be wrong. The girl could have been wandering around aimlessly. In fact, if you think about it more broadly, couldn't she have been the cause of the terrible accident? Stepping out in front of a certain Land Rover, forcing the driver to swerve and lose control. In the end he couldn't avoid her, knocking the poor creature into the air by quite some distance. That would explain so much. As for the girl herself, sadly she remains unidentified and is likely to stay that way.'

Chase didn't know whether to be angered or merely disappointed. But he was definitely curious. 'What exactly are you suggesting?'

'I'm suggesting you complete your investigation along the lines of the scenario I laid out for you. I provided a blank canvas and painted a perfect picture for you, Sergeant.'

Swallowing back his annoyance, Chase said, 'I don't see that happening. Besides, we're getting closer to identifying that poor kid all the time.'

'But are you? Are you really? And… do you actually need to?'

Chase felt his flesh tingling as it grew warm. Not only at the indignation of having this man attempt to steer his investigation, but also at the implied threat if he didn't. He assumed the two silent men in the front seats were there to prevent this odious creep from having his face smashed in. He wondered what their reaction would be if he pulled out the rubber mallet.

'Where's all this coming from?' he asked around a huge lump in his throat. 'Did her Ladyship send you? Is that what this is all about? Some old school tie establishment muscle?'

'Do you honestly believe it matters, DS Chase? Put your mind to it for a moment. Think about how I know so much about the case.

How I was able to find you. You, your wife, Erin, and little Maisie. By all accounts, you're not a stupid man. Neither am I. We both know I'm not actually suggesting, Sergeant. Nor even asking. I'm telling you how it has to be.'

Chase shuddered at the mention of his wife and daughter. The man he was sitting alongside was extremely powerful. That much was obvious. He swallowed and said, 'It's not as easy as you make out. Whoever you work for, whatever channels you move in, you're a day late to the party.'

'How so?'

'Precisely because I'm not the sort of copper to sit on my arse and do nothing. There's an investigation running. People have already been spoken to. There's a part of the story already out there, and no matter how much you might want it not to be, it is. There's nothing you can do about that. Nothing I can do to row it back.'

The man scoffed. 'We both know that's not the case. You are not so naïve, Sergeant. People can be placated. They can be bought off. They can be warned off. They can become… irrelevant to the bigger picture. You must realise what's at stake here. And therefore you must also realise there is nothing we will not do in order to protect the best interests of those whose reputations must remain unsullied.'

'And you include threatening a serving police detective in that, do you?'

Maurice offered a shrug. 'If necessary. Look, at the moment we're having a polite conversation. Our first encounter could have gone any number of ways, but at this stage we're merely two men discussing options. But know this: my powers of persuasion are without either remit or scope. Everybody has a weakness. If required, I will exploit that weakness. If coaxing alone will not suffice, then I am unrestrained in what I am able to do in order to ensure the satisfaction of my paymasters.'

Chase slowly slid a hand inside his jacket. He gripped the wooden handle of the mallet. It was three against one. He would lose. But not without a fight. 'I could arrest you,' he said, eyes boring into those of the man who sat undaunted and unfazed.

'You could certainly try. However, you would fail. I've made no overt threat to you. And my credentials are impeccable. I would consider a swarm of patrol cars and blue lights bathing the homes of your neighbours as the first shot in a war. A war you cannot hope to win, be assured of that if nothing else. And for what? A thirty second phone conversation will see them all drive away again. Leaving you where exactly? Leaving your wife and daughter where, exactly?'

'You mention them again and I'll break your skull,' Chase snapped.

The man in the passenger seat turned swiftly to look at him. 'If I see that hand emerge from inside your jacket with whatever your holding, I'll do more than break your bones,' he said.

If the man was pumped up with adrenaline and full of bluster, Chase didn't notice. There was a calm air about him that had to be respected. He nodded and loosened his grip on the hammer's shaft, sliding his hand back into view. 'There are too many people involved in this,' he said, hearing the lack of certainty in his voice. 'The investigation has already gone too far.'

The man sitting beside him shook his head. 'There are never too many people involved, DS Chase. As I said before, we have our methods. What will not work for some will work for others. If you think about how willing Stacey Brownlow was to protect her partner, imagine what she would do to save her own neck and that of her unborn child. Frankly, I don't imagine anybody will consider a bitter old drunk like Mr Radcliffe to be a reliable witness to anything you told him. The man is barely conscious much of the day, and we can easily find a way for the DNA analysis to go missing. As for ex-Detective Inspector Riley, he'll not want any harm to come to those grandchildren of his. And if your friend Trevor Shipman wishes to maintain his current career progress, it's unlikely he's going to be quite as helpful to you as he has been thus far.'

'You're sick,' Chase said, appalled by what he was hearing.

Maurice nodded. 'And completely without conscience. I'm also a man with an extraordinarily long reach. Something worth bearing in mind as you consider your approach when you get to Little Soley later on this morning.'

After a lengthy pause, during which all manner of responses flashed across his mind, Chase eventually said, 'I don't know how to go about fixing this the way you want.'

This time the man gave a slow smile of satisfaction. 'You're a good man and a good detective, Sergeant. I'm sure you'll think of something.'

Chase stared him down, a knot of flesh forming above his nose. 'All this to protect the name and reputation of a dead, drunken paedophile.'

Maurice's eyes flickered. He considered his words carefully before responding. 'The world is not about the dead, Sergeant. It's about the living. I'd advise you to remember that.'

SIXTEEN

THE BIG DECISION FOR Chase later that day was whether to take Claire Laney into his confidence. He had told his wife nothing about their early morning visitor. He'd already decided it was not safe for PCSO May to make the calls he'd assigned her, but he thought he could talk his way out of that situation. How he took the case forward, and the degree to which he let Laney in on his predicament, was still in question when he arrived at the village station.

He was early, and grateful for some additional time on his own. He hadn't tried to sleep following his impromptu meeting, and had thought of little else since. The implied threat had been obvious, and the man had appeared to be both capable and ruthless. Yet Chase was still undecided how to react. If Superintendent Waddington was not a party to the external intrusion, he would surely listen with an open mind. The Super was too good a copper to dismiss what he had to say merely because it was Chase doing the talking. Yet two questions remained: how far would the DSI be willing to take matters, and how far would he be allowed to?

Chase had heard of this sort of interference occurring, but today was his first experience of it. Politicians, major business leaders, celebrities, and royals major and minor, were all human beings beneath the thin veneer holding them all together. When it came unglued, those who held the balance of power generally rallied round to prevent it from falling apart entirely. Occasionally the public got to hear about these private disgraces, because the story got blown wide open. Most of the time they lived their lives oblivious to the deals being made behind closed doors, threats handed out, money changing hands, promotions obtained, and even the people who went missing never to be seen again.

Making grubby little deals in order to protect reputations was the stock in trade for some people. Maurice was the official point of that particular spear, and as such was a man to be feared.

Chase ran the meeting through his head time and again and continued to take the threat seriously. Its source interested him. More than likely it was something the widow had implemented, terrified of her husband being exposed as the kind of man who abused young children. But if not from the Webster camp, then where? And who? Sir Kenneth was dead. His reputation had to be preserved at all costs. Chase pondered the possibility that the police structure itself had turned against one of its own in order to protect an ex-luminary. Yet, if the Tier One club was the key to everything, then the dead Knight was not its only member. Nor founder.

In his own manipulative way, Colin Shakespeare was as big a fish as Sir Ken Webster, though they swam in vastly different oceans. Webster had known only money and privilege, and his years spent policing the area had been nothing more than a way to appear as if he were giving something back to the public in the same way his father had done by serving in the military. Conversely, Shakespeare had pulled off the clichéd rags-to-riches rise after investing every saved penny he had in his first local newspaper. If the investigation was going to continue, then he might be the man to tell them more about the club.

As Chase continued to weigh up his options, Laney came bundling through the office door shaking rainwater from the same leather jacket she had worn the previous day. 'Bloody weather,' she moaned, her voice deep and cracked, suggesting she'd had a late and heavy night. 'Forecast says it's going to be dry but overcast all day, and yet I get caught in a bloody downpour the moment I step out of my car.'

'Cup of tea or coffee improve your mood?' he asked.

'If you're volunteering. I don't suppose you have any hot chocolate, do you?'

'Alison has a mug of that every now and then. Cadbury's, I think. Mind you, it is her own jar.'

'She won't mind. Especially given the leg up you gave her yesterday. Injecting a PCSO into this was a slick move, Royston.'

As he made their hot drinks, Laney joined him in the small kitchen and leaned against a wall, arms folded. 'I spent much of last night reflecting on our day together, and you in particular.'

'Oh? I doubt that was fascinating.'

'Actually, it was. I must say, your bluntness shocked me at first. But the more I thought about it, the more I decided it was fresh and interesting.'

He'd used May's hot chocolate after all, reminding himself to buy her a new jar. He stirred both mugs vigorously, delaying while he considered his response. The truth was, he'd always been direct with people, occasionally to the point of rudeness. The injury to his brain had simply provided him with a medical excuse to carry on as before, though the filter aspect was true and had required management.

'I was especially rude to you yesterday,' he admitted, passing her a mug. 'I know I already apologised, but I truly am sorry.'

Laney took her drink and they walked back through into the office. 'I've heard worse,' she said. 'And besides, I was also abrasive and arrogant, and not at all respectful. I was unhappy at being dumped here rather than posted to Gablecross or the Devizes, HQ. It felt like yet another sign of defeat, and I took it out on you. It wasn't a great start, but I think we got it together throughout the day. Perhaps it was good for us to have such an important case to investigate.'

You have no idea how important, he thought. 'I'm sure we can put it behind us. We're very different people, Claire, but I've often found that works well. It means we'll bring diverse attributes to the table.'

'That's certainly true. Though I have to say, I've never met a Royston before. I seem to recall the village in that TV show *The League of Gentlemen* was called Royston Vasey. But that came out in the late nineties, so you can't have been named after the programme.'

'No, but you're warmer than you know,' he said, dropping into his chair. 'You ever heard of a comedian called Roy "Chubby" Brown?'

'I don't think so.'

'He's still around, though no longer performing regularly. On stage he wore garish clothes and an old style flying helmet, complete with goggles.'

'Sounds like a bit of a prat if you ask me.'

Chase smiled. 'You'd have liked him. His humour was coarse, offensive, and completely lacking any form of political correctness. Hugely popular in the north, where he became something of a folk hero to many. Anyhow, his real name is Royston Vasey, and it was from him that they took the name of the fictional village.'

Laney narrowed her gaze. 'Is that true or are you winding me up?'

'Why would I do that?'

'To screw with me. Having me tell that same story to somebody who knows it's all bollocks would make your day, I reckon.'

Chase shook his head. 'It's gospel. Give it a go on Google if my word is not good enough for you.'

They sipped their drinks slowly and began discussing the day ahead. It was now or never for Chase, and before he could stop himself he was telling his new partner all about his unexpected visitors in the early hours of the morning.

'Spooks?' she said when he was done.

'I'm not entirely sure. I got the impression these men were the kind even the security services call upon when they want something handling, no questions asked.'

Laney puffed out her cheeks. 'We must have struck a nerve.'

'I'd say so. And whoever they are, they have some pull. I had to update the crime log before I went home last night. Made sure DSI

Waddington had a copy waiting for him in his inbox when he went looking for it.'

'You saying he forwarded it to the man in the Jag?'

'They had information that could only have come from the crime log. Even so, I'm not sure that's how they acquired it. I got the impression these people have ways of intercepting mail. Even mail that only went through the police's own system. Plus, I like to think Waddington is not that kind of copper. I hope not, at least. We may yet need to confide in him.'

Laney gave a glum nod. 'Stands to reason. If they are who you think they are, they'd have connections through GCHQ.'

'Are you suggesting our own intelligence gathering services spy on the police?'

'No, Royston. I'm saying they spy on whoever they want, whenever they want. Do you think this goes beyond Sir Kenneth?'

It was a good question. Perhaps *the* question. Feeling more than a little lost and anxious, he nodded. 'I do. They're looking to pop the genie back into the bottle, but I'm not sure they would go this far to save one man's reputation. In fact, having given the matter a great deal of thought, I wondered why they didn't take the opportunity to throw him under the bus. A one man disgrace they could all claim had them fooled.'

'Too risky,' Laney said. She took another slurp from her mug and smacked her lips. 'Admitting to him having a thing for young girls brings it out into the open where it becomes fair game. There are investigative journalists out there who would see the story behind the one being told.'

'I agree. Which is why the approach they made to me makes sense. They want it to disappear before it opens up into the public domain. The cover-up almost certainly began with a quiet word in the right ear, and several words in several ears later you appear in this station. But then the moment they heard we were working the case and actually getting somewhere with it, they closed ranks and those words became demands, demands threats, and threats actions. All of which leaves us… where?'

Laney wrinkled her nose as if she had a bad smell beneath it. 'Up to our necks in shite, my little cupcake.'

'It certainly feels like it. By the way, I'm telling Alison May none of this.' He checked his phone and frowned. 'Which reminds me, she's not in yet and I've never known her to be this late.'

Laney held the mug of hot chocolate to her lips. She gave it a guilty glance and set it down on the desk on top of a folder. 'You think she got her own early morning visit?'

Chase shrugged. 'I wouldn't put anything past them, but it doesn't make a lot of sense to pay her and me a visit and leave you out.'

'That's true. You worried about her?'

'Not yet. I'll give it a few more minutes and then give her a bell.'

'They wouldn't hurt her, would they? As a warning to you, I mean?'

'Again, I'm not sure if they have lines they won't cross. But I think they'd wait to assess my response before taking action against anyone else involved.' Chase swallowed hard. 'Mind you, I gave Erin and Maisie a tighter squeeze before I left this morning.'

'I do hope that's your wife and daughter and not the names of each testicle.'

Chase laughed so hard he slopped hot chocolate over his desk. 'Don't tell me… I'm guessing you dated somebody who did precisely that.'

'Not precisely. Be a bit weird if he named them after your family members. But yes, he did have names for them. It's one of the reasons I married him.'

'Really? So what happened?'

'What do you mean?'

'Between the two of you.'

'Oh, I see. Nothing. We're still married. We have a son in the merchant navy.'

'I hadn't realised… sorry.'

Laney raised her eyebrows and bobbed her head. 'You assumed somebody like me had to be single.'

'No. Not at all. I… I don't know what I thought, or why.'

'It's okay. No offence taken, Royston. I can see why you came to that conclusion.'

'It's just that when you told me you drank too much, smoked too much and… well, fucked too much, I did imagine that was because you lived alone. I apologise.'

She flapped a hand at him. And then gestured at herself. 'You notice I eased up on the makeup today? No scary clown to terrify my new partner, DS Chase, this morning.'

He smiled. 'Actually, I did clock the appearance. Other than that bloody rank jacket, you're looking half decent today, Claire.'

'Half decent? Please, don't gush. You'll embarrass me.'

'You know what I mean. Anyway, if I say you look good, I open myself up to some hashtag or another and get sent for sensitivity training. I don't want to be offered up as a sacrifice to whatever new version of the #MeToo movement is flavour of the month.'

Laney's face twisted as if she'd bitten into a lemon. 'You're entirely safe with me on that score, cupcake. I'm all for banter in the workplace, and I really don't think you can offend me more than you did yesterday. Plus, I think I've demonstrated the ability to give back as good as I get.'

'And more,' Chase agreed. He glanced at his phone again. 'Okay, I'm officially worried. No Alison, no call or text to say she won't be in. I'm going to find out where she is and what's going on.'

He brought up his contacts and hit dial on a number. A few moments later his call was answered. 'Alison? Is that you? It's DS Chase.'

'Oh, hello, Sergeant. I was just this second thinking about you.'

'You were? Why's that?'

'I was wondering why you didn't need me back in until Monday. Other than today, I was due in tomorrow morning as well. Did something come up?'

Chase muted the phone. 'They got to her,' he told Laney. 'Not in a bad way. But another warning. Showing me how easy it would be.' He took the speaker off mute. 'I'm sorry, Alison. I think there must be a glitch in the matrix somewhere. Did you receive a call or a text message?'

'Did I… sorry, I don't understand. You texted me, sir, remember? It came with your name on it, from your phone.'

He took that in and grew more concerned. 'Hence the glitch, Alison. Actually, it's fine. Carry on with whatever you're doing. I was just checking. Somebody made a mistake and things got switched around in the system somewhere. Have a nice long weekend. We'll see you here bright and early on Monday.'

'Are you sure? Only, if there was an error, I can still come in. I don't live far away from Little Soley.'

Chase repeated himself, insisting there was no problem and that he'd already decided not to go down the path of recontacting either Mr Radcliffe or Donovan Riley again so soon. He said he hoped to have something more interesting for her to do on Monday morning. Before she could come back at him, he said goodbye and thumbed the call closed.

'I got the gist,' Laney said. Then she frowned. 'Hey, how come your mobile is working fine this time?'

He shook his head. 'Crazy signal.' He then checked his text message app. No outgoing text to May's phone was logged.

'That's scary,' he said, looking up at his colleague. 'The call they placed to me this morning isn't registering. Also, supposedly my phone sent a message to Alison May telling her not to come in until next week. Yet it's not in my list of text messages, and you can bet it won't be in hers, either.'

Laney whistled. 'That's a real abuse of power.'

Chase nodded. Took a deep breath and released it. 'And I'm betting it's only the beginning, too.'

SEVENTEEN

THE SPEED WITH WHICH somebody holding enormous sway had acted against them gave Chase considerable pause. He was not a naïve man, and had not imagined having an easy ride. Any investigation would have been hard enough if the errant man behind the wheel had merely been guilty of causing death by careless driving while under the influence of drink or drugs. That alone would have tarnished his memory, perhaps ruined it in the eyes of some. But under age sex, with or without consent, would inevitably shatter the man's reputation beyond all repair. Deservedly so, in Chase's opinion. To his mind, human beings couldn't sink any lower than engaging in acts of paedophilia.

But this particular man had been knighted. Sir Kenneth and his family going back many generations had been pillars of the establishment, he being both a wealthy landowner and onetime Chief Constable when he died. The embarrassment factor was bound to crawl its way into the very core of several major institutions. Little thought would be spared for the poor young girl whose life was lost alongside the pervert who somehow procured her and had been indulging in various sexual activities with her at the point of their deaths.

'Which way are you leaning, Royston?' Laney asked, disrupting his flow of thinking. She regarded him with genuine concern from the other side of his desk. 'I've only known you for a day, but I see you as a man of principle. I suspect your instincts are crowding around insisting you fight this. Equally, you're aware of the impact on others, so you won't take the threat lightly. If you want my advice, I'd caution you not to be bullied by either.'

'What's that supposed to mean?'

'That the louder and more strident voice is not always the one to listen to. Fuck me, you only have to spend an hour on social media to know that. You're a man of integrity, so the most natural approach is to carry on as you were and hope they are bluffing. But this is not your fight alone. If they're not blagging this, then there's bound to be collateral damage. All I'm saying is, pay attention to both sides of that internal debate.'

Chase nodded, uncertainty causing his stomach to clench. 'You're potentially part of any collateral damage,' he said. 'How do you feel about that?'

'I suppose that depends on how far they're willing to go. I want to nail Ken Webster if he's what we think he is. I want to put a name to that poor girl and find some closure for her. On the other hand, she can no longer be saved and I don't think I'm prepared to lose my life over the repercussions.'

'Perhaps I'm being naive, but how likely are they to take things that far?'

'I wouldn't put anything past these people. They mentioned your wife and daughter by name. The threat in that particular instance might have been implied, but are you willing to gamble everything on it?'

'So we meekly step aside?'

'I'm not saying that.' Laney shook her head. 'Only that you have to do what you think is best for you under the circumstances. I'll back you up if you step away from this case. It's what the likes of Crawley and Waddington want, anyhow. They won't push back. Far from it, they'd probably welcome it with open arms.'

'I don't know if I could live with myself.'

'I understand. So let's discuss both options. You know, if you wanted to put it to bed by this evening, the scenario he suggested might not be a bad way to go. Then we have Sir Kenneth driving home on his own. The naked girl rushes out from somewhere in the shadows and runs straight in front of him. He tries to avoid her but ends up hitting her, throwing her in the same direction as his own vehicle. At night, with everything that happened, witnesses could be confused about what they saw. And they could probably be convinced of it, too. Either that or their statements get altered, paper versions destroyed.'

'You're forgetting our own people. The SCIT crew were all over the scene. By now they've talked, pieced the whole incident together in intricate detail. Maggie O'Donnell herself told us at the meeting over at Gablecross that what took place was clear cut. First of all, there were no tyre marks, so there's no way we can claim Ken Webster tried to avoid the kid. Second, there's evidence of the impact and how it ejected the girl from the passenger seat of his Land Rover. And even if we had neither of those facts working against the idea, it's still pretty hard to suggest that scenario then explain away her having half his dick in her mouth.'

Drawing both hands down her face, Laney said, 'Yeah, that's pretty conclusive and hard to ignore. Officially, you may be able to build a wall of silence, fudge the DNA, and have the scene forensic photos go missing. But too many people have that snippet of information to make it go away for good. So there's your answer, Royston. No matter how much you might try, you can't let this slide without causing more than eyebrows to be raised. It's an impossible task.'

Chase squinted. His partner was right. There was no chance whatsoever of him being able to twist the circumstances of the events in the way the man in the car had suggested. But the mysterious stranger was privy to the exact same information, so he had to have known that at the time. He looked up at Laney. 'He *was* bluffing. But it was a purely tactical move. The start of a negotiation. You begin by asking for too much in order to be haggled down to what you find acceptable. That way both parties walk away from the deal believing they have precisely what they wanted from the outset. Smart, eh? So, knowing I can't ignore what happened, what do you suppose he will accept as a result?'

Laney's mouth twisted. 'Let's walk it through logically. He knows he can't save Webster's reputation. Details that sordid will leak, and it's also right there in official documentation that people have already either compiled or seen. We can do nothing about the girl being a minor, so that's another avenue closed off to us.'

Nodding vigorously, Chase said, 'Yes, they must surely have accepted defeat on that specific issue. But what else is there? If they understand we can't back down on the cause and circumstances of the deaths, what is it they're looking to protect?'

'The girl's identity?'

He gave that some thought. 'That's a genuine possibility. We know she's Mandy Radcliffe's daughter, but that's as far as our intel goes. There may be something about her or her past that they want to keep hidden. But we also can't ignore the very real probability that this was not the first time that Ken Webster had done something like this. So maybe they'd like us to make sure the truth of that never emerges.'

'Then there's this club of his, of course. We don't yet know if that's where he met the girl. Nor do we know where he was taking her, for that matter. You only assumed he was on his way home because of the road he was on. But would he really risk taking her back there?'

Chase pointed a finger at Laney. 'Yes. Yes, the club. What if there were more girls in the past? And what if they were also taken from the club? What if that's what this club is all about? A place where high rollers can quench their repugnant thirsts for underage children.'

'Meaning it may not be about Sir Kenneth alone. He could be the tip of this squalid little iceberg.'

He reeled back, visibly shaken by the suggestion. 'You think that's it? You really think that's what this Tier One club is all about? A place where like-minded people of influence can obtain exactly what they want, when they want it? Jesus…' He swallowed twice in quick succession. 'I feel almost physically sick just thinking about it.'

'Me too. But it's feasible, Royston. The powerful receive powerful protection. If such a place exists, an investigation could result in a lot of influential people being exposed as child molesters and worse. An elite paedophile ring. You pop by, you have your choice of young flesh, and after an evening of who knows what kind of mass debauchery, you get to take one home with you if you wish.'

Rubbing a hand across his mouth, Chase took his time to digest what they were both considering. There was nothing outlandish about the suggestion, because such rings existed. In fact, it made a lot of sense. It also explained his early morning visitor. But did this theory leave them better or worse off? It was one thing to leave Sir Kenneth Webster strung out as a sacrificial lamb, but there was also the death of Mandy Radcliffe's daughter to investigate. Not to mention the club and the potential for other young minors to be exposed to the awful urges of men who believed themselves too superior to be caught.

'I want to know more before I decide one way or the other,' he said before the thought was fully formed.

'About the club? The girls?'

'Both. If we're right, if other girls are being exploited in the same way, we have to have hard evidence of that.'

'And how do you propose we go about finding out?' Laney asked.

'You hungry, Claire?'

'I could eat.'

Chase nodded. 'Me, too. But we're going to need a table for four.'

EIGHTEEN

Ed's easy diner at Swindon's outlet shopping centre made great waffles. Chase had only ever tried their breakfasts, but he liked the place. It was decked out like a traditional American roadside diner, though in his experience nobody did such eateries like the Americans themselves. Still, coffee and waffles were good enough for him. The meal was on Chase, so Laney treated herself to a cheese and ham omelette. Their two companions tucked into hearty all dayers, which did not hamper their conversation one bit.

Mark Pascoe and Harriet Fisher had worked together for the better part of five years, and their experience as a partnership and in sex crimes and vice overall was second to none when it came to the Wiltshire county as a whole. If they didn't know what was going on, nobody did.

Chase had put the question to them with all the finesse he could muster. It was important not to give too much away, but the whole point of speaking to the two detectives from the Gablecross sex crimes division was to elicit information. Both he and Laney had decided it was worth the risk of stoking their intrigue. When you poked the bear, you expected it to poke back, but this was an entirely new path for Chase to follow and he thought he'd feel a lot better with a tour guide.

As had been discussed on the drive over, Chase's biggest problem with their theory was the girls themselves. Their current victim had to be an anomaly, a complete one-off. Her background was unknown to them, even if the circumstances regarding her mother suggested a tragic or at least difficult upbringing. But if there were other girls, young kids being made available to a number of men, from where were they sourced? Were they trafficked? Prostitutes? Homeless kids picked up off the street? A combination of the three? And if so, were they simply released back into the environment from which they had come after an evening of servicing these men? If that was the case, then word surely had to have spread. The girls might even have done well out of it in terms of basic pay and tips, with perhaps a night of warm and luxurious accommodation thrown in to sweeten the deal.

It was Fisher who responded first, though her eyes narrowed as she did. 'You're not thinking of trampling all over our turf, are you, Royston?'

'Absolutely not,' he insisted.

'But you can't or won't tell us why you want to know?'

'I can't. Look, I'm doing a favour for somebody. It's no big deal. And believe me, whatever emerges from this I will deliver to you on a silver platter.'

The female DC looked sceptical, but she eventually shrugged. 'Okay. So, if I'm understanding you correctly, you want to know where these young girls might gather if they're hoping to get picked up by a group of nonces willing to pay good money for a night of whatever sick shit these scumbags get up to.'

'That's about it, yes. Eloquently put. Also, I'd be keen to know if there was anywhere in or around the city that you could think of that might hold… events of some kind along these lines. You know the sort of thing I mean. A big party at a hall or some such place.'

'Like a paedo orgy?' Pascoe asked in between bites of his toast liberally spread with raspberry jam.

'Something along those lines.'

The two detectives from sex crimes looked at each other, and in that moment Chase felt his insides lurch. They knew something. They had something.

'Rumours are rife,' Pascoe continued. 'But don't you think if we knew where parties like this were going on we'd raid the place and bang these sick fuckers up?'

Chase leaned in across the table. Waggled his fork. 'But there *are* rumours?'

'Of course. Time was when you'd hear them about children's' homes, even foster homes. And every so often when we get a sniff, it pans out. But we're talking strictly small time here. A handful of these freaks bandying together with a bunch of kids.'

'Jesus.'

'Yeah, tell me about it. I've seen so many of these perverted wankers I seriously wonder if I'm going to come out of this job even halfway normal.'

'You don't mean...?'

Pascoe's head jerked up. 'What?! No. Fuck off! No way am I about to get turned on by that shit. I meant it's all so depraved and sickening. I'm not sure how much more of it I can take. But, like I say, it's generally a family and friends thing. No big Caligula-type orgies. Not that we've ever been lucky enough to get wind of.'

Fisher was nodding. 'Mark's right. There's nothing solid along those lines. We hear talk, but that's all it is. So far as we can tell. If there is something like that going on, it's well organised and well hidden.'

Chase wasn't at all disheartened as he wrestled down a piece of waffle slathered in strawberry syrup. 'How about the girls themselves? Any sense of groups of them gathered together, hanging around waiting to be picked up?'

'Other than a few red light streets, there's nothing remotely like what you're suggesting. Fact is, if we hear of young girls out there, we flood those areas with cars and either scoop them up or flush them away. Yes, there are a number of rough sleepers who sell what they have for a few quid. And yes, there are blokes who cruise by looking for the kids. But nothing like you're implying. Do you have any specific place in mind, Royston? If so, you could do worse than check in with Monkton Park in Chippenham. They have a small sex crimes unit working out of there.'

'Do you know them personally? Do you have their contact details?'

Pascoe grunted. 'What, you think we all hang out at sex crimes parties?'

That drew a laugh from around the table.

'No, I thought you might have run across them at some point.'

Fisher pushed her plate to one side. She gave a satisfied belch and polished off her tea as she bumped a fist against her chest. 'If you want an introduction, I can call ahead. Let them know you might be popping by. I'll ask them to provide you with the same level of courtesy you've enjoyed with us.'

'In other words,' Chase said, 'you'll tell them to make themselves available at meal break and bag themselves some free grub.'

'We pigs have to look after each other, Royston.'

He narrowed his gaze. 'I am one of you still. You do know that, don't you?'

Laney put a hand on his arm and patted it. 'Oh, you poor deluded bugger. You were only ever a small fish in that big bowl of theirs, but you were at least swimming among them. Now you're on the outside peering in, cupcake. From a great distance.'

Chuckling, Pascoe said, 'There you go. Your new partner knows what's what. My friend, you get to stand on the other side of the glass where it's nice and dry and we're still getting ourselves wet. It makes a difference.'

'I'm still a bloody copper, Mark. Same rank as you and a rung up from Harriet, so a little respect would be appreciated.'

Hands up in surrender, Fisher laughed and shook her head. 'Oh, Royston. You always were too bloody easy. We're pulling your leg, mate. Look, I know you're probably still feeling narked about being turfed out of GC and sent to Siberia, but look at the investigation you've landed yourself. You soothe a few wounds here and you can slide on back before your chair is even cold.'

Chase nodded along. He was having his leg pulled, but not entirely. There was truth to everything his colleagues had suggested. He felt like an outsider because that's precisely what he was. Little Soley wasn't exactly the arse end of the universe, but being dismissed from Gablecross left its mark. Even if only on his pride.

'If you can give your Chippenham friends a heads-up, that would be appreciated,' DC Laney said to her fellow detectives. 'I'm not sure when we'll get around to them, but we'll arrange a suitable time.'

'So what other leads are you following up on?' Pascoe asked.

Laney looked at Chase, whose eyes had already found those of the man seated opposite. 'The usual,' he replied.

'The usual? When it involves Ken Webster? I don't think so, old son. In fact, I reckon it must be about as far from usual as you can get while still be investigating.'

'What do you already know, Mark?'

'If you're wondering if we've heard about the kid having been in the motor with him, then yes. And as for her biting off half his todger, well that just makes me tear up. That kind of news travels faster than a fucking Vindaloo through my digestive system. Probably burns the old ring-piece about as much, too. But we hear she's proving difficult to ID.'

Chase nodded. If they knew that much, he might as well open the door a little wider. 'Other than a bizarre connection to a case two decades old, we have bugger all to go on. Even the little we had led us nowhere, so we're starting again today. Lady Jane is proving to be a bit of a hurdle, as you might imagine.'

'I met her once,' Fisher said. 'At some function or another. Has she had that stick surgically removed from her arse, yet?'

Laney came close to spitting her tea across the table. 'Not that we could tell. Upright, uptight, and better out of sight. In my experience, if it walks like a bitch and talks like a bitch…'

'I got the impression most of it came as no surprise to her,' Chase admitted. 'As if she'd been preparing for this moment for quite some time. Hard to feel too much sympathy for the woman when she continues to look down on you after her drunk of a husband has caused the death of an underage child he was having sex with. But I'm sure she couldn't give a toss about the likes of me, nor what I think of her. She'll have an entire army of sycophants to fuss over her.'

'Including the current Chief Constable?' Pascoe wondered out loud.

'That,' Chase said, wagging a finger his way, 'is a very good question. If I were a betting man, I'd say he'll sit on the fence as long as he can and feel which way the wind is blowing before committing himself. Hopefully, that will give us enough time to find out what the hell is going on.'

NINETEEN

THEY WERE CLOSING IN on Aldbourne on the way back to the station when Chase's phone rang. 'Trevor,' he said, making use of the onboard Bluetooth. 'You're on with me and Claire.'

'Ah…' Chase heard the hesitancy in his friend's voice. Then Shipman said, 'Give me a call when you're free, mate.'

'Is it about the case?'

'Yes.'

'Then feel free to talk. Claire is fully briefed. We share common goals.'

But Shipman refused to continue, insisting Chase call him the moment he was free to.

Laney didn't say a word, but Chase could tell she was disgruntled. Rather than make excuses for his friend, he ignored it as if it were nothing, slipping back into the conversation they had been having.

'So… you'll find out where we can find this Paul Daniels chap. While you're doing that, I'm going to see if I can hunt down Colin Shakespeare. Given his job, he could be anywhere in the world, I suppose. Still, it's worth a try. Even if we can't locate him, there's a good chance of him heading our way to comfort the widow.'

Laney grunted more than replied, but he let it go. He had more important things to worry about than his partner's hurt feelings. They had yet to arrange a visit to Chippenham, and Chase was eager to learn more about how the sex worker scene worked locally. It also gnawed at him that they still had no idea about the location of the Tier One club. With a bit of luck, a single trip out to Monkton Park police station would give them a break on both.

Before his theories became a hypothesis upon which the investigation might flourish, Chase had to understand more. Stronger evidence would come if the focus of the operation narrowed, but he understood how infirm the ground was beneath their feet.

'What did you make of Pascoe and Fisher?' he asked Laney, his mind having wandered back to their meeting. 'Did you get the impression they were holding anything back at all?'

'They were all right. A bit on the arrogant side, and nowhere near as laid back as they try to pretend. But no, I think they were straight with us. Why? Was it that remark they made about us trampling all over their patch?'

He nodded. 'I thought they might be over-protective, but my sense is you're probably right. They gave us as much help as they had to give.'

She turned to look at him, a faint smile thinning her lips. 'It was certainly hard to tell if they were fans of yours or not, my love.'

Chase groaned and began gesticulating with one hand. 'This is what happens when you get cast adrift. I wouldn't consider either of them to have been my best buddies, but we were far from enemies. We were colleagues. I respected them, and I like to think it was reciprocated. We always found time for more than a nod and a quick greeting. But when you're shunted beyond the walls of GC, people you once worked alongside start to wonder if they'll be tainted by rubbing shoulders with you in the future.'

This time, Laney dipped her head to acknowledge what he had said. 'I get that. More than I care to admit. My rise up the ladder wasn't without its bumps, but I've been clobbered far more than I deserved to be on my way back down. It's like I have a bell in my hand and have to ring it to tell others I'm unclean.'

'Something we have in common,' he said. 'Let's think of a way to use that to our advantage.'

When they reached their destination, Chase remained outside the front door of Little Soley's station, while Laney went in to begin her search for Paul Daniels. Trevor Shipman answered on the second ring.

'You on your own this time?' he asked.

'Yes. But what the hell was that all about, Trev? Laney and I are working together, at least for this case. She's my partner, and it was embarrassing for both of us when you excluded her.'

'I'm sorry about that, Royston. But I have to protect my back, and I have my reservations about DS Laney.'

'Such as?'

'What if she was placed with you deliberately?'

'I think she was. We both do. We're assuming the big cheeses put two misfits together in the hope of creating one larger misfit, incapable of running this case properly. Moreover, a misfit they could control.'

'But what if that wasn't the reason they put her with you?' Shipman asked. 'What if she's there to spy on you at best, sabotage you at worst?'

Chase had not considered the possibility, and the suggestion gave him pause. Laney was unconventional, a bit of an enigma, but in their short time together she had not come across as somebody determined to do him harm. Quite the opposite, in fact. She was sharp, keen, and above all dedicated. If she was working against him, he felt sure he'd know it.

'Let me worry about that,' he told his friend. 'What did you call me about?'

'I thought you might be interested to know that Lady Jane Webster has a friend of the family on his way to see her later this morning.'

'Oh, and who might that be?'

'Sir Colin Shakespeare.'

'Really? That *is* interesting. Do you have a more precise time?'

'Not precise. But I do have details. He's flying in from Dubai, due to land at Heathrow at around ten-thirty. I reckon that puts him at the Webster estate sometime around noon.'

'I'm not sure what I'm supposed to do with that information, Trev. With him being a close friend of the family, we might have good reason to talk to the man. But I just don't see how that's going to be possible.'

Shipman laughed. 'I'm simply the messenger. Thought you'd want to know. What you do with the intel is entirely up to you, my friend.'

Chase thanked him and disconnected the call. Tucking his phone away, he paused to consider the conversation. Nobody other than he and Laney knew of his suspicions relating to the Tier One club, its founders and members. In his prior conversations with Trevor Shipman he'd not so much as hinted at any special interest in Shakespeare. So why had his colleague made the call? What made him think Chase would be interested in the man's whereabouts, or that he was about to visit Sir Kenneth's widow?

Did Trevor know more than he was letting on? Was he acting as the mouthpiece for someone else? Somebody who wanted to put Chase and Shakespeare in the same room together? He couldn't think why that might be so, but it nagged at him and by the time he headed inside he found himself unable to let go of the idea.

*

Meanwhile, Laney had managed to get hold of Daniels. The man no longer earned a living from roofing, having blown two cervical discs, causing some nerve damage in his neck. Instead they discovered him working at the Wiltshire Museum in Devizes, less than a five-minute walk from his home. Chase had tossed the Volvo's key to Laney, preferring to think than drive. The market town was only twenty-five miles away, but it took them forty minutes to get there. They broke silence only to discuss how they were going to handle Daniels, eventually agreeing that their initial approach should be to the friend of the family that he was, rather than the suspect he might be.

Tall but stooped, Daniels was lean and looked to be as fit as he must have been in his roofing days. His hair had turned grey, but it remained plentiful and thick. An attractive man with rugged good looks, Chase could see why he had been described as a bit of a womaniser in the past. He'd arranged to take a break, and took them into the large conference room which currently housed an exhibition of archaeological finds in the modern era. Most of them were behind glass display cases or Plexiglas pods.

'Some interesting relics,' Daniels told them. 'This county is awash with pottery shards, coins, brooches, weapons… you name it. We receive around five thousand items a year to evaluate.'

'Any major treasure hauls?' Laney asked.

'Several in recent years. Some running into valuations in their millions. It's all supposed to be handed in, but occasionally a large find will be divided up and sold in small quantities and we only come to know about it afterwards.'

Chase swiftly moved them on to the subject of the Radcliffe family.

'If you've been to see Harvey,' Daniels began, 'then you already know life has never been the same for him since the night Mandy went missing. He not only lost a daughter, her disappearance wrecked his marriage and ruined him as a person. Understandably so, I reckon.'

'I take it you've not heard from him recently,' Chase responded carefully.

Daniels squinted with one eye and cast the other to the ceiling. 'It must be a good five or six years since we last talked. His choice, not mine. Said all I had become to him was a reminder of everything he'd lost. As hard as it was to hear, I understood that as well.'

'What was Mandy like as a child, Mr Daniels?' Laney asked, steering the conversation in the direction she and Chase wanted them to go.

This time his eyes stared at nothing at all, except perhaps for the past. A wide smile spread across his face. 'She was a little cracker. Inquisitive, strong, brave, intelligent. Precocious in many ways. She loved life, that girl. Loved it.'

'You were fond of her?'

'Of course. She was my Goddaughter. My best friend's daughter. Sometimes it felt as if she were one of my own.' His gaze narrowed, and he looked suspiciously at the two detectives. 'You're not here to rake all that muck up again, are you? I'd understand it if you looked hard at me these days, given how people are. But back then you could like a kid because they had something about them, without being thought of as some kind of perv.'

'We're not suggesting otherwise, Mr Daniels,' Chase was quick to say. 'It's only natural that you were close to Mandy, given your relationship with her parents. Do you have children of your own?'

'I do, but didn't at the time. I think that's one of the reasons why I doted on her. She was a sweet, lovable kid. My wife and I were struggling in that way, but about eighteen months after Mandy disappeared, it came good for us. We have two, girl and a boy.'

'I expect losing Mandy came as a huge shock to you.'

He blew out his lips, his expression pained. 'You can say that again. Thing is, none of us knew what to think. You hear stories about how when kids go missing and aren't found quickly they never usually are, or are found murdered. In some ways it might've been easier on Harvey and Miriam if she had been. It's cruel, Sergeant Chase. People having to sit and wait for the knock on the door, hoping for the best but always fearing the worst. Bloody cruel.'

'I take it time never gave you pause for thought? You never had even the slightest inkling what might have become of her?'

'Nothing like it. I had no clue at the time, and I'm none the wiser now.'

'So it would be something of a shock if you were to learn that Mandy didn't die that night, nor any night soon after. That we have evidence she was alive at least until thirteen or fourteen years ago, and might very well still be.'

Chase concentrated only on Paul Daniel's facial features. The creases forming on the brow, bushy eyebrows arching, mouth falling loosely open as if suddenly unhinged from the jaw, and a gradual dawning horror tinged with fierce excitement. None were the expressions of a guilty man.

'She... Mandy may be alive, you say? How... how on earth is that even possible?'

'We can't know for sure about her current circumstances,' Chase insisted, raising a quietening hand. 'But we do have evidence telling us she survived well into her teens at the very least.'

'What kind of evidence?' No trepidation in the question, only genuine curiosity. Unless he was a better liar than Chase had previously encountered.

'I'm afraid we can't go into detail about that,' Laney told him. 'But be assured, it's the truth. We asked this of Mr Radcliffe, and I'm going to do the same with you: knowing Mandy survived, does that change your impression of what happened the night she disappeared? And if so, in what way?'

Daniels appeared to consider this for quite some time, but eventually he shook his head. 'Other than a massive sense of relief, I have nothing,' he said. 'I knew Harvey and Miriam weren't responsible, and to have their reputation cleared vindicates everything I've said in defence of them over the years. Myself, too, I suppose. But like I told the police back then, unless Mandy thought she was playing a game of some sort, there's no way she would have run off.'

'Playing a game?' Chase prompted.

'Mandy was a great one for immersing herself in fantasy stories. She had one or two decent friends, but most of her pals were imaginary. She was inventive. Had a great imagination. If I'd been told she'd gone off on some kind of quest during the day, it wouldn't have surprised me. But not at night. Never at night. Pretty much the only thing that would lure her out after dark were fireworks.

Bonfire night and New Year's Eve were among her favourite times of year for that reason.'

'Could there have been a firework display on the night she went missing?'

'I don't imagine so. But I was living here in Devizes, so I probably wouldn't have known about it if there were. Perhaps Harvey will remember.'

Chase wasn't sure about that. It seemed to him that Mandy's father had left the past behind in the dregs of the bottles he kept lying around like discarded trophies, each one a tribute to the loss of memory each application of alcohol had afforded him. But he thanked Daniels for his time, leaving the museum with the sound of rockets exploding in the air and showers of sparkles falling to earth in a cascade of light filling his head.

TWENTY

THE NARROW, CURVING DRIVEWAY that led to Webster Manor ran for some fifty yards or more before the entrance gates barred the way. The opening into the drive was concealed, and it was there that Chase told his colleague to park up the SUV. From this position they'd spot vehicles approaching from some distance away, which would afford them sufficient time to block the turn the moment they identified Shakespeare's Range Rover.

'You do realise this is something both Waddington and Crawley are going to hear about,' Laney warned him as she slotted the transmission into neutral.

'I know. But I'd rather be bollocked for gaining additional intel than gain none at all.' The accompanying nod he gave was more assured than he felt. The Superintendent and Chief Superintendent were bound to be furious with him, but his argument would be that nobody had ordered him to steer clear of this particular Knight, and the questioning would not strictly take place on Webster property. His senior officers might well be angered by what he was about to do, but they had not expressly forbidden it so they couldn't exactly discipline him. Yet at the same time he knew this was more than likely his one crack at Shakespeare before the man was drawn into the circle of privileged untouchables. That alone came with its own pressure.

After a short silence, Laney turned to him and said, 'So why did your mate Shipman not want to talk to you with me listening in?'

Chase's fingers had been tapping out a rhythm on the door's armrest. He paused to consider his partner's question. 'Trev is both over-protective and ultra-secretive. Paranoid as well, I imagine. A high-profile case like this has him rattled.'

'Meaning he doesn't trust me. Does he think I'm the Little Soley version of Guy Burgess?'

In drawing that conclusion so quickly, Laney was proving how sharp her mind could be. Chase liked her all the more for it. 'I wouldn't go that far,' he said. 'Anyway, you're surely more Mata Hari than one of the Cambridge Five.'

'A spy is a spy, Royston. Never to be trusted.'

'Does it matter if Trevor doesn't trust you? I do.'

'You shouldn't. You don't know me well enough to trust me.'

Chase grinned. 'I'm of the opinion that even the likes of Waddington and Crawley are intelligent enough to send in someone halfway normal to spy on me if they were going to do it at all.'

Laney laughed. 'Thanks for that. I think. A backhanded compliment if ever there was one: you can be trusted, Claire, because you're clearly bonkers.'

'Tell me I'm wrong.'

'I wish I could, cupcake. Oh, and car.' She pointed straight ahead.

It was the first that had come their way. Within seconds they were able to make out the distinct wedge shape of the squat Range Rover Evoque. As it drew closer, Laney confirmed the registration belonged to the vehicle leased by one of Sir Colin Shakespeare's companies. She slotted the automatic gearbox into drive and gently rolled forward across the driveway. Chase hit a switch to put on the blue flashing lights so that the driver of the approaching vehicle would know they were police.

Laney reached down to open her door, but Chase put a hand on her arm. 'Not yet,' he said. 'Let's see who gets out of the Rover. There are no other vehicles, so if Shakespeare has security they must be riding in the motor with him.'

Sure enough, after the car came to a halt, a man stepped out of the passenger side and walked towards the Volvo. He was neither tall nor bulky, but his eyes were narrowed and took everything in. He approached them with all of his senses heightened it seemed to Chase, who powered down his window as Laney did the same.

'You here to see Lady Jane?' she asked the man who studied them both closely.

'Who's asking?'

Chase fumbled around in his pocket and eventually came up with his warrant card.

The man frowned. 'I was told to expect a marked car and uniforms.'

'You'll find them further along the drive at the gate. We're an added precaution.'

It was fascinating to watch the passenger at work. In a single casual sweep, he took in the whole of the vehicle's interior. He was alert and suspicious, but would have perhaps been pacified at spotting the switch for the two-tone siren. In return, Chase gave him the once over. It was illegal for a personal security detail to carry firearms, or any other weapon for that matter. But he'd heard stories suggesting it was not unheard of, so he remained wary.

'I have a close friend of the Webster family, Sir Colin Shakespeare, on board,' the man finally admitted. 'Plus three, including myself and the driver.'

'Do the uniforms at the gate have your names?'

'They should do, yes.'

Chase nodded as if it were of little concern to him. He met the man's gaze and reached a hand out across Laney. 'ID?' he said.

Wordlessly, the man dipped into the breast pocket of his suit jacket and produced a card identifying him as Lawrence Reid, a Close Protection Operative working for Centurion Security, based in London. Chase exaggerated the amount of time it took him to compare the photo on the card with the man standing beside the door.

'Please return to your vehicle,' he said, handing back the identification. 'I need to run a few checks.'

Reid seemed about to argue, but instead muttered something about running checks of his own, before turning on his heels and striding back to the Range Rover.

'What was all that about?' Laney asked him.

'A bit of cat and mouse. I want to give them time enough to make a call to ask about us.'

'And you want this why? Royston, we'll get told in no uncertain terms to fuck the fuck off.'

Chase shook his head. 'No, we won't. They won't be able to get through to anyone. The signal is rubbish here.'

'Which means we can't dig up any information about them, either.'

'They don't know that. We could have Airwaves, which work on a different system altogether.'

Laney smiled at him. 'You crafty bugger.'

He grinned back, but let it drop quickly. 'I'm going to pop over for a chat. It might be best for you to wait here. Plausible deniability. Plus, if we march over mob-handed they'll know something is wrong.'

'I'm not sure two of us constitutes a mob, Royston. Besides, I don't really want to be left out entirely. How about you crack on and I'll join you in a minute or two?'

Chase didn't pause long enough to second guess himself. He nodded once and got out. He wondered what those in the Rover were thinking as he approached. Wondered if they had weapons inside the vehicle. As he reached the SUV, the same door started opening again, but he used his hip to nudge it closed and instead rapped his knuckles on the rear window. The tint on the glass was too dark for him to see inside, but he took a chance that the man he wanted words with was sitting directly behind the front passenger, as was often the case in close protection mobile security.

When he got no immediate response, he tapped again. 'Sir Colin,' he said. 'I need a word before I can allow you to pass. It's protocol, sir. I won't keep you any longer than necessary.'

The window eased down and Chase immediately recognised the face from some of the research he'd done after learning about the club. White hair swept back off the forehead, rounded cheeks and a full beard the same colour as the hair on his scalp. He wore oval rimless spectacles with a blue tint.

'Thank you, sir,' Chase said, noticing the other CPO in the back seat watching every move.

'We attempted to establish your authority, but were unable to call out,' Shakespeare said, looking to institute his alpha role in proceedings.

'Poor reception around here, sir.'

'And yet I have visited the estate on several previous occasions without noticing any disruption whatsoever.'

Chase gave a caustic nod. 'Yes, sir. They recently made so-called improvements, which probably explains the awful service. But while I have you here, you can save me some time. I was going to have to speak to you anyway, so this is fortuitous.'

'Oh? Speak to me? Why would that be?'

He appeared more offended than concerned.

'You are one of Sir Kenneth's business partners, sir.'

Shakespeare shook his head. 'You've been misinformed, Sergeant Chase. I have no… had no business dealings with my dear friend.'

'You're forgetting your club, sir. Tier One.'

Chase noticed a slight flicker of surprise on the man's face, but he reacted swiftly. 'Ah, I see your mistake, Sergeant. The club is a joint enterprise, not a business partnership. Tier One is a non-profit organisation.'

'I see. Still, what with all that being semantics, you'll be able to help me out, I'm sure. The thing is, we know there's a Tier One close by, but we can find no record of it.'

Shakespeare's features grew curious. 'Why would you need to? My friend died in a road traffic accident. What has our club to do with anything?'

'A good question, sir.' Chase smiled and leaned forward so that he was at face level. 'The answer to which is that we believe Sir Kenneth may have been at the club prior to making that fateful drive home. We'd very much like to speak to both staff and guests present on Tuesday evening.'

'To what end, Sergeant?'

'To satisfy my curiosity. As part of the official police investigation I am conducting.'

'And mine,' came a voice from behind. Claire Laney had joined him, and she was staring intently at Shakespeare. 'You see, as I'm sure you are aware, Sir Kenneth was over the drink-drive limit at the time of the incident. We need to ascertain whether that is true, and to do so we'll need to carry out a wide range of interviews.'

The man's rounded cheeks bulged further still as he smiled. He pulled a square of cloth from the breast pocket of his suit jacket, then removed his spectacles, whose lenses he began to polish. 'I'm afraid that won't be possible at the moment. One of the benefits we offer our members is strict confidentiality. We simply cannot release their details upon request. You understand, I'm sure.'

Chase nodded. He'd expected this reaction, and was prepared for it. 'Of course. We can always compel you legally to provide us with a list of club members if you prefer. However, your staff are not covered by that same commitment to confidentiality, so there are two pieces of information I'd like from you: the first is the address of the club itself, and secondly I'd like the name of whoever manages it for you.'

Shakespeare swallowed and moistened his lips. 'I would have to run your request by my legal team,' he said.

'In which case, please be sure to inform them correctly. Mine was a demand, not a request.'

'Even so...'

'Are you really taking this stance?' Laney said, feigning shock well, Chase thought. 'I would have expected your full cooperation at such a sensitive time, Sir Colin. Surely you'd like to see this whole sorry mess put to bed, especially with the media. I don't suppose they're going to be happy at being stalled because of your refusal to help the police with our inquiries.'

'I don't believe I refused. I'm simply not entirely aware of my legal responsibilities in respect of my staff.'

'But you'll provide us with that information as soon as they tell you to provide those details to us, yes? Which they will.'

'Oh, of course. I'm only too willing to help as and where I am able. You can't be too careful in these data-sensitive times. I'm sure you appreciate that.'

Laney shook her head, no hint of amusement in her expression. 'Not really, sir. My first instinct is always to be helpful, not to cover my arse. But that's me.'

'Me, too,' Chase said. 'Mainly because I have nothing to hide. Even so, sir, while you may shelter behind your legal duties in respect of your club members and staff, the location of the club itself is a different matter entirely. So, if you'd be so kind as to let us have the full address, we'll be on our way.'

Having earlier discussed the prospect of questioning the man, Chase and Laney had role-played the possibilities. They had concluded that Shakespeare would use data security and legal implications as a way to prevent providing them with the information they sought. In realising this, their aim had always been for the man to rule things out in a specific manner, leaving the issue of the club's location uncovered by the same loopholes.

Chase kept his attention on their Knight, and he could tell they had provoked a reaction. Shakespeare fidgeted with the knot of his tie, fingering his shirt collar and shifting restlessly in his seat. It all occurred inside two seconds, but it revealed his level of discomfort.

'Sir?' Laney prompted.

Hemmed in, the man gave a reluctant nod. 'It's called The Grange,' he told them in a voice far less assured than it had been earlier. 'We're on the other side of Calne if you go from here, approximately halfway between Ratford and Studley. The property is adjacent to the river Marden.'

'Thank you, sir. Most helpful.' Chase gave a mock tip of an imaginary hat.

Shakespeare's anxiety became a tight sneer. 'Not that it will do you much good. Our staff won't provide any information without consulting with me first.'

Chase raised a sneer of his own. 'That's not a problem, sir. We'll make sure they are advised of their rights before interviewing them. And you can be sure we'll make a thorough job of it as our way of thanking you for your full cooperation.'

Shakespeare huffed a low sigh and partially turned his head away. 'Well, if that is all, Sergeant? I'll be sure to discuss this intrusion with Chief Superintendent Crawley.'

'You do that, sir. Meanwhile, I'll get on with obtaining warrants for that membership list.'

He uttered the final sentence to a raised, tinted window. It was Shakespeare's way of having the last word. Chase's way was to keep his vehicle where it was for a further five minutes before pulling away and heading back to Little Soley.

TWENTY-ONE

THEY PICKED UP A hot sausage roll and an iced apple doughnut each from a family run bakery in the village. Having washed down their lunch with tea, Laney stepped out into the back garden for a cigarette. The moment she returned to the office she broached the subject of their next move.

'How long do you reckon we have before Waddington comes in here all guns blazing?' Chase asked in response.

'Depends. If Sir Bard made his call before meeting with Lady Snooty, then the Super is probably already on his way and we'll hear the screech of brakes and the smell of burning rubber before the dregs of our cuppas are cold.'

Chase scrunched up the paper bag his food had come in and lobbed it into the wastebasket by his desk. 'That's what I was thinking. On the other hand, Sir Colin may well wait until after his visit with her Ladyship, which gives us a bit more time.'

'Time for what, though?'

'I can think of three things off the top of my head: we drop in at The Grange, we have a chat with sex crimes over at Monkton Park, and we also drop in on Harvey Radcliffe again.'

'Mandy's father? What for?'

'Firework displays. I want to know more about them and if there was one the night she disappeared.'

Laney nodded. 'What do you hope to achieve at the club? There's no way anybody there is going to speak to you. Whether Sir Bard put a call into Gablecross at all is debatable, but he sure as shit will have called his manager at The Grange. You can bet your pension on that one.'

'True. But it would be good to have a nose around, just to get a feel for the place. Besides, we may be able to apply pressure to whoever answers the door.'

'If anyone does. If I were them, I'd cop a deaf'un.'

'Still nothing to stop us snooping around. A club like that may even have members there looking for a quiet drink in a quiet room.'

'What good does that do us if nobody opens up?'

Chase grinned. 'They have to leave at some point. Others are bound to arrive.'

'They're not going to talk to us, Royston. None of them.'

'Don't you be so sure. If we take them by surprise, who knows what they might tell us.'

She gave that some thought before speaking again. 'What was your take on Sir Bard?'

'I'd say Shakespeare is the kind of man who wouldn't appreciate being called that, for starters. Overall, though, I think we ruffled a few of his feathers. From the various clips I've seen of him, he comes across as gregarious and friendly and not at all aloof, so he's clearly capable of putting on a show. That said, he was definitely on edge from the moment I mentioned Tier One.'

'He's a cool one, though. Calculated, too. But I agree, he didn't like the thought of us poking around in that side of his business.'

'Hmm. Did you notice how he went on the defensive right from the off? Made sure we knew his involvement was little more than a coming together with Sir Kenneth rather than any formal partnership. Still, given we're talking about something on a par with the Masons, there's bound to be some official documentation lying around somewhere. We just have to sniff it out.'

'To what end?'

'So's we can apply pressure. If he's already figured out that distancing himself from the club means he distances himself from Ken Webster's related behaviour, the sooner we can disabuse him of that notion the better.'

'He didn't seem the sort to crack easily.'

'No. Which means we use his immediate aim to our advantage. If he's desperate to distance himself enough that he can't be tainted by anything we prove against Webster, then we must first educate him on that score. After which, we suggest we might be willing to work with him along those lines provided he gives us more about his friend and whatever ugly things the man was up to.'

Laney gave a mock bow. 'We are not worthy, Sergeant Chase. That's a cracking idea.'

Chase thought so too. 'I have my moments. But we start by applying the pressure, and that means we have to get something from our visit to The Grange.'

*

A collection of three original stone houses and sensitively refurbished barns surrounding all four sides of a substantial cobbled courtyard, lent The Grange the kind of grand appearance its name demanded. Two of the buildings were three-storied, while the one facing the line of barns had additional attic space and a central tower at the same level. Woodland lurked behind the houses, close enough to be almost a part of the development, with a large meadow providing open land to the rear of the barns.

This was as much as the two detectives could see from beyond the perimeter of the grounds. And only then after they had squeezed their way past a line of tall bushes. It had taken them a good amount of time to find the place, eventually stumbling upon a small wooden signpost for The Grange, having driven up and down country lanes on both sides of the river. At the entrance to the property, however, they had encountered a sturdy steel gate which was closed and locked. Chase noticed a keypad fixed into one of the metal posts on which the gate was hung. On the other was an intercom, above which hung a security camera. Laney pushed the button several times, but if anybody heard they chose not to respond.

Chase parked the Volvo close by but out of sight of the camera, waiting for a visitor to either emerge or arrive, deciding he probably had enough time to follow them through the entrance before the gate swung closed again. Ten minutes later he lost patience and suggested a recce. Up close, much was obscured by trees and bushes, so they had to go back and up to obtain a better view. He was impressed by what he saw. Whatever its operational status, it also undoubtedly acted as an investment from which both the Webster and Shakespeare families would benefit at some point in the future – assuming the pair had shared the initial startup costs.

'Did you know Shakespeare isn't Sir Bard's real family name?' Laney asked him at one point. Without waiting for him to answer, she continued. 'They were Polish Jews who went by Silberman before coming here in the mid-thirties. They decided to change it upon registering at arrivals, perhaps fearing what was to come.'

'And they opted for Shakespeare instead? Talk about bringing attention to yourself.'

She grinned. 'I know. The story goes that they didn't know too much about England or the English, and for some reason thought it was quite a common name of the time.'

'Well, whatever the name, he won't be hiding behind it much longer.'

Prior to driving out to search for The Grange, Chase had put in a call to Gablecross. He asked for any and all information pertaining to the property, including its owners and the club's standing as a non-profit organisation. He'd also sought clarification on the legal niceties regarding access to the names and details of club members, in addition to finding out who worked for Tier One and what their roles were.

None of that information had become available by the time Chase and Laney resumed their vigil in the car outside the property.

'Perhaps they can't reach us,' Laney suggested. 'You said yourself how random the signal is out here.'

But Chase shook his head. 'Not here, precisely. It's fine in this neck of the woods.'

'Good job our lot have their Airwave devices. At least they don't get stuck on their own with no communication.'

He snapped his fingers. 'Damn!' he said. 'I forgot the bloody device Waddington couriered across. It's sitting on my desk back at the nick.'

Her gaze narrowed. 'If Waddington has been trying to reach you on it, he'll never believe you simply forgot.'

'Believing and proving are two different matters. Oh… heads up.'

Chase had spotted a silver BMW purring up the lane towards them. Since only the river lay further along its path, Chase guessed this was a visitor to The Grange, so hit the button to start the engine. As predicted, the car pulled up to the gate, and a hand reached out to tap in an entrance code. The gate began to swing inwards. Chase edged his own vehicle forward and added some pressure to the accelerator the moment he was certain the Beemer driver could no longer see them. The gate paused for only a second or two before it started closing on them again, but he was quick enough to squeeze through without the sturdy steel bumping against the bodywork.

'That was close,' Laney said. 'I thought for a moment we were going to get squished.'

He nodded, keeping an eye on the car ahead. The driveway was not long, and soon they were approaching a flat, paved open area clearly designated as a car park. Chase came to a halt well away from the BMW, whose driver was quick to exit his vehicle. Risking only a sidelong glance, the detective was able to make out the querulous look the man gave in their direction. He appeared to pause, perhaps waiting for them to climb out. When it became apparent that they were not about to do so, he walked briskly over towards a solid oak door set into the closest building.

'Damn!' Chase said, turning to his partner. 'He's using another sodding keypad.'

Laney glanced over his shoulder. 'They take their security seriously. Still, any door can be knocked on.'

Which was precisely what they tried moments later, but to no avail. Laney turned a full circle, her head raised. 'I can see a couple of cameras. They're the dome type, so I have no idea if they're looking at us, but I'd bet good money on it.'

'I wouldn't take that bet. Still... this may be private property, but they're not going to call the police if we have a nose around.'

Laney liked that idea. 'Let's split up,' she suggested. 'You go right, I'll go left. There are five sets of wheels in the car park, not including our own, so there could be other members here.'

'All right. But, Claire, don't do anything stupid or reckless.'

She smiled benignly at him. 'As if. Do I look the type?'

Chase winced. 'Please don't make me answer that. You know what I'm liable to say.'

This made her chuckle. 'No, that's fine, Royston. I think we both know what this feisty old bint is capable of.'

TWENTY-TWO

CHASE WORKED HIS WAY around the house towards the courtyard. Carefully tended ivy clung to wooden trellis frames affixed to the thick stone walls, whose roughened surfaces and joints appeared to have been waterproofed with a sealant, leaving them with an eggshell finish. He noticed limestone lintels and sills above and below the windows, the sashes themselves constructed from wood rather than uPVC. He considered himself a down to earth man in many ways, but when it came to homes, he envied the choices available to the well-heeled.

At every opportunity he pressed his nose to the glass. Other than the imposing décor and furnishings, he saw nothing of interest. No movement, nobody sitting in a leather Chesterfield reading a musty old tome. What he did notice was the sense of tranquillity. In the gentle breeze, plants and foliage stirred, and from rooftops and the woods in the distance, Chance heard birdsong. It was peaceful here, but that did not mean the place was deserted. He knew one man had entered, while the number of cars in the car park suggested the presence of others. The age and quality of those vehicles told him they were more likely to be members of staff rather than members.

Shakespeare had evidently made his call to the manager. Chase could imagine the urgency of the message: *get all the members out of there, seal all staff away in a centrally located room where they can't be spotted from the outside. Don't answer the intercom down by the gate, and if the police happen to gain entry to the grounds, don't respond to their knocks or demands to enter the premises. As a matter of urgency, contact all members and warn them not to attend until further notice. Should any slip through the net, make sure they are out of sight.*

That gave Chase an idea. He made a mental note for when he got back to the car park.

He was impressed by the layout of the courtyard, which provided a viewpoint from which the entire property could be seen from a central position. It was a sprawling old place, grand and impressive in the way only old money can truly provide. Though he considered gentlemen's clubs to be archaic, he was also aware of the good work many of the modern day establishments did for charitable causes. The attitudes of the men who made their second homes here might be stuffy and outmoded, but who was he to judge how other people lived their lives provided they did so legally?

Which was the big question he had yet to resolve: what actually transpired behind these old stone walls inside its stately rooms?

He paid some attention to the barns, which looked to have undergone significant modernisation and repurposing. The original huge and heavy doors had long been closed off, with sturdy but smaller versions erected in their place. Chase tried each of them as he moved along the paved walkway, but not a single one yielded to his touch. By the time he turned back towards the courtyard, Laney had appeared from the other side and was moving in his direction.

'No luck I take it?' he called out.

She shook her head, a mass of wavy hair rippling. 'Locked up tighter than Scrooge McDuck's wallet. It's almost as if they don't want us here, Royston.'

He cupped his hands around his mouth. 'You're not fooling anybody!' he cried, his voice bouncing off the walls.

'What do you think?' Laney asked as they came together.

'I think they've battened down the hatches like a Texan farmer in tornado season. At this very moment they're watching us and trying to guess what our next move will be.'

'Have to say, I was wondering that myself.'

Chase nodded. 'I have something in mind. Come on, let's get back to the car.'

As they reached the car park, he pulled his phone from his pocket.

'Don't bother,' Laney told him. 'I can't raise a single bar.'

He winked. 'Let me do what I wanted to do first, then I'll give mine a try.'

Striding beyond the Volvo, he carried on until he was directly behind the BMW they had followed into the grounds. He made a show of taking photographs of the car and its surroundings, before getting a close-up snap of the number plate.

'I'm hoping whoever is inside saw that,' he said, making his way back to Laney. 'Especially the owner.'

'You going to run it through PNC when you get a chance?'

'I'm going to do it right now,' he said.

With that, he placed a call and requested information on the owner of the vehicle whose index number he reeled off.

'How is it your phone always works for you but other people get signal problems?' Laney demanded to know, looking put out about it.

Chase sighed. 'I'm not going to be able to keep this up with you, am I?' He dipped a hand into his jacket pocket, and when it came back out he was gripping a small, thin box not much larger than his phone.

'What's that?' she asked him, squinting at the item he held in his hand.

'It's a signal jammer. I find them useful at times, especially when I don't want anybody I'm with or close to having access to their devices.'

Laney stared open mouthed at him for a good while, then formed her lips into a tight slit as she back-handed his arm. 'You sneaky bugger. Aren't they still illegal?'

He shrugged. 'I hate going out to a pub or restaurant and having my evening or lunch spoiled by loudmouths on their phones or kids playing noisy online games. Cinema, too. So I switch this on and enjoy the peace and quiet once the hubbub of disappointment has died away. But it's handy for the job, too. Such as when I didn't want Sir Colin getting through to Waddington or Crawley, for instance.'

'You do know you're a headcase?'

'If you say so. I prefer to think of myself as prepared.' He raised a hand as news came back about the owner of the vehicle. He gave his thanks and disconnected. He then began to dial out. 'Name, address, landline, and mobile,' he told Laney. 'They're used to me, so they know I want the extras when I ask for information. Hold on... it's ringing. Hmm, he's let it go to voicemail.'

'Hardly unexpected,' Laney said. 'Not when he's probably watching you as we speak.'

Chase nodded before leaving a message. 'Mr Reece. My name is Royston Chase. I'm a Detective Sergeant with Wiltshire Police. As I think you're well aware, I'm calling you from the car park of a place called The Grange. In fact, I'm looking at your BMW in the very same car park. This is, we believe, the home of an exclusive club called Tier One. We'd like to chat with you about the club, sir. Please give me a call back on this number, or you can find me at the Little Soley police station. It might be better for you if you talk to me now, Mr Reece. That'll save me asking awkward questions if I have to visit you at home. Thank you.'

He and Laney climbed back into the Volvo, but Chase sat there without putting his seatbelt on. Laney looked across at him.

'What's occurring?' she asked. 'You think he's going to make a dash for his motor?'

'No. I think he might listen to that message, weigh up his options, and decide to talk to us here and...' Chase let his words tail off as the door through which Reece had entered opened up and the man stepped out, closing it firmly behind him afterwards.

'You're on fire today, cupcake,' Laney said. 'If you've got numbers for the Lotto, please do share them.'

He winked at her before opening up and exiting the vehicle once more, Laney not far behind. He met Reece halfway, but did not extend a hand in greeting. 'Wise decision,' he said to the man. 'At least for our first encounter.'

As he made the implied threat of further action, Chase assessed Reece. A little over six foot. Swimmer's build and in shape. Late forties, perhaps a smidgen older. Clean shaven, hair slick with product. Expensive suit. Vain, Chase thought. But scared, too.

'What can I do for you, Sergeant Chase?' Reece asked, a slight tremor in his voice.

'Would you mind telling me what your business is here today, sir?'

Reece struggled to keep hold of his equilibrium. His lips twitched as he tried to inject firmness into his voice. 'Actually, I'm not sure what business that is of yours.'

'Just asking questions, sir. No need to take that tone. If you're refusing to answer, allow me to offer a suggestion: you're visiting your club. The Tier One club. Do I have that right, Mr Reece?'

The man hastily cleared his throat. 'I didn't say I was refusing to answer. But I don't understand what it has to do with the police.'

Chase nodded. 'I see. Fair enough. So, are you going to answer me or not?'

'And what if I am visiting my club? Please do tell me how that's suddenly against the law.'

'Visiting your club? Of course it's not. Why would you even suggest such a thing? Are you telling me there's something unlawful happening here, Mr Reece?'

'No! I… you said… look, what do you want with me? Have I done something wrong, detective?'

Chase frowned as if bemused. 'Surely you're in a better place to answer that than I am. Have you done anything wrong, sir?'

Reece sighed heavily and tossed his arms in the air. 'That's not what I'm saying. You're deliberately confusing me.'

More softly this time, Chase said, 'That's not the case. I'm simply attempting to ascertain why you happen to be here today. It was you who mentioned wrongdoing, Mr Reece. Tell you what, how about we start again? You're here to enjoy what's on offer at the Tier One club, yes?'

'Yes.'

Chase smiled. The first admission. 'Good. We're off to a better start this time. So, tell me, are you a frequent visitor?'

Reece paused to consider. Chase waited him out. The man was probably asking himself if attendance logs were kept concerning his visits and, if so, whether the police might be able to access them. Eventually the man shrugged and said, 'It's my club. I drop by occasionally. I have no idea how often.'

'Were you here on Tuesday night?'

Again the pause, only this time Reece's face broke out into a smile of genuine relief. 'No. As it happens, I was at the other end of the county on business. I was with four other people, Sergeant.'

'You can provide me with their names, I assume?'

'You assume correctly.'

Chase glanced across at his partner. She nodded and took a step closer. 'What exactly is the Tier One club, Mr Reece?' she asked. 'What do you club members get up to behind those sturdy walls?'

Being on familiar territory seemed to have calmed Reece's nerves. 'It's what you might call a gentlemen's club. It's a place where we can come and simply be. We can choose a quiet room for reading and drinking, or one of several lounges in which we might get together with friends and acquaintances. Stuffy and antiquated to you, I'm sure. But we like it. And we pay well for discretion.'

'I'm sure you do. I suspect you form close bonds here.'

'That's true, yes.'

Nodding along, Laney said, 'So how well did you know Sir Kenneth Webster?'

Reece was back to being a creature caught in headlights. 'I... I'm not sure what you mean by that.'

'Let me put it another way: how well did you know Sir Kenneth Webster?' Laney laughed and feigned embarrassment. 'Oh, do excuse me. I guess there's no easier way to ask that question, after all.'

Reece swallowed a couple of times before responding. 'I knew *of* Ken, of course. Can't say I knew him well at all, though. Tragic what happened to him.'

'Quite,' Chase said, nodding solemnly. 'For all concerned, given how many deaths he was responsible for that night. Tell me, Mr Reece, does anybody ever keep on top of what members drink while you're here?'

'I'm sorry, I'm not sure I understand the… what are you asking me?'

'I apologise. Allow me to explain. I suspect many of you arrive here in your own vehicles as you did today and as Sir Kenneth did on Tuesday night. I'm wondering if your drinking is encouraged to continue unchecked and then you're simply allowed to drive home, or if your drink intake is monitored and keys taken by bar staff if they suspect you're over the legal limit to drive?'

'I'm still not sure if that's a genuine question or if you're trying to insinuate something, Sergeant. Let me explain this to you: this is not a rugby club or a boozer's paradise. This is a respectable private institution. Drinking in moderation is welcome. But we are grown men, and we make our own decisions. There are also expectations of us. Expectations we have to meet, or we will find ourselves on the outside looking in.'

Chase shrugged as if unimpressed. 'A worthy notion, I'm sure. None of which prevented Sir Kenneth driving while drunk on Tuesday night when he left here.'

'I wouldn't know about that. I wasn't here. As I already told you.'

'But there must have been talk since. It's not as if he was a nobody, after all. You must have heard mutterings, Mr Reece.'

'If I heard anything, what was said came with an expectation of privacy. I will not comment on idle speculation or chit-chat.'

'Of course. Quite right. Still, him being here that night suggests this is where he imbibed. And he was then allowed to drive off while impaired. Does that surprise you, sir?'

'All I know is that he was said to have been in fine fettle. Good humoured, happy with his lot. As for how much he drank… I've genuinely not heard a single word spoken about that.'

Chase was happy enough. Reece had confirmed what until this juncture had been pure speculation. Sir Kenneth had been at the Tier One club on the night he died. He tucked that away for later. He desperately wanted to go for the throat and ask about the girls, but in this case he felt it better to keep his powder dry. He was pretty sure Reece would clam up and mention legal representation. No sense in warning them all if it could be taken no further. In fact, this was an ideal opportunity to make them think the investigation was unaware of the girls – if, indeed, girls were involved and the one who lost her life choking on Sir Kenneth's appendage was not an anomaly.

He gave a curt nod. 'That's it, then, Mr Reece. We have no further questions for you. There was no need to hide away inside the club. All we wanted to confirm was how much Sir Kenneth had to drink that night. Wasn't too hard, eh?'

Reece could not have looked more relieved if he tried. Nor could he have looked more guilty at the same time.

TWENTY-THREE

CHASE DIDN'T WANT TO go straight back to the station in case Superintendent Waddington was waiting for them. He pulled over at the Poachers Croft bus stop opposite the Cherhill white horse and Lansdowne monument. Of sixteen such white horses dotted around the UK, only two were older than the eighteenth-century figure up on Cherhill Downs. Chase was largely unimpressed with the symbolism, but respected the history of such places.

'I think we need to talk this through,' he said to Laney as the big SUV rumbled to a halt. 'And I'd like to begin by asking you a question, to which I need an honest answer.'

Beside him, his partner settled herself in her seat. 'You'll get that whether you ask for it or not,' she assured him.

'Good. My problem is this, Claire: our time is currently being split between our ongoing investigation and one from twenty years ago. I can't decide if they are connected, and I also can't make up my mind if any of what happened to Mandy Radcliffe is relevant to what happened to her daughter. Logic is telling me it has to be, but because I'm not seeing how, I'm beginning to question my reasoning. It could be flawed. And I don't want to waste time solving somebody else's cold case when we have a live one ready to detonate in our hands like a grenade with its pin pulled. I want to know what your thoughts are.'

Laney nodded as if she'd been expecting to be asked. Or had possibly hoped to be. 'Let's come at the same issue from a different angle, my love. However hot our case is, what do we actually have going for us? Nobody on Ken Webster's side is about to offer us a smoking gun. His influence means even the top people in our own organisation would rather we didn't solve this case. We've already seen at close quarters how difficult it is going to be when dealing with the Tier One club, its members, and its only surviving sole co-founder. All I'm seeing there is us rolling rocks uphill.'

Chase grunted. She made a fair point. 'Okay. But given what we managed to get Reece to admit to, isn't there a way in through the club members? If we look long and hard enough, we might come across one or two who had no loyalty to Webster. Indeed, we could find some who are angered by him drawing attention to the club.'

'You're forgetting the girls, Royston. If that club is where Ken Webster picked up Mandy Radcliffe's daughter, then you can pretty much guarantee there are other girls just like her. Which means those club members have more than their membership to worry about. Whatever they might think of him, it's not in their best interests to talk to us about it.'

Chase nodded. 'You're right. And I'm convinced that's what they have going on there, even if perhaps not all of them are involved.'

'I think they are. I think that's what Tier One is all about.'

'Yes. I have to say I agree.'

'In which case, our approach might have to be from a different perspective altogether. It could well be through the Mandy Radcliffe investigation. If we can somehow find a link between her and Sir Kenneth or the club, then we have our way in.'

'This time it's you who is forgetting something,' Chase said. 'The staff. The Tier One members might have something to hide, but the staff…'

'What?' Laney asked quickly as he failed to finish his sentence.

'I was going to say the staff aren't in the same boat. But what if they are? In fact, doesn't it make more sense that they would be? Who else could be entrusted with such an ugly secret?'

'I think you've answered your own questions, cupcake. And I'm right there with you.'

Chase inhaled deeply. 'Do you think Lady Jane knew all about her husband's... particular tastes?'

'I do. Perhaps not the finer details, but the broad strokes, certainly. My guess is he never discussed it and she never probed. That way she knew, but didn't *know*.'

'And Mandy? Why has she not come forward to report her daughter's disappearance?'

Shrugging, Laney said, 'There could be a dozen or more reasons for that, Royston. She may be dead. If not, she's possibly not even aware of what happened the other night – she and her daughter might have been estranged. Or she could know what went down but hasn't come forward precisely because she *does* know.'

He closed his eyes for a moment. 'It's all pretty grim, Claire. Whichever way you look at it. There's also one small matter we haven't spoken about for a while. My nocturnal visit from the spooks.'

Laney gave a sniff of derision. 'I haven't forgotten about those shadowy buggers. You know, it occurred to me that them changing your PCSO's shift might not have been an attempt to disrupt us at all. It could be their way of clearing her out of the firing line so that we could go about our business more freely.'

Chase shook his head. 'Isn't that the exact opposite of what they want?'

'To a certain degree. But remember what we discussed earlier. They understand and accept that you have to investigate. You have to go through the motions at the very least, so you can't not follow up on the Tier One lead, you can't not interview relevant people. Whatever happens here, there will be a formal inquiry. Your investigation – our investigation – will have to stand up to that test. It has to not only be robust but be seen to be so. Everything we're doing needs to be done. It's the end result that counts as far as they are concerned, not how we achieve it.'

Hearing it said out loud, he had to agree. He had no idea where the investigation would ultimately lead, but he did know how the man known only as Maurice wanted it to end. Chase, on the other hand, had to know the truth, irrespective of what made it into his case file and reports. And the next phase had to begin where it all started.

*

When Harvey Radcliffe opened the door to the two detectives, his head slumped to his chest, which wheezed out a long, wet sigh. Mandy's father looked to have aged ten years in a single day. He wore the same clothes as before, and by the smell of him if he'd bathed at all it had been in undiluted alcohol.

'What now?' he asked. 'You going to tell me my wife has come back from the dead, too?'

'Not at all, sir,' Chase said, keeping his tone on the right side of sombre. 'But we would like to ask a few more questions if that's all right by you.'

To his surprise, Radcliffe stepped outside onto the flagstone step to join them. 'Ask away,' he said. 'We have no need of privacy here.'

Chase thought the man might be embarrassed by the number of additional bottles they were bound to discover if he asked them inside. Then he remembered something that had caught his eye as he and Laney had walked up the path towards the cottage. On their previous visit, he had pulled open the curtain to a window overlooking the front garden. He'd not drawn them closed again, and as they'd approached had noticed he could see inside the room.

'You've taken to looking out for her again,' he said gently, indicating first the window and then the view across the road and the meadow leading towards the woods. 'Mandy, I mean.'

Radcliffe licked his lips, his eyes red and watery. Chase doubted he had slept at all. On two occasions, the man opened his mouth as if to reply, but instead said nothing. Broken capillaries spread like a rash across both cheeks until they became lost among the thick stubble. His nose had taken on the appearance of a fat strawberry, swollen and pitted with open pores.

'If she's out there we'll find her,' Chase told him reassuringly.

This time he got his response, which was all pure contempt and anger. 'Like you did last time, you mean? My little girl was alive at the time, and all you lot did was waste it trying to blame me, my wife, even my friends.'

'There's no point in going over old ground, sir. I understand your frustrations. I genuinely do. But things are different this time. Different personnel, fresh information. Something we can work with.'

The man scratched his head, flakes of skin falling from his scalp. He held up a hand as if to ward off any promises. Chase bit down on them and turned to the reason for their return visit.

'Mr Radcliffe, we spoke with your old friend Paul Daniels. Seems he thought a great deal of you and your wife. I can see why the original investigators were interested in him as a suspect, but they eventually concluded he had nothing to do with your daughter's disappearance, and I have to agree. During our conversation with him, Mr Daniels mentioned something about Mandy loving firework displays. It struck me as something that could have lured her outside. Tell me, can you recall any displays being on around that time? Were there any events close by during which a firework display might have been scheduled?'

Radcliffe closed his eyes. His chest rasped once again as it rose and fell. 'Shall I tell you a sad irony, Sergeant Chase?'

'Please do.'

'Since Mandy disappeared, barely a day has passed that I've not taken a drink. Or two. Or more. At first I thought it was out of sorrow, or perhaps even depression. Miriam always insisted I was stuck on that stage of the grieving process. But by the time I realised why I was drinking so heavily, it was too late to put it in reverse and go back to how things were. See, to begin with I drank to forget. I thought if

I drank enough I'd eventually wipe out all memory of even having a daughter, let alone losing one. That way I wouldn't miss her and break my heart over it. Can't miss something you've never had. Only, I didn't realise any of that for many years. When it eventually came to me, I started drinking even more heavily so that I might break through some invisible wall and actually start remembering again. With every sip I tried to squeeze out a memory. And the more she came back to me, the more I needed to drink. As for now… here's where the irony kicks in. Because these days I find myself neither forgetting nor remembering. I'm caught in some hellish middle ground. A place in which my Mandy exists but doesn't exist. She could be a memory, or she could be an hallucination. That was until yesterday. When two police detectives came to push the knife deeper still by telling me she survived, that she lived until she became a teenager at least, but also that there was no longer any trace of her. Maybe alive, maybe not. Memory… or hallucination.'

Chase didn't know what to say. Pain radiated off the man in waves. He was broken so completely that one loud sound might shatter him into a million tiny pieces. How he was alive was a miracle. Yet he was surely not living.

'Mr Radcliffe,' he said. 'If I have brought you only further pain, then I am more sorry than you will ever know. It's true that I can't know one way or another if Mandy is still alive, only that we have no reason to assume otherwise. She remained out of touch and off our grid for a number of years. That might well still be the case, given the only reason we're aware of her at all is the discovery of her own daughter. So, I won't speculate. And while I do understand how difficult it is for you to take yourself back to that night, it could help us if you were able to recall whether there was a firework display anywhere close by.'

Further shrunken, Radcliffe's shoulders slumped and his arms sagged, hanging loosely by his sides. 'I have no memory of a display, but that's not to say there wasn't one. They weren't exactly unknown around here.'

'They weren't?' Laney said. 'How come?'

'Webster and his cronies often ended the hunt with a celebratory firework display.'

Chase felt his skin prickle. 'Sir Kenneth hunted in these parts? On his own property, you mean?'

'Yes. Over there, inside the woods.'

'I see. Were they fox hunters?'

'No. Birds, I think. On a still night with the breeze blowing in the right direction you could hear them charging through the woods making fake trumpet noises as if they were hunting foxes, but then you'd hear the shotguns blasting out and the cries of what I assume were birds but might even have been wounded animals. I don't suppose their sort much care if animals are caught up in their little games.'

Chase slowly shook his head. It sounded like the ridiculous behaviour of a bunch of wealthy men with nothing better to do than run around like children making silly noises and playing make believe. He imagined them dashing through the trees and undergrowth, all red cheeks, light-headed with booze, taking pot shots at grouse or pheasant and thinking of themselves as great white hunters.

'Could they have had a hunt that night?' he asked. 'Was it the right time of year? Is it possible, is what I'm asking?'

After some thought, Radcliffe nodded. 'It's possible.'

'And after the hunt, the fireworks. Fireworks that might have drawn Mandy's attention.'

'I suppose. Yes. I mean, I don't remember hearing any of that the night she went missing, but as you can probably imagine, the days from so long ago all merge into one. I remember reading to my little girl and saying goodnight, I remember us finding her missing the following morning. But that's it. Everything else that happened in or around that time is vague.'

'That's all right, sir. The fact that you can't positively rule it out is potentially helpful.'

'You really think my Mandy left the house that night to get a better look at the fireworks? That's why she was out there?'

'At the moment it's all conjecture,' Laney told him. 'It was such a long time ago. Yours aren't the only memories of that specific night that are bound to be a bit of a blur. You retain those specifics because that evening was of such enormous importance to you. For pretty much everyone else it was just another summer night. However, if there was a hunt, if there were fireworks, then your daughter might not have been the only one standing outside her house at the time. It gives us something to work with. Something nobody has had before.'

Chase nodded along. Only his mind was focussed more narrowly. If Sir Kenneth Webster had staged a hunt that night, along with his pals, then what if a curious eight-year-old girl had wandered too far and strayed across their path? What if she had seen something she wasn't supposed to see? What if she had been scared by it and run away? Or, perhaps equally as likely, chased away by rampaging men fuelled on drink and high on adrenaline?

Ken Webster was no longer around to ask. But his wife would know precisely who he hung around with in those days, who his fellow huntsmen were. Yet how on earth was he going to compel her Ladyship to discuss the matter with him, let alone cough up those names? Chase had no answers, but that did not quell his determination to find them.

TWENTY-FOUR

CHASE COULDN'T QUITE WORK out who was the more dumbfounded: himself at attempting to arrange the meeting, or Detective Superintendent Waddington for agreeing to it. As it was, when he and DC Laney arrived at Gablecross and were led into the conference room, neither was particularly surprised to find Chief Superintendent Crawley also waiting for them.

Laney had considered him insane when he first suggested the idea to her. She had not altered her opinion since. She argued that the more time they spent out of the clutches of senior leadership, the more they were likely to achieve. Chase believed they had run into the buffers and had nowhere else to go without seeking help from those with the authority to move goalposts around. He'd told her she could remain behind at Little Soley if she preferred, but she wasn't having any of that.

'If you have to endure a grilling before moving this case forward, then so will I,' she'd insisted, for which he was immensely grateful upon seeing the county's finest sitting together at the conference table. Outranked we may be, Chase thought, but at least we're not outnumbered.

'Before you begin making the requests you hinted at earlier,' Waddington said, his piercing glare aimed squarely at Chase, 'you first have some explaining to do.'

'If it's about being out of contact, sir, that's my fault entirely. I hold my hands up to that.' Chase sat on the edge of his seat, leaning forward as if eager to confess his sins. 'I'm not used to carrying an Airwave around with me, so when we left the station I completely forgot all about it. Actually, I did so again when we drove over here. It's still sitting on my desk. I apologise. An oversight on my part.'

His bluff and bluster seemed to have taken the wind from Waddington's sails, but the Det Supt recovered swiftly. 'That really is unacceptable, DS Chase. If your mobile phone is unreliable in so many locations in your area, then it's your duty to ensure you remain in communication at all times. I thought I'd made it clear to you that the Airwave was mandatory, not an item you could simply ignore.'

'I understand that, sir. I'm sure it will become second nature to me, eventually.'

'Immediately would be better.'

'Yes, sir.'

'Very well. Let's move on to more pressing matters. Would you mind telling me why you and DC Laney prevented Sir Colin Shakespeare from visiting his close friend's grieving widow?'

Chase was prepared for this as well. 'We didn't do anything of the sort, sir. With respect.'

'Then what precisely did you do, DS Chase?'

'I stopped them at the entrance to the estate so that we could have a chat. They went on their way afterwards. There was no prevention.'

'A chat? At such a stressful time for all concerned you decided to block the way in to Webster Manor in order to have a… a chat with one of this nation's foremost business entrepreneurs?'

'Yes, sir. Under the circumstances, I thought it better to have an informal chat as opposed to a more formal interview. You see, we have information suggesting Sir Kenneth and Sir Colin jointly owned and operated a club known as Tier One. It's a sort of Masons-lite, exclusive, and I'm guessing popular with a certain kind of person.'

'And you're telling me this is a crime, Detective Sergeant? Something worthy of grilling a highly influential man suspected of absolutely nothing, and who could not have been involved in the terrible accident that killed his close friend because he was abroad at the time?'

Chase took his time to reply. Silently counted off a few numbers. Steadied his breathing. Attempted to close the filter inside his head.

'None of that bears any resemblance to what I said, or to the conversation that took place between myself and Sir Colin,' he finally said, unable to keep the edge from his voice. 'I don't suppose I need to remind you, sir, that no man is above the law irrespective of his influence. But do I really have to mention the contributing factors in respect of that road traffic collision?'

'No, you most certainly do not,' Waddington replied, barely moving his lips. 'And if you value your job, DS Chase, you will control that tone of yours.'

At this point, Chase chose not to buckle. 'Any tone you perceive is a matter of opinion, sir. If I'm being vociferous, it's because I believe in what I'm saying, and I'm attempting to make you understand. The fact is, I believe Ken Webster visited that club of theirs on the night in question. I believe he arrived on his own, but left with the young girl – a minor, let's not forget – and I want to know how and why that happened.'

'Good grief! What are you suggesting, DS Chase?' Chief Superintendent Crawley blurted out. 'Are you saying you think this Tier One club is closer to a knocking shop than it is a Masonic Lodge?'

'That's close enough, sir, yes.' Chase remained in his chair, but standing his ground.

'And if I'm understanding this correctly, you're also suggesting that in addition to Sir Kenneth engaging in underage sex with this girl who was killed along with him, Sir Colin Shakespeare also indulges in this same unforgiveable behaviour.'

Chase shook his head. 'No, that's not it at all, sir. I have no evidence to suggest that might be true. Neither do I have any to indicate this young kid was not an anomaly. However, I do believe something sexual and sinister takes place at the Tier One clubs, and that even if he doesn't engage in any of it himself, Sir Colin is aware of it. He may even encourage it, perhaps in order to entertain those he wishes to do business with.'

The room became still and quiet, each person in it lost in their own private thoughts. Crawley eventually broke the silence. 'How much of this can be proven, and how much is idle speculation?' he asked.

'Hard evidence can only follow as a result of you agreeing to the requests I'm about to make, sir,' Chase admitted. 'What we have to go on is the situation we discovered in the aftermath of the RTC. Our subsequent investigation tells us Sir Kenneth left his home earlier that evening. When he did so, he was on his own. He returned later that night with the underage girl, who was naked, and the two were engaging in a sexual act at the time of the incident.'

'But you have no proof that he was ever at this Tier One club on the night in question?'

'No, sir. Not proof, exactly. Although earlier today we met with a club member outside the property, and he confirmed Sir Kenneth's presence there on Tuesday.'

'This man was there? He saw Sir Kenneth at the club?'

'Not quite. He wasn't there, but subsequently heard about it.'

'So hearsay is the best you can offer?'

'At the moment, yes. Remember, it's why we're here.'

'And what did this club member have to say about the girl?'

'I didn't ask, sir. I thought it better to have them believe we were not looking at a connection between the two. I mentioned seeking verification only of Sir Kenneth being at the club and being drunk when he left.'

Crawley blew out a long breath. 'That's one small mercy, I suppose. And yet still the only evidence you have linking the club with Sir Kenneth is that he is a co-founder and may have been there on the night in question. That's it, correct?'

Frustrated, Chase had to almost bite his bottom lip off in order not to reveal his contempt for the senior officer's attitude. 'Correct.

However, the girl was naked, and no clothes were found at the scene. It defies belief and all logic that he chanced upon her walking along the pavement in that state. He was known to frequent his club and drink more than he ought to when climbing back behind the wheel. His alcohol levels were through the roof according to his blood test afterwards. He had to have been somewhere, and wherever he was there's a very good chance that's where he picked up the young kid. The fact that his club sits in the right location has to be more than a coincidence.'

'I agree.'

'You do?' Chase was stunned by the admission. He regarded Crawley with renewed interest.

'Yes, Sergeant. It's stretching credulity too far to believe otherwise. However, it's also circumstantial. You can connect Sir Kenneth with Sir Colin by virtue of the fact they co-founded this Tier One club. What you cannot do is link the Tier One club to the events of the night in question, nor are you able to offer any evidence to prove such behaviour ever took place on the property you know as The Grange. It's thin, DS Chase. Too thin. The CPS will laugh at us if we go to them with this. Do you honestly believe you have sufficient evidence and intelligence to request even a Section 15 or 16 warrant?'

'No, sir. Not specifically in relation to this unnamed victim, though I suspect we would find evidence there in the form of sex workers at the very least if we raided the place on any given evening. My gut also tells me we could well find other underage girls inside the property, too.'

'And your instincts may well be right. But that's not enough. Besides, don't you think that if these girls do exist, they will by now have been moved on in the wake of what happened to Sir Kenneth?'

Unfortunately, Chase did. But as he'd been taught, he'd reached for the stars but would settle for the moon. 'Then how about a list of their members? Surely we can compel them to hand that over at least?'

Crawley frowned, steepling his fingers and pressing them against his lips. He worried over the question briefly, before taking out his phone and making a call. He asked whoever he was speaking to if they had time to come over to the consultation room. Having put his phone away again, he turned to face the others seated around the table. 'I've asked Kaitlyn Dee to join us,' he said. 'She's my go-to expert on all things legal, and part of our senior admin team.'

Chase was intrigued. He'd expected a harder fight, but if Crawley was summoning a legal mind to the meeting, then the Chief Super might be taking the matter seriously. He glanced at Laney, who caught it and gave a slight nod. She had to be thinking along the same lines.

Kaitlyn Dee entered the room in a flurry of arms and legs. All purpose and confidence. Chase estimated she was somewhere in her late twenties. Her light brown hair was braided and pinned to the back of her head. She was slender and tall, wore a pale grey skirt suit and expensive-looking shoes. Her eyes gleamed behind black-framed glasses, and her cheeks glowed with vigour.

Following the introductions, Crawley explained their dilemma. The newcomer nodded throughout, her gaze firmly fixed on her hands which lay clasped on the table. When he was done, she eased back in her chair and tilted her chin upwards.

'An interesting quandary,' she began. 'This is where the Police and Criminal Evidence Act meets the General Data Protection Regulation and we're glad to have acronyms and initialisms to fall back on.' Kaitlyn smiled at her own joke and moved swiftly on. 'I suspect our focus would be on Section 29 of GDPR. Our goal would be to convince the relevant data controller that we have an obvious exemption by way of a clear objective to prevent, detect, or prosecute a criminal act. I'm happy to advise on the necessary language for any application you submit.'

'Do we have such a clear objective in obtaining this list?' Superintendent Waddington asked.

Chase jumped in before anyone else could. 'Absolutely we do. Interviewing the members provides us with a specific investigative action aimed at detecting criminal acts taking place inside The

Grange by members of the Tier One club. Those actions are designed to lead to prevention of further acts and a number of eventual prosecutions. It's not even a matter of debate.'

'It's always a matter for debate,' Dee said. 'But I can make that work. The potential stumbling block being how we get the application into the hands of the data controller.'

'I say we go the linear route,' Laney suggested. 'Present ourselves at the gate showing the application in our hands. A couple of uniforms and a marked vehicle in full view of their security cameras ought to do the trick.'

Crawley appeared to agree. At least, he did not immediately disagree. 'Do we have an address for their head office or registered office?' he asked.

'We can look it up. Even if it's not obvious from their website, they're a non-profit outfit so they'll be on the charities database.'

Chase gave an admiring nod towards his partner. 'Good call. So we send a copy of the application to them as well. And I suppose somebody has to address the elephant in the room: do we also directly hand Sir Colin a copy? After all, he is the co-founder and he did refuse to cooperate.'

Crawley tossed Waddington a sidelong glance and gave an almost imperceptible shake of the head. 'I think we may need to take that under advisement,' he said. 'This whole sorry mess may yet become a toxic political minefield.'

'Which leads me to my second request,' Chase stated flatly. 'Thanks to Kaitlyn, we seem to have a reasonably clear path towards obtaining our membership list. However, that represents only one aspect of this investigation. Another may have ties to an unsolved case which could yet involve Webster Manor.'

Waddington's sigh drew their attention, but it was Crawley who asked the question. 'Ties? What ties?'

Both Chase and Laney spent the next ten minutes outlining the Mandy Radcliffe disappearance, followed by the startling revelation in respect of their victim.

'Good grief,' Waddington said, looking visibly aghast at the implications. 'This is fast becoming a bloody nightmare.'

'What precisely do you need from us, Sergeant?' Crawley calmly asked.

'Permission to talk with Lady Jane Webster, sir. There really is no alternative.'

Crawley closed his eyes. 'You'd better explain,' he said with a weary sigh. 'And this had better be good.'

'I don't know about "good", sir,' Chase said. 'But I think you'll find it interesting.'

TWENTY-FIVE

ONE OF THE REASONS Chase had wanted to meet with his Superintendent was to look the man in both eyes to see how much he really knew. Having the Chief Superintendent in the room at the same time was a bonus. However, he'd left the meeting believing neither was working with the spooks. A relief in many ways, it nonetheless posed more questions than it answered.

The result of the conference was that Crawley himself agreed to communicate with Lady Jane over the weekend. He felt it was impossible – and unreasonable in the circumstances – to compel a meeting before Monday, but would do his best to ensure it took place early in the day. As ever, Chase was keen to make progress and didn't want to wait almost three whole days, but this was not a hill to die on. There were protocols to adhere to, certain niceties expected, and nothing good could come of any attempt to force the issue. Patience wasn't his greatest virtue, but he understood he'd need to rely on it this time.

Immediately following the meeting, Chase had sent Laney home, telling her he had admin to catch up on and would see her first thing Monday. He was at his desk and deep in thought while composing an update for the crime log when he heard a throat being cleared.

'Good evening, DS Chase,' Maurice said from the doorway. He smiled and entered the room.

Chase looked up and did his best not to appear startled by the intrusion. 'What's the matter?' he asked. 'Can't sleep? Conscience keeping you awake?'

The man's smile broadened. 'It's good that you find humour in this. Please do let me know when that's no longer the case.'

'I'll be sure to. What can I do for you this time? Have you come to admit who you work for?'

'I work for everybody and nobody.'

Chase rolled his eyes. 'You think that makes you sound enigmatic? Mysterious, perhaps? It doesn't. You sound deranged.'

The smile fell away as if it had never been. In its place, an implacable gaze. 'Is that the wisest course for you to follow, Sergeant Chase? Baiting me? Do I need to remind you of my reach or unlimited remit?'

'And do you need reminding of my lack of filter? Things occasionally slip out, no matter how hard I try to repress them.'

'Then I suggest you try harder.'

'Okay. Whatever. You here for a briefing? Or do you already know as much as I do?'

'What I know is my business, Sergeant. You've been a busy boy today, though. Put yourself about like a bloodhound snuffling at the soil. Almost as if you ignored my sage advice earlier today.'

Shaking his head, Chase said, 'Not ignoring. That would be foolish of me. No, in fact I think I even managed to read between the lines. You will have been aware that even if I don't do what's expected of me, I have to be seen to be doing precisely that. Going through the motions at the very least. Nobody can be aware that I'm deliberately tanking this investigation, so I've been going where the leads take me. If I happen to miss some of the lines when joining the dots, it won't be seen as wilful.'

Maurice stood square and upright, staring down at Chase who sat rigidly behind the office desk. He angled his head before responding. 'You wouldn't be trying to play me, would you, Royston? While I'm a perfectly reasonable chap for the most part, like each of us I do have a darker side when roused. It would better for you not to rouse me.'

'I have no intention of doing so.'

'Then what are your intentions? Now that you've had time to think, time to act, time to dwell upon the outcome and the resulting consequences?'

Chase took a breath. 'I intend on doing my job as I have been doing all day long. This is a puzzling case with many loose ends. You know what limited evidence we have. That's no different to how it was when we last spoke.'

'Are you doing the most or the least expected of you?'

'I'm doing precisely the right amount of what's expected of me without causing anyone to become suspicious of my motives. I mentioned loose ends before. Well, those loose ends still have to be followed up on, even if they cannot ultimately be tied off.'

'And your visit with Harvey Radcliffe today? What exactly was the purpose there?'

Chase had to think quickly. Was it possible that Radcliffe's home had been bugged? Could listening devices have been installed. Hidden cameras, perhaps? Radcliffe had confessed to rarely straying off his own property, but the likes of Maurice could probably do everything he needed to do in the early hours of the morning without waking the drunk lying in his own vile soup of sweat and neglect.

'Something unexpected came up during an interview. There was mention of fireworks possibly luring Mandy Radcliffe from her home the night she went missing. Not following up on that would have been noticed. I didn't want anyone becoming suspicious.'

Maurice nodded amiably. 'And the result of your conversation?'

'Mr Radcliffe told us about the displays Sir Kenneth put on every so often. He couldn't say for sure if there was one that night, but neither could he discount it.'

Chase neglected to mention anything about the hunts, and his stomach lurched as he waited for this omission to be pointed out. But instead, Maurice nodded to himself in that same quiet way of his. Nonchalant, as if none of what they were discussing was of any real consequence. His eyes were guarded, however, and Chase couldn't tell if the man knew or not. Perhaps his silence was a bluff to match his own.

'Is there anything else?' he asked.

Maurice shifted his stance a little before settling firmly once more. 'Come Tuesday, perhaps Wednesday at the latest, this notion of Sir Kenneth being in the car with a naked minor will be denounced as pure speculation. Any mention of it, or the presence of his sexual organ in the girl's mouth, will be eradicated from the records. At that point she becomes a statistic, quite possibly the cause of the collision itself. Sir Kenneth's intoxication will also turn out not to be proven by blood tests if we decide to go that way. In short, the RTC will be precisely that, and in no further need of investigation. Are we quite clear on that?'

'Yes.'

'Good. I want us singing off the same hymn sheet ahead of any case wind-up and subsequent coroner's verdict following the inquest.'

'There will be insurance investigators involved as well, I should think. People other than Webster and our unidentified girl died, after all.'

'We'll take care of everything, I assure you.'

'Very well. I want you to know I continue to object.'

'I want you to know I continue not to care about your objection.'

Chase shook his head and got to his feet. 'Do you not care at all about that poor girl? And potentially many others like her? What they might have been subjected to?'

'Whether I do or not is irrelevant. I have a job to do. I don't question my instructions. Neither should you.'

'Except that I don't work for you.'

Maurice smiled once more. This time it was broader and more genuine. 'Believe me, DS Chase,' he said, turning away and heading for the door. 'You don't have the foggiest idea who you work for.'

TWENTY-SIX

CHASE AWOKE ON MONDAY morning with a sluggish stretch and a weary yawn. He reached out for Erin but touched only an unwrinkled sheet beside him. He closed his eyes and instantly remembered why he was alone.

His wife had sensed his unease when he arrived home on Friday night, and over a shared bottle of Rioja, Chase told her about Maurice. They'd spent all day Saturday discussing their options, but as the clock ticked over into Sunday his wife finally agreed to spend a few days with her best friend who lived on the south coast at Goring-by-Sea. Despite the spook having mentioned his reach, moving both Erin and Maisie out of the direct crosshairs made Chase feel an awful lot better. It was the sensible thing to do, though he would miss them dearly.

Following an early breakfast, the Chase trio set off on the long drive to Brighton, where they'd decided to spend a few hours together before heading west along the coast road. Delays caused by an accident on the M25 stretched the journey out to almost three hours, but Chase was in no hurry. He spent most of the time checking his mirrors, certain he was being followed but unable to spot any vehicles that might be involved. If he was wrong and the spooks were not physically following the Volvo, then he imagined they were tracking its GPS. He took it for granted they were doing the same thing with his phone, and probably Erin's as well. Subverting their digital surveillance was also part of his overall plan.

After leaving the SUV in an underground car park, they headed for the seafront and entered a cafe adjacent to the British Airways viewing tower. The West Pier Tea Room had become a familiar haunt over the years, its multiple entrances and exit points ideally suited to the next phase of Chase's strategy. They each had a snack and a cold drink. Erin and Maisie then ordered ice creams, at which point Chase left his mobile with his wife before ducking out to find the local Curry's store, inside which there was a Carphone Warehouse outlet. There he bought two cheap prepaid phones, loaded each of them with credit, before making his way back to join his wife and daughter. All three then went for a stroll along the pebbled beach, the moist, salty breeze at their backs.

'Are you certain about this?' Erin asked him one last time, giving his fingers a squeeze.

Chase moistened his lips. 'Not at all. I just can't think of a decent alternative. I had to tell you about the threat, and I'm glad I was able to share it with you. But I can't function knowing you two are close by, and I won't allow anything bad to happen to you. Still, you'll both have a great time with Kathy and Jordan, and a week is not so long.'

'Maybe you'll worry about us less, but I'll be in pieces, Royston.'

'I know. And I'm sorry. I've put the numbers into the phones, and I'll call you every evening. Which reminds me…' He took a phone from his pocket and handed it to her. 'Let me have yours so's I don't forget it.'

As they traded, Erin said, 'Are you sure all this is necessary?'

He shook his head. 'No. But better safe than sorry. These people are a law unto themselves, so I don't know if they followed us, if they listen in, if they have our phones bugged, nor even if they are tracking us at all. They probably aren't. But if they are, they'll see the two signals together, then they'll see both joining the Volvo's and staying together all the way back home. That's why we're putting you two in a cab. You'll go off to Goring, I'll be the decoy.'

His wife nodded. She said nothing, and Chase couldn't tell if the tears in her eyes were prompted by sadness or caused by the breeze. They continued to hold hands, strolling along some distance behind Maisie who enjoyed clattering through the pebbles at speed. For all he knew they were being observed at that very moment, but if so they'd also be followed back to the car park. Chase had a plan for that, too.

His mind drifted back to that precise moment as he pulled up outside Little Soley police station at the start of another working week. Before heading below ground he had called for a taxi to meet them by the Volvo on the first level. There they piled the luggage into the cab and gave each other hugs. Maisie was upset that he wasn't going to be enjoying their holiday at the seaside together, but this was largely offset by her eagerness to spend a few days with Jordan, a girl just a year older than her and who she thought of as a big sister.

Maisie had sobbed as they said their goodbyes, while Erin had been mostly silent. Knowing they were out of harm's way was a small crumb of comfort to Chase as he entered the station. At least now he might be able to concentrate on the job at hand.

'Good morning, Alison,' he said brightly, throwing a smile the way of the young PCSO standing behind the reception counter. As usual, she reciprocated wider and brighter in every way.

'Morning, Royston. Good weekend?'

Different, he reflected. 'Yes, pretty good, thanks,' he replied. 'You?'

May's eyes sprang open enthusiastically. 'Shopping with my mum and sister in Swindon on Saturday. Family dinner at a restaurant in the evening. Then I spent all day yesterday at Longleat.'

Chase nodded his approval. 'We took Maisie there a couple of years ago. Erin and I have been there on several occasions. You're too young to remember, but they had a Dr Who exhibition there at one time. I'm pretty sure there was even a Tardis.'

'I'm not much of a fan. Odd thing to have at Longleat, though.'

'I thought so, too. I think it was there for thirty-odd years, so it must have had a following. How were the animals yesterday? When we went with Maisie, they were a bit sluggish; I think they'd recently been fed. Apart from the monkeys. I had to squirt one to stop it from ripping off my windscreen wiper.'

May laughed. 'No, they were all in good spirits. I still feel sad in a way to see them out of their natural habitat, but they have plenty of space and I know they're treated well because one of my friends works there.'

He was about to reply when the front door was thrown open. A young man wearing a serious frown and dressed more like a youth than the mid-twenties he appeared to be, swaggered in off the street. Hands plunged deep into the pockets of his jeans, his head jerked up and his eyes switched between Chase and May, but he said nothing.

'Can I help, sir?' May asked him. 'I'm PCSO Alison May.'

'I'm here to speak with the lady detective. Lane, I think her name is.'

'Laney. DC Laney. She's not here at the moment, sir. May I ask for your name and what it's concerning?'

'It's Guy. And I have no idea what it's about. I got a call first thing from my boss telling me to get my arse over here to meet with a detective called Lane… Laney. That's all I know.'

The door crashed open again as the woman herself entered. She took them all in with one sweep of her gaze. She stopped when her eyes reached their visitor. 'You must be Guy Maddison?'

When he nodded, still quite sullen, Laney turned to May. 'Keep him entertained for a few minutes will you please, my love. I need a quick word with the boss before we speak with this fellow.'

Without another word, she bustled on through towards the office. Chase raised his eyebrows at May. 'Take the usual contact details,' he said. 'We won't be long by the sound of it.'

Laney had already slumped into her chair without removing her favoured leather jacket. Her facial expression was taut with fury. 'You're not going to like this, Royston,' she said as he followed her into the office. 'Not one little bit.'

'And good morning to you, too,' he said, remaining standing until he knew what was going on.

'Yeah, good morning. What a lovely, bright and breezy autumn day it is. And I had a fabulous weekend, too, thank you very much. Filled with candyfloss and unicorns. So, can we crack on with the job and get stuck into Guy Maddison?'

Chase shook his head, more amused than affronted by his partner's bullish behaviour. On Friday she appeared to have softened a little, but it seemed she was back to her fiery self. 'Go on then, Claire. Who is he and why has he soured the start of your week?'

'He's going to shit all over yours, too, believe me. So, Crawley's legal bit of skirt, Kaitlyn, must have got straight into it after we spoke with them on Friday. Whatever she said or did worked a treat... up to a point. It seems that all the IT stuff for Tier One is provided by a tech company specialising in engineering and support. They are a framework provider with local government contracts up and down the country. It just so happens that they have premises in Swindon, which is where our Mr Maddison is based. One of his clients is Tier One.'

'And I'm guessing the delightful Kaitlyn rousted his bosses from their slumber over the weekend and instructed them to rustle up the membership list.'

'Yes. Apparently, the staff at Tier One can enter the details of new clients into the system, and can look up the records of existing ones provided they have a name or number, but have no way of collating them all into a single file. But when Mr Maddison's supervisor attempted to do that on our behalf, he encountered an unexpected problem.'

Chase put back his head and closed his eyes. 'Don't tell me... all the data was missing.'

Laney raised two fists and growled in the back of her throat like an animal. 'The fuckers. At least, that was my initial reaction. I assumed – as you probably do – that somebody at Tier One deleted them all. But then I reasoned that if they couldn't even compile a full members list, they surely wouldn't be able to delete them, either. Not easily, at least.'

'And you dealt with all this yourself?'

'I'm big enough, and certainly ugly enough according to you. cupcake.'

He chuckled. 'Low blow, Claire. Low blow.'

'Kaitlyn contacted me yesterday. I thought you'd probably be off somewhere with your wife and daughter, so I handled it. Or tried to, at least. But when I realised I was out of my depth, I lit a fire under an arse or two at the IT company.'

Now he understood. 'All right. Let's have a word with the young man.'

Moments later, the three of them gathered in the same office. Chase sat behind his desk while Guy Maddison and Laney faced him from the other side. It was she who kicked them off.

'Tell me, Guy, how long have you been servicing the Tier One club?'

His seemingly permanent frown deepened, but he replied immediately. 'Going on two years. There or thereabouts.'

'Much to do? I mean, it doesn't seem to me as if there'd be a great deal of technical expertise required with such a small establishment.'

'There isn't. I do monthly health checks on their servers, make sure they are up to date with security software, updates, that sort of thing. Usually they need basic maintenance, but then I also get the occasional support call when something's not working. I can handle the majority of requests remotely. I've never actually been on site, though I've had to send a technician over on a couple of occasions.'

'I see. We may need to speak with them at some point. You mentioned servers how many and where are they located?'

'They have two, and both are part of our virtual server farm.'

'Virtual?' Chase interrupted.

Maddison didn't quite roll his eyes, but he seemed put out at having to explain something which for him must have been all too apparent. 'Yeah. Basically, you have these powerful physical servers, and using specific software you can create what we call virtual servers by allocating disk space, RAM and CPU resources and then installing server software to each of them.'

Chase nodded at Laney for her to continue, which she did. 'Tell me about the system used by Tier One staff.'

'It's proprietary, developed by one of our programmers. Simple enough, and made that way so's the end user can't screw things up too badly.'

'They have limitations, then?'

He nodded. 'Of course. They can add new members, archive those who leave, and they also have a basic search facility if they have to look up details on any individual member. That's about it.'

'Tell me more about the archive facility.'

'It's a way of removing them from the system without fully deleting them. They get stored in archives for ninety days, in case a mistake was made or members decide to reapply. After that they are automatically purged.'

'So there's no possibility of a staff member accidentally deleting the membership list?'

'Is that what this is all about?' Maddison said, still surly. 'If they can't locate a member on the system, then it's down to user error. I guarantee it. But what's it got to do with your lot?'

Laney leaned forward, drawing his attention. 'This works better if we do the asking and you do the answering, my love. So, what would you say if I told you the entire membership list was missing from the system?'

'I'd say you were mistaken. But even if that were true, it won't be gone as in never to be seen again. It'll all be on the backups.'

'And what if I were to say it's missing from the backups as well?'

For the first time, Maddison seemed uncertain. He reclined as if recoiling from the possibility, only to ease forward again as he spoke. 'The only way that happens is deliberately. Are you telling me we were hacked?'

'I'm telling you the data is missing, Guy. As for the how, that's what I'm hoping you can tell me. Especially as Tier One is your client.'

Maddison looked up in alarm. 'Woah, hold on a minute. Is that why nobody would tell me what this was all about? No way, man. You're not pointing the finger at me. You say Tier One is my client, but they're actually my employer's client. There's a big difference. I service their account, that's all. Any tech or engineer can access the same data. Not that I'm saying they did, just that they could. Is the Tier One data the only data missing?'

'We believe so, yes.'

'Then it's a hacking. Bound to be. Somebody wanted that particular data gone.'

'We actually have some of your colleagues looking into that as we speak, Guy. Your supervisor said much the same thing as you, so he has a couple of chaps running checks, searching for an external breach. Apparently you have software that can detect that sort of thing.'

Maddison nodded. 'Of course. So did they wipe everything on both servers?'

'They did.'

'And the backups?'

'Unfortunately, yes.'

This time Maddison grinned. 'If it's an external hack, then you're in luck,' he told them.

'Oh, why is that?' Chase asked.

'You can thank data retention requirements. See, we have what we call three degrees of separation for our data. Server, backup discs, backup tapes. Server data is backed up to disc throughout the day. Overnight that data is backed up to tape. All three devices are located in different areas. If your hacker knows what they're doing, they will have found a route in to the tapes as well. But once a year we replace all of our backup tapes, which we then store in a fireproof safe in a central vault. I last did that job about three weeks ago.'

Chase understood immediately. 'So you're saying you can pull data from those tapes that is at most only three weeks out of date?'

'That's right. I can restore the entire system as it existed at that point.'

'I'm no tech guru, as you've probably spotted. But even I have heard of the cloud. I was under the impression that most tech companies rely on cloud storage, especially for backups.'

Maddison nodded. 'That's true to a certain degree. But when you shift anything off site, you relinquish some control. I mean, you have access and you can restore data, but it's a legal arseache when it comes to disputes. Our company is a bit old fashioned and prefers to keep everything in-house.'

'The benefit of which is...?' Laney asked.

The tech engineer interlocked his hands behind his head and stretched out his legs. He looked pretty smug. 'No cyber hacker can remove tapes from a safe.'

TWENTY-SEVEN

CHASE WAS DEEP IN conversation with DC Laney when Chief Superintendent Crawley called, inviting him to a meeting arranged with Lady Jane Webster. By the time he left the office to make his appointment, several actions had been agreed upon.

Guy Maddison's revelation about the backups in storage had lifted the mood considerably. Somebody had gone to great efforts to prevent them from obtaining a list of club members, but it seemed as if they would get their hands on it, anyway. The plan was for Maddison to access the tapes and recover the data from them as unobtrusively as possible after returning to work. He would then send the membership files to a personal email address Chase had provided. After the engineer had left, Laney was curious as to why her colleague had asked the man to carry out the task discreetly rather than working under police supervision.

'Because I'm paranoid,' he'd replied. 'Maddison works for Gateway Technological Enterprises. They're a big hitter, and as I understand it they have contracts with police authorities up and down the country. So let's say I'm not entirely convinced this security breach came from the outside.'

'You think somebody high up in the company might be on that membership list?'

'I'm not ruling out the possibility.'

They'd agreed that while he was gone, Laney's first task was to speak to Kaitlyn Dee to make sure the main addresses associated with Tier One had been emailed all relevant requests and appropriate warrants. Her next job was to contact the main switchboard in order to request a meeting with the manager of the local Tier One club, and that he or she should be instructed to provide the names and contacts details of staff members. Both detectives were encouraged by their progress.

As arranged, Chase met Crawley at the entrance to Webster Manor. He left his vehicle parked up on the grass verge before joining his Chief Superintendent inside the man's gleaming silver Audi.

'What's your intended plan of attack?' Crawley asked as he nosed the car along the drive into the estate.

'Two-pronged, sir. First of all, I'll ask her Ladyship if she's had any further thoughts on who the young girl might have been and how she came to be with Sir Kenneth that night. Secondly, I need information about the hunts, specifically the names of those who would have taken part in them around two decades ago.'

'And if we draw blanks?'

'I'm not expecting her to offer me anything on our victim. In all honesty, I doubt she knows a single thing about her. But I do want to impress upon her that this is not something we're going to drop, that it won't just go away if she ignores it. Once I have that thought fixed in her head, she may be more willing to work with us regarding the hunts. Hopefully, I can convince her that they represent safer territory, carrying no immediate threat.'

Crawley nodded. 'My presence there will only go so far, Royston. After all, she was married to a Chief Constable, so even I am too many ranks beneath her as far as she is concerned.'

'You sound as if you know her reasonably well, sir. I'm aware that Superintendent Waddington was a friend of the family, but I didn't realise you were.'

'I'm not… entirely. But I have met them as a couple on a number of occasions. We've attended several of the same functions over the years. And yes, I am fully aware of how she perceives herself. I did wonder if I should go as far as asking our current CC to intervene and attend this meeting, but although he and I discussed the matter briefly over the weekend, I sensed he might prefer to maintain a respectful distance.'

'In other words, if there's a sword to be fallen on, better it's yours than his.'

As he drew up outside the entrance and switched off the engine, the Chief Super regarded Chase with frank scepticism. 'I thought you understood how it worked, Royston. How the game was played. I'm here to wedge the door open for you. You'll be the one walking through it. If there is a sword in play here today, it'll be yours alone.'

Chase gave an amiable nod and chuckled to himself as they got out of the car. His interactions with Crawley over the years had been limited, but he appreciated the man's candour. The buck seldom stopped at DCS level or above. Which was why the man currently in that post was able to confront a difficult situation with such alacrity. And Crawley was absolutely right; of the two of them, only Chase's job was on the line.

Her Ladyship kept them waiting, but on this occasion she was only a couple of minutes late for their appointment. Once again they gathered in the drawing room. Chase was surprised to see her accompanied by another woman, more so when she announced herself as Lady Jane's legal advisor.

'Is your presence absolutely necessary?' he asked, unable to help himself. He gave them both a look of bewilderment.

The woman, who had introduced herself as Ms Logan-King, smiled before replying in a gentle Scottish lilt, 'Time will tell, Detective Sergeant Chase. Time will tell.'

Lady Jane's response was more strident as she fixed Chase with a hostile glare. 'Following our previous encounter, I felt more comfortable being joined by somebody who is both a friend and my legal representative. I have no intention of being bullied a second time.'

'Of course,' Crawley said as they each took a seat. 'It's entirely your right, and if it makes you feel more at ease, Jane, then I'm happy for Ms Logan-King to join us at what must be a difficult time for you. Before we get started, I want to apologise for not having dropped by sooner, and to offer my sincere condolences.'

'Thank you, Bruce. Your apology is quite unnecessary. I of course understand completely how busy you are these days.'

Chase set his features, not wanting to reveal his surprise at how close the two appeared to be. If they were at the Jane and Bruce stage, then their relationship was stronger than Crawley had earlier intimated. Either that or the DCS was better at putting on a show than he had realised.

Two trays bearing pots of tea and coffee, together with cups for the former and mugs for the latter, arrived within seconds of them taking their seats. The legal advisor poured their chosen drinks, before settling back in her chair and drawing attention to the purpose of the meeting.

'Our understanding is that you wish to ask further questions of her Ladyship in connection to the incident that took the life of her husband. Is that correct?'

Chase had to admire the skilful oration. Reducing the loss of several lives in a terrible crash caused by Sir Kenneth to nothing more than an incident, while at the same time mentioning only his demise, was thoughtful word play. He and Crawley had agreed that he should do all the talking in reference to both the RTC and the disappearance of Mandy Radcliffe, while the DCS smoothed the surrounding waters as necessary. That left him in the chair to take the first swing at a response.

'Broadly speaking, yes. And I'd like to begin by asking you, Lady Jane, if since we last spoke you'd had any further thoughts regarding the young victim known to have accompanied your husband that night?'

He switched his gaze to her Ladyship, but it was the woman's legal counsel who responded. 'Lady Jane has no knowledge of who may or may not have been with her husband at the time. As you are well aware, her Ladyship was residing at their Cornwall home at the time and her husband made no mention of guests or visitors when they spoke earlier that day.'

Chase took a slow count. As disgruntled as he was at having a spokesperson doing all the talking so far, he could not afford to show his displeasure. When he felt more in control, he kept his eyes on Webster and said, 'The young girl in question was neither a guest nor a visitor. That much we have been able to ascertain. We believe your husband met with her during the evening while at the Tier One club. We'd very much like to know how that meeting came about, and also why Sir Kenneth had the young girl in his vehicle later that night and where they might have been going.'

Webster glanced at Logan-King and gave a slight nod. 'Detective,' she said. 'If you believe they met at the club then I suggest you aim your questions in their direction. As previously mentioned, I was not here at the time. Therefore, I cannot attest as to where my husband went, how long he spent there, who he met, or where he was headed when the crash occurred. I feel we've sufficiently covered this matter now, so does that satisfy your curiosity?'

'Not in the least,' Chase said, shaking his head before he could snap the filter into place. 'But we are making progress in respect of the club, so let's put that to one side for the time being.'

'Very well. I'm pleased to hear it. But what else is there?'

'I'm interested in expanding upon some information that has come our way as part of this investigation. You see, although we have yet to identify the poor child who was sitting alongside your husband at the time of the RTC, we do know more about her. It's most peculiar, in fact, because DNA evidence tells us that her mother was Mandy Radcliffe. Does that name ring a bell, Lady Jane?'

Her shrug was intended to be haughty, but he could tell she was intrigued. 'Not as far as I can recall. Should it?'

'It's possible. You see, Mandy Radcliffe lived on the edge of Little Soley, not too far from this estate. In the summer of 2001, when she was eight years of age, Mandy vanished from her home. There was a major investigation into her disappearance at the time, so I imagine you would have heard about it.'

Lines converged across the woman's brow. 'I dimly recall something of the sort, yes. It was twenty years ago, after all.'

'Of course. But it's interesting, is it not? A local child goes missing and is presumed long dead, and then her daughter turns up in the same vehicle as your husband. An odd coincidence to my mind.'

'Coincidence? How so? I'm not quite sure what you're getting at, Sergeant.' She threw an exasperated and withering glance at DCS Crawley, as if to suggest it was time he got this idiot out of here and stopped pestering her.

'Oh, I'm not getting at anything,' Chase replied quickly, pressing on. 'But here's the thing: nobody could work out why Mandy might have been lured out of her home that night. Until, that is, we heard about the firework displays you and your husband occasionally put on following the irregular hunt nights held on your property. I'm not for one moment expecting you to remember if you had a hunt on the night in question, but I'm quite sure you will recall some – if not all – of the men your husband went on hunts with at the time.'

You didn't have to be Sherlock Holmes to notice the reaction this provoked. After fumbling with her necklace, Lady Jane looked to her advisor for a way out. Logan-King must have sensed the woman's discomfort, for she leapt straight in.

'I'm going to have seek some advice on that myself,' she said. 'I wouldn't want her Ladyship being exposed to litigation by revealing any of those names.'

'There's no data protection involved,' Chase protested. 'These were private guests, here by invitation. There's no legal expectation of privacy in such circumstances. We ask for verification in such matters all the time. It's routine, Ms Logan-King.'

'Need I remind you that her Ladyship is not a suspect in any crime, Sergeant Chase? Lady Jane is not being asked to provide evidence of an alibi.'

'I didn't need to be reminded, but thanks anyway. Of course her Ladyship is not a suspect, but in this specific instance she is a witness.'

'To what exactly?'

'Those who attended hunts during that period might have come across young Mandy Radcliffe on the night she went missing. If she happened to have been with an adult at the time, they probably didn't think anything more about it, but they might remember her all the same. We'd like the opportunity to interview them, in the hope that if they do recall anything they might be able to describe who this adult was.'

'It was twenty years ago,' Webster said. 'A night like many others our friends would have enjoyed here, if indeed it was even on the same night this poor girl disappeared.'

Chase was insistent. 'One night among many, perhaps, but surely such an encounter would have been rare? It would have stuck out, possibly even lodged in their memory. All we're asking for is the opportunity to speak with them.'

'Are you telling me I have no choice but to cooperate?' Her voice rose, and still she toyed with the chain around her neck. Both hands shook as if she had a fever.

'We're not here to tell you what to do, your Ladyship,' DCS Crawley said calmly. 'That's not our place. But I am wondering why such a request is proving so difficult for you to agree to. There is no legal or ethical component here. Your assistance, however, could lead to a successful outcome in our investigation. I can't imagine why you would not agree under those circumstances.'

Impressed, Chase nodded his agreement and sat looking at the woman, whose eyes were downcast. Clearly she was struggling with a dilemma, and he wondered why. Was the hunt something else such people sought to protect, their presence during the event something to keep secret?

Closing her eyes, her Ladyship finally drew in a deep breath. Her hands came together, fingers interlocking. When eventually she turned her head to speak to Crawley, her tone was firm, poise having returned.

'I'm sorry, Bruce. You are more familiar than most when it comes to the standing of people we entertain here at the manor. Despite private gatherings falling outside of the legal framework as you suggest, there is, nonetheless, an expectation of discretion when it comes to attendance at specific functions. I cannot possibly provide you with these names you have requested. What I will ask my advisors to do is contact as many as I can remember, and to ask them if they are happy to speak with you. However many of them respond positively, their details will be made available to you.'

She expressed herself as if she were doing them a huge favour, refusing to meet Chase's gaze while she spoke. Although he attempted to catch her eye, she continued to look only at Crawley. There was little appreciation written on his face as he responded.

'That is extremely disappointing, Jane. In all honesty, I expected more of you.'

Her lips puckered slightly. 'In all honesty, *Chief Superintendent*, what you expect of me is no concern of mine. I have a duty to my friends, Kenneth's friends. My husband would approve of my decision if he were here.'

'I'm sure he would,' Chase said, eager to have the last word. 'But then he didn't exactly set the bar high, did he?'

TWENTY-EIGHT

'What's your honest take on this, Royston?' Crawley asked him. The two men stood close to their vehicles outside the manor entrance. Chase had expected his Super to speed off as soon as it was humanly possible, so he was pleased the man had stuck around to discuss their meeting and the wider case in general.

'Which aspect in particular, sir?' Chase asked, the wheels inside his head still spinning.

'Let's begin with these hunts. Do you really believe one of them came upon this child and perhaps the person who lured her away from home that night?'

'I think it's possible. And if it's possible, then it's worth exploring further.'

'And what do you imagine happened at that point?'

Chase exhaled deeply through his nose. 'Any number of things, I suppose. But if these people were charging about through the trees, one or more of them could have startled Mandy. Their presence might have terrified the girl, causing her to panic. In the woods at night, it would be easy for an adult to get turned around, let alone a child.'

'You sound doubtful.'

'It's not my prime theory. If she'd run around in circles and got lost, we already know she didn't remain there. I can think of no reason why she would not have eventually returned or been returned home. It's all conjecture, sir, but if there was a hunt that night, and if there were also fireworks, then I do think they could have enticed Mandy out of the house. It's possible that somebody – and I have no idea who – spotted her and took her. She could have gone as far as the road, stood there looking up at the display in the sky. Car comes along and the driver is the right kind of deviant. It happens. It could easily have happened that night.'

'Agreed. In which case, nobody on the hunt would have seen her.'

'True. If it happened precisely as I said. Equally, Mandy could have entered the woods in order to see the fireworks up close. She could have been taken there by whoever she met along the way, or run into them there. I'm reaching. I do realise that, sir. There are probably a hundred ways it could have gone. But we do know she vanished without trace at that point, so I'm willing to consider all possibilities.'

'I think you're right to, Royston. Because, unfortunately, that's all you do know. For certain.'

'Well, we also know she survived, gave birth to a daughter of her own, and that her daughter was killed during a sexual encounter with Ken Webster. The same Ken Webster who might have organised a hunt on the night Mandy Radcliffe went missing. There's a connection there, sir. I can't see it yet, but I can feel it. There's every chance that whoever took Mandy also fathered her child. It wasn't Webster, but what if he knew the man responsible?'

'Yet more speculation. I'm sure you haven't discounted Colin Shakespeare, either.'

'I haven't. We don't have any DNA of his to analyse, so of course he remains a suspect as far as I'm concerned.'

Crawley stroked his chin. 'I'm wondering if we need to bring this into Gablecross, Royston. It may be time. You and DC Laney working out of that pokey hole in Little Soley no longer feels suitable for an investigation of this magnitude.'

Chase regarded the man for a moment. He could see why the DCS was in favour of such a move, but wondered if there was an unspoken motive behind the suggestion. 'Does that mean you agree there's more to this than meets the eye, sir?'

'Believe me, what happened last week is bad enough. We've managed to keep a lid on it for the time being, but soon everybody is going to know the kind of man Ken Webster was. A Knight and an ex-CC for this police authority proven to be a drunkard who drove while under the influence and as a consequence was responsible for the death of several people is… it's unthinkable enough. But a paedophile as well? And from what you say, perhaps the one we're aware of from an entire club full of them.' He paused to shake his head. 'I can't even begin to comprehend the damage this will cause.'

Chase thought about Maurice, and how much manipulation was going on behind the scenes to avoid those truths emerging into the public domain. He wondered when the man might next pop up, expecting it to be sooner rather than later. Meanwhile, he had to ensure the investigation made progress.

'I have no problem working out of GC, sir. I doubt Claire will have, either. We might need to arrange a uniform to man Little Soley with PCSO May, though.'

Crawley turned to him, pensive this time. 'I'm sorry, Royston. I obviously didn't make myself clear. When I mentioned bringing it into Gablecross, I meant the investigation. Superintendent Waddington is already SIO, and he's a good man to take over the fine work you've already put in. He'll assign a worthy DI or DCI to take up the fight from here.'

Chase had to look away as he bit into his lip and began a countdown. If he reacted immediately, what he felt like saying might very well end his career. Instead, after a pause of several seconds, he simply nodded, saying. 'If that's the way you want to go, sir.'

'It's a high-profile case. One that will only escalate from here on in, Royston. You don't need this in your life.'

'And yet it was my investigation to run with, sir. Then Claire Laney was sent to work with me. I thought those were your decisions. Or that perhaps they'd come from even higher up the food chain.'

'No. Superintendent Waddington approached me the moment he learned you'd attended the scene, and then the next morning had spoken to a member of Sir Kenneth's staff. He suggested we allow you to do what you do best while he steered from the sidelines. He also thought you might need help, and DC Laney was available at short notice with no caseload of her own.'

Chase nodded. 'I see. In that case, I think I'd better shoot off and update the crime log. Best make sure I've dotted every i and crossed every t before handing it over.'

'He may still want to use you for information gathering, Royston. You and Laney remaining at Little Soley doesn't necessarily mean you're off the case entirely. But I'm sure you see the sense in basing the op in a major investigation room at Gablecross. It's more a matter of resources than anything else.'

'If you say so, sir.'

Chase got into his car and drove away. In his heart and a large part of his stomach, he was furious at being removed from the investigation – despite Crawley having insisted otherwise. But his head and a much smaller portion of his gut told him it was for the best. At the very least, he was off the hook with Maurice. That alone would make sleep a little easier to find. Erin and Maisie could come home early if they decided to. He nodded and muttered to himself beneath his breath. 'It's all right. It's okay. It's for the best.'

Except that it wasn't. The fire burning inside of him was proof enough of that.

When he drew up outside the station and saw the pavement swarming with journalists, photographers, and TV news crews, Chase instinctively knew the bag was currently catless, the can devoid of worms. His heart sank, but at the same time he saw an early and unexpected opportunity to remain in control of the situation. Steeling himself, he emerged from his vehicle to a cacophony of noise, harsh demands for quotes. and updated information. He had no choice but to respond, but first he had to calm them down.

'Please!' he cried, raising his hands before lowering them gradually. 'If you all shout at me at the same time, none of you will get answers because it's just one big noise to me at the moment.' He looked at the crowd wedged together, each of them shuffling forward, using arms and shoulders to create a better position. One man towards the centre stood his ground and seemed faintly embarrassed by the actions of those around him. Chase jabbed a finger in his direction. 'You,' he said. 'Ask one question.'

The man seemed taken aback at having been selected, but he was quick to react. 'Detective Sergeant Chase, do you have any comment on the speculation that Sir Kenneth Webster was not alone last Tuesday night when he was killed in a road crash? That he was, in fact, accompanied by a young woman?'

Chase was relieved by the wording. 'I won't respond to speculation. We deal with evidence and hard facts.' He turned to walk away, but the media people erupted as one. Once again he managed to quieten them down. 'Do you have a source for this speculation?' he asked, confident they did not. He knew how it worked when rumours spread. Each time the story was told it changed a little, and by the end the bare bones were unclear.

'I didn't think so. And even if you did, you'd refuse to share it. Like I said, I'm not about to discuss pure speculation with anybody. Come to me with allegations that will hold up in a court of law, then we'll talk.'

Amidst the subsequent din, Chase heard one female voice. He hushed the crowd and asked her to repeat the question she had asked.

'You are investigating this case, Detective. If you're unwilling or unable to respond to speculative questions, can you at least tell us if you have any information relevant to the incident? Was there somebody in the vehicle with Sir Kenneth Webster the night he was killed? And if so, was that person a young woman?'

Chase's heart felt as if it skipped a beat or two. Blood pounded in his temples. The same questions, phrased differently than before, required a full response. He knew what he wanted to say, but he also knew what he should tell them. Breaking the story to the media could not possibly help his investigation. It could only hinder it. He swallowed thickly before offering a reply.

'I suspect you already know I am unable to comment on the specifics relating to an ongoing inquiry. My understanding is that you were provided with information at a media briefing held by Detective Superintendent Waddington on Friday evening. All I can add to that is that we have no additional information for you at this time. I'm sure you will be briefed appropriately as and when we have news to release. For the time being, I'd like to get on with the task of resolving my investigation if you'll give me some breathing space.'

'Does that mean you're continuing with your inquiries, Sergeant Chase?'

'Of course.'

'And when do you expect to be able to conclude them and have answers for us?'

'Soon,' he said confidently. 'Provided we're left alone to pursue the case.'

This time he turned and strode away, pushed open the door to the station and was grateful to close it behind him and lean his back against it. He smiled. He'd enjoyed that last part. Whatever happened from this point on, and irrespective of how Crawley truly felt about making progress in the case, there was no way he could push aside the two officers who'd so far been responsible for investigating the events surrounding Sir Kenneth Webster's death.

'You okay, sir?' May called out from behind her desk. 'Bit hostile out there, was it?'

He pushed himself away, glad to hear the chatter outside starting to die down. He extended his smile to the PCSO. 'Nothing I can't handle, Alison. And for once, they might have actually improved our situation.'

TWENTY-NINE

LANEY GRILLED HIM ABOUT everything: the meeting with Lady Jane, his discussions with Crawley, as well as the media ruckus outside their front door. He realised what a fearsome opponent she must be inside an interview room. He wouldn't want to piss her off by 'no commenting' throughout, and could imagine her tight stare being unnerving under the right circumstances.

It remained a pleasant autumn day. They had wandered into the garden and wound up at the edge of the river, which barely stirred as it flowed languidly beneath their feet. Chase had needed some fresh air, while Laney had lit up and smoked her way through their conversation. He revealed as much as he knew, before shrugging and wrinkling his nose.

'I don't see us shifting her Ladyship,' he admitted. 'And I can't see any way of compelling her to provide us with the information we requested. I did consider embarrassing her further by leaking it to the media, but doing so might cause her to retreat even further into her shell. We're going to have to wait and see on that one, especially since the journalists have their snouts in the trough.'

'I'm not as convinced as you are that it matters,' Laney said. 'The chances of those hunters running into Mandy Radcliffe are remote, and encountering the kid together with her potential abductor even more so. I agree there has to be some kind of link, Royston, but I don't think that's it.'

Chase understood his partner's reservations, some of which he shared. 'I'm by no means certain, either. It's only logic that pulls me in that direction, and I'm aware how often rationality doesn't come close to breaking a case wide open. As for DCS Crawley, either I've lost it completely or he is not the one who put us together in order to see us fail. That means it had to be Waddington, which is disappointing but not a total shock. He and I generally get on okay, and I like the man. But as much as Crawley might have wanted to bring the investigation into Gablecross, thanks to that mob outside, there's no way that's happening now.'

'So who do you think leaked to the press?'

'No idea. And before you say another word, it wasn't me. What concerns me a little is that anybody who knew Ken Webster had a young female with him that night, also has to have known the girl was underage and naked. So why leave that out when leaking? That's a much bigger story to break, so why would you tell only part of it?'

'Perhaps they held it back in order to increase its value. Feed the media a snippet to establish your credentials, and then if the investigation team acknowledges that minor infraction, go back to the well and drain it dry next time.'

Chase nodded. It was a good theory. It fitted perfectly with the information they already had, and was potentially a good strategy. Get the media to bite and then have them swallow. 'Still doesn't tell us who,' he muttered. 'And there are so many candidates.'

'Too many. You'll go crazy even thinking about it, Royston. So instead, let me tell you what I've been up to while you were swanning around with the high and mighty. Kaitlyn Dee did her job to perfection. I didn't even need to call the Tier One main switchboard, because they contacted me. By email initially. I followed up with a phone call, and they had no choice but to do as I asked. They agreed we could speak to the club manager, but on the proviso that we did so at the offices of a local solicitor, with a legal representative present during the interview.'

Chase was fine with that. 'No problem. If we dragged them in here or over to GC, they'd have insisted on doing the same thing. Okay, so when do we do that?'

'We have an appointment at 2.45pm. That's if you decide we even need it after I've told you what else I have. Because, I've also heard back from our tech friend, Mr Maddison.'

'That was quick.'

'I was on the phone to him while you were outside with that rabble.'

'Good news?'

'Good and better. Good news is, he is able to recover the data and is copying it down to a separate hard drive. Once he has it, he's going to upload it to Dropbox for us and then send you a link to it. He'll also forward it to cloud storage, to ensure there's yet another copy available to both of us. As soon as he's done that, he'll send over the access details. Oh, and everything he sends us will be encrypted, and I have the encryption key in here…' Laney tapped the side of her head.

'Is that wise?' Chase asked. 'You've a brain like a colander.'

'Up yours, cupcake. I'll have you know my mind is like a steel trap.'

He grinned. 'Seriously, Claire, that all sounds terrific. What's the better news?'

'I'm glad you asked. While he was waiting for the data to copy down, our Mr Maddison also looked into the breach. He has a backdoor way of interrogating their own software, which means nobody will know he was even there. He told me the hack was both external and clumsy. Too clumsy to be a genuine hack. That alerted him to the probability that it was an insider trying to make it look like the work of an outsider.'

'And does he happen to know who this insider is?'

'Yes, he does. The man who deleted the data is none other than the company Managing Director, a Mr Otto Baumann.'

*

Chase roped in May to help them out, but with the shadow of Maurice the spook still providing a threat, he kept her involvement to background work only. While he and Laney pored through the evidence, actions taken, and hypotheses so far investigated, he had the PCSO scour the internet and various database engines searching for a link between Baumann and Tier One. The former included the man's Gateway Technological Enterprises company, the latter both Knights of the Realm.

After settling either side of Chase's desk, the two detectives attempted to find a view of the overall picture from the scraps they had managed to piece together so far. There was more to sift through than he had realised, but each thread was disparate. Despite making progress, in terms of hard facts they had little more to go on than they'd had when they started. Without the DNA link between a missing girl case from twenty years ago and their unidentified victim, they'd have nothing more than crumbs. Yet it was the connection between the two events that continued to drive Chase's thinking.

'Am I completely wrong?' he asked Laney at one point. 'Am I allowing myself to be sidetracked by what might yet prove to be a simple coincidence? Because we've learned more about a twenty-year-old case than one we've had for less than a week.'

'There's not a lot you can do without an identity, Royston,' Laney pointed out. 'Our underage victim is central to the entire operation, and the little progress we've made lies along a road littered by stumbling blocks. This is the job, isn't it? Picking things apart bit by bit until they start to unravel in our favour. Sad to say, but our investigation is not a race against the clock. Our victim will be no more dead than she was last week. In that respect, it doesn't matter if it takes time.'

Chase nodded. 'You're right. Of course you are. Which means I'm allowing myself to be led by a case that's not even ours. I'm putting Mandy Radcliffe's disappearance ahead of our unidentified victim, convincing myself there's a link beyond the familial.'

'Which there still could be, don't forget. So don't be too hard on yourself. You can't manufacture evidence out of thin air. What we've done so far will shortly have us a list of Tier One staff and the full club membership. Our job is to identify potential weak links, isolate them, get them to tell us what they know. Let's see where we are then rather than criticise where we are now.'

'Who knew you could talk such sense?' He grinned and gave a nod of appreciation.

Returning the acknowledgement, Laney said, 'Who knows what treasures we might unearth in that list of members? It could be pure gold.'

'What's the betting we find the name of one Otto Baumann on there?'

'I was thinking the very same thing myself. He was in a big hurry to delete the list. I suppose it's possible he owed a favour to somebody, but like you I reckon he knows more about Tier One than first appears.'

'And I think I'm now able to confirm that,' Alison May said, walking through the open doorway. Her round cheeks bulged, and she hit the pair full beam with one of her dazzling full-toothed smiles. 'Eleven years ago, Mr Bauman's company GTE received a Confederation of British Industry award for best new startup. The accolade came with a financial package sponsored by Sir Colin Shakespeare.'

Chase got to his feet. He walked over to May and put a hand on each arm. He squeezed affectionately but did not draw her into a hug. 'You are going to be a superstar, Alison,' he said. 'And as your reward for that critical piece of information, you can take my seat while I fetch us each a celebratory cold drink.'

*

As he emerged from the small grocery shop fifty yards away from the police station, Chase almost blundered straight into the man he knew as Maurice.

'Bloody hell, you startled me,' he said, putting a hand to his chest. The other clutched the handle of a plastic carrier bag containing chilled carbonated drinks.

'You made a mistake,' Maurice said bluntly. He did not look happy. 'Yours was a good plan, I'll grant you that much. But you're insane if you think it was anything other than temporary relief.'

'I don't know what you mean. What plan? What relief?'

'You had the foresight to take your wife's mobile from her. You were also right not to remove the battery and have it go dark as that would have been a red flag and we would have been all over that. I suspect Erin and Maisie are currently far from home, and certainly your wife is nowhere close to her phone.'

'If that's all true, what mistake did I make?'

'I'm guessing you tossed her phone into the glove box of your vehicle. Your error came in not removing it again.'

Chase felt a twinge of anxiety. He refused to buckle to this man, however. 'Ah. I'm assuming you saw her signal alongside mine this morning. Moving in sync with my own.'

'Precisely so. Not smart, Royston. Not smart at all.'

'It doesn't mean anything. It certainly isn't an indicator that I'm looking to tackle you people head on.'

'Is that so? What does it mean, then?'

'Only that I wanted to remove my wife and daughter from immediate danger.'

Maurice seemed to consider that. He began to laugh, his shoulders steadily rising and falling in unison. 'Who do you think you are, Royston? Some failed state warlord? Some terrorist intent on doing us all harm? You think when I mentioned your family that I was threatening to harm them? What do you take me for? I'm a civil servant, Royston. No more, no less. My remit is to resolve existing problems, not create more of them.'

'Why did you mention Erin and Maisie, then?'

'Because both will be affected if something bad were to happen to you, won't they?'

Chase arched his eyebrows. 'I see. No threat to them, but happy to intimidate me?'

Again the deep chuckle. 'Once again, you do me a disservice. When I say something bad might happen to you, I mean you might end up looking completely foolish spouting your conspiracy theories when the truth emerges. I mean you might end up even further out on a limb, or perhaps gone from your job altogether. Do you seriously believe I go around taking people off the map entirely?'

This time Chase caught his response before it came out. He counted off, thinking about their conversations so far. Eventually, he nodded. 'Yes, I do as it happens. I think you're probably capable of anything if you put your mind to it. If you deem the cause worthy enough.'

Slowly, Maurice allowed the smile to fall away until he was regarding Chase with a cold, dead stare. 'Then stop playing silly buggers,' he said. 'If you think I am a serious man, Royston, start taking me seriously. The genie is forcing itself out of the bottle. I can't allow that to happen. I won't.'

'You mean the media circus? I had nothing to do with that?'

'I know. That was all my doing?'

'You… but why on earth…?'

'Something was bound to emerge today. Better to control the news than react to it, Royston. Tossing the sharks half a story at this stage is better than them having a feeding frenzy later on with the truth. Speculation, especially that coming from the media, hardly holds up an entire twenty-four-hour news cycle. I wanted this one blowing over, so we fed them a little something and let them run with it. Rumour and social media chirping consumes its own oxygen, and is easily forgotten when the facts emerge. Because nobody apologises when they get it wrong these days. Have you noticed that, Royston?'

'So let me get this straight… you released the story in order to kill it?'

'Naturally. I'm sure you've read about or seen on TV how sometimes fire crews set controlled fires to burn ahead of the wildfire coming their way, so that the racing flames have nothing more to feed upon when they reach that point. Same thing.'

'Is it? Wildfires tend to be less intelligent and a bit more predictable than media reporters.'

'Perhaps, but it's the same general principle. Kill that one, the next one becomes even harder to believe. After all, what do they have? Sir Kenneth accompanied by a young woman when he died? Hardly crime of the century, especially when we eventually reveal there was no crime at all.'

'But the real investigative journalists will pick up on it. They'll want to know who this young woman is. They'll dig deeper for that answer at the very least.'

'And they will find the police offering their own version of a no comment. Not while investigations are in progress. Full disclosure as soon as all inquiries have taken place. Only, by then we'll be able to pull a sheet over it and declare nothing to see here.'

'Provided I don't do anything to spoil things for you,' Chase finished for him.

Maurice winked. 'There you go. You've got it. Please do continue your investigation while we work behind the scenes. But if you are putting together building blocks, better remember how unstable it will all be without the correct foundations.'

THIRTY

BY FOUR THAT AFTERNOON, Chase and Laney were back from Swindon, having met with Tier One manager, Marcus Thresher, together with a senior solicitor representing the club itself. After a lot of posturing and statements insisting Thresher could only provide essential knowledge in reference to other members of staff due to the club's IT system having failed, eventually they came away with a compiled list including two dozen names.

The detectives had discussed the merits of meeting with the man at all, knowing the same information was on the way in a file restored by Guy Maddison. Chase had argued that talking to him might prove worthwhile if they could force him to make a slip, plus it would also reveal to them how Tier One intended fighting them on all fronts. But Thresher had been solid and determined, responding like one of Pavlov's dogs as if to a bell only when prompted to do so by the solicitor. She was a pleasant woman in a top-notch business suit, and she knew her stuff. She kept Thresher on a tight rein, but Chase got a sense that she had no idea what went on within the walls of Tier One, nor what some of the people she was protecting were capable of.

Before heading out to the meeting, Chase had given Maddison a call. They'd been told going in that the full data recovery process would be slow and depended entirely on how much of it there was to begin with. However, Chase was impatient to get started and asked the engineer if it was possible to send whatever data had already been restored.

'I'll let you have what I can,' he told Chase. 'But you have to understand that digital data is recovered in chunks, so while a filename might exist on the disk I'm restoring to, not all of its component parts will necessarily be there. You may find some of what I send out at this stage to be corrupt.'

Chase had settled for a better to have something than nothing approach, and was delighted to see a link to a dropbox account when he checked his mail upon their return to Little Soley. He clicked the link and downloaded the corresponding folder containing a vast number of files. He then obtained the encryption key from Laney, and together with PCSO May they worked their way through the various folders looking for files with relevant names. Locating a staff list from a folder called *HR* was easy enough, but the file refused to open.

'It's too small,' May pointed out. 'Look, it's only about three kilobytes. That must have been selected for transfer before it had recovered all of its data.'

'Not to worry,' Chase told her. 'We have the list from Marcus Thresher. I'll want to compare the two before we're done with this. To make sure he didn't leave anyone out. Still, we have our starting point as far as members of staff are concerned. Though I must say I'm much more interested in the members.'

At that point, May asked what these people were suspected of, beyond being members of an elite and exclusive club. After exchanging nods with Laney, Chase told the PCSO some of what they knew and had speculated upon. May was horrified, paling as the repercussions of their search became more obvious to her.

'There will be people I've heard of in here, won't there?' she said falteringly.

Laney nodded. 'That's what we're expecting to find, yes. We believe one of them went to a great deal of trouble to make sure we'd never lay eyes on this list. But it's our hope that somewhere here lies the evidence we need to solve our case. One or more of these members is bound to confess everything in exchange for a deal. It's our job to find them and get them to talk when we do.'

The task proved to be harder than Chase had imagined. There were membership applications separated alphabetically by surname and into years, with as many files refusing to open as did. Chase hunted through what they had, looking to find a membership acceptance and number associated with Otto Baumann. He was unable to find any such file. Then he noticed the year folders only went back as far as 2004, and he guessed the remainder were only just being recovered from the backup tapes.

Frustrated, he decided they should work on a revised strategy. He created a folder which he named *Search* and another called *Searched*. He told Laney and May to open relevant membership files at random. Any that did were to be copied to the *Search* folder. Inside that container he generated three more, each marked with their own initials. He then divvied up the files equally between them. By the time they were finished, they had thirty-seven files each. The idea was that any they regarded as being potentially valuable would remain open, and those checked off were moved into the *Searched* folder. They were only a few minutes into the job when May gasped.

'Ohmygod!' she said in a voice barely louder than a whisper. 'Please don't tell me he's a nonce. I don't think I could stand it.'

May revealed the name of a beloved afternoon TV chef. Laney followed up with an actor famous for an eighties situation comedy that at its peak pulled in millions of viewers, while Chase discovered an ex-MP and current environmental campaigner among the files he was able to open. It was a treasure trove of information, and nowhere near yet fully formed. It was time to start separating the wheat from the chaff and strategising over whom to approach first, and deciding upon the level of pressure they might bring to bear.

As he examined the files and studied the occupations of the men whose names were not immediately familiar, Chase started to formulate an idea that nagged at him long enough to catch hold of his attention. His initial thought after learning about the proximity of the Webster estate to the Radcliffe family home had been based on little more than a dislike of the coincidence. The possibility of a firework display at the end of an obscure hunt on the Webster property attracting Mandy Radcliffe closer to the grounds, had sent his enquiring mind in search of answers. By this time the gateway to his imagination had also opened up, and he could not be sure which possibilities were feasible and which were mere fantasy.

The one that stuck with him lodged inside his head and refused to give way to logical assaults and the oiled wheels of natural scepticism. But the more he considered it, the more the idea fed off the adrenaline sluicing through his bloodstream.

Mandy Radcliffe had vanished into the night at the age of eight. The possibility existed that she somehow found her way onto Webster land, where the hunt was in full flow. That scenario could easily have led to a terrible and tragic accident, one in which the young child stumbled across the path of a huntsman pulling on the trigger as he saw what he thought had to be a bird crashing through the undergrowth. Except, as they were now aware, Mandy Radcliffe went on to give birth to a child perhaps five or six years later. So, he asked himself, what if some or perhaps even all the huntsmen that night were also members of the Tier One club? If the club was a cover for a major league paedophile ring, as Chase surmised, then maybe some tastes were not restricted to young teens.

Put it more plainly, Chase told himself. *Make it clearer even to yourself.*

Okay, then. Did Mandy Radcliffe stray across the path of a pack of deviants that night? Was she removed from the Webster property and taken to The Grange for the pleasure of members of the Tier One club whose sexual desires allowed them to consider an eight-year-old child fair game? And had she remained there or close by over a number of years, had she given birth to a child there, a child who herself later became the target for sickening and repulsive yearnings? Perhaps before ripening into the age range preferred by a certain Knight of the Realm?

Chase cast his mind back to the meeting with Marcus Thresher. So far they had spoken to a Tier One co-founder, and a terrified member, but as the manager, Thresher had to be involved right up to his scrawny neck in every sordid detail. Chase had felt distaste and nausea lurking in the pit of his stomach throughout the entire interview. He had refused to shake the man's hand or call him Marcus as requested. The idea had been to keep the man at arm's length both emotionally and physically. Especially the latter, because if what he read in Claire Laney's demeanour was correct, he was not the only one who had wanted to reach out to choke Thresher.

The man had come across as genial if unhelpful, normal by modern-day standards. He treated the entire meeting as if he were being put out, insisting the police were wasting his and everybody else's time. You odious freak, was all Chase could think when forced to look Thresher in the eyes and watch his moist lips move. *You odious freak!*

Chase heard his name being spoken. He blinked a couple of times, before looking up into the curious and concerned eyes of both DC Laney and PCSO May.

'Where did you go, Royston?' Laney asked. 'You blanked out on us there for a moment.'

'I was… thinking,' he said softly, his mind still lingering on those awful thoughts.

'Yeah. That's some deep thinking. It's like you were in a trance.'

Ignoring the observation, Chase said, 'If Otto Baumann is on that membership list, I want him in a room at either Gablecross or Monkton Park. Swindon or Chippenham, either suits me. When he's being interviewed, he has to know we're taking things seriously. A back office in Little Soley won't cut it.'

'Why, what have you got?'

'Nothing more solid than I had before. And nothing I want to talk about here and now in case I'm wrong. But I've had an idea.

And it's so awful, so fucking twisted, that I genuinely believe I have to be right. Perhaps not in every sickening detail, but enough to waterboard the fucker if I need to.'

The laughter from both Laney and May was half-hearted at best, perhaps because neither was entirely convinced he was completely joking.

'Come on, Royston,' Laney said, cajoling gently. 'We're both on your side. Both on the side of good triumphing over evil. Whatever you have, or think you have, you can share with us.'

'Absolutely, sir,' May added, nodding as her features became a deep frown.

But Chase was adamant and shook his head with conviction. 'No. Not yet. I need some time to think, to go over it again one last time. Plus, there's something you both need to know and fully appreciate. If I'm right, exposing the truth is going to cause devastation and upheaval without parallel. I won't be able to control the butterfly effect. Anyone who comes anywhere close to it will get caught up in a whirlwind, and who knows which way that will blow. You might want to take several large steps backwards, away from me at the very least if I am right and I expose what I think may be going on.'

'I… I suspect I might have an inkling,' Laney said tentatively. 'But then, I know more than Alison does, so I'm already in much deeper.'

'I realise I'm paddling away in the shallows compared to you two,' May said, 'but I'm not afraid. I want to be you two at some point, so I'm happy to be pulled in.'

Chase was shaking his head. 'Trouble is, I'm afraid for you, Alison. If I pull you in at this point and allow the ripples to do their work, you might drown along with the rest of us, and then you'll never be what you want to be. Sometimes it's better to learn from the sidelines, where it's dry and no harm can come to you.'

May looked crestfallen. 'I thought we were in this together, sir. I thought I was part of the team.'

'You were. You are.'

'Then let me get wet. Let me be a part of it all the way. Because anything other than that makes me an outsider, and I'm better than that.'

Chase put back his head, inhaled a huge lungful or air. Releasing slowly he said, 'If I tell you what I'm thinking, then at the moment it's just another possibility. But if I'm right, your lives may never be the same again. Are you both sure you're ready for that?'

Laney and May nodded as one.

His head came all the way back down until his chin was resting on his chest. He gave it a good count. Only this time he saw no way out. Looking up again, he gave a single nod. 'All right. But remember, when all this is over and the dust has settled, you asked for it.'

THIRTY-ONE

SHORTLY BEFORE SIX THEY decided it was going to be a late night after the remaining data was downloaded from Dropbox. One by one they slipped outside to call home. Alison May to her mother, Laney to her husband, and, using the burner phone, Chase hit the only number in the contacts App to speak to Erin.

'Please tell me it's all over,' she said.

He chuckled gently. 'It's not that bad down there, is it?'

'Sweetheart, I'm sitting out on the deck gazing at the tide coming in. I have one hand wrapped around this phone and in the other is a tall glass of wine. The sun is setting and there's a gentle, cooling sea breeze. But I'd happily trade all that to know you were safe and that this horrible job was at an end.'

'It's going to be fine,' he assured her, though he had his doubts about how that might happen. 'A couple more days at most I'd say.'

'And this Maurice bloke? Have you spoken to him again?'

Chase was okay with omission if it kept Erin from having darker thoughts, but he did not want to lie to her. 'He and I bumped into each other earlier, actually. He's aware of what we did with the phones.'

'Oh, no. Was he angry? Is he looking for us? Will it help matters if we come home?'

'Steady on, love. That's a bit quick-fire even for me. If he was upset, he didn't really show it. More irritated than anything, I think.

He's used to people doing as they're told. As far as I know, he's not searching for you. It's too big an ask for so little reward. And no, it will only confuse matters if you come home today. I promise, if I get this wrapped up by the end of the week, I'll drive down to collect you both on Saturday. Any earlier and we'll talk – you might decide to enjoy a few more stress-free days away.'

He said goodnight to Maisie and went back to his colleagues. He ordered from the Indian takeaway on the main road down by the town's central shopping area. It sounded larger and more grand than it was, comprising only a dozen shops in all. Thankfully they included a bakery, a grocer, and the Indian restaurant. They ate as they worked, the time that passed liberally sprinkled with further gasps of amazement as the names of yet more well-known men and women were unearthed.

Unsurprised, Chase was both delighted and appalled to see the name of Otto Baumann on one of the files. Delighted because he had final confirmation to back up his hunch, and appalled to find another figure of prominence and stature involved with one of the worst crimes imaginable.

Chase kept his own mental list of crimes worth life imprisonment… or worse. He had no problem including murder, although in many cases a momentary loss of control could not compare with premeditated brutality. Rape, too, he believed, was worthy of the maximum sentence. But right at the top he put child abuse and paedophilia. Most murderers never went on to commit the same crime, but studies proved the majority of paedophiles were unable to stray from the path they were on.

At around eight, Chase puffed out a long sigh and said, 'We're going to have to be choosey. There are too many names here. This is a national enterprise, remember, with club bases all over the country. I want a sufficient number of locally based members to feature, but I'm also willing to travel up and down and from side to side around the entire bloody United Kingdom if I have to.'

'Choosey in what way?' May asked.

'We have to narrow it down so that it becomes more manageable. I suggest we separate these names into, say, four individual lists. List A will contain the twenty names we decide are the most likely to be vulnerable to the kind of pressure we can bring to bear. Famous, married, the kind who'd do anything to keep their names out of it. List B to D will have the remaining names in descending order of their likelihood to break. I'm of the opinion that we won't need to push past the first list in order to obtain the evidence and statements we're looking for. But I also think we should interview or have interviewed everyone on those four lists by the time the case is over.'

'What does that mean for those who don't make lists A to D?' Laney asked.

'We'll get around to them. Eventually. But as part of a much larger case. I'm thinking of proposing an Operation Yewtree type of investigation to continue after this one.'

'Yewtree?' May said, frowning.

Chase nodded, swinging around in his chair to face her. 'It was the nationwide child abuse investigation that first identified Jimmy Saville as an abuser and which looked to follow up on allegations against him, allegations against him with others, and allegations against others excluding Saville. It began back in 2012 if I recall correctly. Stuart Hall, the TV presenter, was one of the big name convictions, as were Rolf Harris and Max Clifford. Others were acquitted of all charges, and then there was all that nonsense with Cliff Richard. It spawned a number of other ops as well, which picked up several more celebrities and famous faces.'

'I've heard about most of those, though not all,' May confessed. 'I didn't know they all came out of a single op, though.'

'Yewtree was massive. Some branded it a modern day witch hunt. And in truth, a lot of people were brought under the microscope with very little evidence based on some pretty dubious allegations.'

'But surely the aim was to give victims a voice, sir?'

'True. And that's a worthy goal. The problem is, sadly for us and those innocently caught up in the net, we got it badly wrong at times. We caught a lot of nonces, Alison, which is clearly a good thing. But I also think about the men whose lives we may have ruined after they were named and shamed but had nothing to do with it. Entire families were torn apart because of false allegations. Careers and reputations died on that particular altar. That's why we have to narrow things down, keep it on the QT for a while, and start with only those people we can nail and who may be able to give us answers concerning our victim.'

'And possibly even Mandy Radcliffe,' Laney chimed in. 'Her father is not the only one who'd like to know what happened to her.'

'Absolutely. And top of group A for me has to be Otto Baumann. With the information Guy Maddison provided us with, Baumann is due a pull for contravening the Data Protection Act. If we can make him edgy about that, then we can escalate into why he removed Tier One data and his connection to it.'

'I'm not familiar with the act,' May mentioned.

'It's simply an offence covering the erasure of information with the intent of preventing disclosure. I previously worked a case we found difficult to prove because the woman in question claimed to have deleted files in error. But with Baumann, we have him deleting off the server and the backup server and tapes, so he's not talking himself out of that.'

'You want me to have a word with the CPS?' Laney offered.

Chase nodded. 'Please do. Firm up the charge with them, and ask if we have enough for an arrest warrant. I'd really like to put him under pressure from the off. Also, make it clear that we'd like to offer inducements in exchange for information. I'm thinking a decent prison close to home if he's a family man.'

'And meanwhile?'

'We don't want to go in there all bullish. So let's put together a package on Mr Baumann. I want to know a lot more about the man and his links to others before we get him in the room. If we can identify his weaknesses, it gives us another way in. I'm confident of the DPA breaches, but for those alone he'll get bail. I'd much rather he left in one of our vans.'

'Is there anything I can do, sir?' May asked.

'Yes. Give Monkton Park a bell. Inform them that we are likely to make an arrest early doors tomorrow and may want to use one of their interview rooms. It all depends on where we pull him, because I'd rather not travel huge distances if we can help it. We might need to call whatever local nick is available to us instead, but let's be fully prepared for either.'

With these minor actions agreed, Chase set about drilling deeper into Otto Baumann's life. LinkedIn, Facebook, Twitter and Instagram were good places to start. The man ran a major IT company, so he was pretty much omnipresent across social media. Chase also read the man's profile on the company website. He printed off relevant pages, all of which combined to provide a frank and detailed outline of the professional businessman, with a touch of his personal life thrown in for good measure.

Otto Baumann, forty-eight, born in Leipzig in Germany. Moved to England in his mid-twenties. Came from new money, his father owning a manufacturing business with international appeal. Married Rosaleen Sullivan shortly before his thirtieth birthday. The couple were still together and had two teenage children. Chase nodded to himself; the three people in this man's life would be his weaknesses. But he feared they might also be a reason for Baumann to fight the charges, not wanting his family to believe him capable of such repugnant desires. It was something to ponder.

He moved on to search for newspaper articles and video clips, of which there were many. In an interview for a BBC series on commerce in the UK, he noted a remark made by Baumann that seemed to reveal a chink in his genial and professional demeanour. In answer to a question concerning why he had chosen to become a provider to the public sector exclusively rather than embrace the private one as well, Bauman's glib response was to suggest he could get away with padding the quotes more when it came to public money. He finished by laughing, the implication being he had spoken in jest. But Chase saw and heard it differently.

When he was done, he asked for updates before they called it quits for the night. May had arranged for them to use IR2 at Monkton Park, which Chase knew to be a decent room in terms of size and temperature control.

'We might need a rethink,' he said. 'I've discovered Baumann lives on the outskirts of Oxford. It'd be better for us to speak to him close by. I know the nick out at Cowley quite well, and they're usually fairly accommodating if they can be. When we're done here, please see if you can get us a room there instead.'

'CPS are a go,' Laney told them, her face wreathed in smiles. 'They'll inform the Information Commissioner's Office, at which point ICO and the CPS will work together finessing the specific wording of the charges. They'll wait until we give them the word in case anything changes, but we have the green light on an arrest.'

Chase stroked his chin. 'Now all we have to do is hope it stays under Gablecross's radar.'

'I don't think DCS Crawley is going to be too happy with you, Royston. Nor Waddington, for that matter. As SIO, he'll be raging that you went ahead with all this without giving him a chance to update the policy book and authorising the actions.'

'It's a fluid investigation, Claire. I felt the need for a swift response to our findings. I felt I had no time for the niceties.'

She chuckled. 'Yeah, good luck with that one, cupcake.'

He shrugged. 'I realise you don't know him, but the man is a careerist, so his arse will squeak like a balloon being mauled by a toddler once he hears of Baumann's connection to Colin Shakespeare and, by virtue of his Tier One membership, to Ken Webster also.'

'I'm happy to be guided by you. So what did you find out about the man?'

Chase spent ten minutes going over the intel he had gathered. Otto Baumann's prominence was indisputable. He was a major player with a huge finger in a pie belonging to the British tax payer. His business, his connections, and his family, were all areas worth probing when they got the man in the room. But if he didn't break, there were seventy-nine other names up for grabs.

THIRTY-TWO

A GREY, OVERCAST MORNING SEEMED befitting of a dawn arrest. An unexpected muggy heat lay like a physical barrier beneath the clouds, but Chase and Laney had focussed only on Otto Baumann. Overnight, May had arranged for the use of an interview room at the Cowley police station. She had also requested the presence of local uniformed officers to assist with the arrest, and a transportation vehicle should their suspect forcefully resist. Chase was delighted with her contribution. A judge had issued a section 32 warrant, which allowed the police to search the property in which the arrest was made and to seize any items associated with the reasons outlined in the document.

Though clearly both shocked and dismayed by the unexpected intrusion, Baumann's initial bluster died in his throat when he first heard those reasons described for the first time. Given the serious crimes he was suspected of, a man like Otto Baumann might well have been expecting this kind of knock every morning of his life. At first he seemed almost relieved to hear mention of him illegally erasing data, but after a few seconds it appeared to register with him that this was something he might not be able to easily or successfully defend.

Having been detained for interview and held in custody, Baumann spent the next ninety minutes in a holding cell waiting for a solicitor to arrive. With no prior dealings with the police, his only legal representation was provided by a company specialising in business contracts. They had referred him to a criminal defence solicitor who'd had to travel down from Banbury. Not so long ago, Baumann's actions might have been worthy of the financial equivalent of a slap on the wrist, but data protection and cyber security was the new big thing.

Half an hour later they were all set, and the suspect together with his solicitor were escorted to the interview room, where Chase and Laney joined them moments afterwards. Laney rattled off the elements of the interview required by the Police And Criminal Evidence act, while Chase set up the recording device, entering the names of those present.

Baumann's solicitor and the man himself might have been siblings. Both a little under six foot, balding, piling on the timber, similar right down to their bushy eyebrows and the same kind of tinted spectacles. Chase had wanted to suggest they wear name badges to make their identification more clear, but he kept the thought to himself.

'Mr Baumann,' he began. 'Tell me what you know about Tier One, the club co-founded by one of your benefactors, Sir Colin Shakespeare.'

Baumann glanced at his brief, who gave an almost imperceptible nod. Both of them had been watching too much TV, Chase thought.

The reply when it came was crisp and clear. 'My company has a contractual arrangement with Tier One. We supply them with IT equipment, engineering, technical support, and network management services.'

Chase opened up a folder thick with hard copy printouts, at the top of which was a page from the Gateway Technological Enterprises website listing services and products offered by the company. He ran his eyes over some of the blurb, then flicked his gaze back to Baumann.

'I'm confused. Perhaps you can help lift some of the fog. Everything I read on here, every interview I've read and seen in relation to your company, categorically states your full commitment to public organisations at the expense of private industry. So how is it that you came to do business with Tier One?'

Almost too eager to bat that one away, Baumann said, 'Tier One is a nonprofit organisation. Charitable status. I see no conflict there with our core philosophies.'

'Quite. But am I right in saying it is the only charitable organisation on your list of clients?'

Baumann nodded, less assured this time. 'It is, so yes, you are correct.'

Chase detected only the faintest of accents. It was there in the sibilants. 'So why Tier One?' he asked.

'Sir Colin chose to invest in GTE after we were given an award to mark our achievements. He invited us to provide technical services for Tier One, and I felt obliged to comply.'

'Obliged?' Chase was intrigued by the word. 'Does that mean the investment felt more like a bribe?'

'My client has no comment to that question,' James St John said abruptly.

Chase eyed the solicitor, but decided not to pursue the matter. 'Very well. Mr Baumann, would you like to explain to me how it was that between 7.35pm and 11.17pm on Saturday night, you deleted all data stored on two virtual servers allocated to Tier One?'

'Do you have any evidence to back up that allegation?' St John asked. He shook his head slowly, as if expecting an answer in the negative.

'We do indeed.' Chase withdrew several pages of A4 stapled together, then flipped them around to display the top sheet for their inspection. 'This is a log of actions carried out on the Tier One servers between those hours. And before you suggest to me that anybody could have hacked their way into the system to carry out the removal of those folders and files, I ought to inform you that this same log identifies the IP address of the source device.'

'Cloning goes on all the time,' Baumann said. This time his voice was neither calm nor collected. 'And what with VPNs and proxies, it's virtually impossible to precisely locate a true source these days.'

Chase nodded along, allowing his lips to thin into a wry smile. 'Clearly as a technical man yourself, Mr Baumann, you'll have far greater knowledge about that sort thing than either myself or my colleague, DC Laney. You're probably also speculating that, given their pay, our own tech people are probably not the pick of the bunch. That said, this information wasn't initially gathered by our own specialist teams. It has subsequently been verified by them, as highlighted on another information sheet here in my pack. However, the original search was carried out by one of your own members of staff.'

Baumann stiffened. St John put a hand on the man's arm and leaned forward in his chair. 'Somebody with a grudge, then,' he suggested, laying out the pathway to his proposed rebuttal.

'That's yet to be decided. However, we have no reason to suspect this person of being anything other than a content employee who simply carried out the search at the behest of Wiltshire Police.'

'In that case, I suggest a short break so that I might consult with my client.'

'If you think it necessary.' Chase eyed the man sitting directly opposite. 'Is it necessary, Mr Baumann? I imagine your brief is going to advise you to admit culpability, citing accidental erasure of all data. Why not cut out the dramatic pause and go with that?'

'Really, I must object,' St John said, rising to his feet. 'It is not your job to counsel my client.'

'It was nothing more than a suggestion. If I'm wrong, you two can go off and find a consultation room if you prefer.'

'Don't bother,' Baumann said, waving off his solicitor's objections. 'Detective Sergeant Chase, it may surprise you to know that despite being the owner and managing director of GTE, I am also willing and able to offer my own engineering and technical expertise to the day-to-day operations. Tier One happens to be an account I service myself on occasion. On Saturday night, I executed what I believed to be a simple archiving procedure. I realise now I must have made a dreadful mistake.'

Chase shrugged and leaned away. 'It happens. We all do from time to time.'

As he shifted one way, Laney moved the other. 'So is that what happened to the backup disk as well, Mr Baumann? You ran precisely the same incorrect process on those disks and erased the data on them as well?'

Baumann froze. His body tensed and his eyes became instantly alert. There was fear in them, too, Chase thought. For the first time that morning. 'I… I suppose I must have,' he said weakly.

'Interesting. Because as has been explained to us, the data on the backup disks is stored in a completely different way. The files are not simply replicated, they are compressed and stored inside an array of folders and they cannot be deleted by using any of the standard deletion methods. It's a safety feature of the software. We are reliably informed that any deletion procedure used to erase the original stored data could not possibly work in the same way to remove the backup data. What's more, our informant has identified the exact method used regarding the backup disks. The software has logs which he was able to interrogate.'

'Was there a question in there somewhere?' St John snapped.

Laney gave him a wide smile. 'Do I need to refer you both to my original question?'

'What do you want?' Baumann demanded, arrogance seeping through the fragile veneer of his compliance. 'What is this all about? So some data went missing from some disks. It happens.'

'It wasn't only disks in this case, though, was it?'

'I'm not sure I understand what you mean.'

'Only that accidentally erasing data from the servers might be considered unfortunate. Erasing the same data from a set of backup disks considerably more damaging. But an entire set of data storage tapes as well?'

This struck a nerve, yet Baumann waved it off. 'ICO will investigate and perhaps issue a fine, which we will pay. Sir Colin will not press additional charges. I can assure you of that.'

'Thank you for neatly leading us back to Tier One, sir. Earlier, you mentioned that your connection to the club was limited to your company and its business arrangement with Sir Colin Shakespeare's own organisation. Is that still your position?'

'Of course. What else?'

Chase thought he detected a thin sheen of moisture sitting over the man's top lip. Interviews such as this often came down to timing. He sensed anxiety eating away at Baumann, and decided to skip a stage in the progression he had discussed with Laney before heading into the interview.

'So you're not a member of Tier One yourself, Mr Baumann?'

That one connected. The man's eyes rounded, and his breathing became heavier. He shook his head dismissively, almost angrily. 'Not that I am aware of, no.'

'That's an odd response. You either are or you're not.'

'I don't believe I am. I'm a busy man. I join many things, and it's not always easy to keep tabs.'

'Would you like to reconsider? Only, we have evidence to suggest otherwise.'

'I suppose it's always possible that I was made an honorary member. But I have no knowledge of it if so.'

Nodding, Chase reached into the folder. He pulled out another sheet of A4. He made sure both men could see what was printed on it. 'If that's the case, Mr Baumann,' he said, in no rush to blurt out the words, 'how do you explain this membership application?'

'It... it... it's just that. You didn't ask me if I had applied. You asked if I was a member. Applying for membership is not the same as being granted membership.'

Playing along, Chase continued to nod. 'That's true. Although in your case, I find it astonishing that any club would turn down your application.'

'Frankly, I find myself in agreement with you, Sergeant Chase. But turn me down they appear to have done.'

One more time, like a magician pulling a rabbit from a previously empty hat, Chase selected another sheet of paper and pushed it across the table. 'And yet here is your acceptance letter, Mr Baumann. A copy of it, at least. With your signature at the bottom.'

Trapped by his own denials, Baumann closed his eyes and turned a pained face to the ceiling. St John cupped a hand around his mouth and whispered in the man's ear, but by this time Baumann was no longer listening. In truth, he hadn't done so since his sense of superiority had boiled over.

'So what?' he said eventually, switching a narrowed gaze between the two detectives. 'So I am a member of the Tier One club. Big deal. It's hardly crime of the century. I had forgotten all about joining. It was such a long time ago, and to be honest with you I've had more important matters on my mind since.'

'Ah, so you were a member in name only?' Laney suggested. 'Something to mention in quiet corridors – if you happen to remember you're a member, that is.'

'Quite so. It seems to me you're making a fuss over nothing.'

'So you never took up your membership? Never paid the club a visit?'

'Not that I can recall.' He gave a smug glance in the direction of his solicitor.

'That is interesting. Do you have a recognised medical condition relating to your memory, Mr Baumann.

'Don't answer that!' St John cried.

'I beg your pardon?' Baumann regarded Laney as if she were a specimen far beneath his own exalted level of the stratosphere. 'How dare you disrespect me that way?'

'I apologise for my colleague's comment,' Chase said, quickly jumping in to deflect the man's attention. 'Only, I do understand the point she makes with that question. DC Laney must be as bemused as I am at how you seemingly can't recall visiting the Tier One club at The Grange on any of the dozen times in August. Nor the ten in July, it seems, or another ten visits in June. I could go back further, but I think you get our drift…'

'How can you possibly know any of that? All historical records are digitally stored. All of that data was… unintentionally erased. You cannot have evidence of what you are suggesting.'

'Oh, we can. And we're not suggesting. Do I really have to pull out another piece of paper? You see, Mr Baumann, when you erased the data on the servers and from those backup disks and even the tapes, you either forgot about or you may have even been unaware of a further precautionary process carried out by your own company. Either way, you clearly did not take into account the fact that for archiving purposes, once a year those tapes are stored in a secure, fireproof safe and replaced by a fresh batch. In fact, this was done three weeks prior to the erasure of the data on Saturday night. Those tapes were removed from the safe and their data restored yesterday, all of which provided us with some extremely interesting intelligence.'

The film of moisture had become a full flop sweat. Otto Baumann stared at them in a way that told Chase the man knew he had been outwitted and all that remained for him was damage limitation.

'What do you want?' Baumann asked. 'And what will you do for me if I give it to you?'

THIRTY-THREE

SUPERINTENDENT WADDINGTON'S IRE REVEALED itself in the pinched contours of his face, the cheeks of which burned red. He was not alone, with Detective Chief Superintendent Crawley cutting an equally enraged figure beside him. The bollocking – mostly aimed at Chase, but with a little reserved for Laney in blindly following her DS – went on for close to twenty minutes. According to both men, Chase's reckless behaviour and actions were provocative, idiotic, and borderline insubordinate in respect of him not running the arrest by his SIO beforehand.

When they had blown themselves out like a passing storm, Chase took a breath and said simply, 'I take it there's no gold star award for us getting the man to cough?'

'You are on the thinnest ice, DS Chase,' Crawley said sharply. 'I am not your enemy, and it was my impression I had earned your respect over the years.'

'If it's any consolation, sir,' Laney interjected, 'I've not known you long and I already hold you in great esteem.'

'You think this is funny, Constable? I amuse you, somehow?'

Laney's mouth opened wide. 'Wow!' she said. 'I thought you were going to do that entire Joe Pesci scene from *Goodfellas*. "I'm funny how, I mean funny like I'm a clown? I amuse you?"'

'That's enough, Constable Laney!'

'Is it, sir? If you ask me, this entire thing is a joke. DS Chase and I worked this case against all odds. My Sergeant here is a complete brainiac, and he is one resolute and determined bugger, too. You have no idea what he's had to wade through to come this far in a case nobody wanted solving. Not successfully, anyhow. But now we have a major player coughing like he has a forty a day habit, throwing out quality leads left, right, and centre, and all you two want to do is whinge and whine and tell us both how awful we are.'

Waddington shot to his feet. He stuck out an arm and pointed towards the meeting room door. 'You are dismissed, Constable Laney. If you are unable to conduct yourself in the proper manner, you will be debriefed on your own when we are through with DS Chase.'

Laney stood. She said nothing, but took time to glare at both senior officers before striding off in the direction of Waddington's extended finger. Chase followed her with his eyes, before also rising and starting to follow her with his feet.

'Where do you think you are off to, Sergeant Chase?' Crawley demanded to know.

'I'm aligning myself with my colleague, sir. No offence intended, but I agree with her. This is all a bit of a joke when you stop to think about it. You both appear to be more galvanised by what we did wrong than what we got right. And what we got right is massive by comparison. It may blow this entire investigation apart at the seams and leave us in a far healthier position. But I'm starting to wonder which of us here are actually looking to resolve this one and which would rather hoover it up and toss the dust bag in the river Ray.'

'And what exactly do you mean by that?' Crawley asked. 'Is that an accusation, Sergeant Chase?'

'No, sir. It's a postulation. I'm wondering aloud, because it seems to me that we are not all on the same side here.'

'You had better explain yourself. And I mean right now, this very second.'

Chase nodded. 'I'm willing to do so, sir. But not unless I have my partner here alongside me. Everything I have to say involves DC Laney, too. She deserves to be here for this.'

'That sounds like an ultimatum,' Waddington said. He lowered his hand but remained standing.

'I suppose it is in some ways. But if we don't all thrash this out together here and now, the next time you speak with me, I will have my union rep alongside me. Maybe even a solicitor.'

'This display of outrageous arrogance may be the last act of what has been a chequered career, DS Chase.'

'If that's the case, then I find myself strangely okay with that, sir. But I don't think that's the way this is going to go. We have matters to discuss, and you're going to want to hear them off the record at first. Believe that if you believe nothing else.'

With great reluctance and resentment still permeating the air, those who had stood retook their seats. Chase caught a nod of thanks from Laney for his support, but he dismissed it with a shake of his head. They were a team on this, but he wondered which of the two on the opposite side of the table was playing for the other side.

'Let me be clear about what it is I'm saying,' he began cautiously. 'Earlier today, a businessman by the name of Otto Baumann was arrested for the deliberate erasure of computer data belonging to the Tier One club run by Sir Colin Shakespeare and Sir Kenneth Webster. Baumann subsequently confessed to his part in the sordid goings on taking place inside a property known as The Grange. This is the location of the Tier One club, co-founded by our two Knights. He went on to provide further information in connection to the club, its purpose, and its members.'

'This information has been verified from a separate source?' Crawley asked.

'Not yet, sir. I'm confident it will be as soon as we break other members. Baumann was the first, but he won't be the last.'

'And…?'

'I'll be blunt: Tier One is nothing more than a permanent home for a paedophile ring. It has a certain exclusivity, though on one day every month its members are entitled to invite guest visitors. Members are allowed to bring their own… minors, if they so wish. However, Tier One provides a number of young people of all ages should members and guests choose to make use of them. In terms of our investigation, Mr Baumann confirmed in a written statement that last Tuesday night, Sir Kenneth selected a young girl who we believe is our unidentified victim of the RTC. Against advice, he not only decided to drive himself home, but also took the girl with him. Though frowned upon, it was apparently not unusual for Sir Kenneth to do this. But as it was his club, nobody argued.'

'And Shakespeare?' Waddington asked, his eyes wider still, all anger having evaporated.

'Sir Colin is, of course, implicated. As are dozens of men from a broad spectrum of our everyday lives. People we have heard of, people we have looked up to, people we may even have met. We are in possession of the membership list, and I should say at this point that there are no serving police officers from this area among them.'

To say both senior men looked relieved would have been an understatement. The news they were coming to terms with was bad enough, without having to clean their own houses as part of the resulting investigative manoeuvres. Waddington was the first to state the obvious. 'Your deliberate phrasing suggests there are from other areas.'

Chase gave a grim nod. 'Unfortunately, yes. Sir Kenneth is also not the only ex-police officer. There are two more, both of whom retired at the rank of DCI. We have one from Cleveland, and one from Bedfordshire. As for serving officers, we have a DCS from the Met, a DS in Berkshire, and two inspectors working in Derbyshire.'

'Corroboration?' Chief Superintendent Crawley asked again.

'Not yet, sir,' Chase admitted. 'But then, as I mentioned before, Otto Baumann is the only person we've brought in so far. I'm here to request authorisation to arrest a number of other men.' He explained about the A-to-D lists, asking for the remaining nineteen members on the first to be scooped up in a coordinated sweep.

'I take it Sir Colin Shakespeare is on your list?' Waddington said.

Chase nodded. 'He is, sir. But as you'll see from the names I'm about to provide you with, he's by no means the most important or influential figure.'

Waddington let out a groan of dismay and put his head in his hands. Chase understood the man's anguish. When you were shooting for Chief Constable, a case like this was likely to shape your destiny.

'Not every single one of these men will fold the way Baumann did. Many will fight us every step of the way. That said, I'm confident we will turn at least one – probably more – to obtain that corroboration the DCS mentioned. However, I feel I should remind you that this is a completely different case to the one I began investigating a week ago. My focus, as it was then, is to identify our unknown victim. Baumann told us the minors arrive at The Grange at pretty much the same time, which suggests the use of a coach or mini-buses. I don't for one moment believe these people are naïve enough to hire the vehicles, but I will have relevant companies spoken to in order to tick the right boxes.'

'Are you any closer to identifying this poor girl?' Crawley asked.

'No, sir,' Laney told him. 'The curious thing is, we had our investigation, which subsequently led us to a case from twenty years ago. We appear to have solved one we had no idea was even there to solve, but without putting a dent in the other. We know she was brought to Tier One. We know she was chosen by Sir Kenneth. We know he took her from the club, presumably intending to take her to his home for the night. And we know what happened to her as a direct consequence of all that. As to who she is, where she came from, or where she's been… we're no closer to knowing that than we were when we set out.'

'Will greater resources make a difference, Royston?' The DCS asked, turning to Chase. 'A larger team, perhaps? We could bring you back here to Gablecross for the duration. I know when I suggested it before, I'd intended you and Laney to remain in Little Soley. But that won't be the case this time. If the investigation comes here, then so do you two. And you continue to manage it.'

Chase took a breath, pausing to consider the offer. 'There may be an appropriate time to do that, sir. But as much as DC Laney and I have our hooks into it, we're finding it increasingly difficult to even know where to start. That said, I have a feeling we'll catch a break during further interviews with Tier One staff and members. After all, those minors had to come from somewhere. If we can identify who brought them there and from where, perhaps even speak to some of the older ones ourselves, I should think one or more of them will be able to tell us what we want to know.'

Nodding, Crawley said, 'Very well. As far as any earlier outbursts and disagreements are concerned, I suggest we put our differences aside and move forward with a common objective. There is some truth in your earlier argument, DS Chase, but given we now have the full picture, I'm sure Superintendent Waddington and I are both equally keen to put an end to these sordid practices. The odd embarrassment at perhaps knowing one or more of these men is trivial by comparison.'

'I agree,' Waddington said, nodding with purpose. 'Tell us what you need, Royston.'

'The coordination of nineteen arrests to begin with,' Chase said, allowing the merest glimmer of a smile to touch his lips. He felt disappointed at being no closer to naming their dead girl, yet he was proud of the work he and Laney had done. Their success had been hard-earned. Then his thoughts turned darker, the leering features of Maurice filling his mind's eye. He debated for a moment mentioning the spook to his bosses, but could not see what it would achieve. It was one for him to consider, and it made him wonder what the man's reaction would be when he learned of Otto Baumann's arrest.

THIRTY-FOUR

FOR THE NEXT FEW hours, Chase and Laney worked together with Superintendent Waddington and a DI familiar with the process of coordinating arrests across different police authorities. In this case, they had nineteen men spread over five counties. The moment all the documentation was in place, Superintendent Crawley gave the green light. Each of them accepted this initial operation was unlikely to net all of their suspects at precisely the same time, but the officers dispatched to each address would continue trying until they had their target in cuffs.

With one exception.

As soon as word came in that Sir Colin Shakespeare had not been at any of the three addresses police visited, Chase requested they stand down until further notice. He asked for permission to call the man directly, and Waddington gave him the nod. Their suspect did not pick up, but Chase left a precisely worded message on his voicemail.

'Sir Colin, this is Detective Sergeant Chase, Wiltshire police. Officers are at this moment in the process of arresting Tier One club members and searching their homes, including any computer devices and phones. Your name is on that list, and although your addresses will be searched, I've decided to offer you a break you almost certainly don't deserve. You can call me back on this number immediately, or news of your arrest warrant will be released to the media. I know how men like you enjoy being in control. Calling me is the only way you get to have a say in how matters proceed from this point. I advise you to take this opportunity. If not, I can assure you it will turn ugly.'

Chase and his partner were on their own in the incident room Waddington had commandeered, when Shakespeare called back eleven minutes later. 'Where are you?' Chase asked without preamble. 'I'll come to you and we can do this quietly, with the minimum of fuss.'

'I don't think that's going to happen, Sergeant. I'm a little over an hour out of Miami, which means I'm about three hours out of Turks and Caicos.'

Chase bit down on his lip. The man had chosen to run rather than fight to clear his name. He took a beat before responding. 'Isn't Turks and Caicos still British territory?'

'Yes, I believe it is.'

'And don't we have an extradition treaty with the islands?'

'Quite possibly.'

'Why there, then, given we can come for you or have you arrested and extradited back to the UK?'

'I'm not on the run, Sergeant Chase. I realise I'm making it more difficult for you to interview me, but it's a beautiful part of the world in which to lie low and wait for the hysteria to die down.'

'I can have the local police pick you up the moment you arrive.'

'You could, yes. But they won't hold me in jail. At worst, I'll be bailed and have to hand over my passport. Either way, there's a beach and a stiff drink in my near future, Sergeant. Not a cell with bread and water. Sorry if that's not what you wanted to hear.'

Chase thought of the children losing their innocence to men like this one, and he felt the anger push through like fire in his bloodstream. 'What I'd like to hear, Sir Colin, is the truth. Tell me, is there any part of you capable of offering that? After all, your partner in crime is dead, so he's of no use to our inquiry. You still could be.

Your help may be invaluable, and I'm sure the new Chief Constable will be more than happy to work out a great deal for you if you are.'

'I appreciate the offer, Sergeant. But it sounds to me as if you have matters in hand. I'm not sure how much genuine help I can be.'

'Let me worry about that,' Chase said. 'And we're not going to play any games of accusation and denial. We're both adults. We both know what went on at The Grange and, I have to assume, other Tier One locations around the country. But let's focus on The Grange for the time being. Sir, I am offering you this one time only proposition. You can cooperate by explaining precisely how the operation at The Grange works, or you can opt not to, at which point you become just another suspect whose name we will drag through the mud. Only, I'll ensure yours is dragged deeper, through the worst of it. I'll hang you out to dry afterwards, and will enjoy every moment of it. It'll be a modern-day version of putting you in stocks on the village green.'

There was a long enough pause that Chase was concerned the call had been disconnected. But eventually Shakespeare replied. 'You make a compelling argument, Sergeant. Be more surgical with your questions and I might have some answers for you.'

Relief flooding his veins, Chase took a seat and put the sound through the speaker. 'We have DC Laney on the line with us,' he said. He followed up by cautioning the man, as he was also recording their conversation. 'Let me begin by telling you what we know. Tier One is a paedophile ring for the elite. Underage children are transported to The Grange, allowing the wealthy and influential to indulge their sickness beneath an umbrella of security and comfort.'

'If you know so much, DS Chase, why do you need my help at all?'

'So you admit to what I have alleged?'

'I admit to being aware of it. In point of fact, I had arranged to speak with Ken Webster about this very matter to express both my concern and displeasure. I strenuously deny taking part in these sordid practices, and fully condemn my friend's role in them.'

Chase glanced at Laney, who was shaking her head, lips curled into a snarl. 'You're throwing Sir Kenneth to the wolves, then, are you?'

'Not at all. I'm merely helping the police with their inquiries, like any good citizen. I am both hurt and embarrassed by these terrible actions. Actions I was wholly unaware of until very recently.'

'You're saying the paedophile ring was Sir Kenneth's idea? That he planned it all and set it up to operate out of The Grange, using the Tier One club as a base for like-minded men and women to rape and abuse children?'

'Sadly, that is the conclusion I have reached, yes.'

'You do realise we'll be interviewing every member of staff and every single Tier One member, Sir Colin? Their recollections will, I'm certain, differ from your own.'

'That may be true, but that's what the legal process is for. Let's see what charges you have against me once the dust has settled. You never know, it could be that the staff and members are more interested in their own fate than discussing mine.'

'Have you threatened them?' Chase asked, feeling repulsed at having to deal with this man in such an amiable manner. 'Is that why you sound so relaxed? Do they know going in what fate awaits them if they spill their guts about you and, previously, Sir Kenneth?'

'If I sound relaxed, Sergeant Chase, it's because I am an innocent man.'

'And yet you've admitted knowing what goes on inside Tier One.'

'Indeed. And was on the point of remedying it when my friend was killed.'

'So you say.'

'Yes. So I say.'

'In that case, tell me one more thing. Answer me this and I'll leave you be until such time as we're ready to come for you.'

'If I can, I will. Of course.'

'Where did the girls come from? From where are they transported at the beginning of the evening, and to where are they taken when you sick perverts are done with them?'

'Please don't include me in your sweeping generalisations, Sergeant. But, as it turns out, I can provide you with no answers. I was privy to few details. As you might imagine, I would rather not hear about such matters in all their ugliness. I'm afraid I can be of no help to you regards the movement of these young people.'

'Children,' Chase snapped. 'Let's call them what they are.'

'If you insist. Look, if I were to hazard a guess, I'd say Ken used his inner circle of friends to supply him with children as and when required. I'm guessing he had either a financial or reciprocal arrangement with them. I imagine he had them collected from their homes and dropped back off again afterwards.'

Chase shuddered at the notion, but was losing patience. 'That all sounds perfectly reasonable. And considering the source, it also sounds like bullshit!'

Shakespeare responded calmly, his manner angering Chase all the more. 'Please, I really must prepare for landing. Let me leave you in no doubt as to my involvement: I had none. The terrible nature of these events came to my attention only recently, and I was in the process of putting an end to them.'

'Is that documented anywhere? Did you inform anyone of your intentions?'

'No, and no.'

'In that case, I don't believe you, Sir Colin. Not a single word of it.'

'Be that as it may, I've given you my verbal statement quite freely. Anything more and you will need to talk to me with my solicitor present. I may make a statement to the media when the story breaks more fully, but it will not deviate from the one I have provided you with. I think that's our business concluded.'

'Other than one final question I am duty bound to ask. Why did you tell me none of this when we spoke the other day?'

'Let's call it grief, or the confusion that so often comes with it, shall we? My friend had just been killed, I was on my way to comfort his widow, who is also a close friend. I was not in the right frame of mind, Sergeant.'

'Speaking of Lady Jane… did she know, Sir Colin? Was she aware of her husband's abhorrent tastes?'

'You will have to ask her that yourself.'

'I'm asking you.'

'Then, in all honesty, I don't have a clue what she knew or did not know. We didn't speak of it, so how could I?'

'How indeed.' Chase felt his fists clench and his jaw firming. 'You have an answer – or no answer – to everything, it seems.'

'That's often the way with innocent men, Sergeant. Goodbye.'

Chase called out the man's name, but the line was dead.

THIRTY-FIVE

SATISFIED WITH THEIR EFFORTS throughout the day, Chase checked his watch and realised there was nothing left to be accomplished that evening. Content that he and his DC would feature in the interview stages at some point the following morning, he said goodnight to Laney and pulled out of the Gablecross car park shortly before 8.30pm. He paused at the junction, worrying at something lingering towards the back of his mind. Instead of turning left to make the short drive home, Chase hung a right, opting to pay a second visit to The Grange. His unsatisfactory conversation with Shakespeare gnawed at him. He decided to have a second chat with the Tier One manager, in the hope of learning more about how the underage children came and went.

This particular aspect had wormed its way beneath his skin. During his career he had brushed up against child abuse and paedophilia, and in the wake of Operation Yewtree the existence of a ring comprising the rich and powerful came as no real shock. His thoughts kept returning to the children themselves, and the possibility of them being bussed in and out of The Grange took hold of him deep inside his gut. He could not shake the thought of those poor little mites stepping onto the vehicle knowing what awaited them at the end of their journey. He felt coiled and clenched, desperate to discover the whereabouts of the victims.

At Tier One he ran up against a brick wall – or rather, the unmoving solid metal gate. He tried the intercom, brandishing his warrant card at the security camera mounted high above the supporting pillar. Keeping a finger pressed on the intercom button, he made it abundantly clear that if Marcus Thresher avoided speaking to him, he would regret that decision. Chase received no reply despite returning to the gate on two further occasions, the barrier remaining stubbornly in place. He sat in the car for a while, allowing his frustration to bubble under. No cars entered or exited the property to provide him with an opportunity to sneak his way onto the grounds as he had done previously.

Somewhere around 10.00pm he accepted defeat and pulled away. On reaching Calne, Chase initially indicated to make a left turn towards Wootton Bassett, looking to find his way onto the M4 for a short hop eastbound. But a flash of pure instinct prompted him to head on through the town and out the other side, taking the route home that Sir Kenneth would have followed the previous week. As he encountered the Devizes roundabout, he wondered more about where Ken Webster had been taking Mandy Radcliffe's daughter that night.

Had the man known Mandy Radcliffe herself? Known her in ways a grown man should never know a child? And if so, when he selected the unidentified girl who would later that same night become the victim of a terrible road collision, had he known she was Mandy's own child? Could that have been his sole reason for choosing her that night to endure his special kind of attention? Chase felt disgusted with himself for even imagining such a wicked scenario, but the terrible image refused to withdraw.

The inspirational notion that came to him as he'd approached Calne, had developed out of speculation concerning what became of the children after the Tier One club members were done with them for the night. According to Baumann's statement, they either arrived together or in large batches at around the same time, so presumably they usually left the same way. In which case, if Ken Webster had been bringing the girl to his home, he also had to know precisely where to bring the child when he had finished abusing her. And the closer Chase came to reaching the outskirts of the Webster estate, the more he thought he knew where that might be.

Dusk had long become nightfall by the time Chase found himself parked up at the entrance he and Laney had discovered the previous week. He mulled over what he was about to do, knowing he should call for assistance – even if it was only the presence of a heavily caffeinated Claire Laney. But although his imagination had been sparked by the earlier flow of inspired thinking, he accepted there was as much chance of him being wrong about his new theory as there was him being right. Going it alone until he uncovered verifiable proof felt like the correct decision.

From his bag in the boot of the Volvo he took out a torch and his walking boots. He exchanged his shoes for them and with one final furtive glance around, climbed the gate and jumped down into the field on the other side. It didn't take long for his calf muscles to remind him of the incline, and once again as he reached the plateau he began to crouch-walk his way forward until he could see over the brow and down into the gulley below.

As anticipated, his surroundings looked completely different at night. Out here in the rural areas, with no city lights to add colour to the sky, darkness was complete enough for it to feel physical. As if it could be grasped by hesitant fingers if you reached out far enough. Chase thought he had to be in approximately the same position in which he'd stood the other day. He strained his eyes to get a better lie of the land, but the darkness was all-consuming.

This time there was nobody around to blow the horn, summoning him back to the vehicle. This time he gathered his courage and picked his way slowly down the hill, not daring to switch on his torch at this early stage. Without any illumination to guide him, Chase focussed on the ground immediately ahead of each step he took as he continued to follow the dusty trail.

After inching his way forward for the better part of ten minutes, he eventually made out the vague outlines of the diggers and bulldozers that he had noticed during his first visit. They stood silently, static like fossilised, hulking creatures. He realised he was close to the trenches he'd seen being dug out, and stuck closer to the track to avoid blundering into one of them. But as the trail petered out and became nothing more than tyre tracks setting off in two different directions, Chase realised he had reached the initial thin layer of trees.

He did a complete 360 degree turn before continuing on.

The night air felt distinctly cooler beneath the canopy of leaves, which although not dense further diffused what little light he'd enjoyed prior to entering the fringes of the copse. Tentatively he pushed branches aside, taking care not to let them whip back as he made his way through the trees. Moving seamlessly into heavier woodland, he felt a trickle of fear slide between his shoulder blades. Chase shuddered once, but quickly pushed it aside. He could not identify the driving force that encouraged every step, only that whatever it was had subsequently consumed him.

Wait!

Stop!

He sensed something amiss more than saw it. Precisely what he had become peripherally aware of, he had no idea, but some detail on the landscape ahead of him had altered. He dipped lower onto his haunches, breathing steadily as he surveyed the wooded terrain; straining to see and hear more clearly. As he was about to move on again, Chase finally realised what he was looking at.

The wall of trees had vanished before his eyes. In its place stood nebulous grey shapes, which eventually became solid objects; structures built upon a clearing carved out of the woodland. The sight of them confirmed his earlier fears, when his thoughts had drifted to the groundwork being done on the land, and he'd asked himself a question: if they're building something in that location, had they previously done so close by? Somewhere sheltered. Hidden away.

As he shuffled forward, he finally made out the sturdy-looking profiles to be huts or cabins of some description. In one of them, the corner of what was most likely a blackout curtain up at one of the windows, had been pulled back to reveal a triangular sliver of light coming from inside. Moments later, as his vision became attuned to it, the light was extinguished. Chase waited, holding his breath as he concentrated.

Five seconds.

Ten.

Fifteen…

There it was again.

The same illuminated wedge. Only this time a face peered out, a person's head almost obscuring the glow, creating a halo effect around it.

Chase froze, managing to catch the resulting gasp in his throat moments before it emerged. His heart began to hammer stronger and harder than before, an electric pulse thrumming in both temples.

The light snapped off again.

He waited to see if anybody came dashing out, but when both silence and darkness continued to reign, he crept closer still, pleased to find the ground finally levelling out. Blood rushed inside his ears and the night was anything but silent. For one moment of stark panic, he imagined the roaring gush inside his head could be heard for miles around. Chase gathered his wits and braced himself; having come this far, he was determined to go all the way. At the back of his mind he realised the huts might be housing the men and women he'd seen operating the heavy machinery and working the soil.

And yet he did not believe it.

Eventually he reached the closest of the cabins, laying a hand against it and testing its texture with his fingertips. The timber was planed smooth. He crept along its exterior, listening intently, eyes blinking every few seconds in an effort to improve his vision. He came upon two windows, but was unable to see any chink of light between them through which to view whatever was taking place inside. He moved on with all the stealth he could muster, locating a door four paces later. It was solid wood with a perfect fit all round, and as with the windows it gave up none of its secrets.

The next building was no more than a dozen paces away, so Chase scuttled between the two. He leaned against a wall, panting heavily. Adrenaline provided a fine buzz, but it also kept him alert. If only he could hear beyond that blasted thunder of rushing blood. As he reached the first window of the second building, he noticed a small fissure between the curtains. This had to be the one through which the face had appeared, and in replacing the corner flap they had not fully overlapped.

Moistening lips that felt impossibly dry, all at once Chase did not want to look inside. He feared what his sneak peek might reveal. Feared seeing working men, laughing and joking while they drank, played cards or watched TV. But most of all he feared he might lay eyes on all he had imagined he would find here, and the very thought devastated him beyond belief. Despite these misgivings, he inched closer, lowering himself down to squint through the crack of light.

Chase snapped his eyes closed again. He felt sick to his stomach and instantly light-headed. He thought he might actually vomit at his feet, but instead he forced himself upright and took several deep breaths. What he had seen inside the building had come as no shock, but he was nonetheless horrified by it. As he began to work his way towards the door, fully intending to gain entry by force if necessary, the whooshing sound inside his head increased.

At the same time he sensed movement from behind, felt the air shift as a result of someone or something approaching at speed. Chase reacted in an instant, turning swiftly. But as his head came around, a blow struck the back of it. He teetered, head spinning, dots like a cloud of midges tumbling before his eyes. He lurched sideways, stumbled against the building, vision blurring as his head lolled like a toddler's. Before he could cry out in alarm, a second blow seemed to cut him down at the knees, sending him crashing to the ground.

For a moment, Chase felt as if he were swimming in a pool of darkness. Seconds later he realised he was drowning in its bleak embrace.

THIRTY-SIX

When Chase finally regained consciousness, he found himself bound by the chest and ankles to a wooden chair in the centre of an empty room, and being loomed over by Miles Radford, the Webster estate manager. Sir Colin Shakespeare's close protection operative, Lawrence Reid, cast a long shadow beside him. The latter stood with both hands clenched by his sides, while the former cradled an unhinged shotgun broken over the crook of his arm.

'Sorry about the bump on the old noggin,' Radford said, looking anything but apologetic. 'Though in all fairness, you *were* trespassing. Tell me, Sergeant Chase, why were you lurking about outside?'

Chase raised a hand and reached around to probe the back of his head. His fingers came away bloody, though whatever had been spilled by the blows he'd received appeared to be congealing in his hair. He looked up at Radford, wincing in response to a stab of pain from one of his wounds. He wriggled once, testing the strength of the heavy nylon cord bonds.

'Do you have any idea how much trouble you are in?' he said. 'Wounding, causing GBH with intent… easy to prove and easy to prosecute in this case. You could do ten, maybe even fifteen years for attacking me.'

'Really?' Radford frowned. 'Good luck proving which of us attacked you. In fact, good luck proving either of us did. Our version of events is that we stumbled upon you already lying on the ground, completely unconscious.'

'And tying me to this chair afterwards? How will you explain that?'

'Good point. We stumbled upon you in this condition, already tied to the chair.'

'But then not letting me go…?'

'Don't dick around,' Reid snapped. He flexed his hands before making tighter fists of them. 'We know why you're here. We know what you saw. But understand this, Sergeant Chase, by the time anybody else thinks to search this place – if they ever do – those women and children will be long gone, and there won't be a single sign that they ever existed.'

'If you think that, then you're a bigger moron than I had you down as,' Chase sneered at him. 'Our forensic teams need only the smallest trace, and believe me they'll find it.'

Radford sniggered. 'That will be a good trick. Because by then, not only will the women and children have been relocated, but the buildings themselves will be no more; razed to the ground and then burned, after which this entire section of land is going to be ploughed and whatever fine ashes remain will later be buried beneath mounds of earth and completely turfed over. New saplings will stand in their place. It'll be as if none of this ever existed.'

Chase felt hope sink like a lead weight, but his mind reached out to all that he had seen through that minute gap between the curtains. Two women, a dozen or more children of both sexes, ages ranging from toddlers to young adults. They did not appear to be undernourished or physically injured, but each pitiful face appeared pale and despondent, eyes sunken and lacking the lustre of life.

'Do what you like,' he said. 'I'd back my people against yours any day of the week. And we'll find them. We'll find every one of those women and children. Either way, you lot are done. With the number of arrests we made today, nobody connected to this repulsive undertaking is going to walk away from it.'

'You seem fairly confident about that.'

'More confident than you, that's for sure.' Chase turned to look at Radford. 'Are you one of them? My gut tells me Mr Reid here simply follows orders, but you... I reckon you're a nonce just like your boss was.'

'Fuck you!' Radford snarled. 'Like I give a damn what you think.'

'No, I don't think it, Miles. I can smell it on you. You're not here to defend your boss's reputation, nor to clean house on behalf of his equally nauseating wife. This is as much about you as it is them. You have their same sick and twisted desires, don't you? You enjoy sexually abusing children. You disgust me.'

Chase saw no remorse in his captor's eyes, but had noticed Reid frowning, a small tic pulsing beneath his left eye. He jerked his head up and said to him, 'How can you stand to be in the same room as this perverted freak? How can you breathe the same air, which his foul presence makes toxic?'

Reid ignored him, but squinted at Radford. 'How much of what he says is true, Miles?'

'What? None of it. Don't listen to him. He's stalling for time, trying to turn you against me.'

'So you're simply doing your job? Like me?'

'Yes.'

Reid continued staring at the man for a full ten seconds, before switching his attention back to Chase. 'How close are your people to obtaining confessions?' he asked.

'I won't discuss my investigation with the likes of you.'

The close protection man took a step forward and delivered a solid punch to Chase's midriff. He coughed up a lungful of air before collapsing in on himself, curled forward and knees raised as much as his bindings would allow. For a moment he thought he might vomit, but each deep breath pulled him back from the brink.

'How close?' Reid asked again.

'Why don't you call your boss and ask him?' Chase managed to spit out. 'I notice he left you to clean up his mess while he basks in the Caribbean sunshine.'

'I'm asking you, Sergeant. And I'm only going to do so one more time.'

Chase made no reply. He'd expected at least one more punch, perhaps even a succession of heavy blows, but this time Reid merely looked over at Radford and shook his head. 'Let's not waste any more time. Get rid of him and then we can get to work.'

Radford snapped the shotgun closed and raised it to his shoulder, staring down the long barrel. From Chase's position, it looked the size of a Transit van's exhaust. He accepted his fate and closed his eyes, but when the shot came, it was muffled. And as its echo faded away, he realised he was still breathing and very much alive.

THIRTY-SEVEN

In no situation Chase could ever have imagined would he have opened his eyes to see the spook, Maurice, standing there in the room as his saviour. But there by the open door was the man himself, his muzzled pistol aimed centre mass at Reid. Radford lay writhing on the floor, gasping for breath, blood bubbling from his lips as he moaned in pain. The shotgun lay out of reach.

'He'll be fine provided we get an ambulance out here soon,' Maurice said in a completely unruffled tone. 'But before I so much as consider making that call, he's going to have to help me understand more about what goes on around here.' He made circles with the gun, which was still pointing at Reid. 'You… do I need to put one in you as well?'

Hands in the air, Reid stood quite still as he slowly shook his head. 'No. I am unarmed. Whoever you are, I am no threat to you.'

A smile flickered on Maurice's lips. 'Oh, I suspect you don't genuinely believe that. I imagine a man with your training and skillset considers himself perfectly able to get the jump on someone like me. But you should know, Mr Reid, your instincts are wrong on this occasion. Listen instead to your own words, be guided by them. You are no threat to me, whereas you, my friend, are in grave danger. So, what we're going to do is this: you are going to free Detective Sergeant Chase, after which you will replace him in that chair and he will bind your hands and feet to it. Don't worry, he's a complete novice at this sort of thing, so I'll be checking his handiwork when he's done. Once I'm satisfied that you are fully neutralised, you can observe while Mr Radford and I have a bit of a chat.'

To Chase's amazement, the following couple of minutes went exactly as Maurice had implied. To his even greater astonishment, he found himself going along with it despite the illegality taking place.

'Keep an eye on this one,' Maurice told Chase, nodding at the man sitting in the chair. He then crouched down by the side of the wounded Miles Radford. After a few seconds of close examination, he reached over to slap the man's face on both cheeks. 'Come on, now. Stay awake. You really don't want to miss all the excitement.'

Through his searing pain and flowing tears, Radford growled at Maurice and told him in no uncertain terms where he could shove his gun.

'Tut-tut. Mr Radford, I should inform you that a gut shot like that starts off as painful, develops into utmost agony, after which you'll be suffering so much you will start hallucinating. But prior to that you will be conscious, intimately aware of everything that goes on. I dare say your wound is starting to feel as if it is on fire. As a mild taster, let's see how much worse it is if I jab my gun into it.'

The wild howl of a man experiencing excruciating torment was terrible to hear. Chase had to turn his head away in order not to see the man's agony emblazoned upon his face. He met Lawrence Reid's fearful gaze and realized the domino effect this first act of torture was having. By poking around inside the gunshot injury, Maurice had made it clear to everybody in the room that there were no longer any rules in play.

'Make me understand, Miles,' Maurice continued. 'Prior to my arriving here, I'd been made aware that The Grange provided a nest for creatures too uncivilized and savage to be truly regarded as fellow human beings. Hence the reason why I have no qualms about what I am doing and am prepared to do to you here tonight. I understood that underage boys and girls were brought to the Tier

One club, where they would endure a living nightmare at the hands of monsters. Having seen this… compound, I understand where they come from and where they go to again afterwards. But who are they, Miles? How do they all come to be here?'

'Go… fuck… yourself…' was the estate manager's exhausted reply.

In response to which, Maurice dug the pistol into the man's open wound a second time. On this occasion, however, he exerted greater pressure and twisted the weapon at the same time. Radford shrieked like an animal, screaming and jerking around on the floor as if he had bitten into a live electrical cable.

'I can keep this up for hours,' Maurice said. 'Can you?'

As Radford settled down, his cries fading until all that remained was a prolonged whimper, Chase looked on, knowing he ought to intervene. Each of them there had a specific role to play, a job to do. He wasn't doing his, though. Not even close. He was both fascinated and appalled by the comfort and ease with which Maurice went about his work. Torture was not something Chase had ever given a great deal of consideration to, but whenever he had, it seemed to him that it was inhumane. Seeing it up close and personal for himself, he was more convinced than ever that he was right. And yet…

'What you see here is the reward for decades of hard work,' Radford said between gasps of breath and bodily tremors as pain continued to flow throughout his system. 'It began purely by accident when… when one of the members got a girl pregnant. Prior to that, the small membership ma… managed to slake their thirsts by taking advantage of orphanages, church groups, children's homes, and… the like. It was risky and there were never enough kids to… to go… round. But Ken had the idea of keeping hold of this pregnant girl, making it appear as if… she had run away, allowing her to be declared miss… missing, but all the while keeping her locked out of sight. It seemed like a… natural evolution of the idea to then make the child she gave birth to available to members whose tastes included the very young.'

Maurice swallowed thickly. 'And having seen this opportunity open up, you people decided to make it work for yourselves on a much grander scale. Does that about cover it?'

Radford nodded, his eyes already ringed and sunken as the constant pain did its work. Tears continued to spill from them, though Chase imagined they were for himself, rather than the poor kids whose lives had been so brutally ripped apart.

'Over a period of time more children were… were taken. The older boys were forced to impregnate the older girls, which was pref… erable to the members risking their own DNA. Some chose to take that risk anyway, eventually getting the… opportunity to enjoy their own children. That really seemed to up the stakes for those men.'

'Jesus,' Maurice whispered, appearing to wince as if in physical pain. 'I've never heard of anything so repulsive in my entire life.'

'Perhaps so, but if you've seen the full list of members, then you'll know how many of us there are.'

'Did you ever do that?' Maurice demanded to know. 'Did you get a child pregnant and end up satisfying your demented urges with one of your own children?'

By this time the man on the floor had curled up into the foetal position, hands clutching his stomach. He managed to shake his head, drool sliding from the corner of his mouth. 'No. I never took the risk of having my… DNA out there. But some of those kids in those cabins… you're going to find some unbelievable familial connections.'

'You basically set up a production line,' Chase said, choking out the words. 'Made it so that you'd never again need to risk taking another kid from the outside. Twins or triplets must have been a time of genuine celebration for you all.'

'It filled a need and… it solved a problem. We thought of it as our own form of human farming. What began as a few seeds became… a glorious crop.'

Maurice slowly shook his head. 'You have no misgivings whatsoever, do you? Not a single pang of regret? Nor a scrap of remorse.

I bet you're one of those sick bastards who doesn't believe there's anything wrong with your perverted tastes.'

'You mean like homo... sexuality was once regarded?' Even through his agony, Radford managed to scoff. 'This is the new progressive society. In time, how we choose to live our lives will be every bit as commonplace. I foresee a day not too far in the future in which a man... will marry the child he fathered. You two can't see it because your minds are guarded and stale. But I can. And so can others like me.'

'Leaving your delusions to one side, you sadistic prick, I can see how you've created your own conveyor belt of children to molest and abuse. Why risk obtaining children from the outside world when you can create your own supply chain, eh? It's all provided for your members up there at The Grange. Just one thing... who takes care of these kids when they're here?'

Radford actually had the gall to smirk. Even Chase wanted to dig the heel of his boot into that gut shot. 'We hold back a few of the older girls until they reach full maturity, at which point some of them are given the task of taking care of their own group of children – often actually including their own kids.'

'What does all that work you're having done on the other side of the woods have to do with all this?' Maurice asked, changing tack.

'We were expanding. Redeveloping, too. It was time to... to run in additional facilities and improve on... the utilities. The cabins are a little primitive. We're preparing the foundations, digging trenches for water pipes and cables.'

'So your disgusting little club was growing?'

'At a rate of knots.'

'You said you keep a few,' Chase interrupted. He had barely been able to look at the man directly, but this time he did. 'What do you mean by that? What happens to the others? If this has been going on for decades, then there must be a large number of men and woman unaccounted for here. Where are you keeping them, or what have you done with them?'

'Oh, no, we certainly don't keep them. After all, what's the point of having children around when... when they are no longer children. Where's the fun in that? Other than those we choose to help raise the little ones, as soon as they reach the age of consent we... remove them from the equation.'

Chase could barely breathe. 'What do you mean by that? Exactly.'

Again that self-righteous grin that Chase wanted to wipe off with his fists. 'That's what the hunt is for,' Radford said, tiny bubbles of blood popping between his teeth. 'We set the children free and then we release the hounds – as they are referred to – and we take care of business. We do this three or... four times a year, culling their numbers and burying the bodies in underground chambers deep enough so that no dog, not even one trained to sniff out cadavers, will ever find them.'

'Why? Why would you do such a monstrous thing?'

'Why?' Radford gasped out a wet laugh. 'Because there really is nothing quite as useless as child you can no longer play with.'

The sound of a single gunshot snatched Chase from the sheer horror of what he had heard. When he looked across at Radford, the man sported a bloody hole in his forehead directly above his nose. Chase turned his gaze to Maurice, who met his eyes and offered a disaffected shrug.

'That's how you get rid of vermin out here in the countryside, Sergeant,' he said. He seemed unwilling to expand further.

'I take it that didn't just happen?' Chase said, though he could hardly hear his voice above the clatter of his own heartbeat.

'What didn't just happen? There's just the three of us here.'

'You think he's going to keep his mouth shut?' Chase gestured towards Reid, who'd silently taken everything in from his chair.

'I don't know. What do you say, Mr Reid?'

At first, Shakespeare's close protection operative looked as if he would refuse to talk, but after a few seconds he said, 'You need to know a few things. First of all, prior to today I had no clue what my boss nor any of these men were up to. I never accompanied Sir

Colin to the Tier One club; that was a destination he was happy to travel to himself. Second, I'd have put a bullet in that man's head myself if I were armed. Third, whether you trust me or not, what I've seen and heard here tonight sickens me the same way it does you both. I came here under instruction from my boss to work with Radford. I ask few questions and I get my job done. Usually. I have no intention of dropping either of you men in the shit.'

'Does that answer your question?' Maurice said to Chase.

'In truth, I'm not sure. I'm having a hard job taking any of it in. That includes you being here and ending up on my side. If I'd seen you approach earlier on, I would have assumed it was me that gun of yours was intended for.'

Maurice chuckled at this. 'I'm sorry, Sergeant, but I have far more important matters to address. Yes, of course I wanted you to do as I asked. Usually that's sufficient. But once the lid has been removed from the can of worms, there's very little point in persecuting the person who opened it up. In point of fact, I felt you were getting close to resolving the matter more fully, and I realised I could eventually use that to my advantage. I tracked down your vehicle, followed you from a distance. I suppose I could have waited for Radford to dispose of you, but I carry no malice towards you, DS Chase. I rather admire you, actually. Of course, that's not to say that if you decided to come after me for what I did here tonight, you wouldn't find my shadow overlapping yours when you least expect it.'

The threat was implicit, yet Chase got the impression it was mentioned merely out of a sense of duty as opposed to any genuine malice. It also struck him that, of the three of them, he was the only one empowered to take the next step.

'How long do you need to clean up after yourself?' he asked Maurice.

'I suspect a crew is waiting outside the perimeter as we speak. I made a couple of calls earlier.'

'And what precisely will you be cleaning up?'

'Two bodies – one dead, the other not. This hut also has to go, of course. Can't risk cleaning it, though. Better to set it alight and see any potential evidence of our presence go up in flames.'

'Leaving the cabins and the people inside them for me to report to my people.'

'Precisely. Also, I don't know if you spotted them, but there are minivans parked up on a small patch of land not far from the trail. They're tucked well out of sight, so it was by pure chance that I came upon them. Still, plenty for your forensic team to get their teeth into, I imagine. You and the flames can guide them in. As for me and these two, it'll be as if we were never here.'

'And if I agree to all this, how long will you need?' Chase asked.

'Give us an hour.'

'It's a big ask.'

'Is it? Really? Surely the alternative, given the advantage I have over you, is even more unthinkable.'

Chase heaved a desperate sigh. 'I no longer know what to believe when it comes to you.'

Maurice angled his head. 'I suspect that's not entirely true, Royston. I also believe you know my way is the best solution all round.'

He was right. Even so, Chase felt his shoulders sag as he nodded. 'Agreed. And… thank you.'

'For what?'

'Saving my life.'

'Ah. Think nothing of it. But remember, if you speak of this, what I failed to do tonight will merely be a postponement of the inevitable.'

Chase grinned. 'There was no need for the threat. I understand what's required of me here.'

Maurice nodded. 'I'm sure you do. But will you be able to live with the choices you made here tonight, Sergeant?'

'I suppose we'll find out.'

'I suppose we will. The future is uncertain. Which is why there's always a need to threaten. Always.'

THIRTY-EIGHT

By the time the emergency services circus had its full complement of clowns, Chase had broken down the doors of all four buildings containing women and children. In the background, the smaller structure in which he had been tied to a chair and in which Miles Radford had been shot dead, was burning fiercely. He'd waited until it was fully alight before making his calls. Its impressive heat caused his flesh to prickle as he wandered from cabin to cabin, trying to keep everybody calm. Mostly the inhabitants were frightened or confused, often a combination of the two. Chase did his best to manage the scene before the trained professionals arrived; people better equipped than him to handle massive, deep-seated trauma.

As emergency responders took over, Chase stood back to admire them from a distance. Firefighters went to work dousing the flames, the hut itself long beyond saving. A fleet of paramedics tended to the women and children, whose underlying health surely had to be questionable given the circumstances in which they had lived. Child services had also provided an impressive out of hours response, and carried out their jobs with grim determination and warm compassion. Uniforms sealed off the area and policed everything taking place within the boundary they had set, while detectives from stations in Chippenham, Devizes and Swindon surveyed the scene and began the process of narrowing down an investigative pathway. As usual, the crime scene was far less chaotic than it initially appeared.

Chase sat down on the incline of the hill just short of the treeline, arms wrapped around his raised knees, so captivated by the action playing out like a movie scene that at first he didn't realise he'd been spoken to. He looked up at the woman who stood only inches away, and could tell immediately from her gaunt expression and the way she was dressed, that she had been imprisoned inside one of those wooden cabins. His cheeks flushed as he scrambled to his feet, brushing himself down.

'Sorry about that,' he said. 'I was engrossed by what I was seeing.'

'You're the man who saved us. The detective.'

If it weren't for the sheer misery etched into her eyes, paper-thin flesh wrapped close to the bone, and clumped mass of tangled hair, Chase imagined this woman would be stunning to look at. From somewhere deep within all she had to have endured, a radiance still clung to its faint glow. His heart broke in that moment, and he had to choke back his tears.

'I am,' he replied. 'I'm only sorry it wasn't sooner. Are they taking care of you down there?'

'They're certainly trying their best… Detective Chase, is it?'

'DS Chase, yes. Royston. Please, call me Royston.'

'They're going to be taking us away from here soon, Royston. And I expect you'll be extremely busy once we've gone. But before I leave, I need to ask you something.'

'Of course.' Chase nodded eagerly, though he feared what the question might be. Or rather, he feared the answer he might have to give. 'Please do. Anything.'

'I have to know what became of my daughter. She was taken from here about a week ago. Driven to a large house along with the other children. Only, when they returned, Miriam was no longer with them.'

Chase felt his brow tighten. The name sounded terribly familiar, though he couldn't immediately place it. He stared at the woman whose own gaze implored him to provide her with good news; perhaps for the first time in her wretched life.

He knew the answer to his own question before he asked it.

'What's your name?'

She touched a hand to her chest. 'Mine? It's Amanda... Mandy.'

His flesh pulsed before a chill settled over it. Hairs rose on his arms and the nape of his neck. He could barely breathe. It felt as if his heart had stopped pumping blood, and for a moment his legs became so weak he thought he might fall back to the ground.

'Mandy Radcliffe,' he whispered.

Her eyes sprang open wide and she gasped. 'How could you possibly know that name? Do you know who I am?'

Nodding, Chase said softly, 'I met your father recently, Mandy.' At which point he remembered where he'd heard the name Miriam, but by then he'd caught the flash of additional pain etch itself into her face. 'You named your daughter after your mother,' he said, closing his eyes as if hoping to blot out the next cruel twist of the blade already so deep into this poor creature's soul it might never be removed.

'So my... my dad is still alive?' she said, clinging to that single strand of hope.

Instead of answering, Chase said, 'Mandy, I believe I know some of what you have endured all these years. So I have to ask you this rather than simply do it as I would very much like to.'

'What? What is it?' A flicker of anxiety punctuated her question.

'Will you allow me to hug you? It would be my absolute honour.'

She nodded and put her head down. Chase pulled her into an embrace that he felt shudder through his entire body. Emotions clawed at him like naked branches in a dense wood, but he held her tight and allowed her to sob in his arms. He had no idea how long the two of them stood there like that on the hillside, but after a while her own arms came up around his shoulders and she hugged him as if they were long-lost friends. When eventually she drew away, Mandy sought his eyes with hers.

'Miriam's gone, isn't she? My daughter, I mean.'

Chase nodded. 'I'm so sorry. It was a terrible accident. Of all the things I suspect could have happened to her, in the end it was a stupid, bloody car accident.'

Mandy tapped her chest and said, 'I knew. Deep inside, here where it counts most of all, I knew. When she didn't come back later that night, or the next day, or the next… I felt the ache, Dete… Royston. I felt the kind of ache you can only understand when a piece of you goes missing and you know it can never be replaced.'

'How old were you when… how old was Miriam?'

'She was twelve. Not far off a teen, actually.' Her words prompted a fresh low moan of misery and gentle sobbing. 'After everything my poor little girl endured, if she could have survived just one more week…' Her voice trailed off, and she turned her head away.

'I can only imagine what life must have been like for the pair of you. Only, I don't want to imagine. This is my case, so unfortunately I will eventually come to know every sordid detail. But for the time being, I want to think of you like this. As you are. Free again. You have many years ahead of you, and you have a father who I'm sure will help you heal those wounds you carry until they become scars.'

'And my mother? What became of her?'

'As I understand it, she grieved for your loss every day. But she passed away, I'm afraid. Your father never really recovered, either. But tomorrow, once you've been through the process of being interviewed and making a formal statement, I'll take you to him myself. I'll take you home, Mandy.'

Opening her mouth to reply, her chin trembled and tears began to fall once more. Chase held her for a second time. Long after the smoke from the fire had cleared, long after Crawley and Waddington arrived, long after DS Laney approached them and stood patiently by. He knew he could not take away this woman's searing emotional agony, but he would hold her for as long as it took to make her feel safe.

THIRTY-NINE

SHORTLY BEFORE NOON THE following day, DS Chase presented himself at the front door of Harvey Radcliffe's cottage. When the man answered Chase's knock, Radcliffe had at least changed his clothes since the last visit. His hair looked clean, too, though he sported additional growth around his face.

'What is it this time?' he grunted after a lengthy sigh. 'Won't you people please leave me be?'

'May we step inside for a few moments, Mr Radcliffe?' Chase said cheerfully. 'We have some important news for you. After today, I don't see any reason why we'd need to bother you again.'

He and DC Laney followed the dishevelled man into the still-gloomy house, perpetually ripe with the stench of stale alcohol and failed personal hygiene. Laney was stern faced as she had been all morning, having laid into Chase for excluding her the previous night. He'd apologised, profusely, on several occasions, but his partner wore her rage on her sleeve, the twisted and sour expression on her face bearing witness to that.

'This about my daughter or her own?' Radcliffe muttered, facing away from the two detectives.

'Both,' Chase replied. 'Sir, the other day I mentioned my observation that you'd kept the curtain pulled back as I'd left it during our first visit. I notice it's not moved since, either. Does this mean you harbour a little of your late wife's hope?'

'I don't know what it means. Nor if it means anything at all. Sometimes things are where they are just because they are.'

'Mr Radcliffe, we're here to tell you that you'd be well advised to keep these curtains drawn back. And in approximately four hours' time, you should stand by the window and gaze out of it as Miriam did. Because when we return, sir, we'll be bringing your daughter with us.'

Radcliffe snapped his head around, the rest of his body following more gradually. 'You… you what?'

Nodding, Chase said, 'We found Mandy. And later today, she's coming home to you.'

'My Mandy?' Radcliffe gasped softly. 'My daughter?'

'Not as you knew her, of course. The eight-year-old you must see inside your head when you close your eyes is, sadly, long gone, sir. This Mandy is the woman your daughter became. Twenty years older, twenty years you can never have back, but still very much your little girl.'

'How… how is that possible?' Radcliffe struggled down into his armchair, staring at them as if he feared having become the victim of some malevolent ruse.

'There will be plenty of time for you to find out all the details, Mr Radcliffe,' Laney told him. 'I don't know how much Mandy herself will want to share with you, my love, but when it comes to our investigation, one or both of us will make ourselves available to you as and when you have need of further information. In truth, we'll be gathering intelligence for many months to come.'

The man's hands shook, his glazed eyes flickering from side to side as he took it all in. He sat silently for several long moments, shaking his head as if almost unwilling to believe what he'd been told.

'Is she… is she unharmed?' he eventually managed to ask.

'Physically?' Laney nodded. 'For the most part, yes.'

'And in other ways?'

Chase crouched down so that they were face to face when he spoke. 'Your daughter is only barely aware of the memories she had come to believe were nothing more than dreams or fantasies. These always featured both you and your wife; her parents. Mandy named her daughter Miriam, though she wasn't at all sure why at the time. This house was also in those dream-like recollections, too. However, I have to tell you that the past two decades have not been kind to your daughter. In fact, her existence has been one long tale of misery and degradation. But her story is her story, and Mandy insisted that only she tell it to you. She wants to see you as soon as it can be arranged, to spend time in your company, with you once again inside this house. She's as nervous about that as you probably are at this very moment. Her sorry tale will not be easy to listen to, but when you do listen, remember that she was the one who had to live it. You've both spent far more time without each other than you had together, which makes you relative strangers. Only you share the same blood, so that will never be entirely true.'

'And it really is her?' Radcliffe said, seemingly unaware of the tears spreading freely down both cheeks. 'You found my little girl?'

'Yes, it is. Yes, we did. And while it may be helpful to think of her that way to begin with, you must ease yourself into the realisation that she is now a woman closer to thirty than twenty. Prepare yourself to hear the worst possible story. And also prepare to hold your daughter in your arms when she breaks down and tells her father what became of her.'

Radcliffe pawed at his eyes to stem the flow, but it made little difference.

Chase reached out a hand to pat the man's arm. 'Sir, we're going to make our way back into Swindon. Like I said before, we'll be back around 4.00pm. I suggest you use that time to clean things up around here, including yourself. Make your daughter's home and her father as close as possible to the image she has inside her head.'

Radcliffe muttered something softly.

'I'm sorry,' Chase said. 'I didn't quite catch that.'

'I asked if you did this? Are you responsible for this, Sergeant?'

'I am. Together with DC Laney and a number of other fine police officers, sir. Teamwork, as ever.'

'Then I will never be able to thank you all personally. And I will never be able to thank any of you enough.'

'And you don't have to. But the next few days will be so much easier to bear if I know you are hugging Mandy every moment you can, Mr Radcliffe. I know I'll be giving my own daughter a tighter squeeze than usual when I see her again.'

This time the man lifted his head. 'You can absolutely guarantee it, Sergeant.'

Chase grinned and stood upright, planting his feet solidly. 'Good. But give her time. Give yourself time. It may take plenty of it.'

Radcliffe nodded. 'I will. We will. And it's thanks to you that we have it to spare.'

FORTY

CHASE SAT ON A low wall, his back to the sea whose breeze toyed with his untucked T-shirt like an invisible hand. He stared down at the vast expanse of grass, appropriated here and there by people. Some read or played games, most sprawled on blankets talking and laughing, eating and drinking. Making the most of the conditions before the real autumn took hold. Two figures were headed in his direction, the smallest of them oblivious to his presence.

The investigation was far from over. They were two days in and a long, hard slog lay ahead if they were going to nail everybody involved with Tier One. But he had persuaded senior officers that any formal statement relating to his part in putting the case to bed, could wait for one afternoon.

Laney had been considerably more difficult to handle.

Earlier on, the day after returning Mandy Radcliffe to her home, Chase's partner continued to vent her fury at him for cowboying, demanding to know how he had acquired his injuries. Every silence seemed to be broken by her telling him how appalled she was by his behaviour. His explanation, that of playing a late night hunch, had not doused her fire. It was made clear to him that a price would be requested at some point in the near future, and she expected it to be paid in full. That price being the unadulterated truth.

He decided he could live with salving some of her anger, but he would never fully share with Laney the events of two nights ago. Better he suffer her scorn and distrust than she be submitted to the kind of honesty that encourages only a lingering doubt and a resurgent fear. Also, he recognised the fact that her resentment stemmed from concern for his welfare, and he liked knowing she was capable of that.

Since the night in question, Chase had started to feel his life and career unravelling. He didn't know if he could pull off keeping the facts to himself, not when every time he closed his eyes he saw it all replayed across the blank canvas of his mind. He hadn't yet spoken directly with any of the children. He was no psychologist, and there were mental wounds to heal far more savage than any applied to his own head. Initial conversations with the women and taking statements from them, broke him. The tragedy of their lives quickly unwound, laying out a trail of misery, humiliation, and pain like none he had ever followed before.

Many hundreds of unpleasant hours lay ahead, as he and whatever team resources allowed worked their way through the variety and severity of abuses. Returning Mandy to her home and the loving embrace of her father had been the one bright moment in an unrelentingly dark passage of time. But he had used the drive down to the south coast to flush away those memories and the promise of more bleakness to come. He did not envy the battles that lay ahead for Harvey and Mandy Radcliffe, but at the very least they were together again.

The investigative team knew where and how to lay their hands on Sir Colin Shakespeare, but the CPS had already advised them to make any case they had against him iron clad before committing to his arrest. As for Lady Jane Webster, an agreement had been reached for her to be interviewed once again, this time under caution. Chase doubted anything would be achieved, but he felt he owed it to the children to ensure she felt the loss of more than her husband. Perhaps his senior officers would surprise him by grilling her Ladyship hard enough to crack that hard exterior shell. She might not have taken part, but she had to have been aware of it. For that, she too deserved to suffer.

His own personal spook had called shortly before he started out for the coast. Maurice made no mention of what had occurred in the cabin. He told Chase that the police investigation was no longer of interest to his employers.

'Is that because no royals or senior members of parliament were on that list of members?' Chase asked.

'You really don't have a filter, do you, Royston?' Maurice said, chuckling. 'I may need to keep an eye on you yet. I have a feeling our relationship is not quite over.'

'I do hope to prove you wrong. Whoever you are and whatever it is you do, your world is not one I care to spend any further time in.'

At this, the spook's chuckle became a full, throaty roar of laughter. 'Ah, there's the difference between us, Royston. I thought I had taught you a valuable lesson, but you still don't seem to realise that of the two of us, I am the one who inhabits the real world.'

'And Reid? Does he still inhabit that same world with you?'

'Mr Reid is currently enjoying the facilities at one of our more salubrious black sites. There's a great deal we have yet to learn from him about his paymaster.'

'And what then?'

'Don't worry about him, Royston. I won't be adding him to the body count. He might prove to be useful to us in the future.'

'I'm not convinced he'll regard that as an improvement on a bullet to the head.'

'Me neither. I'll inform him of your concern and get back to you with his response.'

'No. Please don't bother yourself, Maurice.'

'It's no bother. Truly. No bother at all.'

Chase thought back to the exchange and smiled to himself. His encounter with a man so dangerous could easily have turned out badly. Yet, for reasons he wasn't able to explain, Chase felt more secure and safe than he had any right to be.

The children occupying those cabins seldom strayed far from his thoughts, and once again they scrambled for his attention. Far too many of them, ages ranging from a few months to mid-teens. Then there were the women several of the abused children had become, taking care of those brought into the world for a single purpose. Caged like animals for most or all of their lives in many cases, how could they possibly ever adapt to the real world?

If he even knew anything about the real world.

Chase blinked back his own fresh tears as he looked up to see his daughter's face come alive, her gaze having fallen upon him and her delight immediately causing her to beam and utter a cry of pure pleasure. Maisie broke away from Erin and pumped her little pipe cleaner legs as fast as they would carry her across the ground.

A dark thought attempted to worm its way into the core of the moment: can you imagine waking up one morning to find Maisie gone, to believe her dead, to have people believe you killed her, to have her missing for two decades, to have…?

He thrust it aside. It would return at some point. And then again, catching him out when he least expected it. How could it not? But right now, right here in this place, he would allow only sunlight into his life. And there were no brighter rays than those provided by his wife and daughter.

ACKNOWLEDGEMENTS

A CERTAIN DI JIMMY BLISS has been a popular and successful character for me, so it was with some trepidation that I set out to create a new UK crime series. There's always a danger of it falling flat, especially if readers make comparisons as they go along. But I felt the pull of the new characters and the new setting, and while I could also feel Bliss's presence as I wrote this book, I was determined not to feel intimidated by it.

I knew I had to create a new lead who was completely different from Jimmy; likewise his sidekick needed to be an entirely different person to Penny Chandler. I was also interested in seeing how the introduction of a PCSO might work; the setting allowing me the freedom to explore that possibility. Early beta reads by the wonderful Dorothy Laney, Kath Middleton, and Lynda Checkley, suggested I was working along the right lines. This came as a great relief, I have to say, as I loved the storyline and so badly wanted this book to work. As ever, I am extremely grateful to all of you for your help, advice and guidance. My thanks, also, to Graham Bartlett, fellow author and crime fiction advisor, whose specific guidance on police procedure relevant to the profile of the people involved, was invaluable.

As usual, no acknowledgement is complete without thanking my Facebook group, book bloggers, family, friends, and readers – you are part of everything I write.

Finally, if what happened to Sir Kenneth had you asking if such a thing is possible, believe me it is. As a forensic investigation into my Internet usage will confirm, I did do the research; mostly with my legs crossed and a pained expression on my face.

Cheers all – here's to the next time, cupcakes.

Tony
August 2021

Printed in Great Britain
by Amazon

22907339R00169